DOWN FOR THE WORD COUNT

UNLUCKY IN LOVE, #3

PIPER SHELDON

QUERQUE PRESS

To J.R., always

And to the family you find.

1

Harrison

Several weeks ago

PRACTICED SMILE LOCKED INTO PLACE AND EYES MEETING HERS FOR the appropriate amount of time; I nodded to show I was listening and interested.

Truthfully, I had no idea what the shop clerk just said.

"The love they're shown is just as important as the quality of the air or the pH of the soil. Everything has to be just right," she went on.

My head continued to nod in her direction, but my eyes roamed around the tourist shop named Brooks' Baubles and Books. Honestly, I'd checked out two sentences in. If I came across as not listening, it wasn't because I was rude, only that if a topic didn't interest me, trying to hold the thread of conversation felt like trying to track a single cloud as it morphed and shifted with others. And that was on a good day. Today, my focus was more difficult than ever. The woman speaking was charming enough, but I couldn't stay centered when the background music played so loudly, and the couple over by the artesian hand towels argued about the bottles of wine they splurged on. The bell above the door rang at sporadic intervals. A brunette woman with her back to me fidgeted with the postcard rack, and trinkets down the row sparkled for my perusal.

And louder than anything was my concern for my longtime friend and father-like figure, George Sedar. My worry was a man yelling into a bullhorn, demanding the lion's share of my attention.

Once this movie wrapped, I *would* visit more often.

"Hello?" she asked, following my wandering gaze before coming back to my face to scrutinize it closely. "Are you local?"

"Nah. Just passing through." I turned away, not wanting to be studied too closely, lest my features become recognizable.

My inability to focus was one of the many reasons people thought I was a bit thick. But didn't everybody struggle to maintain a conversation? Didn't everybody receive the input around them at full blast all the time? It was impossible to stay focused on the growing conditions of a particular grape when I wasn't a big wine drinker to begin with.

In her defense, being in Sandia, the "hidden gem" wine town in Northern California, typically meant that one *was* interested in the fancy grape knowledge she'd just been sharing. This was probably a spiel she gave to a hundred tourists a week.

"I swear we've met," she said. Her head tilted, examining me closer as I tucked my chin. She couldn't have been thirty, which meant chances were she'd easily know who I was. Not vanity, just statistics.

"Not likely," I said, using *Hank*, my Southern American persona. A slow-talking Southern drawl was like slipping into a familiar character, another layer of defense against notoriety. I tried my best to speak as little as possible as she continued. Not just because I had no idea what to say, but with every second that ticked by, she would likely realize that I was *the* Harrison Evans, uber celebrity.

I picked up another item as she spoke. It was a simple bottle opener with the town name etched on the side. I made it dance by pulling on the square head of its spiral body. Arms up. Arms down.

"Wheee." I brought it higher so she could see it looked like an excited person doing jumping jacks, but she didn't seem entertained. Her brow arched as her spiel trailed off.

"Excuse me. I'm needed over there," she said, scooting away hurriedly.

I set the trinket back down with a sigh. I only came down to town from George's place to get some space to think. His house was thirty minutes away, higher into the surrounding Mayacamas Mountains. I'd been filming so much these past few years that visiting happened less often. Ever since George's other half, William, died, I found it harder to return.

My best friend Emma Flynn would say I was uncomfortable dealing with my own impending mortality, and the loss of someone that close shoved that unavoidable fact in my face.

My other best friend Charlie Downing would just slap me on the back and tell me that time was a gift not to be wasted.

But Charlie had found Kate, and Emma had reunited with Wesley and were happily in love—or pretending not to be, as was the case with Emma—so their optimistic views on life couldn't be taken as gospel.

My truth lay somewhere between. I was wracked with guilt and an overarching sense that something was wrong not only with him but in my own life. I felt stuck between two worlds yet fully in neither. The world of celebrity and fame, and the world of George and my past.

But I was here now. That mattered.

I discreetly shuffled away, feigning interest in goat milk soap as the woman chatted with another tourist. I couldn't shake the feeling of being watched, even with my "normal American" disguise. That was to be expected. I was grateful for my fame, but it came at a cost I'd been paying since I was eleven and made the life-changing decision to join the cast of what would be the international phenomenon *Terraformative.*

George's health couldn't be that bad if he were still writing. I'd been repeating that sentence like a mantra. His last two books were well received not only by the frothing fanbase but also by notoriously hard to please reviewers. So things couldn't be *that* bad. Sure. He forgot my name from time to time, calling me Adam, but that was bound to happen to anybody close to ... How old was George these days? I couldn't recall, but he'd met hundreds of thousands of people in his lifetime, so he mixed my name up with my character from his novels. No. Big. Deal.

I moved to a bin of what appeared to be various miniature farm animals.

Who were these shops for? Who bought these incredibly overpriced knickknacks? In my hand, I turned around a tiny fluffy chick with literal twigs for legs.

"It's alpaca fur."

I jumped slightly. The woman was back.

"There's a farm up the road, and it's locally sourced," she explained, misinterpreting my examination of the petite poultry as interest.

"Very cute." I gestured with it as I checked the price on the bottom of the fluff ball on sticks, *yeesh*—very overpriced rubbish. "But not cheap, cheap."

She gave a polite smile with a glimmer of worry behind her eyes. "Let me know if you have any questions." She smiled as she backed up.

"Cheep." The chick in my hand answered as I waved it at her.

She opened her mouth and closed it again, deciding to make a polite sound of "hmm" before backing away slowly and busying herself with another shelf. On the other side of the store. Away from me.

It was a familiar feeling. Despite being one of the most well-known people on the planet, very few people *knew* me, which was terribly isolating.

Maybe it was that my hair was longer than it'd been since the seventh season of *Terraformative,* and my beard was more unkempt than Harrison Evans's usually beard-free style, thanks to the latest movie I was shooting. I didn't have time to clean up before this surprise visit to George. Between the beast-mode hair, hat, and sunglasses, I must have looked a little less like her usual clientele: the elite on holiday.

After another few minutes of wandering and worrying, *not worrying*, about George, I slipped out discreetly. The shop owner was distracted, and I didn't need to give that awkward wave of "thanks for having me, sorry I didn't buy anything" and risk seeing the judgment in her eyes. Maybe I should have bought that damn little chick to send to Charlie and Kate. Hell, I could probably buy the whole store, but gifts should mean something more than a way to show that you had the means to purchase them.

I left the small shop filled with expensive wooden cheese boards and silver inlaid cutlery and slowly made my way down Main Street. The twists of evergreen around the lampposts and twinkling fairy lights decorating the perfectly manicured tree-lined street hinted that Christmas was just around the corner. The picturesque small town of Sandia thrived with tourists but was still fully in the hidden gem territory. The surrounding mountains protected it, and its famous watermelon wine kept it flourishing.

I wasn't quite ready to go up the mountain and return to George's just yet. When it was just George and me, it could be painful. I sometimes struggled to meet his gaze because of my guilt at my absence in these years since *Terraformative* wrapped. And that made me feel lower than a rubbish bin. At least his tiny ward, Collette, was a welcome distraction. I saw so much of myself in her as a child, a constant reminder of the family I'd thought I'd have by now. My stomach twisted uncomfortably, and I shoved the thoughts and the overstimulating distractions around me away by reaching for my earbuds.

I hit play on my watch, and the voice in my earbuds started the next scene. A female voice with the careful optimism of AI, read the action beat of my current manuscript.

Fade in. Exterior. A small cabin set back in a densely wooded area. A soft glow comes from the windows, but the man on the front step hesitates before reaching for the handle.

Ever since I discovered the magic of listening to my screenplays, memorizing my lines came a lot easier than when I tried to read the words on the page that tended to blur and lose my attention. It also blocked out the outside world so I could fully sink in and focus.

Just one of the many reasons I had been identified as a dumb kid, reliant on my looks and knack for acting. Practicing my lines helped distract me as I wandered the small town, known for its slanting slopes and dry, mild climate.

"This is the end for you," my prerecorded voice said as I spoke quietly along out loud. I tucked my head as a passing retired couple glanced at me.

My mind kept going back to George and the worry that settled deep in the marrow of my bones.

He was the most important person in my life, along with my two best friends. I couldn't lose …

No. I wouldn't go down that path.

"It's too late," the robot voice said.

"Excuse me!" a woman called out.

That was odd. I didn't remember that line. This was a high-budget action flick in the newest mystery detective Simon Harris series remake. I didn't recall a woman in this scene. I frowned and continued to walk.

"You've run out of chances," I said.

"Excuse me!"

That time, I was sure that hadn't been in my earbuds. I stopped and turned just as a woman was halting her jog up to me.

So much for incognito Harrison Evans. I didn't mind a selfie with a fan but was surprised to have been discovered. I straightened my shoulders and slipped on my Hollywood smile. I wouldn't need *Hank* since I'd already been identified.

The woman in question stopped in front of me, halting with her hands on her knees, and took a few breaths. "You ... walk ... really fast," she said through her pants.

I smiled, disarmed by her cheek. I didn't often receive an accusation from a fan right out of the gate. As she straightened, her features focused into view. Full pink lips on a wide smile slightly parted in exertion. High color in her sharp cheekbones, dark, curious, almost sleepy-looking eyes, and soft brown waves of hair flowed down her shoulders. I imagined a camera cutting sharply to a zoomed-in shot of my pulse rapidly picking up its tempo, my pupils dilating, and my intake of breath. Tiny details to show that my very human body was having a very human response to her.

She was astoundingly beautiful and as familiar as a friend in a dream.

"Hi," she said with a wave of a hand.

"Hi," I said in return, still feeling caught off guard and awestruck.

Awestruck.

It hit me then why I felt like I knew her. She had the same coloring and wide smile about her of this early nineties soap star that my mum watched when I was a child. Something about how her lids sat low on her eyes gave her a sleepy look and, combined with her low, raspy voice, was alluring. She was impossible to look away from, not that I wanted to. My gaze was eager to capture every detail of her that wasn't covered by her heavy winter coat.

"This is a little awkward," she said in her American accent.

"Don't worry. This happens all the time," I said.

She tilted her head. "You're British?"

That didn't usually come as a surprise. I have played Americans, even a Russian once, but Adam Abbots was undoubtedly my most famous role. People often yelled, "To be human is to endure!" as I walked down the street, and I'd salute back as I had in *Terraformative.*

"I am. Londoner, I'm afraid."

"Huh." She cocked a hand on her hip. "You know I have a friend ..." Then she waved her hand through the air as though erasing what she said. "Never mind. You don't know him."

"No. I might. All ex-pats here in the US know each other," I said. "We have a group chat where we are remiss over the lack of beans on toast and the strict dental regime." Her glorious mouth split open into a huge smile, revealing a perfect set of pearly whites. I gestured to her mouth. "Case in point."

She self-consciously brought a hand over her dimming smile. I cursed myself.

"Well, now this makes things even more awkward," she said.

"Excuse me." A group of at least a dozen geriatric tourists was headed right where we blocked the walking path.

I stepped out of the way under an awning of another tourist shop, gently guiding her by the elbow. My hand hummed with warm energy when I made contact, even through her jacket, and she glanced where my hand briefly touched.

A passing senior dropped her map, and I quickly grabbed it and returned it to her.

"Thanks, doll," she said, patting my arm and then catching up with her group.

I returned to the cove with the mysterious, beautiful woman. Sparkling white lights hung around us, closing us off.

"Yep. Super awkward." The stranger looked at me with gleaming light reflected in her eyes.

"Why is it awkward?" I asked, my voice lower, as somehow this setting made our conversation deeply intimate.

"It appears that you're both funny and polite." She gestured to the passing group, avoiding my eyes as she said it.

"I'd think that would be a good thing. I'm a professional after all." I gave what I hoped was my most Harrison Evans, good-natured smile.

Her mouth hardened, and her eyebrows slashed down. "Are you admitting to being a professional shoplifter?"

My smile dropped. "Excuse me?" I glanced around, worry growing. "You didn't stop me for a—"

I couldn't even finish the question. It felt absurd now.

"Empty your pockets, buddy. And I won't alert the authorities." Her eyebrow raised with a teasing reprimand, but my pulse thumped in my throat.

"I am *not* a shoplifter, I assure you," I said, holding her gaze with all seriousness. This would not be tomorrow's headline.

"You know, I believe you. But still. Humor me," she said gently.

I checked the first pocket of my Mac: a crumpled receipt and a rock Collette found for me and told me was lucky. I proffered my loot.

"See?"

"Nice rock. Other one." She crossed her arms and tapped her foot.

Earbuds case, phone, keys to George's and ...

"Oh bloody hell," I said in horror.

A little fluffy chick with stick legs and an exorbitant price tag.

"I didn't—I would never," I sputtered.

I looked up and around, trying to collect my thoughts. Was this a prank? Was there a hidden cameraman? The clickbait headline unfurled in my mind, "Intrepid Trio heartthrob Harrison Evans secret kleptomaniac?"

"It's okay. It's okay," the woman who was most certainly *not* a fan said.

She went to pluck the little chick from where it sat in my hand, trembling slightly. Before she could take it, I closed my fingers around it. Our hands brushed, and she pulled back like she'd been zapped. I tucked it away as I reached for my wallet instead.

"I'm mortified," I admitted. "But I'd like to keep it."

I thrust twice the price tag in cash at her, but she didn't check. Her mouth pulled in an indulgent, albeit pitiful smile as she pocketed the cash.

"I know you didn't mean to. I was watching you in the shop. You seemed distracted," she said. "I was kidding about calling the authorities. I'll let you off with a warning. This time."

I ran a hand over my face. "I should go apologize ..."

"It's okay. Really." She reached for my arm before dropping it awkwardly. I wish she'd have completed the gesture. It might have helped keep me from melting from embarrassment. "It's my friend's shop. She's the one who sent me after you. You were talking to her. Well, she was talking at you. She's not concerned about it. Actually, she thought it was funny. Do you know her? She seemed to know you."

"I didn't ... no. I was distracted."

She lowered her head until my gaze found hers again. "Really. It's not a big deal. We won't put your picture by the register."

"Ha." Only a moment ago, I had been expecting a picture. Just not that kind. "Right." I nodded as I ran my hand over my stupid beard. I was suddenly keenly aware of how much I wished she recognized me or at least saw me at my best and not like this. A hairy, self-absorbed, shoplifter.

"Are you okay?" she asked carefully.

I scoffed. "You shouldn't be worried about the criminal. You would make a terrible copper."

She laughed softly. "For many reasons. But are you?"

I didn't feel okay. Hearing her gentle question seemed to unlock this intense pressure in my chest.

I felt absurd and somehow like a child who had no idea what they were doing trapped in an aging man's body. Time passed too fast. People I cared about got older. My youth felt like a lifetime away. My two best friends were creating their own families away from me. It was like I was dunked in the undertow of life, and nothing I could do would get my head above water.

I couldn't say any of that. Basking in the focus of those compassionate green-brown eyes—I hadn't noticed the little flecks of green before—all the thousand swirling thoughts calmed down to one distinct longing.

I swallowed. "Have we met?" I asked without meaning to, avoiding the complicated answer to her simple question. There was something about her. A rising need that almost felt like panic to figure out what this connection was flowing between us. Like a magnetic pulse that couldn't be seen but only felt. "I feel like I've known you," I added, breathless, with my throat too tight.

She hesitated, probably because of my awkward phrasing.

"You know, I thought you looked familiar too," she said after a moment. "Are you a local? Sometimes I help out at my friend's shop, Brooks' Baubles and Books." She gestured back toward the shop I'd visited.

"No. That's not it." I couldn't stop memorizing the details of her face. The swoop of her lashes. The curve of her neck. Time raced by. This odd interaction would end too fast.

She shrugged. "Maybe just one of those faces." She glanced back in the direction of the shop. "I better get back. Just in case she really does call the police."

My eyes widened.

"I'm teasing," she said with a laugh. She reached for me again, looking at her own hand like it was a stranger. When she dropped her arm, still not making contact, I reached out without thinking to hold her sleeve.

"Wait," I said.

Her full lips parted in surprise but not fear. Hopefully.

I couldn't let her go. This couldn't be the end. I felt a frantic desire to get more information and learn something about her. This brief, terrible interaction could not be her only impression of me.

"What's your name?" I asked. Hopefully, the edge of desperation wasn't as noticeable to her.

She chewed her lip, her brow furrowing. "I'm sorry. I really have to go."

I swallowed as my heart dropped to my trainers. "Right. Of course." I let her go and tucked my hands back in my Mac.

She wasn't interested. A distracted, petty criminal didn't attract her. There were a thousand reasons this witty woman would tell herself to get away.

"Good luck with the kleptomania," she said, keeping her voice as friendly as before but already walking backward and away from me.

Forever.

I chuckled once, balling my hands in my pockets, stopping myself from reaching for her and making even more of a fool of myself. I respected a woman's wish the first time she spoke them.

She backed into a street chalk sign advertising lavender lattes and almost fell over. By the time I took two steps forward, my body reacting on instinct to get to her, she had righted herself and the sign, chuckling nervously and dusting chalk off the sleeve of her jacket.

"Oops. How'd that get there?"

I smiled but couldn't get the other half of my mouth to lift.

She turned and took three steps away. Her brown waves flowed down her back. Her long legs shapely in tight jeans. I watched her longer than I should for someone who wanted to come off as *less* weird. She stopped suddenly, fists balling once before turning back around.

I stepped closer, feeling my eyes widened hopefully.

"But I'm around, at the shop sometimes," she called a couple of yards away. A passing family crossed in front of her, and she tucked her hair as they shuffled on. "So you know. If you feel like trying your luck again."

"Right. Brilliant," I called back.

She ducked her head, smiling. "Okay then. I'll see you around. Maybe."

I waved like a big, goofy goober. She disappeared around the corner, glancing back once more with a shy smile. I'm not sure how long I stood there blinking happily in the thin winter air. I didn't even reach for a cigarette. I'd been meaning to quit anyway. Collette had caught me yesterday when I'd thought I'd been sneaky and made me feel terrible when she started asking all sorts of questions about it. The sun shone a golden hue. The birds chirped giddily. Passing pedestrians chatted happily.

Everything felt brighter and more alive.

Today was a new day. A fresh start. I'd be up here visiting George more. He was absolutely fine. I didn't need to worry about a thing. The world was a beautiful place.

2

Frankie
A few weeks after that

THE DOOR CHIMED, AND MY HEAD SHOT UP FROM WHERE I'D BEEN straightening a rack of hand-painted postcards. This rack, coincidentally with a direct view of the door, had been reorganized several times in the last weeks.

The last customer waved as he left. I sighed softly.

A person would hope, at this point, I'd stop getting a bolt of adrenaline every time the door opened.

I feel like I've known you ...

Such a weird way of saying he recognized me, like he was actually trying to say something else, but the words were stuck in my brain, nonetheless. Maybe I should have given him my name. Or asked for his. Literally any speck of information about him. Instead, my imagination played on repeat: Mr. Soulful Eyes, looking at me hopefully, and then that hope crumbled as I hurried away. But I hesitated when he asked for more information for a reason. That hopeful gleam in his haunting blue eyes was all too familiar, all too alluring. There was a time in my life when I would not have hesitated to take his phone and add my number. That person didn't even feel like me anymore. She hadn't in a long time. I had no room in my life for any more unforeseen complications. The neon glowing sign of my life flashed "No vacancies!"

Brooks came to my side, nudging me back to the here and now. "Sorry you had to stay so late, Frankie."

"I don't mind," I said.

Brooks was one of those naturally gorgeous people. Aside from the blond beach waves that flowed down her back and her large dark eyes, she just had an air of someone who knew themselves. She had a nose piercing and wore hats. That alone made her immediately cooler than me. She defined boho beauty before it was a trendy aesthetic. We are close in age, early thirties, yet she ran an entire business in a luxury tourist town. Her confidence was so magnetic every eye went to her in every room.

Except for his. He hadn't looked at her like he'd looked at me. I swallowed a painful lump in my throat.

Brooks twirled the rack, examining my work. When I came across her and this store two years ago, I felt an instant connection to her. She said we were soul sisters and took me in as her friend.

"Did you alphabetize the—never mind." She shook her head. "Your organization skills freak me out. It makes me wonder yet also understand how you could still be working for Sedar after all this time."

"Rome wasn't built in a day, as they say," I said, but it was so much more than the archiving that took my time these days.

She rested her head on my shoulder, and I tensed at the contact. Brooks was so free with affection. So much like Collette in that way. It freaked me out when I first met her, but I learned to go with it. I patted her head.

"That makes you my super extra favorite person. I didn't

expect this holiday rush. I think I would have curled up in a ball under the desk without your help. I really didn't expect you to work so much. Especially pro bono ..." She looked up, cringing a smile.

Of course, I could have used the money, but Brooks needed to keep her business afloat, and having an excuse to be away from George's was helpful.

"I like being here. It's downright relaxing compared to the archiving and organizing a million boxes of loose-leaf paper. Plus, George had company this weekend anyway. I would have just made it weird."

"Well, that's not true but I appreciate you." She straightened off me. "But it's almost Christmas, go home."

"It's not my home," I muttered. It was an important distinction.

"Sure. But *home* is a lot easier than saying that place where you've basically been staying the past few years, keep all your stuff, work most days, and also sort of take care of a man and child."

"Fair."

This transition period with George was only ever supposed to be temporary. I came to my former foster parent looking for help, knowing he was the only person from my past I could count on. I hated that I needed help. I didn't want to be another person who took advantage of his kindness, but I tried to make up for it by doing whatever he asked. He needed somebody to clean up, organize, and archive everything from old handwritten book notes to behind-the-scenes footage from the show based on his books to fan letters and everything and anything in between. Almost every room in his huge home was filled to the brim with *Terraformative* memorabilia in some way. I was still up to my neck in work. Add in a local best friend, a little niece who I felt responsible for, a never-ending to-do list, and absolutely no job skills fit for a résumé, and ... I had yet to move on from this pit stop on the journey of my unpredictable life.

I absolutely did not need anything else added.

Out the front windows, Main Street quieted down and twinkled with lights.

"Seriously. Go. The rush is over," Brooks said as she tracked my gaze and looked outside.

I glanced at the time. "Okay, I think his guests should have left anyway. Are you sure you don't want me to wait and help you close out?"

"Goooo." She pushed me to the counter to grab my coat and bag. "Stop stalling."

Brooks closed the blinds on the main door as I slipped into my coat. If mystery man hadn't shown up by now, I wasn't likely to see him again.

And that was for the best ...

"No word from Joey?" she asked.

I shook my head, a familiar tightening in my chest that felt like stepping out in subzero temperatures. "Still planning to be back after the holidays."

Brooks clicked her tongue. "How can she leave her own kid over Christmas?"

"It's her busiest season with the theater company. They add extra dates to the tour," I defended like a reflex.

To myself, I agreed. Every month, six-year-old Collette became more aware of how time passed and asked more and more questions about her missing mother. She grew and changed so fast. Sometimes, I stayed in town at Brooks's during the week to help at the shop, and when I returned to George's, she'd seemed to have developed years in her speech and grown inches. It made me worry how much Joey was missing, but my sister didn't seem to be as concerned about it. More so, I worried about the long-term impact this would have on this shining star little girl who needed her mom.

Brooks made a sound like she wanted to argue but didn't press. It was a conversation we'd had a lot over these past few years as Joey came and went with the winds. I couldn't think about it without my heart breaking.

"Merry Christmas," I said, only hesitating for a moment before giving her a hug goodbye. Look at me growing and changing.

"You too. Tell Collette I said she's a stinky booty butt," she said as she squeezed me tight.

I chuckled. "I'll pass that on."

I was exhausted when I hit the incredibly packed—and only —grocery store in town and made my way back up to George's. My social batteries were drained after answering the same ten questions to tourists all day, and I was ready to call it a night.

An unfamiliar car parked in the driveway caused a pang of dismay. I'd have to plaster on a polite smile for a little longer. I sighed as I loaded my arms with the groceries and last-minute Christmas gifts. Piano music and singing voices reached my ears before I made it to the front door. The people inside sang a slowed-down cover of the old song "What Are You Doing New Year's Eve?" Only Collette's voice was recognizable. My little niece and George's temporary charge was always eager to put on a show for whoever would listen, but the other voice had me stopping in my tracks.

The rich, male voice was reminiscent of old Hollywood crooners, complete with a decent level of professional lessons. Joey had once explained that not everybody was born with raw talent (like herself), and most singers require years of breath control and pitch training.

I tried not to encourage Collette's understandable obsession with performing. Between her mother's career and George's multitude of contacts in the business, it made sense why the little girl was drawn to it. But I didn't like it. My experience with actors showed them as vain, flighty creatures by nature. Those who reached any level of success were the worst, adding ego and entitlement to the mix. They were detached from reality and only saw to their own needs, and the people in their orbit fed that fantasy.

Still, I let myself listen to the duet for a moment longer, noting how the hairs on my arm stood on end as the male voice held a long, particularly lovely note at the end.

If I were to go in now, I'd ruin the fun. I didn't earn the name Frowny Frankie for nothing.

I never used to be the buzzkill. I used to be the life of the party ...

As the piano stopped, I opened the door. Collette spotted me first, instantly launching herself at me, and I dropped the groceries just in time to stoop to catch her. My heart ached as she squeezed with all the might her tiny arms could muster. I've missed her so much, and I only just saw her a few days ago.

It still felt shocking to be loved by this child, so free with her affection. I should have grown accustomed to her hugs and snuggles, but every time was surprising. It felt like a special kind of gift to be loved without any expectations. Just because I existed. My love for her was never a choice. When Joey introduced her to me all those years ago, she looked at me with big, wide eyes like "Oh, there you are," and my heart was hers. I still felt undeserving and scared. She shouldn't be alone without me here. It was becoming increasingly apparent that it would be irresponsible to do so. I would have to add it to the list.

After Collette released me, I stood to take in the guests, all of whom felt familiar but not anybody I knew.

Then, my gaze snagged on the man leaning casually against the piano. I felt his searing, watchful eyes before I met them with my own. He straightened as we took each other in, and my breath stuck in my throat.

Dark eyes framed in thick black lashes that said mischievous, wounded, distracted.

I feel like I've known you.

The room around me seemed to fall away like I stumbled through a wardrobe to an unexpected world. It was him. His beard was gone, and his brown curls were trimmed short, but those mesmerizing blue eyes were unmistakable. They zeroed in on me, intense and delighted as they'd been the day he accidentally shoplifted. I hadn't stopped imagining those intensely piercing eyes that contradicted his good-natured affability.

Those eyes that were so familiar even through our painfully short exchange. After all these weeks of hoping to see him again, just to get his name ...

I almost stumbled with the pure shock of it.

"What are you—" I caught myself in time, unsure how much to reveal. Would I give away how much I thought about our brief interaction? What would that say about me?

He schooled his features as well, glancing at a beautiful redhead and back at me.

It was so jarring to see him. Here. At George's. I wanted to ask so many questions, but all at once, the tension in the room was palpable. I couldn't handle all these people looking at me expectantly. If only I'd taken a few more minutes to get here. I felt awkward and bored in the presence of all these accomplished people. How would I explain who I was? I'd let George decide.

"Grandpa, who are your guests?" I asked lightly, feeling silly that he told me and all his former foster kids to call him that. Also, a small part of me liked that the familiarity made me less of an intruder here. In *not* my home.

Then came a blur of introductions. I shook hands without

soaking much in. I couldn't get my mind to slow down enough to absorb any details. Only one face held my attention, and I had to force myself to glance at it in careful, measured-out looks so as not to be suspicious. Every time we accidentally met eyes, we jolted apart like getting caught doing something wrong. Not like last time, when he wouldn't look away. He had made me feel like the most interesting thing when he studied me. But of course, he could make me feel any way he wanted.

He was an *actor*.

The revelation was met with disparity and relief. I had been right to ignore his flirtation. I found myself explaining for the hundredth time that I hadn't seen the show *Terraformative*. Yes, George had helped raise me, but I'd never had the time. It was the quasi-truth I usually went with. Of course, I read the books. It was a stubborn personality trait that I wasn't about to delve into with a group of strangers. Strangers who made their careers from said show.

But that had to be why he had looked so familiar. Harrison *freaking* Evans. He was the prodigal son from another family that George spoke of as though he walked on water. He was in half the pictures on the walls. He was a man who had his whole world thanks to George, and this was how I finally met him.

How could I have been so stupid? How could I have not put it together sooner? Brooks had to have recognized him. She was always up on pop culture references, where I purposely kept myself in the dark. She subscribed to that Nosy Nellies podcast and read ChicChat for salacious details. She must have sent me after Harrison to watch the chaos unfold. *That* was why she had been so interested in how it had gone when I got back and also huffed in annoyance when I said I got money back but didn't elaborate. She'd been waiting for some drama, some insider info.

That was why she kept encouraging me to work up front and

pretended not to notice when I asked if the shoplifter with the magical eyes had come back. She totally knew it all along.

The next time I saw that woman, I was flicking her boob.

I felt silly and off balance. This wouldn't have happened to a woman who had a normal childhood. Every other person in my generation would have known him in a moment. I was always a marked outsider, and this was just another example of it.

I wasn't sure of all that I said. I felt like I was outside my body, watching it operate but not in control. I needed to get out of that room and organize my thoughts. I might have come off rude or flighty, but I couldn't think when I felt Harrison watching me. If I wasn't careful, would he try to get me alone? Or was he as happy to let that brief meeting slip by unnoticed? Why had I built it up so much in my head when chances were it was just another day for him?

I collected Collette and left George to say goodbye to his friends. Once Collette was in the bath singing as her bath toys did a talent show, I slipped into the closet to be alone. I let out a long breath and dropped my head back against the door.

It figured. The first time I'd have the hint of an inkling of feelings for someone since I moved here, and it had to be one of Hollywood's, according to Brooks, most eligible bachelors. Care-free, as he should be, doing whatever he wanted.

Another unattainable, flaky actor in my life.

It was fine. My initial instinct to avoid getting close to him was right. My instinct hadn't failed me yet.

"Frankie?" Collette called out.

I squeezed my eyes tight. "What's up, girly-pop?" I called.

"Are you okay?"

"Of course. Why?"

"Because the closet is where you go to cry."

How was it that this six-year-old girl could simultaneously

be the most distractible and unfocused child yet manage to notice every little thing I tried to keep locked down?

I chuckled, but it came out like a growl. "I promise I'm fine."

I would be fine. Harrison and I had miraculously managed not to cross paths yet, and we would continue that way. He was always off shooting movies and lived in LA the rest of the time. George often lamented he visited even less after William died. I wasn't going to be here forever, either. I would just push our weirdly memorable meeting out of my mind and focus instead on my job here until I could finally get away.

"Okay," Collette said. "Wanna see me hold my breath?"

"Sure. I'm coming," I called and put Harrison Evans out of my thoughts once and for all.

3

———

Harrison

Present Day

I STEPPED INTO MY TRAILER, EAGER TO SHOWER THE NEW MEXICO dust off my body. The end of March in the Southwest desert meant being pummeled with hurricane winds while standing in the middle of a sand field with nary a single plant or tree to block the blasting gusts.

"At least I'm exfoliated," I said to my reflection. It became increasingly disconcerting how often I spoke to myself these days. There weren't many other options around. Wesley and Emma were finally united—called that—and Kate and Charlie raised chickens with Agata in Devon, England.

I was here. Alone.

Heavy-lidded eyes closing in disappointment ...

The second Frankie found out who I was, the light I had seen initially faded from her eyes. She had been guarded and leery the next, and only two times I'd been able to visit. The first in January when George had taken a tumble (but was okay, thankfully) and the second more recently, between award shows and Wesley Cole's dramatic love confession to Emma.

Frankie's smile was polite enough, but she always had an excuse to move out of my company quickly. It felt like I had imagined the connection between us.

In my suitcase, I lifted out the tiny chick tchotchke I'd eventually purchased the day we met. I'd meant to give it to Charlie and Kate but found I couldn't quite relinquish it.

I sighed as I twisted it around. Maybe I had projected more onto it.

Maybe seeing my two best friends recently find the loves of their lives had painted that entire interaction in a more hopeful light. After all, I didn't know her. I'd spent so much time lately thinking about building a life outside my career that maybe I had put too much pressure on an awkward one-time encounter. I may have never felt like that before with someone, but I would never want to force unwelcome advances on a woman. They got enough of that.

I cleared my thoughts of Frankie to make a plan.

The last day of shooting meant no more beard and, even more pleasing, no more sand in my unmentionables. I could head home.

Cut to a shot of a typical LA mansion set in the Hollywood Hills: glass, steel, concrete. Show a man with dark curls and sad eyes sitting alone at a sterile countertop, staring into the emptiness around him.

I shook my head, sand flying loose.

The sleek amenities and chic, modern architecture had felt like such a crowning achievement when I first purchased it, a physical sign of my success as an actor, post-*TF*. But now it was just so much, so big, so quiet.

I imagined George and Collette arguing over Legos and felt

myself longing for the lower back ache caused by hours spent on his well-worn furniture.

I'd been so busy with this shoot and award season that I hadn't been able to visit much since Christmas.

I wasn't avoiding Frankie and her shuttered gaze or the blatant disappointment when she found out who I was. My reputation preceded me. A vapid actor with the attention span so much that of a gnat that I hadn't even noticed when I committed petty theft. She looked at me like so many others: a funny, charming, lucky-in-looks bloke not to be taken seriously. I was smart enough to recognize the blatant lack of respect but not smart enough to change opinions.

It was time to let this projected fantasy go.

The water ran brown for the first two minutes of my shower, but before long, I was so fresh and clean and ready to head back. Filming wrapped. Award season was over. I was not contractually obligated to anybody for the foreseeable future, and instead of the peace that should come with a break, a bleakness of unending, similar days unfurled in front of me, blurring from one day to the next with nothing to distinguish them.

I leaned against the shower wall, replaying the last time I spoke to Frankie—the only time after our initial meeting.

"I guess we do all know each other," I said, finally managing to get a moment alone after Collette and George went to bed. I'd found her in the living room, tucked into the corner of the sofa, sipping tea. She'd been hunched over a notebook, focused. I stayed at the edge of the room, not wanting to impose too much on her quiet moment. When I spoke, she shut her book and slid it into her lap to slowly set her teacup down, making almost no sound. She looked up at me, confused. I slid on my affable smile like a shield. "I'm assuming George was the ex-pat you mentioned?" It was the only time we'd mentioned the meeting on Main Street.

She smiled, but it was a dark alley knockoff of the real thing. "Yeah." She tucked her hair behind her ear and looked around. "Small world."

I physically cringed at myself. I'd searched for something clever to say, a recall to that easy repartee we'd shared. The more I tried to find the right words, the more they all got muddled up trying to form. It was so much easier when these things were scripted. She smiled politely, but the exchange was stilted and heavy. I had to leave back for LA, and I had ruined the moment. I left frustrated with myself but at least more sure of where I stood with her.

Not that I was still thinking about it.

After I got dressed, I sat staring at my phone, debating the merits of returning Emma's call.

She'd been checking in a lot more often lately. Ever since we'd all gone up to George's before Christmas, she became more of a mother hen.

Tell me what's going on, Harrison.

You seem so distant.

You will have to talk about it eventually.

Agree to disagree, my friend.

"Christ, I'm being morose," I said to myself as I got dressed.

Even before she and Wesley Cole, our former costar, admitted their feelings for each other—*finally*—she'd been prying more and more into my personal life. I was relieved that I hadn't told her about my "not actually a moment" with Frankie. I hadn't mentioned it at first because of the ribbing that would have followed when I told them I had expected to give an autograph and instead had almost gotten a misdemeanor.

It wasn't that I avoided her questions; it was that I didn't have an answer. I wasn't sure what was wrong. I felt unmoored and listless. I wanted to be there for George but didn't know how. I wasn't sure that I was a person he could rely on. I didn't know what my life would look like from month to month. I was used to being the good-time friend or even the reliable paycheck to my family back in England. I never felt like I'd be the friend you called when you needed help moving or a ride from the airport. Not that people in my circle needed help with those things.

I wanted to be, though.

My phone vibrated in my hand, causing me to almost drop it. It was Bob *Cratchit*. I answered the video call after collecting myself. "Hey, Bob," I said, waving to the man on screen. "How are you?"

Bob Caddick was George's agent and nearly as old as George himself. They'd been in the business together since the beginning. At this point, George was his only client, and they both should have retired a couple of decades ago. His name wasn't actually Cratchit, but Emma, Charlie, and I got in the habit of calling him that after ... honestly, I couldn't remember. When we were young, we interchanged him with the famous Charles Dickens character, and it sort of stuck.

"Still kicking. How are you?" he said. If George Sedar was a retired author and Englishman old—think hunched back, bushy eyebrows, and a weathered smile—then Bob Cratchit was LA old. He'd been tanned, tucked, and injected so much that he had a perpetual sneer that made it hard to tell if he was smiling or grimacing in pain.

"Just wrapping a film," I said. If Cratchit was calling me, then he either needed a favor or to tell me something about George. Neither option filled me with effervescent joy.

He wasn't a bad guy, but he had been in this business his entire life and didn't care for small talk.

"Great," he said distractedly. His dyed eyebrows didn't move on his tanned forehead, but I got the impression he was trying to convey concern. "I'm calling about George."

"What's going on?" I asked; my palm grew slippery where it gripped the phone.

Bob reached over his head with his left hand to scratch his right eyebrow. "I'm hoping that's what you'll tell me. The thing is, uh, George hasn't been responding to me. Not returning my calls or emails."

"We both know he's never been keen on either of those things." I tried to keep things light but heard the tightness in my throat. "He still uses a typewriter for crying out loud."

"Yes, true. That's why I don't want you to worry. However, the thing is. I've gotten quite a few calls from his publisher. Now, this is NDA information, but apparently, George has asked for an extension on his current manuscript four times now. They absolutely cannot push this release back any more."

"Bloody hell," I swore softly. "I didn't know that." The *drip-drip-dripping* of the shower blared loudly. I stuck a finger in my free ear and closed my eyes to focus as worry hunched my shoulders.

"We aren't trying to publicize. This book is supposed to be the final book in the series. Ever. The expectations are massive. As you can imagine."

"Right," I said. The anxiety about George's health had already been at the forefront of my mind. If George wasn't responding to his oldest friend ...

"The *Terraformative* books had always been massively successful, but after the show's fans aged up a little, there was a lull in sales. The last two books brought the focus back to George. Add in that the reunion special and Millennial sentimentality sweeping the nation. The publisher wants to strike while the iron is hot," Bob explained.

"Anything to squeeze every penny from our aging generation," I mumbled.

"Business. You know how it is. But the fact of the matter is that they need this book written before the end of this year."

"That's barely eight months."

"I know. That's why we need to know where he's at. I'm fairly certain he started writing it, at least. Last we talked, he mentioned having a good amount of words written. But he was also a little confused. I've noticed he's been mixing some things up. Have you—"

"Hey listen. I have to go," I cut him off. "But, uh, I have a break in my schedule. I'll head up there now and check things out. I'm sure it's all fine. Just being George. He's probably so deep in the writing cave that he can't be bothered. I'll give you a status report as soon as I have one."

"Thanks, Harrison. I really appreciate it. I would go up there myself, but it's quite a journey for me these days."

"I understand."

"George thinks of you as a son. Always has. If anybody can help him, it's you."

And I saw George as the father I wished I'd had. The father in sitcoms and movies that had long talks about life and taught his sullen teen to drive.

I swallowed, jaw clenched. "I'm sure he's fine," I rasped, desperate to believe my own words.

There was a long pause. Bob held my gaze with his sharp eyes. His mouth was pursed, stubborn wrinkles bracketing his mouth. Eventually, he nodded. "I'm sure you're right. You're a good kid, Harrison. I appreciate you."

I nodded with my lips pressed in a tight line. Once we ended the call, I replayed the last few times I'd visited George. He hadn't even been writing that I knew of. It made my chest tighten with the worries I'd been keeping at bay.

I'd go up there and reassure myself, but mostly Bob.

It was probably just some sort of mix-up. Everything was fine.

4

———

Frankie

Tension sat heavy in my shoulders, setting my jaw on edge as I walked back into George's house.

Some mornings, getting a six-year-old dressed and ready for school felt more vigorous than any fitness class could ever be. Collette overflowed with confidence and curiosity—which was great; I constantly worried how having an absent mother might impact her—but she was as argumentative as a lawyer and sharp as a fox. She would negotiate every step of her routine, as though we didn't perform it five times a week.

"Let's save the animal ears for after school," I said.

"But I'm a cat. How will I be able to hear?" she said.

"You have to wear a coat. It might rain later."

"But it will clash with this shirt, and I'm fashion," she said with a snap of her fingers.

And on and on about every single obstacle that stood between her and first grade. Maybe I should set firmer boundaries and be harsher? But I wasn't her mother; I wasn't that person in her life. Plus, the world would find a way to crush her on its own, let her feel safe here to be free to be who she wants to be.

This and a thousand other thoughts had me feeling defeated before I'd even made it to a second cup of coffee.

I slumped into the couch, mentally planning what was in store for my work today. I hadn't even come close to finishing the attic, but it was so cold up there I wanted to wait until warmer months. Plus, bringing those boxes down the shaky wooden ladder made my palms sweat.

I had almost motivated myself off the spot on the couch, from where I'd been staring into space for twenty minutes, when George shuffled into the room.

"Where's Josephine?" he asked.

My heart skipped; the clenching in my jaw tightened. Wasn't that the question of the decade? Joey was meant to be back three months ago for Collette and had barely called but a handful of times.

"I'm not—"

"Did she make the bus okay?" George clarified.

I blinked at George. He stood stooped over his cane with deep creases etched on his forehead.

"Oh. You mean Collette?"

"Yes, yes. That's what I said."

I let out a slow breath. I drove Collette to her private school, paid for graciously by George. "Yes, George, she's at school. Would you like some tea?"

"Please. Bring it in my study. I need to talk to you," he said and turned to shuffle back to where he'd appeared from.

I sighed with great gusto and heaved myself into action.

Ever since his scare a few weeks ago, a misstep that led to him falling, his moods seemed to be less predictable and more often leaning toward the ill-tempered side.

I needed to look into getting some help soon. George wasn't

getting any better, and I worried constantly about him. His moods, his mobility, and his mind worked in tandem against him. Every little bump in the night, I worried he had fallen again. Whenever he forgot a name, I worried he'd never remember it.

It was easier before to say this wasn't my life and that I was just passing through, but I couldn't consciously make excuses anymore. George needed me. More importantly, Collette needed me. I couldn't stay in town with Brooks anymore, I had to be here twenty-four seven just in case.

My arms laden with the tea tray, I backed into his office. Somewhere within the stacks of books and papers was an old desk and typewriter.

Instead of sitting behind the desk, George sat in one of the two wingback chairs facing the fireplace. He leaned forward, resting much of his weight on the cane as he stared into the flames, his mind a million miles away.

I softly cleared my throat and set the tray on the table between the chairs. When he blinked back to himself, his eyes gleamed, and the skin around them was reddened.

"Good. Thank you. Have a seat," he said.

"Everything okay, George?" I asked.

He made a thoughtful sound as he brought a tea cup shakily to his lips. "I don't know how to answer that. You tell me."

I blinked at him, my mind going to worst-case scenario. George had been my foster parent, and I'd always looked up to him. At this moment, all I could think about was how I was falling short. I was a student expelled for truancy. I was sitting in the back of a shop, scolded by a store manager for shoplifting. That was how I knew Harrison wasn't stealing that day. He was far too earnest to be sneaky.

I wished my brain would stop finding excuses to think of Harrison.

"Are you unhappy with my work?" I asked carefully. It had been slow going, but he knew better than most of the factors that played into the delays.

"I'm thrilled with your work. That's part of the reason I wanted to talk to you. I believe you know more about my health than you are leading on. I suspect that, in fact, you know that I'm not doing well."

I swallowed a sip of tea to avoid speaking. Truthfully, I'd rather it had been about my performance than his health. I wasn't ready to have this talk.

"I saw a ghost last week," he said.

My hand stopped midway to setting down my cup.

He frowned as he continued. "It is as absurd to me as it sounds to you. I saw it clear as you are sitting there."

I shifted uncomfortably. I had no idea how to answer this. He obviously told his version of the truth, but what did somebody say in this sort of situation? "Who was it? Are you okay?" I asked.

"It was a man, could have been anybody. Standing just outside the office there. He didn't seem to notice me."

"Ah."

"You can't tell anybody," he said.

"Okay." I hoped that was a promise I could keep.

I wasn't sure of where I stood on the afterlife and spirits. I'd seen too much of the world to have my mind firm on one set of beliefs, but this felt entirely foreign to me.

"Something is happening to my mind. We both know it. When the doctor saw me, after my tumble, I shared some things that had been happening. Sleeping a lot. Waking angry. Things are not where I left them. He wants me to come in for more tests but believes that I have the early signs of dementia," he said matter-of-factly.

I nodded stiffly as immense sadness made my bones feel

brittle. "I'm very sorry to hear that, George." I sat perfectly still. It was as though if I breathed too hard, all the barely contained emotion would spill over, like the surface tension on an over-filled glass of water.

"Are you sure you aren't British? That's quite a stiff upper lip," he teased.

"I'm so sorry." My voice shook as I spoke.

I was so still a bird could land on me. This was how I handled big news: my mom being arrested, the schools kicking me out, and my sister leaving her child on the doorstep. I couldn't move or react. People thought I was emotionless or heartless, but sometimes, I felt things so big that my brain couldn't even communicate the situation to my body. If people could see my thoughts, they would never think I was a calm person. No one noticed my clenched hands, the knots in my stomach, or the sharp, shallow breaths. It all covered the swirling maelstrom of pain, fear, and confusion of the blows thrown by life.

"I know you are, Francesca. I'm only giving you trouble. But this composure is a quality I admire in you. It is why I knew I could trust you with this information. I need someone who can be levelheaded about what comes next. There's much to do."

I knotted my fingers in my lap. A plan. A plan, I could handle. I may not know the right things to say or how to act, but I could help. "What can I do?"

"You aren't going to like what I say next."

I nodded once. My ice-cold fingers balled into fists.

"I need you to finish writing the last book in *Terraformative*."

I heard the words. They bounced around my head, but I couldn't process them. "George. You shouldn't say stuff like that."

"You and I both know you mostly wrote those last books," he said, ignoring me.

"That's not true." My head shook once. "You can't tell people that."

"You did, and you know it." He slammed his cane.

My head shook slowly. This couldn't be right. I misunderstood. "I helped you type here and there. Maybe gave a suggestion."

"Francesca," he said somberly. "I've already made a video. Collette helped record me on her device pad thing. It was notarized, and I'll explain it to the publisher. Just as soon as I asked you. I've been avoiding Bob and the others as much as I can, but they'll come knock down the door soon if I don't start producing words."

My hand was plastered to my chest, and my heart raced under my fingertips.

"There has to be somebody better suited for this. I didn't even graduate from high school technically," I sputtered, embarrassed, but he knew most of my sketchy past.

"Pish." He waved his curled fingers in the air. "What does a piece of paper prove that I don't know in my heart?" He brought his balled fist to his own chest. The crepe-paper skin revealed aged spots and yellowed bruising from the IV weeks ago. "You know this world better than any other person. You have every note I've ever taken at your disposal. You made those characters come to life in a way that this old, out-of-touch brain could never. You were the reason those last two books were so successful."

I blinked into the fireplace. My brain was a *Terraformative* encyclopedia. When George and William took me in, I was at my worst. I needed hope, and I found it in those stories. I was obsessed. It was that loyalty to those stories that never allowed me to watch the show. It would taint the purity of his craft.

"You are incredibly detailed oriented, you know my voice

and my style. I have left it at your discretion how much credit you get. Of course, you will get a bonus for your effort."

"I don't want your money. Not this way," I clarified.

It was one thing to work for it, but this felt wrong. Dirty somehow.

"You work that out with my team. I don't need any more money. It's all going to charity when I go anyway. Might as well take advantage while you can."

"No," I said vehemently. "Do not let people take advantage of you."

I could see it now. Former foster children he helped over the years coming out of the woodwork, trying to get a piece of George as his health declined. As he forgets if he already wrote a check to this or that person. Much like Joey had.

Much like I had.

Somebody had to be here to protect him. Another wave of guilt made me determined.

"This job was only ever supposed to be temporary for you. We both know that." His deep, emphatic voice shook the room as he spoke. "It's been years now, and you're still here. This is the last thing I will ever ask of you, and then you can be free to go. This money will help you. You've done so much to take care of Collette. I pray her mother will return for her, but together we will figure out the best plan for her."

My head shook as he spoke. Yes, I wanted freedom to find my own path. I didn't want weights of responsibility on my shoulders. I wasn't meant to take care of people at such different ends of the spectrum of life, but both needed full-time care. I didn't want freedom this way, not with the decline of the man in front of me.

"It's not about the money," I said.

"I know that. It's about your life. You're young and beautiful, and you're stuck here. Finish this last task for me and be free.

"What I care about is how this series ends. It has to be how we talked about. There is nothing more important than the Intrepid Trio getting the ending that I wanted for them. You know it all. You know how this has to happen. Now, if you absolutely refuse, I cannot force you, of course. I just worry that if I don't make it ... if the publisher picks somebody else ..." He leaned closer, his watery gaze holding mine, the earnestness changing his voice. "It would mean the world to me if you did this. Consider it your grandpa's final request."

"George ..." His name whooshed out of me in a gasp of pain. There was no way I could say no. I wanted to help him. I wanted to do whatever he ever needed or asked of me. He'd been there time and time again when nobody else had been.

"Of course," I said. "Nobody can know I'm behind it. I will help as best as I can."

He nodded. "I will protect you. This video and Bob will make sure things are taken care of. But we need to get this squared away."

The corners of his eyes were tense with fear as he looked past my shoulder. I was tempted to turn around and see if there was a ghostly figure standing there now.

"I feel myself running out of time, Francesca. I wouldn't ask you if I could do it without you."

"You don't have to. I'm here." I reached out without hesitating and took his shaking hand.

He sat back with a long sigh, his shoulders relaxing back against the chair. "Good. Good girl."

He squeezed his eyes shut, and a small tear gathered at the corner and leaked down the side. I stood and bent to kiss his cheek before tucking a blanket around him.

I managed to contain myself enough to reach the second-story room where I slept. Fresh, cool air met me as I opened the door to a small balcony that overlooked the rolling vistas of the Mayacamas Mountains. I took deep inhales in and out and still felt dizzy.

I could run away. I could just pack up and run away. It was how I handled everything hard before. My life had always been about moving forward, racing toward safety and independence. How did I even get here?

I looked across the tree-filled vistas, imagining all the different people in their little houses, living a thousand different lives from mine. Are they feeling pressure to try to smother them? Are they sure of who they are meant to be?

What were my priorities? Who would I be if I never ended up here? What would I be doing?

I closed my eyes, the wind whipping my hair around my face as all the growing pressure in my life stung the back of my eyes. George's weathered face, almost childlike in its fear as he asked for help. His mind was tricking him, but there was enough to know something wasn't right. It had to be the scariest feeling in the world not to be able to trust yourself. Another image. Collette sat on my lap and squished my nose with her finger before telling me I was pretty. Eyes wide and trusting, putting faith in me that I didn't deserve.

Now, I was the one seeing ghosts.

My throat tightened, and I gasped in a breath.

Except these people were tangible and real and lived in my heart as well as my brain. They made me feel like maybe I could be worth more than my past. I tried to picture what would happen if I left them, truly let myself imagine their expressions, worry, and concern. They wouldn't understand another person in their life leaving them, and a pain so acute robbed my breath from my chest. Eighty-plus years between them, yet equal in their need for love and protection.

I couldn't do that to them. As badly as the road called to me, as much as I wanted to travel life alone and figure out who I was, I couldn't leave them. Not yet. Not until I knew they would be okay.

5

ARCHIVE FILE: *2348*

Telly News Magazine Interview with Harrison Evans, May 2010
Attached video MP4 format
Transcript:
TellyNews [TN]: Thanks for being here today, Harrison.

Harrison Evans [HE]: Hullo. Thanks for having me.

TN: How does it feel to have wrapped the final season of *Terraformative?*

HE: It still doesn't feel real.

TN: Did you ever think this series would be the massive success that it was? The series finale broke every record.

HE: It's mad but not surprising. The Intrepid Trio and the world of Terraformative have impacted so many people. I'm just grateful to be a part of it. Feel very lucky.

TN: You have grown very close with your costars. Are you planning to stay in contact?

HE: Of course. Every summer, we go up to George and William's. They've got this massive pool and the best American snacks.

TN: Is that G.S. Sedar, the author of the books?

HE: Yeah, sorry.

TN: Oh? Your costar Emma Flynn said she had plans for university and was headed back to England soon.

HE: Oh. Well, we haven't firmed up the dates.

TN: Any truth to the rumors that you and Emma—

HE: No.

TN: She's quite lovely.

HE: She's like my sister. Next question.

TN: What about university for you?

HE: Erm, I've never been great at the studies.

TN: Well, thankfully, you're one of the biggest stars on the planet.

HE: Right.

TN: And what about your other best friend and costar, Charles Downing? Did he really show up to set drunk several times during the last season?

HE: Next. Question.

TN: What are your plans for life after this?

TN: I can't imagine it will feel possible to return to any sort of normalcy after being a part of such a phenomenon.

TN: Harrison? Mr. Evans?

HE: Sorry. Right. Erm, not sure. Hopefully, make a few movies, if I'm lucky. My agent has something lined up. Then, one day, get married, settle down, and make a load of babies. Hopefully, with my two best mates and their families living on either side of me.

TN: Well, I'm sure the world will be waiting to see who the lucky lady will be.

HE: They're gonna have to wait. I'm only eighteen.

—End transcript —

NOTES:

FRicci: Archived.

That interviewer was a jerkwad.

6

——————

Harrison

solo from LA in my Mercedes and was ready to stretch my legs and move around. My steps slowed, crunching in the gravel of George's driveway as I pricked my ears to listen. Not yelling, a form of singing.

Collette seemed to be testing the capacity of her lungs while simultaneously beating her fists against the piano.

I flinched as I reached for the door. "Hello?" I called, ducking my head to look past the foyer. Sure enough, Collette was "practicing" at the piano, where we had put on our show before I left at Christmas. She sang a song centered around macaroni and cheese, chicken nuggets, hot dogs, and bologna. She didn't notice my arrival as in the moment as she was.

When she paused to take a large inhale in, a much more distressing sound made itself known.

George *was* yelling.

I dropped my weekender bag and ran down the hallway to

his office. As I got closer, I heard another voice, soothing, rich, and a little raspy.

"George. It's me, Francesca. Frankie."

Collette noticed me as I ran down the hall.

"Scarecrow!" she called after me.

She launched her entire body weight at my leg, buckling it and almost knocking me down. Her arms and legs gripped to barnacle herself to me just outside George's office. "I've missed you most of all," she said.

"I don't know who the bloody hell you think you are, but you have no right!" George's muffled yell came through, followed by a crash of what sounded like a heavily tombed hardback slamming against a desk. My heart lurched with alarm, but I didn't want to frighten Collette.

Collette stared up at me in hesitant horror. "Papa George used a bad word."

"Pretend you didn't hear that." I unsuckered Collette from my leg and hefted her up into my arms. "Missed you too, Dorothy."

"I'm a kitty now. Not Dorothy. Don't worry, I still like *Wizard of Oz*. But Dorothy was before yesterday."

"Right. Noted." A pair of faux animal ears made of sparkles sat in her auburn curls.

"A lot can change in lots of days," she said with a hint of peevishness.

"No doubt about that," I said.

Another crash and yell came from the other side of the door. I fought the urge to storm in proverbial guns blazing. I loved Collette's reaction to seeing me, but I couldn't focus on one single thing as my attention was split between her and the conflict. My palms went sweaty as I held her, glancing back to the door.

She scrunched her tiny face up. "Papa George is upset."

Collette stuck out her bottom lip as she grabbed my cheeks and squeezed them with both hands. "I like your beard better. You look weird now."

"Thank you for the feedback."

She squished my cheeks together even harder, face twisting in concentration. "At least it's not as pokey."

"Dats chew," I said, lips puckered like a duck. I shook my head to free myself. "Can you go practice more? I need to check in on the grown-ups."

"Okay. I'll play my new song. I'm really good."

"I heard." I set her down, and she zipped down the hall.

I gently pushed open the door. George stood at his desk, trying to lift his ancient typewriter protectively in his arms. Frankie stood on the other side, palms up, hardly moving.

"I won't let you have it!" George bellowed.

"I'm not trying to steal it. I'm helping you. You hired me." To her credit, Frankie was calm, her face open and friendly, patiently waiting and not matching George's chaotic energy. Her gaze flicked in my direction and snagged. Her eyes widened briefly before returning to normal.

"Hello, Harrison," she said calmly, showing very little emotion.

"What's going on here?" I said brightly, tucking my hands in my pocket as I entered the office. Despite my pounding heart, I played it cool.

"Oh. Oh. Harrison. My boy," George said, and my throat tightened at his visible relief in seeing me. "This ... this swindler is trying to steal my manuscript." He scooted awkwardly from behind the desk and approached me faster than I'd seen him move in some time. His arthritic finger jabbed in Frankie's direction. "Trying to steal my words."

Frankie didn't speak. There was a stillness to her that reminded me of when you came across a bunny in the field, as if not moving would somehow make them invisible. I couldn't decide if that made her distrustful. I interrupted something volatile, and she wasn't exactly trying to explain the situation.

"Let's see if we can't clear this up," I said affably as I hugged George. I glanced at Frankie, who met my gaze solemnly. She glanced away, jaw clenched.

"I'm going to go check on Collette. Excuse me." She brushed past, head down, as she walked briskly out of the office.

"Where's William? He handles this sort of stuff." George looked left and right, patting his pockets. "And where are my damn glasses?"

My blood went icy. Was he really asking about William? He couldn't have possibly forgotten about William's passing. Not when that had been the worst year, probably more, of his life. He didn't leave his room for months. He couldn't write for over a year.

Here now, George looked around, distressed, shaking hands reaching, then tucking back in at his sides.

I wasn't even sure what he needed. There wasn't anything I could do. This was too much. Why was he acting like this? The child inside me wanted to cower, but the man's fear drove me to help him through this. I kept my tone light and easy. I bent for his bifocals on his desk and handed them over. I didn't feel equipped to handle this.

He put them on, hands shaking so much I had to assist him. "Thank you. Yes." He cupped my cheek. "Harrison. Bloody good to see you, my boy."

I swallowed with effort, trying to smile. "Hiya, George."

"Now." He looked away and leaned over the mess of papers on his desk. "Where is—what was?" He shook his head again. "Blast it! I know I was doing something."

"Are you working on a book?" It was the only thing I could think to ask. My brain felt mushy and slow, with worry-soaked thoughts. I couldn't keep up with myself, but one instinct was clear. If I got upset and succumbed to the nauseating fear that seeing him this way caused, I would only escalate the situation.

Calm. Happy. I was great at this role. The carefree, unbothered charmer.

George was still looking around. His face contorted in that way, saying he'd been just about to say something but lost the train of thought. I was familiar with that face.

"I, uh ... I don't ... Harrison?"

I smiled brightly and felt the edges of it tremble. Absurdly, I could hardly keep myself together seeing him so lost in his thoughts. But he hadn't been this bad before. He'd not ever been angry. Just confused at the worst of times. This was not normal.

"Hey, George. Just popped in for a visit. I hope that's okay?" I said as he clasped my arm, steadying himself as he shifted to look at me more closely. His eyes watered, his hand cupped my cheek.

"Yes. Oh, my boy. My Adam. Of course. You are always welcome. You know that." Tension melted from him, and he sighed.

"Thanks, George." My throat was so tight I could hardly get the words out. "Would you like a cuppa?" I asked him.

He settled himself into the chair, rubbing his forehead. The injustice that had been fueling him quickly burned out. "Wait. Wait. Before I forget. I feel it shifting away. Like the flashes of a dream when you first wake up. Something about the money." He rubbed his brow with one hand as he pointed at his overcrowded desk with the other. "The ledger. Something with the ledger and that woman. Stealing my book." His voice faded as his eyes shut, and he leaned back.

"I know what you're saying," I lied. "I'll take care of it."

"Good, yes. You'll take care of it." His words began to slur as exhaustion took over.

"Of course, George. You rest for a minute."

"Good. Good. Yes. Maybe just for a moment. Check the back of my eyelids." He chuckled with strain as he crossed his arms and settled deeper into his chair. His head lolled to the side, brow relaxing as he slipped quickly into sleep.

I braced myself on the side of his desk, head dropping. This was more intense than I let myself imagine. Watching him struggle before hurt so bad, but this felt like an entirely new stage of trouble that couldn't be denied. My eyes moved over his messy desk and caught on a thick, ancient-looking ledger. I reviewed the accounts, handwritten, month by month, specifying the various expenses to keep up the estate.

Francesca Ricci repeated monthly with a modest sum and "archiving" next to it. It went back for years and years. A growing suspicion. I flipped to the most current entry.

"Final book - Francesca" and a sum I couldn't even fathom being worth any sort of note-taking or archiving. The worst sort of thoughts swirled around my brain. Who was this woman? She worked at the shop? She looked after Collette? She was always here, yet I knew absolutely nothing about her. Was this why she hadn't wanted me to know her better, wouldn't even give me her name, because of her connection to George? Christ, I'd been a fool. She probably knew who I was from the beginning. Emma and Charlie would have warned me.

Something we all learned the hard way in the film industry was that almost everybody you met was in it for their own benefit. They would do whatever it took to get what they wanted, no matter the cost to any supposed friend. A peer who swore he didn't want the role you were auditioning for would throw you under the bus the first opportunity they got to get a callback for that same part.

Was this a woman taking advantage of an aging man? Hadn't

I known everybody in his life? She felt like a stranger who had recently become a fixture.

George's outburst wasn't irrational. He must have seen this entry and wondered the same thing I was now. She fled the room when I came in, not even trying to defend herself.

I needed answers, and I wasn't leaving until I had some.

I slipped quietly out of the office. Collette had switched to playing outside. I spotted her dancing in the grass before I saw Frankie leaning against the kitchen counter, watching her through the window and worrying her thumb. Her posture stiffened when she noticed me enter the room. Her hand dropped, and she slipped into that hard-to-read place of neutrality.

"Is he okay?" she asked.

"Napping."

"You calm him down." She stepped hesitantly in my direction.

"I've known him most of my life." My body leaned to step toward her, but instead, I exhaled sharply. "What's going on?"

Her nostrils flared subtly, but that was the only sign that she'd reacted at all. "Can you be more specific?"

"George is ... He wasn't this bad when I was here at Christmas. Not even the couple of times I visited since then," I said.

She took a steadying breath in and out before answering. "Well, if you came more often."

"I tried." I ground my molars. "I'm sorry, who even are you?"

"Who am I? Who are you? You show up every few months and walk in like you have any right to question anything?" she said in return, pressing where I was the most sensitive.

"I've known George most of my life, and I've never even heard of you."

"I'm Frankie Ricci. I work for your—for George."

"Yeah, I saw the payments." Frankie, I knew that was her name, but it just occurred to me now that this Frankie,

Francesca, were the same person as the Frankie that George often spoke of. I had assumed it was a man.

She crossed her arms and scrutinized me, and I stepped forward to meet her in the middle of the room.

This was the opposite of our interaction on Main Street. Now, I was suspicious and careful. Full lips and sultry eyes wouldn't fool me.

"Looking through his books? If you were worried about him, you would be here every day. Like I am." She lifted her chin and narrowed her eyes at me.

I reared back. I opened my mouth to defend myself, but she was right. I should have been here. I should have been here every day.

"You are—" She braced herself as I spoke. "You're right. I'm sorry."

Her gaze moved over my face, and shame burned my neck, but I let her see my sincerity. She sighed out a long breath. "I'm sorry too. That wasn't fair. I'm defensive because ... I don't know. He's never acted like that with me. He looked at me like I was worse than a stranger." She stopped speaking abruptly, tucking her thumb tight in her palm before hugging it to her body.

"He's getting worse?" I hadn't meant for it to sound like a question.

She nodded. "He's been more scared lately, I think. Since his fall. Gets more confused easily."

"Why haven't you gotten help?" I asked.

"I'm doing my best. It wasn't like this before." She tossed her hands out to the side. "I didn't ask for any of this. I-I didn't want —" Her mouth pinched shut tight, and she looked to the side, arms crossed.

"Something else is happening here, and I need to understand," I said sternly. Or as stern as I could manage.

Her foot tapped as she brought her thumb up to gnaw. She caught herself in time but continued to avoid my gaze.

"George accused you of stealing his manuscript. Payments in that ledger seem pretty high for just archiving work. Which, by the way, you've apparently been doing for over two years, yet when you look around this place, it doesn't seem like much progress has been made." Her fists balled tighter, her jaw clenched, but I wouldn't stop now. I'd been fooled before. I wouldn't let George take a hit on this. "George didn't mention writing last I talked to him, but now he is? His publisher says this book has been pushed back so much that no more extensions are available. I'm getting so much conflicting information." I waved my hands around my head. "And ultimately, I still don't understand your role in all this."

"I don't know what to tell you. I don't know what I *can* tell you." She worried her bottom lip instead, with her teeth having given up on the thumb still safely tucked away in her palm.

"Can you start from the top? Who are you, and what do you want?" I asked.

She ground her jaw. "Who are you? I don't know you—"

"—from Adam Abotts," I finished, offering a hint of a grin.

She huffed a laugh. "Exactly," she said.

"Pun intended." I finished lamely, glancing up at her and reading her reaction.

Suppose she wasn't out to get George? Maybe she was here all the time and privy to something I wasn't. Maybe, to her, I was an interloper demanding answers. She glanced to the side, but the subtle joke managed to break the tension.

"I guess there is really only one question I need to understand," I said. She swallowed but nodded once. "Are you here to help George or hurt him?"

She cocked her hip out. "You know, I was just about to ask you the same thing."

I tossed my arms out.

Logically, we're strangers, but there was no doubt that the fierceness in her eyes spoke of protectiveness. That was a common ground to start on. One of us would have to take a small step of faith.

I cleared my throat and stepped forward. She mirrored my actions whether she meant to or not. We met in the center of the kitchen. Her arms still wrapped protectively around herself, but she was close enough that her soft breaths were audible.

"I can count on one hand the people I would die for, and George is one of them. He's the only father I've ever known." As I said that, she took a slight intake of breath. "I owe him everything. Everything good about me comes from him. I need to help him through whatever is going on."

Her eyes narrowed as she scrutinized me. Her gaze traveled my length, completely exposing me under her inspection. It was the same look she gave me when we first met, and I had promised I wasn't a shoplifter.

She dropped her arms to the sides. "Okay." She shook her head at the ground. "I better show you something."

7

———————

Frankie

THE VIDEO ENDED, AND I CLOSED THE LAPTOP CAREFULLY BEFORE slowly spinning to face Harrison. I'd set Collette up with a movie, something I only allowed in the most rare and desperate times of uninterrupted focus. George had moved to the living room to watch with her as I played this in his office. I sat rigid the whole time he watched, waiting for any sign of what was coming.

Maybe it was a mistake to trust him. My past certainly told me that trusting anybody was always a way to get screwed over, but he seemed to genuinely love George. George loved him too. That much was clear. Maybe that alone would have been enough, except that George was so open with his home and heart, my sister and I included, that it made me wary of anybody I didn't know personally. Harrison's career did little to help invoke trust.

Harrison's only focus was on the older man as George spoke from the screen. With every bit of news about his health and the book, Harrison curled in on himself like a sheet of paper in a fire.

"So ..." I sat in the chair across from him, waiting patiently for a reaction.

"Right." He closed his mouth and leaned back, running his hand over his mouth and turning to look at me.

He studied me with those strange, wounded eyes as though he'd never seen me before. It shouldn't hurt. We were essentially strangers, after all. It was as though the distance between us grew with every second when there had already been an ocean between us.

I feel like I've known you.

"I apologize for questioning what is obviously already a well-established plan for this novel, but how and I mean *how* did this happen?" he eventually asked.

I stood, unable to keep still any longer. Now that the truth was out, the weight of it was no longer chains around my shoulders, and I moved freely.

"It was one of those things that happened gradually," I began. "I never in a million years would have ever thought I would be in this position." I almost said how badly I didn't want to be here, how it was a thousand ways to disappoint millions of fans. And more importantly, George. But I didn't want to seem ungrateful, not when he'd done so much for me. Wouldn't people love to be in this position? Didn't people dream of this? Maybe even me, on a good day when I thought there was a chance I could pull this off.

"Are you a writer?" he asked, those eyes so hopeful.

I shook my head. "Not exactly."

His shoulders slumped more. "I'm trying to make any sense of this."

"Me too," I said quietly.

He stood and paced, which caused me to sit back down,

tucking my hands under my legs as though there could only be so much movement in a room at one time.

"He said in the video that you had co-written the last two books, and that was one of the reasons he asked you to do this." He scrubbed his hands through his hair. "Christ, Emma and Charlie aren't going to believe this. Those last two books were huge. They loved them. Kate, Charlie's girlfriend,"—he explained as an aside, forgetting that I had briefly met her—"specifically said they were his best books yet."

A soft groan escaped me, and I fought the urge to dig a hole and bury myself in it. Instead, I defaulted to frozen protective mode, arms pulled in tight, emotions safely tucked away.

"I'm trying to keep my temper. I'm trying to understand this, but I have to say you seem awfully cavalier about all this," he said.

This wasn't the first time somebody had gotten me all wrong. I was not easy to read. I kept my emotions locked deep down inside, and my face rarely gave anything away. My heavy eyelids always had an air of being disinterested, and my lips naturally turned down. That was a distinct advantage when you had no idea what life would throw at you next. It felt like a shield.

On the other hand, he couldn't be less self-contained as he paced in front of me, the quick back and forth causing second-hand motion sickness.

"I'm very worried," I said flatly.

"Well, clearly. Calm down."

"Not everybody wears their hearts on their sleeves, Harrison," I said. Or, in his case, those dark, wounded eyes that seemed to telegraph every passing thought and emotion.

"I've barely even heard of you, and somehow, you're now the person who is responsible for his crowning book in the series?"

"It wasn't intentional. None of this was. My place here was

meant to be temporary. I'm sure George spoke of me. I was hired to help archive everything related to *Terraformative*."

"Everything?"

"Book notes, fan letters, old screenplays, journals, photos, and videos from the set. His hand-typed manuscripts. Boxes and boxes of memorabilia. You've seen it around here. A long life makes for a lot of work. I'm sure he mentioned me."

Harrison frowned in a broodingly handsome way that made his lips pout. He really was distractingly good-looking. His jawline alone was meant to be documented. How I hadn't suspected he was an actor from the get-go was a glaring oversight on my end. It must have been the beard. And the thievery.

Maybe even subconscious wishful thinking.

"I suppose he did." He looked into the distance as he thought. "Sometimes I know several facts to be true, but my mind doesn't always connect them as they relate." He waved his hands around his head. A dark-haired, perpetual motion machine. "It's hard to explain. He mentioned a Frankie, I assumed maybe he'd been seeing somebody. I don't know."

"No. Just me." I sighed.

"How did it go from scanning files to all this." He'd finally stopped pacing, choosing instead to sit across from me, leaning forward and giving me the full blast of his direct attention.

I looked over his shoulder as I spoke, finding those eyes a little too unnerving for long periods. "At first, I was the only person around, you know?" He opened his mouth, most likely to defend himself for his absences, but I went on. "When George hired me to digitize all his old notes and manuscripts, we never thought it would take so long. There were additional ... complications." Collette wasn't his business and not pertinent to this part of the story. If he wondered who she was, he hadn't asked. "I was around. A lot. If he needed a sounding board for his ideas. If he wanted to read a scene out loud for flow." I hadn't planned on telling anybody, but the words kept uncharacteristically flowing out of me. "Soon, he asked for my input about potential plot ideas. Then I was typing for him on that ancient typewriter when his hands got too stiff—which is no easy feat. Then I'm filling in the brackets he left for me, adding suggestions in the margins. I never meant for him to take any of them. Sure, I had a few ideas and fleshed out a few scenes, but I never expected him to keep my changes in the final drafts."

I gasped in a breath.

"I believe you," he said, falling back into his chair. I could see his mind working things. Every single thought telegraphed over his roaming gaze. This was what made him so good at his job. He was impossible to look away from. Even just in thought, he was compelling.

Harrison paled. His features contorted in pain. He slumped back again, once lively hands were limp in his lap. "I kept telling myself things couldn't be that bad with George, not if he could still write the way he was. That his mind was still sharp. Maybe he mixed up some details here and there, but nothing concerning. I told myself we still had plenty of time—" He cut himself off sharply to look up at me. The hope in his features broke my heart. He wanted me to reroute his train of thought. He wanted me to tell him that things weren't that bad.

I couldn't do that. There was no going back to a different version of the man Harrison held in his memories.

I glanced at my lap.

"It's not good." His eyes closed as he took a moment to collect himself. Eventually, he blinked up at me. "He wouldn't have asked for help if he wasn't sure he would need it," Harrison concluded on his own. I nodded. He dropped his head into his hands, shaking it side to side.

"I'm so sorry, Harrison." I reached out hesitantly to comfort but stopped before I touched him. I balled my fist and brought it back to my lap.

He lifted his head to look in the distance. "I've wasted so much time."

"You're here now," I said firmly. "It's more than most."

He shook his head. "Not enough."

I understood the helpless feeling that nothing would ever be enough again. How could any person ever make a totally unfair and unfixable situation better?

He processed in silence. I fought the urge to get up and check on something, work on something. I understood his pain, but I also had so much to do. Every moment that passed was another moment lost. When George had an episode like this, it was a harsh reminder that time was fleeting.

Maybe I hadn't been as subtle as I thought. He caught me glancing around the study, calculating how much work was ahead of me. I was putting this room off for last. It would easily take the most amount of time.

"What are you going to do?" he asked.

I let out a long, slow breath. "Everything I can," I said with a shrug.

My throat was tight, and I had to look away lest I fall into his concerned and worried gaze.

"People can't know," I said. "Readers want G.S. Sedar. Not some nobody. You have to keep this to yourself. I'm trusting you." I finally locked my eyes on his and poured in the importance of this request.

His gaze flicked back and forth between my eyes and briefly moved over my face before he swallowed and nodded. "I understand."

We stayed stuck at that moment.

"It's going to be okay," he said to us both. I wished I believed him. "You aren't doing it alone, right? George is going to help write still."

"Yes," I said carefully. "That is the plan. In theory. He has lots of notes." He wasn't exactly reliable, but he had his moments of writing bursts, and I would be able to find a way to organize his scribbles.

"Okay. Okay," Harrison said.

We had moved to stand in the center of the room. We both seemed to realize it at the same time. His gaze flicked to my lips and moved over my face. Why was he always looking so intensely at me?

"What?" I asked, and it felt loud in the silent room, even though it could have only been a whisper.

"Did you know who I was? That day in town?" he asked.

"Did I know who you were in relation to George?" I asked in return.

He shook his head. "Well, yes, but also, did you know I was a"—he cleared his throat—"an actor?"

"No. I had no idea that you were super mega star Harrison Evans." I dropped my arms as a thought occurred.

The tips of his ears flushed, and he looked away. "I guess I thought when you came up to me—never mind."

"Wait. Wait. Did you think I was a fan?" I asked, amusement growing.

He ducked his head, cringing. "Maybe."

I snorted, "And then I ..." I sucked in my lips to keep from laughing. "I'm the last person on the planet who would ever recognize a celebrity." I couldn't help a small laugh that escaped.

"Okay. Very funny. In my defense, that had never happened before," he said.

"The theft or the lack of an autograph?" I laughed harder. The relief of having the truth out there lightened me more than I'd felt in years.

His smile grew as I continued to lose my composure. "Both. Stop laughing at me."

"I'm not. Sorry. I'm just—" I waved my hand at my face, where tears gathered at the corners. "Laughing with you. It's sweet."

"Hardly." He pretended to frown but only looked more charming.

"Okay. Sorry." I gained some composure.

He had a quirked smile as I took a deep breath in and out. Somehow, as I bent forward to hide my laughter, he had moved even closer so that when I straightened, he was within arm's reach. He stood a few inches taller than me; his intense eyes flicked, moving over my face as if trying to figure out the feelings I kept locked away. His strong jaw had just a hint of a five-o'clock shadow. A tangible heat radiated from him, carrying the warm scent of something slightly spicy and exotic but laced with the familiarity of fresh laundry.

And these were all things I didn't want to be noticing. This kept happening, this drifting together. The smile melted off my face as determination filled his eyes.

One breath.

Two breaths.

He cleared his throat to speak, "It's just that the day we first met, it seemed—"

The door swung open, and Collette burst in. "Frankie! I finished the movie. Can I have a snack?"

Harrison and I stepped apart in a flash, as if there were any reason to feel guilt. I avoided his gaze as George came in behind my niece, heading to his desk. All evidence of his previous accusations gone.

I rubbed at my temple. Break over.

"Frankie. Good. There you are." He moved to his chair with

effort and *oomphed* as he slumped back. "And Harrison, my boy! Did Frankie tell you the news?"

Harrison took a moment of blinking before he caught up. "Yeah, yes."

"You can have an apple or string cheese," I said to Collette. "Tea, George?" I asked.

Collette wrapped herself around my thigh with one arm and Harrison's with another. He smiled down at her with a little wave.

"Cheesy crackers?" she asked.

"Or a yogurt. No junk food."

"Cheese crackers aren't junk. They're delicious."

"Those are your options. Dinner will be soon." I started to walk, weighed down by Collette.

"Ugh, fine. Stupid healthy food."

"I guess if you don't want to grow big and smart, you could just have junk food all the time."

"If I stay small and dumb, can I have cheese crackers?" she asked.

Harrison snorted, watching our exchanges with a bemused smile.

"Hmm, no," I said, pretending to think about it.

"I don't want that tea that tastes like bergamot. You keep giving me that tea, and I don't like it," George said.

"That was once, George. I haven't given that to you in a long time," I said on a sigh.

"Well, I didn't like it."

The pressure at my temple grew. "Let me make sure I've gotten everybody's orders right. I'm like a short-order cook."

"Oh, can we play kitchen? I'll be the chef and pour the tea!" Collette jumped excitedly.

"No, sweetie can you go play dolls for a minute while I do this?"

"Nooo. I want to help," she whined.

I looked up at Harrison and found him trying to follow the bewildering conversation that had just occurred, almost overlapping.

"Collette, why don't you show me what movie you watched," he said. "Then you can take my order."

"Okay, but you have to order cheesy crackers," she said, tugging Harrison out of the room.

"Deal."

As Harrison took Collette, and George sat at his desk, I went to set the kettle.

I couldn't believe I shared everything like that. Anybody in George's life this long couldn't be bad, but it was very unlike me. Harrison made me feel safe.

Feelings of safety led to the worst disappointment.

8

———

Harrison

I TUCKED MYSELF INTO THE PANTRY, SQUEEZING ONTO A BOX OF canned goods. Outside, Collette played happily on my extra work phone I'd given her. I'm sure Frankie wouldn't like that, but Christ, I needed a moment to think. The situation at Sedar's was far worse than I'd thought. No way could any one person handle all this. My head spun. Collette and George ping-ponged demands back and forth so fast I couldn't keep up. How had Frankie handled this for two years? I dialed Emma, and she answered right away.

"Harrison? Where are you? I can't see anything." Emma leaned closer to the screen. I didn't recognize where she was.

"Shh, keep your voice down," I said.

"What's going on? Where are you? Are you in a closet?"

"I'm at George's. Are you free?"

"Yes, but turn a light on. I can't see you."

"I'm adding Charlie. Hang on," I said.

Charlie's face popped up a moment later. "Heya," he said loudly, propped against his headboard. "What've I missed?"

Emma and I shushed him.

"Harrison is in a closet, and we have to whisper," Emma said.

"The media would have a field day with that one," he chuckled.

"It's a larder!" I whisper-yelled.

Kate leaned into the screen, her wide eyes glinting as she waved perkily. Her head moved closer, eyes squinting. "Harrison, are you stuck in a closet?"

"It's the larder," Charlie said.

Kate turned to him with a frown. "Is that better?"

"If he gets peckish," Charlie said.

"Are you peckish, Harrison?" Kate asked me.

"Harrison is clearly having some sort of a crisis," Emma added. "Although maybe he is hangry."

"No. I'm not hangry. And it's not a crisis. I just don't want Collette to hear." I dropped the phone, peeked through a sliver of door to check, and found her giggling and making faces at herself in the camera.

"Is Collette okay?" Emma asked worriedly.

"Yeah, she's eating cheesy crackers and taking selfies on my work phone," I explained.

"That's hardly a reason to hide in the closet," Charlie said.

"Larder," Kate corrected sweetly.

I groaned and dropped my head. This had been a mistake. People in love were the worst.

"Okay, okay. Sorry, mate, what's going on?" Charlie asked.

"It's worse here than I thought."

"What do you mean?" Charlie frowned.

"George. His memory." I didn't feel right telling them about the video or Frankie's role in the next story. They didn't know who she was anyway, and I didn't have time to explain. "He's gone downhill since his fall."

"Oh, Harrison. I'm so sorry," Emma said. She paused in

putting in her earrings. Wesley came up behind her and kissed her shoulder.

"What's wrong?" he asked. Then he noticed the phone and a cool mask slipped over his features.

"It's just the guys," Emma explained, and he instantly relaxed. "Do you need us to fly out?"

Emma and Wesley had recently announced their retirement and were in the thick of legal battles to free Wesley from the tyranny of his father. The good news was his awful father was set to be arrested without bail within the next week. Their life was stressful enough without me adding to it.

Wesley leaned down to speak to me. "We have access to the jet any time you need it."

Damn, if that man hadn't grown on me. I used to think he was a proper arse, but he had spent his entire life protecting Emma from his family, unbeknownst to all of us.

"No, thank you." I scrubbed my face. "Things are just hectic here. Really complicated," I explained.

The others nodded back.

I heard Kate whisper to Charlie, "Should we get Agata for this?"

Charlie tilted his head to consider.

"No," I said quickly. I wasn't ready for their sturdy Polish housekeeper to put me in my place, which made me realize just as quickly that I had a guilty conscience. I supposed it was why I called them in the first place. "I feel bad being here. Adding to the stress. I just—I think I'm making things worse. I should probably go, right?" I asked.

"Does George want you to leave?" Charlie asked.

"No, uh, he didn't say that." I thought about the recognition in his eyes when I entered his office earlier. The release of tension as I sat next to him. The nagging guilt intensified.

"What do you want to do?" Emma asked, presumably to me.

"I want to help him," I said with a sigh.

"And you think leaving would do that?" Emma asked.

"I-I don't know," I admitted. I wanted to tell them I wasn't the crisis person people called in these situations. I wanted to explain that things were even more complicated than they knew, that a little girl was here too with no sign of her mother returning, and Frankie wouldn't elaborate.

Frankie. Frankie was drowning in all this. Her stress was evident in the tight lines of her mouth and her constant worried frown when she thought nobody was looking. But I was always looking at her.

I couldn't find the words to express any of that.

"From what it sounds like, George isn't getting any better, Harrison," Emma said. "I know your heart, and while you might be scared, you don't want to have any regrets."

"Regrets are far worse than being there when things get hard," Charlie said, jaw clenching. Kate's hand moved to his shoulder to rub.

"Yeah," I said, my throat too tight to elaborate.

I sighed. I wanted to be better. I wanted to be more than the lowest expectation of me.

"I can't imagine leaving him alone," I said. *Any of them.*

There was a sharp rapping on the door before light spilled into the room, causing us all to jump. "Why do adults hide in closets to cry?" Collette asked as she swung open the door.

"It's a larder," everybody on the phone yelled out.

"I'm not crying," I said.

"Hmm." She narrowed her eyes and leaned forward where I sat on the box that was making my bum numb. Her nose pressed against mine as she looked between my eyes. "You only have one eye. I'm done with my snack, and Frankie said she needs to start dinner, and you're blocking the pasta." She straightened and noticed the phone and saw the other faces there. "Hello." She waved. "I remember you!"

They all smiled and waved back.

"I'll, uh, talk to you all later," I said. I'd been about to hang up when Wesley spoke.

"Think about the person you want to be," Wesley said. "Not the person you think you are."

I held his gaze for a moment before nodding and ending the call.

"Right. Let's get dinner started," I said.

Frankie needed help. Collette and George and the archiving and the book. The book. It all had to be written, and she was one woman trying to do it all. It would be like a screenwriter trying to produce, act, and film an entire movie.

After dinner, I read to Collette and situated George in his favorite chair with a book. He was drowsing before I left the room.

I found Frankie staring out the kitchen window into the now dark evening.

"Tea has been poured. George's way. Lesson learned. I apparently didn't pour it right the first time," I said.

"Ah, yes, I learned that the hard way too. Milk first," she said and smiled.

I shuddered. "Sometimes I don't believe he's from England. And Collette finally fell asleep. I read her the one about the unicorn."

Frankie nodded. "A classic."

"Collette only complained 'that's not the way Frankie does the voice' a dozen times." I slumped into one of the wooden chairs at the breakfast nook.

She chuckled. "Sorry about that. She has this thing where however it was done the first time means it has to be done that way in perpetuity."

"Tough crowd." I pretended to yank at a tie I wasn't wearing.

"Thank you for doing all that. You really didn't have to," she said, finally turning from the view to look at me. She took a deep breath in and out before she met my awaiting gaze. She was so beautiful, but that tension around her eyes spoke of exhaustion on a deep level.

Almost as though she was doing the job of several people.

"You can't do this alone," I said and flinched. "Bullocks. I'm sorry. That's very presumptive of me to walk into one hour of this and say that."

She only raised her eyebrow but didn't disagree.

"What I meant was, you should get help. Can you get help?" I asked.

She spun her mug on the counter by its handle. She had one leg propped up on the other knee, like a sort of flamingo stance. "A cleaner comes every other week for a deep clean. And gardeners. I don't have to worry about anything on the estate so long as nothing changes," she explained.

"But Collette?" I hedged.

"That's a little more complicated. She's staying here for now."

"But you are her caretaker?"

She sucked in her lips, debating. "Technically, George has temporary guardianship. And that's murky at best. But as you probably guessed, that situation needs to change." Her leg dropped from its perch. "I was okay leaving her with George before, but not since the fall."

"Right." Anxiety tightened my gut.

"I'm hoping that they—George's team—might allow a stipend to help with her care. Collette goes to school a lot of days, but if she's off or it's a weekend, I-I could use some help," she admitted as though she were confessing a terrible sin.

"Bloody right!" I said, because *obviously.*

She frowned with a sigh. "I feel like I should be able to handle it all. Like I should be thankful I even have the opportunity to help. So many people would be thrilled to work for George. But there are so many things that need to get done. What ends up happening is that I just feel like I'm doing a lot of things poorly and not a single thing right." She closed her eyes briefly. "God, I'm sorry. I don't know why I'm unloading on you like this."

Because you trust me. Because you need help. Because you feel like you've known me too ...

"So what does that consist of?" I asked. She frowned, and I clarified. "What would you hire someone to do to help with Collette?"

"Oh, that? The rearing of a child? Oh you know, just sprinkle some straw and apple cores in her trough, and she'll be fine."

"Then you're golden." I stepped closer until she glanced warily at me. "Really, what would help?" I asked.

Her gaze moved over my shoulder as she contemplated. "Some of the domestic details. Meal planning. An extra guardian on hand for the unexpected school stuff that pops up, like conferences and field trips. Short days and snow days. Getting her ready and to school. Packing her lunch and doing her laundry. Buying her new clothes as she grows out of the old. Getting her to eat things that aren't neon colored. Picking her up and making her dinner. Wash, rinse, repeat, as needed." She rubbed at her chest.

"Okay. Yes." I nodded, ruminating. "Okay. Now George," I asked.

"What about him?"

"This isn't sustainable. You can't do this."

"I've been managing fine."

"Have you? Because it feels to me that you aren't."

"Look, if you just came up here to tell me all the ways in

which I'm failing, please feel free to keep that to yourself. I know that things are a mess but I'm doing my best."

"I believe that you are," I said. "I can tell you care. Deeply."

She looked away. "I do. And for you to sit here and pick apart my life and sum it up to a few choices, as if I don't spend every waking moment thinking about this, it's insulting. I didn't ask for your opinion. Or your help." She wouldn't look at me as she scowled, head turned to the side.

"That's not what I'm doing here. I'm not saying I have the answers. I just need to break it down into steps so I can understand."

"I don't know." Her head shook. "I don't know how to do any of this. How do you figure out overnight how to raise a child who isn't your own, care for a man who can't remember who you are all while doing your job, and oh yeah, write a damn book based on faded memories and handwritten notes even though you've never done any of things before in your life and you absolutely have no clue what you're doing." She slumped at the end of her speech. Her head dropped into her hands.

"I'm sorry, Frankie."

She glanced to me, and her eyes glistened.

"It's fine. God. I'm sorry. I'm not like this. I was never like this ..." She turned her head away, the upturn of her nose more noticeable in her profile. She was so delicately built yet carried a fierceness. "I have been doing everything on my own. I'm not a nurse. I'm not a mother. Yet I wear so many hats now I cannot even keep track. If you have a better way to do all this, then be my guest."

I blinked. "Good idea." I hadn't even thought about the words before they flopped out of my mouth. The answer seemed so obvious.

"What?" she asked, exacerbated.

"You're right. I'll stay. And help."

"You can't be serious."

"You can't be expected to do this all alone."

"No. That's—" She shook her head. "You have an entire life and career away from here. I'll talk to George's team. I'm sure they'd provide the funds for a caretaker."

"How would he like that, you think? You just told me that he sometimes forgets who you are. Another stranger in his home? Two? Imagine how that will add to the stress. I make him feel better. You said yourself that he's more settled when I'm here, less confused."

"Yes but ..."

"But what? I'm offering." I shrugged with a cheeky Harrison Evans grin.

"This is a lot. The book is due at the end of the year. Collette ..." She glanced up hesitantly. "I don't know how long we will be caring for her."

"Fine," I said.

"Fine?" She shook her head with a guffaw. "What about your massive career as a film star?"

"I'll take a sabbatical. I've been acting since I was born. I've earned it."

"It wouldn't be some fun vacation." I glared at the ground as she spoke. Of course, she'd think that I took this as a fun little romp through the park. "I worry that you aren't thinking this through. You can't commit to-to them, and then leave when things get hard."

I ground my jaw. "I'll sign a contract then. I'll tell my team I need a break. It's true."

"This isn't a break."

"I meant from acting," I said, my frustration growing. I was here offering to take some of her burden, and she would rather suffer than accept my help. "Is it that laughable that I can be of assistance?"

"Have you ever watched a child?"

"Kids love me. Collette and I get on swimmingly."

"This isn't like working together on a movie set. Getting along hardly matters. She needs structure and predictability. Her life has been so"—she hesitated—"messy. Little kids need to have some routine to feel safe. She can't just have strangers coming and going. It's not good for a child. For her." She spoke with vehemence. She spoke with a fear rooted in trauma. This was a woman who wanted to spare a child from having a life she knew too well.

"I understand what you're saying." I stepped closer until she was forced to meet my eyes. "I will be here. That's what you need. You can call my friends and get references if you want. But I'm telling you that I *will* be here. Having an extra adult on hand can't hurt."

She didn't hide her skepticism very well, and it cut.

"I want to be here," I said. "And that's more than most people who are being paid to just do a job. If you want to sign a contract, I will do that too."

"This just doesn't feel real. What will you tell people?"

Good-time guy of the Intrepid Trio, actor Harrison Evans, takes unplanned leave from Hollywood for secret reasons.

"We won't tell anybody. Out of sight, out of mind in this business. By the time I return people won't even realize I'd been gone. But that's not what matters to me." If we drew any attention this way, then there would be issues, but if we slipped quietly out of the limelight, nobody would notice.

She had taken a leap of faith with me earlier by trusting me with her truth, so I would do the same. "The thing is, George is one of the most important people on the planet to me. He literally gave me the life I have. I-I haven't been here when he needed me."

She groaned quietly. "I shouldn't have said that. I'm sorry. I felt defensive." She balled her thumb into her palm.

"But you're right," I half-shouted and lowered my voice, glancing out into the hall. "I should have been here." She sucked in her lips and didn't say anything else. "I feel like I have to do this. I want to do this for him. I can't—" I broke off suddenly, emotion catching my throat. I gathered myself, using more focus than when I was on SNL and couldn't laugh, only this time, I was trying not to lose it in front of a beautiful, stoic woman. "I saw the fear in his eyes in that video. I could hear the worry in his voice. I want to be here for him. I haven't been great at a lot of things in my life. I'm not really a person who others feel like they can count on." Her forehead creased. I added quickly, trying not to shoot myself in my own foot as it were, "I want to be the person George counts on. Collette too." I wanted Frankie to have faith in me, but that felt like too much too soon, and I wasn't even sure why that felt so important.

"In a few days, you and I can reassess. If it's not working and we need professional help, that's understandable. I'll work with Bob and his team and get some. But for now, nobody outside the few who already do need to know about this. We will tell Collette and George that I'm visiting for a while. We don't have to mention that I'm here for anything other than a visit. We can give George the finale he deserves."

It felt like hours as Frankie deliberated. Eventually, she stepped up to me. "Fine. You have a two-week probational period to see if this works."

I grinned so wide that Frankie had to bite back a smile of her own. "Deal." I extended my hand.

"And if and when you commit to this, you're signing your name in blood. Do you understand? I won't let these people get hurt," she said.

"In blood."

Frankie smiled at me and it reminded me of the day we met. "Okay, Harrison Evans. You're hired." She shook my hand, and we both looked at our clasped hands.

"Full-time manny, extraordinaire," I said.

"I don't think we say that anymore. Manny," she said while still looking at our clasped hands.

"Ah."

I would prove myself worthy of something more than acting and being the fun one. I ignored the frisson at her touch and released her, balling my fist and putting it in my pocket.

"Then just call me Mr. Mom," I said.

She shook her head with a snort. "That's worse somehow."

9

———

ARCHIVE FILE: *4308*

George's Terraformative notes: Adam and the others finally ping on a planet that could be paradise. He wants them to leave to give it one last shot.

…

"It's humanity at stake, that's all," Adam said.

"No pressure." Lucy glanced at Freddy.

"It *is* pressure. It's the only thing that matters."

Freddy scrubbed a knuckle over his scarred eyebrow. "We've been down this road before, Adam."

"Then we give up?" Adam tossed out his arms. "What has our entire life been about if not this? This is all we trained for. This is all we know."

NOTES:

FRicci: Would Lucy and Freddie be fighting Adam this hard? Or would they want to take this mission too? None of them even sound like this anymore. Maybe in the early books, but not now. UGH. I need George, but he said he was too tired today, and I'm running out of time. I have no idea what I'm doing. I can't do this. Maybe I should just type one hundred thousand words of "all work and no play make Frankie a dull girl" and see if the publisher notices. I should just quit now before this got too far. I can't do this alone.

HEvans: You're being rather hard on yourself. Also, was that a movie reference? I thought you didn't do movies.

FRicci: Who is this?!

HEvans: The deus ex machina ;p Did I just hear you yelp? I'll give you one guess.

FRicci: Really, Harrison?

HEvans: How'd you know?

FRicci: Because it says HEvans.

HEvans: That's because now you're in heaven, love.

FRicci: If you heard that, it was the sound of gagging. And for the record, *The Shining* was a novel long before it was a movie.

HEvans: Ah, I would never know such trivia because I'm just a beautiful actor, too dumb to know about ... what did you call it a nobel? Noovle?

FRicci: I never said you were dumb.

HEvans: Ah, so you think I'm beautiful?

FRicci: Such modesty. Just explaining how I got the *all work, no play* reference. I don't live in a total bubble. Tell me you didn't choose that username name on purpose?

HEvans: A delightful coincidence, I assure you.

FRicci: Back to the real issue, buddy.

HEvans: Books being made into visual media and the impossible expectations?

FRicci: Don't distract me with a good debate. HOW DID YOU GET IN HERE?!

HEvans: No need to growl. Do I need to worry about you too, Frankie? You gave me a spare key. Remember two-week trial period?

FRicci: Too soon to make a joke about bad memory.

HEvans: You're right. Showbiz has given me gallows humor.

FRicci: Seriously, how are we typing back and forth like this?

HEvans: It's the chat feature on the shared doc you're working in.

FRicci: Yes. But how did you find it?

HEvans: Honestly, I'm not sure, but I suspect it has something to do with Collette playing with my phone. It's scary how tech savvy this kid is.

FRicci: STOP GIVING HER DEVICES TO PLAY ON.

HEvans: How come you aren't using the typewriter?

FRicci: I know you heard me. I don't think my wrists would survive it. I don't know how George managed so many books on that machine.

HEvans: He can be a stubborn old mule sometimes. He still thinks the internet is a passing phase.

FRicci: I once watched Collette try to explain hashtags to him.

HEvans: I would have paid good money for that.

FRicci: Like you did the chicken from Brooks' Baubles and Books?

HEvans: Ouch. Speaking of too soon to make jokes. And if you recall, I did end up paying for Nix.

FRicci: Eventually. You named her after *Terraformative*?

HEvans: It was meant to be a gift for Charlie and Kate, sort of an inside joke.

FRicci: Didn't I spot *Nix* sitting on your dresser?

HEvans: I'm still getting around to it. ;)

FRicci: You are too heavy-handed with the winks. Just like in real life.

HEvans: It's a gift only a few can wield.

FRicci: I'm supposed to be working. This is no place for winking.

HEvans: I beg to differ. But I will leave you be. Collette and I were about to have giant bowls of ice cream anyway and watch telly.

FRicci: Har har.
FRicci: You better be kidding.
FRicci: Harrison?
FRicci: HARRISON!?

10

Frankie

HARRISON'S SNORING FORM WAS SPREAD EAGLE, FACE DOWN ON THE mattress. Sound asleep without a care in the world.

To be fair, it was his room. His temporary room. I'd waited as long as I could before coming to see where he was. The whole house was up, and he slept on. It was a school day and his first morning on duty. This wasn't an encouraging start.

"Must be nice," I mumbled.

It was weird that there was a man in the house. A man who wasn't like a grandfather to me. He was all man. The fact only occurred to me now. In another life, at another time, Harrison would have been a distraction. More than that. With that Hollywood jawline, his perfect ski-slope nose, that thick head of dark hair that looked sturdy enough to grip. It had been so long since I leaned into that side of myself. That *feminine* side.

His face was tucked into a pillow, his flexed arm curled around, giving a lovely show of exposed skin. His entire backside was on full display. His defined muscles were artistically toned and pointed down to where his ...

"He's naked," Collette whisper-yelled at my side suddenly.

I startled and cleared my throat. I had also been chewing on my lip, apparently.

"No. He's got undies on," I said, arms crossed, back to business.

She giggled and covered her face with her hands. "I see his booty butt."

I sucked in my lips to stop a laugh.

"His legs are so hairy," she said, curling her lip.

"That's why they call him Harrison. *Harry*-son."

Collette blinked and then looked up at me with an unamused expression. "Lame joke. Cringe."

I shrugged with a grin. "Where did you learn cringe?"

"Harrison's phone." I grumbled, but she just noted, "He's got lots of muscles."

"That he does," I agreed.

Harrison smiled where his face smooshed against the pillow. "Thank you," he mumbled without opening his eyes. I sighed at his lackadaisical attitude.

I had a book to write, and every second he stayed here sleeping was another minute of my time wasted.

"Collette, I don't think Harrison heard about your other musical talents," I said.

The little girl's eyes widened before she sprinted out of the bedroom and to hers.

Last night, Harrison and I explained to George and Collette that Harrison would be around for a little while. Harrison made plans with his agent and team, keeping the details vague as "family issues" and we made a plan for how he could be most helpful in the next two weeks. I'd gone to bed feeling somewhat hopeful. Cautiously optimistic was a better term.

The other two were, as expected, thrilled with this development. Apparently, Frowny Frankie was a bit of a downer, and the fresh blood enthused them both with new vigor. We will see how long that lasts. Finding him face down an hour after even Collette had woken up wasn't encouraging.

It wasn't that I wanted him to fail. I did need the help, but I worried that he wasn't taking this situation seriously. Or, at best, as some sort of role he was playacting at. There was no room for that here. Better to throw him into the deep end and see how he swam.

At least the view was nice.

"Are you staring at my bottom, Francesca?" he mumbled with eyes still closed. The way he rumbled my full name did things that it really shouldn't have. Mostly in the nether region area that had long ago been closed for business with boarded-up windows and a layer of dust.

My head snapped up from being tilted. "I don't really have a choice." I tossed the comforter up to cover him. "Your tighty whities have traumatized Collette."

He chuckled a deep, sleepy laugh.

Collette slid back into the room, stopping next to the head of the bed. Her recorder in hand. I smiled, subtly covering my ears as she blasted the screeching high notes into the room.

"I'm awake." Harrison shot up and blinked around the room. His bedhead was flat on one side and sticking up on the other.

"Oh. No. Did we wake you?" I said loudly over a halting rendition of what may have been "Twinkle, Twinkle Little Star."

"No. I'm wide awake." A jaw-cracking yawn split his face as he scrubbed sleep from his eyes. "Morning, kitty, ready for school?"

Collette dropped her recorder and flung her arms out. "I'm still in my pajamas," she said with incredulity.

Harrison squinted to look at her. "I thought maybe it was a fashion statement."

"Come on. Get up." She shoved his arm, and he flopped back

over onto the bed, wrapping himself tightly in the comforter and pretended to snore loudly.

"Harrison!" She giggled, and he snored louder as she catapulted herself onto his back.

A loud "Oomph" came from under the blankets. "I'm up. I'm up."

Sure, it was all fun and games, until it wasn't.

"It's after eight," I said. "I'll be getting to work. Breakfast needs to be made. Lunch packed and George needs to take his pills so he needs to eat ASAP. Collette will help. Snap, snap, get to it."

They both sighed. I walked out of the room before curiosity got the best of me, and I could see what he was packing in those undies.

"Come on, Collette. Let's give him a minute to get dressed, and then you can show him the ropes."

"What ropes?" She followed me, and I shut the door as she stood outside. "How much is a minute?"

"Sixty seconds." I began to walk away when it was clear she took the minute warning literally.

"Okay. One. Two. Three ..." she yelled, face pressed against the closed door.

I strutted to the office with a smile as her counting faded away.

As I sifted through the Post-its and sheets of papers with notes scribbled on various scraps of paper, I heard Harrison and Collette chatting happily.

I hadn't expected the anxiety as I finally sat at the typewriter to get to work. Well, yes, I had expected it for the writing but not for listening to Harrison and Collette learn their morning routine together.

"Don't forget my water bottle," Collette said.

I had to bite my tongue from jumping up and running to tell him where it was.

"They'll be fine," George said from the wingback chair where he sipped coffee.

I relaxed back and pretended I wasn't staring down the hallway.

George was having a good morning. It made me want to make as much headway as possible on the book while I had him like this. Mornings like this made it hard to remember that there was anything wrong with his traitorous brain. A stirring of hope that maybe it was Harrison's presence was quickly clamped down. I wouldn't get my hopes up. One day at a time. He would be leaving.

I would be leaving.

This was all a temporary situation.

I glanced at the keyboard. "I'm not worried."

"Okay, good. Because you seem tense."

"There's just a lot of steps to get her out the door in the morning."

"And they will figure it out."

I put my head down and got to work. A little while later, Collette jumped into the office.

"I'm ready!" She was dressed in her uniform, her face clean, and her hair done.

"Wow. Look at you," I said, smiling. Her hair was in two little buns like Princess Leia. A warm, gooey feeling melted in my chest, a feeling that made me want to scoop the both of them up in a big hug. It took me by surprise.

"Harrison gave me space buns!" Collette shouted.

"Very cool," I said genuinely. Meanwhile, my insides continued to flip. It was a battle to brush through her hair most days, and he'd managed to style it. I imagined him intently focused on smoothing her fine curls with product as she squirmed, incapable of keeping her head facing one direction. I wished someone had taken a photo.

Harrison leaned against the doorway, giving a modest shrug. He'd gotten dressed in jeans and a fitted tee. His biceps bulged where his arms were crossed in such a manly man way.

"She told me she wasn't allowed to wear her cat ears," he said. He smiled softly up at me, and I blinked away, aware that I may have been studying him a little too closely.

"Uniform rules," I said with an eye roll.

"It's okay. I'm over being a cat. Harrison was telling me about Star Wards."

"*Star Wars*," he corrected.

"Can I watch it tonight? Please, Frankie?"

"Maybe after dinner. If you don't have any homework," I said.

They both made the same face of annoyance.

"Okay! What time is dinner?" she asked.

I smiled up at Harrison. "What time?" I asked sweetly. I could actually get used to this.

"Right. Well, uh, eight?" he asked rather than said.

I widened my eyes and shook my head. "Collette's bedtime?"

"No. That's too late. Obviously. Six?" he corrected.

"That sounds good. What're we having?" I asked.

Harrison scrunched up his face. "It's a surprise."

"Can't wait," I said.

"Your confidence in me is simply awe-inspiring," he said with cheek.

Maybe my tone had been dry. I smiled again before looking pointedly at the wall clock. "This is about the time we leave. Otherwise, you'll be stuck in the drop-off line all morning."

"All right, kitty, let's roll out."

"I'm Princess Leia now."

"Of course. How could I forget?"

They made their way, and I fought the urge to call after to make sure she had her lunch. Collette would remind him.

Sure enough, I heard her distant voice ask, "Did you make my lunch?"

There was a long pause before Harrison covered smoothly. "Ah, well, I think you will have to buy today, is that an option?"

"Frankie always makes me lunch with healthy food and one little treat. She said the food at school is filled with per-pre-parservartives. Junk."

"Okay. Noted. Tomorrow, I will pack you the best, most brain-fueling, preservative-free lunch that ever there was."

"What's brain fuel?"

Their voices drifted out the door.

I let out a breath and looked at George. He was smiling as his gaze lingered where they had just been.

"Nice to have a full house again," he said. "I miss the chaos sometimes."

I nodded with a tight smile, feeling my throat constrict. Only one more person was in our little collection of misfits, but it made the house feel more full. It was only the first morning, and the second I felt the pings of hopefulness, I clamped them down. That way only led to disappointment.

I dropped my head to look at the notes for this scene. George's handwriting was a slanted and messy half-cursive, which I was a professional at deciphering at this point.

"George?" I asked him where he sat next to the fire. "What would you think if I made Lucy pregnant?"

George's deep, wrinkled brow pinched in thought. "I think that's the exact sort of idea that makes you perfect for this."

"Some readers won't like that."

"Some readers will. You can't worry about that," he said. "Plus, it's the things you don't even worry about that end up bothering them the most. Just focus on telling the story of our hearts."

I smiled at him and ducked my head quickly to type notes on my computer. I'd write on my computer and type the final on the typewriter if I had to. That was what I had done for the last two books. Not to alarm anybody, but that wasn't necessary anymore, and that was one perk of all this. Soon, the soft sounds of George sleeping filled the room. He was like a cat that way, and there was comfort in that predictability.

I worked for a while in the silent house, losing track of time and feeling like actual progress was made. By the time the vibration of my phone startled me from where I'd been working, it was after lunch.

It was a text from Brooks checking in on me.

My wrists were tired from typing, so I called her back.

"What's wrong?" she asked.

"Nothing. I just didn't feel like texting," I said.

"Sometimes you seem so normal, and then you do things like call me, and I feel scared."

"Sorry, sorry. Next time, I will text you that I don't feel like texting and give you plenty of time to mentally prepare. Wrists be damned!"

"That's better," she said. "At least you didn't video call or you'd be getting a whole view of my banoffee pie."

I guffawed and covered my mouth to make sure that I didn't wake George. He snored on.

"That is a visual I could have lived without," I said.

"My humor is wasted on you. How goes it with Brit boy anyway?" she asked.

"Weird. I had this realization this morning—briefs, by the way." She made a sound of impressed surprise as I went on. "That he is very much a man. Like he has these big man feet and hairy legs and strong shoulders and he's just a *man* and I don't know, like virile and masculine."

"Virile? Huh. You are a thirsty bird," she said.

"I mean, it has been a minute," I mumbled. "But no. You know me. I have turned that part of me off, locked it in a box, and buried it under a haunted graveyard, so the only way to get to it is by battling poltergeists."

"Quite the metaphor. I assume by 'it' you mean your sweet, sweet chastity or are you referring to overall level of horniness?"

"Yes." I blushed as I twirled a pen on the desk, hiding a secret smile.

She laughed. "Well, hopefully, he won't be in your hair much longer. Oh! You should come into town, and we can go to the bar and get you a ghost hunter."

"I regret that metaphor."

"Too late, your vagina and all surrounding area are now going to be referred to only as the crypt keeper."

"So much regret." I sighed. "But actually, I'll have to take a rain check on the night out."

Without going into too much detail, I gave Brooks the report that Harrison would stay on to help.

"Just as a trial run to start. Two weeks. And then we'll see," I said.

Brooks was quiet after I finished. "I'm really surprised that he agreed to stay and help out," she finally said. Her carefully chosen words worried me.

"You and me both. But I have to admit, and granted it's only been one day—or one morning—but it went smoother than I expected. He has the boundless energy of a golden retriever puppy."

"That's good." She laughed, but it was the hollow fake one she used with customers. "He just always struck me as the good-time guy of the Intrepid Trio. I feel sort of bad for thrusting you at him that day."

"I knew you did that on purpose!"

"How could I not? I knew you had no clue who he was. Oh, man, I only wish I had been there to see the shenanigans unfold."

"Nothing of the sort."

I feel like I've known you.

She clicked her tongue and said, "Of all the kids from *Terraformative*, Harrison seems the most content to exist in and embrace his bachelor lifestyle. Just seems very out of character for him to pop up and decide to stay."

I worried my lip before I stopped myself. "I thought the same thing. But people change. I mean, in theory, I've heard. He cares a lot about George."

"Of course. And people can change." She let out another breath. "But just be aware. There were rumors of a love child once, you know? And I know your thoughts on deadbeat parents."

It was like I swallowed a rock. "I hadn't heard anything about that."

"That's because you know as much about film and TV pop culture as I know about what banoffee pie actually is." I heard the tippy tap of a pen and pictured her hitting it against the cash register. "Okay. Don't let me stress you out. This is good. You really do need the help. You are running yourself ragged. Plus, I don't have to worry about you. You have oodles of street smarts. You're in the safe zone now if you didn't instantly fall for his charm. The crypt keeper can relax. I know you won't ever let your guard down just for his wounded puppy eyes, and you especially wouldn't let Collette get hurt."

"Yeah," I said softly. I was glad to have her support but hated that her thoughts mirrored the ones that kept me up at night.

Harrison wasn't long-term. Did he even really want to be here, or was he motivated purely by a sense of guilt? How long would that guilt keep him playing house, weighed down by commitments?

"Don't forget, I can always help watch her if you need a night off. After the shop closes. I owe you. And someone has to be the cool aunt," she said.

"Excuse me? I am literally her cool aunt," I said flatly.

She tutted. "You were. Now, you're her primary caregiver. Wah wah. I can be the one that explains PG-13 jokes to her and buy her a training bra way too soon."

It was obviously meant in good fun, but the words cut deeper than she meant them to.

The bell dinged in the background. "I gotta go," she said. "Imagine if we could still communicate even without a customer interrupting our conversation. Like some sort of textual version of a phone call we could send back and forth through the sky. What a wonderful magical world that would be."

"But then I wouldn't get the full force of all this charm. Bye, Brooks."

I stared out the window after we hung up. The wind of my writing sails had come to a sudden stop. Had I taken on the role of a wet blanket parent? I just wanted to keep her safe. Was there a way to protect someone from the harsh realities of the world and still have any sort of zest for life? How the hell did people do this?

"You can't believe everything you read in the papers," George said, startling me.

"Sorry. Did I wake you?" I asked, rising to go to him.

He waved me to sit back down. "No. That was my bladder."

"Need a hand?"

He glared at me. "My legs are fine," he grumbled. He shuffled to stand and made his way out of the room.

"Sorry. Sorry."

George paused to lean on the desk. "Harrison is a good man. I know how he acts like nothing affects him, but don't you be fooled by that. Give him a chance."

I nodded, feeling chastised. I knew how it was to be seen as unfeeling just because of my outward appearance. Was it possible I was doing the same to Harrison, only he wore a different mask, one of a charmer? Or was I simply protecting myself against an ill-timed attraction to him?

George left the room, and I sighed. How could I protect myself from the charms of a professional charmer and still accept the help he offered?

11

———

Harrison

"Go change out of your uniform and bring that skirt right back down. That marker needs to be treated, or I will never be able to get that stain out," I called after Collette as she sprinted up the stairs as soon as we walked in.

"Okay!"

Frankie sat at the counter, a spoonful of marshmallow cereal paused on the way to her mouth.

A yellow moon fell off her spoon and plopped into the bowl. She wore another old band T-shirt that fell off her shoulder, exposing the pale skin of her neck.

"What?" I asked.

She closed her mouth and shook her head. "Nothing." She blinked again. "Nothing. I'm impressed is all."

I felt myself preen under her direct praise. It was less than a week into the new routine, and I was bloody killing it. Sure, I flew by the seat of my pants most days and made a pig's ear of it once or twice, but the thing was working.

"Ah, she's easy," I said, leaning on the counter between us. "I hope you didn't spoil your dinner," I said teasingly.

"I forgot to eat," she said but pushed the mostly empty bowl away. "I wanted to thank you, you've been doing really good with Collette. I know she can be ... combative. Maybe that's not the right word."

"She's confident," I said.

Frankie blinked up at me. "She really is, isn't she?"

I nodded. I wanted to tell her because of all that she had done for that little girl. I'd only been here a week, but I could feel the impression of Frankie in so much of her. Frankie spoke to Collette like a person with bodily autonomy and encouraged her without placating her. She took the time to explain why things worked the way they did instead of just saying, "Because I said so." It was more work, but it was paying off.

"She's great. I've worked with big personalities before. This is nothing."

Frankie smirked at me. "I don't doubt that."

"I have a question," I said.

Frankie sat up and gave me her focus. "What's up?"

"Hypothetically, if someone were to tell Collette, that her laugh was gross, a child, let's say. A classmate. Am I within my rights to absolutely bludgeon them?"

"Oh, no," Frankie said, her shoulders slumping under the loose shirt. I could just glimpse the hot pink sports bra. I dragged my focus back to her face.

"It's America, right? I can just hurt someone and that's within my rights, or something?" I asked.

She winced. "I don't think that's quite how it works." She shrugged. "In theory."

"Bullocks."

The anger I felt on the drive home returned. I stepped closer to Frankie and lowered my voice. Frankie met me, glancing toward the door to make sure Collette hadn't come back. "She told me on the way home that a girl in her class said that to her. I don't think I have ever felt so mad. Her laugh is amazing. And laughter means she's happy. I want to find that kid and—" I balled my fists and shook them.

She nodded and scooted closer. "It's terrible. Kids can be so awful."

"Is it too much to absolutely never let her leave the house and wrap her in bubble wrap and approve every piece of media that she views?"

Frankie shrugged and smiled softly. "That's the dream. But I'm also known for being a sort of buzzkill. And apparently, children are meant to thrive and learn."

I blinked. "Well, that's the most absurd thing I've ever heard. I want to keep Collette here at the house where things are happy and safe and everybody cares about her."

"I know." She had leaned forward, our faces were only a few breaths away from each other. The hint of marshmallow cereal came from her as her gaze moved over my face, eyes wide and almost dreamy, if only for a second, before she swallowed and leaned back.

"What did you tell her?" she asked, putting distance between us.

I swallowed before opening my mouth to answer, but Collette was back in the room and demanding a snack.

"I'll take care of the skirt," Frankie said and reached for it.

"Nope. I got it." I snatched it before she could grab it.

"I'm starting to feel unnecessary," she said.

"Hardly."

"Mommy!" Collette screamed, and Frankie and I looked at each other and then at her. There was a flash of something in Frankie's eyes that went away as quickly as it appeared.

"What?" Frankie asked, looking out the window, her color draining.

"Mommy is calling!" Collette danced with the tablet in her hand. "Can I answer?"

"Of course, of course," Frankie said, forcing a laugh. She didn't meet my gaze as I studied her closely, wondering about that reaction.

As Collette answered the call, I took the skirt to the laundry room to add a spot cleaner to her uniform. It astounded me how a tiny little person could go through so much clothing.

"Honestly, what are they doing in that school?" I grumbled as I dabbed the stain.

When I walked back into the room, Collette was at the table, gesturing wildly and talking to her tablet. "It's not my business what people think about me anyway. They are probably just unsecured and have mean parents."

I felt my eyes widen as I looked at Frankie. She was holding back a laugh.

"Insecure," Frankie corrected. "Where did you learn that word?"

She glanced to me as I went to the cabinet, whistling nonchalantly, to get the ingredients to start supper.

"That girl sounds like a major bi-brat," a voice from the tablet said. "Next time, just punch her."

Collette's eyes went comically wide as they flicked to Frankie.

"Okay, well we should always try to talk first," Frankie said loudly and stepped behind Collette to wave at the screen. "Hey, Joey. How is the tour going?"

"Oh. Hey, Frankie. It's so exhausting. It's just show after show. Fan after fan. I cannot tell you how much they need me. Blah." She sighed loudly. Frankie's fake smile remained plastered in place save for a small twitch.

I could almost hear Frankie's mind screaming *Collette needs you.*

"Mommy's a famous actress," Frankie said to me over the top of the electronic.

"Is that right?" I said.

"Who was that?" Joey asked sharply.

"Scarecrow," Collette said, chomping on a carrot as she spoke. "He says my laugh is the best."

"Don't talk with your mouth full," Frankie and I said at the same time.

"Who?" Joey's voice held an instant defensive tone.

"Uh, my friend," Frankie said quickly.

"Excuse me?" The voice sharpened, and Frankie's shoulders went to her ears. "Who is this man? You just let a stranger into Sedar's house? A man I don't know near my daughter? I expected more from you Frowny Frankie."

"I-I—" Frankie stumbled. She was doing that thing where she went completely still, features blank. I couldn't believe I ever mistook that for indifference when it was clearly her defensive mode. I hated that bloody nickname. Had Joey labeled her that?

I stepped in front of the camera, ducking to wave at the camera.

"Hi. I'm Harrison. I'm a friend of George's," I said, giving my most charming of smirks.

Joey was a blond woman, similar in some ways to Frankie. They shared the same heavy-lidded eyes and full lips. But there was an insincerity in her that rang a warning bell of learned instinct. She was beautiful, but she wasn't interesting to look at, not like Frankie was. Frankie revealed a secret every time you looked at her: a soft beauty mark near her right eye, the cut of her jaw where it met her long, elegant neck when she twisted her hair up into a bun as she was doing now.

"And Frankie's," I added, realizing I was staring at her and brought my focus back to the screen.

Joey's mouth fell open before she caught herself and fixed her hair over her shoulder, glancing discreetly at her own image on the screen. She flipped her hair back, and a slow smile spread over her features. "Of course I've heard of you, Harrison Evans. I didn't know that you and Frankie were *friends*." She said the last word with a raise of a very sharp eyebrow.

"No. It's not—Harrison is visiting George," Frankie stated.

A little quick to correct, in my opinion.

"I was about to say. Could you imagine?" Her sister made a wincing face.

I had the inexplicable urge to scoop Frankie into my arms and kiss her until her knees gave out.

Instead, I said, "Exactly. Frankie is way too good for a shirker like me." Frankie had gone to wash her bowl in the sink, but even with her back to me, the tension in her shoulders was obvious.

"You're an actress?" I asked, changing the subject. "Doing anything now?"

"Oh. It's really nothing. Just until the next movie." Joey lit up, obviously pleased to be talking about herself. "I'm touring with Chicago. Roxie Hart. The lead." She added with a lick of her lips, as if I didn't know that. "Broadway was just too ... pedestrian. I love to see the country. I need to travel and meet the people. You know how it is." She batted her lashes.

"Mommy, Harrison taught me to sing—"

"Shh, baby, the gown ups are talking," Joey said, not taking her eyes off me except when they moved to the lower corner to check herself out.

If I had thought I wanted to punch that kid in Collette's class (yes, in hindsight, I understand how awful that sounded), it was nothing compared to the anger that burst in my chest as I watched Collette's eyes dim at being reprimanded. Frankie always gave Collette a chance to speak. The little girl's ever-present smile fell off her face, and her tiny shoulders slumped.

Maybe I wasn't hiding my rage as much as I thought because a moment later, Frankie was across the kitchen and tugging me out of the room.

"Why don't Harrison and I let you two catch up," Frankie said, calling over her shoulder.

"Oh, but—" Joey's voice was cut off as the door swung shut behind us.

"I know how she comes off," Frankie said when we were in the hallway. "But she's actually ... she's trying her best. Things haven't always been easy for her. She's doing really well right now."

I ran a hand over my mouth. I didn't know the woman, but I was getting to know Frankie. If she felt the need to defend her sister, that was her choice.

It was bad enough when people treated me totally different when they learned who I was. I didn't care about that, I was used to it. It only spoke to the content of her character, but to see Collette so excited to talk to her mother only to have her shot down. It made me furious.

"She has no idea the gift she has," I said.

Frankie shrugged. "She's her daughter. She will always be the most important person to her. Joey's just finding her footing."

I hadn't been referring to Joey and her daughter—though that was true too. Collette was a miracle of a child, but I had been thinking that Joey didn't understand what a gift her sister was. I wanted to tell her that she was more a mother than that woman ever would be. That Joey should kiss the ground that she found someone to raise her daughter with such care and tenderness. But it felt grossly out of line and would only upset Frankie, who defended her sister as only family could.

"Okay," I said.

"She *can* be a good person. She's always been a lost soul," she insisted when I must not have appeared sold.

"I'm not simple enough to see any person in black and white, good or bad. I know that if you care about her enough to protect her honor"—I scratched the back of my head—"then there must be something *honorable*." I shrugged.

She blinked up at me. Her mouth closed as she swallowed. "Your opinion of me can't be that high already."

"I've met a lot of people in my life, and none of them like you."

"I-I'm not sure if that's a compliment or not." She huffed a laugh.

I stepped closer to her, my anger starting to dissipate. "It is," I said.

She looked up and met my gaze. "Harrison there is so much about me that you just don't know."

I was about to say how much I'd like to change that when there was a soft thud followed by a sniffle. She turned away and sprinted back into the kitchen.

Collette sat with her arms crossed and a scowl on her face. The tablet was face down on the table.

"What's wrong?" Frankie asked and stepped to kneel at the little girl's chair.

"Mommy said they need her for another tour." Her jaw jutted out, and she glared at the table. "I hate her stupid show. I hate her stupid job. She said she can't come home yet."

"I'm so sorry, baby girl." The second Frankie scooped her into her arms, Collette's anger dissolved into anguished tears. "She loves you so much. I know she wishes she could be here." Frankie's own eyes reddened as she rubbed Collette's back.

My entire body shook with a feeling of helplessness. It was like when George asked for William. Or looked for the memory that was just out of reach. The intense pain was incomprehensible and unfair, and I could do absolutely nothing to stop the real world from getting in here.

"I know, sweetie. It's okay to be sad. I miss her too." Frankie closed her eyes. I couldn't stand by and watch this.

I might not be able to keep the outside world at bay, that much was clear. But I could help these two.

"Oh my God. You know what?" I said loudly and suddenly. They turned and looked at me with wide eyes.

"What?" Collette asked, wiping at her eyes.

"I forgot to defrost the chicken." I smacked my forehead.

Frankie watched me as I scooted over to block the defrosted meat on the counter. She raised her eyebrow but said, "Oh. No?"

Collette sniffled and wiped her nose, looking from Frankie to me. "What are we going to eat?"

"I guess it's going to have to be a pizza and ice cream night," I said, punctuating with a loud sigh.

"But it's a school night!" Collette said excitedly. She jumped out of Frankie's arms.

Frankie shook her head as she stood and shrugged. "I mean we can't *not* eat."

Collette whooped and jumped around. "I hope Harrison forgets to defrost meat every night!"

Frankie smiled at me, and a tightness gripped my chest. I could do this. I could be the distraction from the pain. That was my job, after all. I was the good-time guy.

"Don't you need to go work?" she asked Frankie.

"There is literally nowhere else in the world I need to be," she said and kissed the girl's forehead.

12

Frankie

HARRISON'S QUICK THINKING HAD TRULY SAVED THE DAY. WITHIN minutes, Collette's tears were forgotten as we selected our pizza and ice cream toppings. I skipped the work I had planned to do after dessert for an intense few rounds of cards instead.

"Uno," I said quietly, hoping nobody would hear me, but Harrison's focus was on me, as it often seemed to be, as he raised a fierce eyebrow. At least, I thought he was going for fierce. The goofy contented grin on his face all night, canceled it out.

I bit back a smile, impossibly charmed even as he tossed down a plus two.

After victory was cruelly snatched from my hands, Collette and I powered through a thirty-minute bath, hair drying, and bedtime routine. I settled in, opening her current favorite book when she insisted Harrison read the story since he does the voices better now. How the tables had turned. What chance did I have against a professional actor? But then, after three stories and much giggling, she still insisted on just one song from me. So, back in, I went, making Harrison go to the other side of the house. I was not a singer and was not prepared to hear any notes about my rendition of "You Are My Sunshine." It was a mystery as to how she could possibly like my singing voice, but I would do it as long as it put her to sleep before the short chorus ended every time. And if I was being honest, it melted my heart to watch as she stilled into that state of fighting sleep, unable to do anything but blink slowly at me, her small hand gripping my pinky. A simple sense of security I could provide her gave me more purpose than anything I'd done.

I should have been bone tired by the time I snuck out of her room, but instead was filled with restless energy. Maybe my lack of progress that evening weighed on me. Then why was there a smile on my lips as I replayed some of the sillier moments from the evening? Harrison could work Collette into a fit of giggles that was music to my ears, especially after such a frustrating call from Joey.

I sighed and leaned my head back against the wall in the hallway outside her room. Routines could be developed so quickly. Collette was already getting used to him even though it'd been hardly a week. George was better than ever. This seemed to be working. We were working.

There was only some slight tension in my rotations around Harrison. I found myself avoiding being alone with him. Hesitant to share too much. Was it the same prickly nature that had me keeping everybody at bay? Or was it that I still wasn't entirely convinced that this was all going to work? Or was it a third option I wasn't as willing to consider, a reason behind the unexplainable draw to him?

I closed my eyes and took a deep breath.

Just yesterday, I'd been headed back to the office to work, and he'd been headed in the opposite direction. We met at this exact spot in the hallway. He smiled as we drew closer.

"Fancy meeting you here," he'd said, stepping to his right, at the same time, I'd stepped to my left.

"Small world," I said. We shared a smile as we mirrored each other.

"Excuse me, Francesca."

My full name was like a feather tickling the back of my neck. He grinned wider as we both, of course, moved in tandem in the opposite direction. Chest to chest, bodies moving in sync, we did that awkward little shuffle step that always happened in situations like these. Absurdly, heat flushed my cheeks.

He stood closer than he'd been since we'd started this arrangement, and that was for good reason. I'd been avoiding this magnetic pull to him. It was that not discussed third option I didn't want to dwell on.

This heat. This draw. Close enough that his blazing gaze seared me up close and personal. His perpetual wounded yet slightly amused quirk of his brow. He was gorgeous. Of course.

"I blame this on American's driving on the wrong side of the road," he said in a low voice as his gaze moved over my face.

"We literally drive on the *right* side of the road. The truth is in the description," I said, a little too breathy for my own liking.

"Such cheek." He grabbed my shoulders, so comfortable in touching, and moved me gently to my right, his left, and completely out of each other's way. His thumbs kneaded my shoulders, just briefly, as though he'd not realized what he was doing. He tucked his hands behind his back. "Right. We should do this again sometime."

I sighed as a fresh wave of heat passed over me at the memory.

"Are you sleeping?" Harrison asked quietly, just inches from my ear now. I jumped, pressing a hand to my chest as he flinched back. I pushed off the wall, guilty at having been caught replaying that innocent exchange.

"Not quite." I fussed with my hair. "Just deciding what to go work on."

"Work? No. It's too late for that. This is the relaxing portion of the evening," he said.

"I wish. I wasted enough time tonight."

A flash of hurt moved over his amicable expression in a quick beat I almost missed it. "Right."

I shook my head. "No. That's not what I meant. The night wasn't a waste. I really appreciate what you did. Distracting Collette like that."

He perked up. "I thought we could all use a bit of fun."

"Well, thank you." Even though I had just been thinking about how much I'd avoided being alone with him, I felt myself longing to draw out this brief exchange.

"You're welcome. You can repay me by coming to watch *Terraformative* with me."

I snorted I was so taken aback by his random request. He quirked an amused smile.

"Oh, you're serious? No. Thank you. I don't think so." I shook my head with too much vigor.

"I will get you to watch the show."

"Sure," I said. "It seems important to you. Is this an ego thing? You want to show off?"

"How gauche. Of course not." He pretended to be offended. "I think you'll like it. The reason it was so well-received was because of how it honored the books. Why are you so against it?"

It would be easy to tell some noble lie in an effort to make me seem smarter about how I was anti-Hollywood and the worship of celebrities never made sense. How society attributed unrealistic expectations to ordinary people only to chew them up and spit them out the moment they showed they were only human. Or how women and children were used up as commodities and rejected when they were no longer cute or appealing. But those were stories I told myself when I was younger to feel better about my snobbishness. My life was never stable enough to have a place to live, let alone a TV to watch shows and movies. It only added to my feelings of being an outsider. When Joey made clear her priorities would always be acting, the hatred of the industry deepened.

In the end, I shrugged. "I just prefer the stories in my head when I'm reading. There's always something lost in translation."

He looked at me for a long time. He was doing that thing where his gaze tried to penetrate to my hidden truths.

"I'm going to try my best to change your mind. But for now, let's try something else. A movie. What's a classic that you haven't seen?"

All of them.

"That's okay. Thanks though," I said, ever the Frowny Frankie.

"Collette and George are sleeping. Just let yourself have the night. You seem tired."

"Thanks," I said deadpan.

"I only meant that everybody needs rest. Are you really in a mood to sit down and work when you've been at it all day? You're only likely to make errors."

"I need to clean up the kitchen."

"I already cleaned up," he said with pep.

I hid a flinch. I'd seen how he cleaned up. There were still pizza boxes stacked by the trash that needed to go out and dirty bowls in the sink. He'd just moved the mess from one surface to the other. But I didn't want to nitpick, not after he'd been so great tonight. The fact that he was still here at all felt surreal.

Could I really do this? Sit down and just be still for at least ninety minutes while we watched a movie? Harrison looked up at me with such earnest pleading I felt my defenses weakening.

More than that, part of me wanted to spend the time with him. And that wily part of me was why I couldn't be trusted.

But before I could think of another excuse, he wrapped strong fingers around my wrist and tugged me toward the living room. I allowed myself to be led to the right side of the couch with half-hearted protests. It was rare that I sat still, but when I did, it was in this exact spot with the little side table to rest my tea, and the good lamp for while I read. Had he already started noticing my habits, or was I projecting more thought onto the situation?

After all, Harrison was charming and talented, dangerously good-looking, but he wasn't detail-oriented. He wasn't careful. The missed dishes and pizza boxes were just the tip of the sloppy iceberg.

But I gave in. In the end, it would be more work to argue, and I suppose it wouldn't hurt to introduce new forms of art into my life. It might help inspire my writing.

"This is a classic from the late eighties," he explained.

"Ancient," I teased.

He narrowed his eyes. "The best things were made in the late eighties. And anyway, this is a movie that is quoted all the time. You need to get the references. I'm here to help you."

"You're so selfless."

"I really am." He clicked on George's only modestly-sized TV. "Going old-school," he said as he slid a DVD into the player. Did he miss what I could only assume was an elaborate home theater setup back in LA? How could he possibly want to spend his evening here when he could call on hundreds of friends or ladies who would happily come over with one message?

I settled into the couch, leaning on my fist, legs tucked up under me.

As soon as he hit play, I felt his constant gaze on the side of my face, waiting for every reaction. This was another reason I hated watching things that were classics or other people's favorites. There was no way not to disappoint.

"I feel you watching me," I said without turning my head.

"No, I'm not." His head jerked forward in my periphery.

"You're stressing me out."

"Okay. Okay, sorry. I'm just excited." The smile was clear in his voice.

Ten minutes in and I began to feel the stress of inactivity make me twitchy. There were files to upload, words to write. I couldn't just be sitting here wasting any hours I wasn't sleeping.

"Frankie?"

"Hmm?" I blinked back to the screen.

"You're missing the best parts."

"Sorry, I zoned out." I dropped the hands I had tightly balled onto my lap.

"It will all be there in the morning," he said in what I thought was meant to reassure me but really just did the opposite.

When I opened my mouth to argue, I found him looking at me with that pleading puppy dog face. This was important to him. I turned back to the TV and gave it my full attention.

I had to admit the movie was very good and even held up over time, which I knew many things couldn't without a certain amount of cringe or offensiveness. Weirdly enough, though we hadn't spent a lot of time together, this was the most focused I'd ever seen Harrison. Now that he'd stopped looking at me, he was fully invested in a movie he had to have seen a dozen times.

"Ohhh," I said out loud without meaning to when we got to a part that I'd heard referenced a ton in my lifetime. Actually, there were several lines I didn't know had come from this movie.

"You've really never seen this?" he asked, watching me again.

"Never," I said.

"Inconceivable," he said with a lisp.

I smiled and nodded. "Nice."

"See. You get that reference now. I can't wait until Christmas and we can debate whether *Die Hard* is more than just an action movie."

"What would I do without you?" I said it lightly but didn't appreciate the bubbling up of emotions that caused a tightness in my chest. Did he think we would all still be here then? Christmas was so long away. I pushed the feelings down quickly. "But seriously, what are you doing here?" I said quickly to change the subject. I hadn't meant it to come out so accusatorially.

He flicked his gaze to the movie and paused it. "We can watch something else."

"No. I just mean." I shifted to turn my body toward him, as I collected the right words. "Aren't there a hundred more interesting places for someone like you?"

"Someone like me ..." He trailed off, and his easy smile faltered.

"A mega celebrity? You could probably helicopter down to LA and party at a moment's notice."

He shrugged. "I've lived that life. As you so nicely noted, I'm older now. I don't want to."

"Yeah, but you have loads more interesting people you want to be around."

"My best mates are a bit spread out at the moment. And also, dealing with their own stuff." He slid the back of the remote on and off repeatedly, focused on that action. I thought of the friends I'd met at Christmas. There had to have been more than that.

"Family?" I asked.

"George is my family," he said simply. "That's why I'm here."

"But what about other family? Anybody waiting for you back in England?"

"You're awfully interested in my background all of a sudden," he said it lightly enough but I couldn't help notice he avoided the question.

"It's important to know about you. For the job," I added quickly.

"You could just look me up online like everybody else."

I actually had thought of that, but it felt weird or icky when I had primary source material right here. Maybe he didn't want to talk about it. I wasn't exactly a fountain of information when it came to my own past. "You know, I'm sorry. I'm being nosy," I said. I went to turn forward when he reached into the small space between us to gently still me with a hand on my forearm.

"It's okay. I'm giving you a hard time. But trust me, if I show you mine, you have to show me yours." His tone was light as the hairs on my arm stood. "The truth is that there isn't much to tell. I'm not close with my family back in London. My mum was older when she had me. She wasn't especially interested in being a mom. I was a difficult child and she pushed me into acting because it was the only time I seemed to settle. But as soon as *Terraformative* started, she stayed in London when she got married and I spent most of my time alone in the States. Well, not alone. I had caretakers she hired and spent so many summers here. She sends a card on my birthday. I send regular checks. We all live in peace." He spoke so matter-of-factly, emotionless. He genuinely didn't seem bothered by any of it.

Alone. This was not exactly an enthusiastic description of his life. "I'm sorry," I said. "I didn't know."

"It's fine. I don't normally talk about it because it's pretty anticlimactic. I've led an incredible life otherwise so I'm not complaining. I just don't have that close family you see on TV. Besides George. That's why I'm here. That's what he's always been to me." I opened my mouth to say something that expressed my complete understanding.

It felt impossible to me that I could have this much in common with a mega celebrity. How could anybody that successful hint at such a lonely existence? It was funny in a tragic sort of way that we both found a family in the same household. Did he know that George had fostered me? Did it ever come up? He had already finished wrapping the show, and his career was skyrocketing by the time I was sent to George's, so our paths never crossed in the short but life-changing time I'd lived with George and William. I had so much that I wanted to say, but my silence was misinterpreted when he turned back to the screen.

"Ready to finish the movie?"

"Yeah. Sure."

"I'll go make some popcorn. We will need sustenance for the final climax and denouement."

I watched him leave and worried I'd pulled a classic Frowny Frankie and ruined the good vibes. The conversation was over. I stared forward, not seeing the television for some time, thinking how impossible it seemed that one of the most well-known people on the planet could be that alone. I didn't like how it clashed with the idea I had of him in my head.

He really did want to be here. His effervescent joy tonight had been genuine. It ached deep in my chest at the thought that a simple night in with us three would have brought him so much joy. And not just him, it was one of the best nights I'd had in a long time.

———

Harrison

I SHUT THE MICROWAVE QUIETLY EVEN THOUGH LITTLE WOULD wake George and Collette sleeping upstairs. The machine hummed to life, and I blinked at the rotating bag. What had started as a distraction had ended up being a healing night for me. Had Frankie seen how much the evening had meant to me? The irony was not lost on me that simple nights playing games with the people I loved was the fantasy for me, while the life I led was the fantasy for so many people. Was it possible to have both? Was I fooling myself?

I thought too long about Frankie's thoughtful reaction to my sad, lonely life. She was still so hard to read in many ways, but I understood those long silences meant she was processing information, carefully choosing her next words. Maybe I should have lied about life or made up some exciting half-truth to make me seem less pathetic. Only, I didn't want anything but whole truths with her. We were working together in a situation that was already hard enough, there was no need to complicate it with deceptions.

A burning smell filled the air. When had the rapid popping stopped?

"Ah, bullocks!" I muttered, quickly opening the microwave and waving the contents. No smoke to set off the smoke detectors, thankfully, but the acrid smell of burned kernels told me we wouldn't be snacking on popcorn after all.

I tugged at my hair, annoyed at myself. It wasn't helping my image of responsibility to burn a food that literally had a preprogrammed button. I tossed the blackened bag into the trash and went back out to the sitting room.

"Funny story about the—"

I cut myself off the moment I rounded the corner to find Frankie sleeping soundly.

She must have been more exhausted than she let on to have fallen asleep so quickly. That or I had been longer than I thought. Both equally plausible.

I grabbed the throw from the back of the couch and gently

covered Frankie, careful not to disturb her. She seemed so different in her sleep, more relaxed. Though she shared that same angry furrow between her brows that Collette had that made them seem slightly annoyed by the act of sleeping, like it was a necessary evil that got in the way of more important things.

I went back to my side of the sofa and turned off the telly. It didn't surprise me that I found my attraction and feelings for Frankie hadn't dulled in these last few days. What had surprised me was this ferocious need to protect her and Collette. It was a primal instinct that made me sit too long on the sofa, staring straight ahead, standing sentry to protect her sleep. She acted without thoughts of herself. She's doing so much. It's as though she was sprinting to a finish line, but what was it? And how far was it? Could she continue at this pace? Who would be there for her if she collapsed?

She sighed and shifted onto her back in her sleep. Her legs stretched out as far as they could until the soles of her feet hit my thighs.

I'd stay here just a little bit longer, make sure she was plenty rested to start all over tomorrow.

13

———

Archive File: 8923

Fan Letter, 1986

Attached photocopy, letter8923.pdf

Dearest George,

I dreamed about you again last night, and then this morning, I saw a pair of mourning doves, also known as Love Birds, sitting on my stoop. This is another sign.

I know we are meant to be. Please believe me.

I love you as I have loved no other man. I think of you all the time. I see you everywhere I go. I saw your hidden messages in your last book. I understand that you need time. I will wait.

I have included several photographs to express my love. I hope you will think of me when you look at them.

Forever yours,

Diana

Attached image, letter8923_1.jpg

NOTES:

HEvans: Talk about barking up the wrong tree.

FRicci: No kidding. I was just debating if I should upload the other SEVEN pictures.

HEvans: Are they all in a similar vein?

FRicci: Yes ... Very graphic.

HEvans: Oh, you definitely should.

FRicci: Perv.

HEvans: It's for history. He did say he wanted everything preserved.

HEvans: Go on, I'll wait.

FRicci: You know, you could literally just walk over here and look at them.

HEvans: You want to look at them together?

FRicci: No judgment here, but borderline fanatic nudies don't do it for me.

HEvans: I'm putting you on. I am not into this either.

FRicci: I just can't get over the fact that this woman somehow set up a camera and then went and got these photos developed at the friendly neighborhood photo lab or whatever. This isn't the only one from dear Diana either, I recognize her ... *name*.

HEvans: Hahaha. Poor Frankie.

FRicci: He gets a lot of these types of letters. Not just women.

HEvans: I don't doubt it.

FRicci: I'm sure you have plenty of your own intense fans.

HEvans: Yeah. Except now they just slide into my DMs with their, uh, suggestive selfies.

FRicci: Poor Harrison.

HEvans: I stopped checking years ago.

FRicci: Sure you did.

HEvans: Really. It's not as exciting as it seems. How could anybody think they know me, let alone *love* me? Fame is ... complicated.

FRicci: I cannot fathom.

HEvans: I'm just a nobody with a recognizable face.

FRicci: You aren't a nobody, Harrison. Not even a little.

HEvans: And anyway. George's love for William was unshakable. He certainly wouldn't be moved by fan mail.

FRicci: They were the real deal, weren't they?

HEvans: A romance of the ages.

FRicci: So sad they had to be "business partners" for so many years.

HEvans: At least George got to see their love recognized in his time. Have you seen his Wiki page recently?

FRicci: You didn't.

FRicci: Oh my God, I just checked. "Life-long partner, lover, and best friend." Harrison, that is so sweet.

HEvans: It was nothing.

FRicci: It's not nothing, Harrison. Not even a little.

14

Frankie

Forty-eight hours since Joey dropped yet another bomb on
Colette that she wouldn't be coming home, and the anger and
hurt were as fresh as ever. If I broke down how her selfish
behavior impacted so many people, I would drown in a sea of
directionless frustration. It was easier to plow on and compart-
mentalize the pain.

"She hasn't returned any of my texts or calls," I added after
filling Brooks in on the unprompted pizza night and how
Harrison swept in and saved the day. If I brushed over the details
quickly, I thought she wouldn't see the surging affection I was
trying to tamp down.

The following morning, I had woken to find myself tucked in
a blanket still on the couch, with my legs sprawled in his lap
where he slept head back but arm holding me protectively even
in sleep. When I tried to pull my legs away, he woke instantly
and mumbled about needing to finish the movie.

We ended up watching the following night. I needed closure
on the happily ever after, even though secretly, I'd read the book

many years ago. Harrison didn't need to know that. Plus, movies and books were so different that I couldn't risk not knowing.

"Unreal," Brooks said, referring to Joey and not my thoughts drifting back to my movie night.

I came into the shop for the day to help her load up boxes for the Sandia Watermelon Wine Festival the next day. Brooks was asked to be a vendor for the first time, and it was a big deal. Harrison volunteered to host Collette and two of her "besties" from her class for an afternoon playdate.

"How could she tell Collette and not me?" I asked.

"She's a coward," Brooks said easily. It was getting harder and harder to defend my sister. Before I could say anything, she added, "I know. I know she's had her challenges. But damn, it kills me that she messes with Collette like this."

"It's hard."

"At what point do things escalate? It's been what, half a year since she's seen her?" I had shared with Brooks once that I looked up the state laws for child abandonment. I felt guilty about it now, in the light of day. I couldn't even let myself go down that road. Not when she still called.

"About. But she calls when she can."

I felt guilty for unloading on Brooks. My mood permeated to her. I should have kept my worry to myself. Brooks opened her mouth to say something more, but I spoke first. "And you are sure you have enough help for the festival tomorrow?"

Brooks held my gaze for a moment before answering. "Yes. I'm good. But I still think you should go."

"Blah," I said. "I don't really like the watermelon wine."

"Shh. Lower your voice. You don't want to get kicked out of town." She looked around dramatically. "You know this town that built its entire financial structure on our watermelons. It's literally in our name."

"Yes. I know. I got the 'Sandia means watermelon' spiel on my first week here."

"Then you understand it's important to the town's heritage. Plus, it would be good for you to get out and meet people."

I hadn't been to any of the fests since I had stopped here. I didn't plan on starting now. I didn't want to make any more roots or connections here. I was already too entangled but didn't want Brooks to take that the wrong way. Not that there was a great way to take that. "I already know too many people," I said.

"Do you hear yourself when you say stuff like that or ..." Brooks teased.

"It's just a lot of people getting wasted." There was a time when I would have gone just for free samples and an excuse to get hammered, but now I couldn't afford the time off or the day-long hangover the next day. "Harrison was really pushing for us to go too," I added without thinking. Harrison happened to slip into conversation a lot lately without meaning to.

"And you said no?" she asked.

"It was hard. The man can really use those eyes to his advantage." I imagined him this morning when he saw the flyer for the festival from Collette's school. He pouted so expertly I had been seconds from giving in. "He really is ridiculously powerful when he yields those eyes as a weapon." I shivered with the sudden chill that went down my neck.

"Poor you. Hot uber celebrity wants to spend the day with you."

"It's not that. It's not really great to take George to crowds or in the heat of the sun. Plus, Collette couldn't even get in." And also, yes, the idea of spending time with Harrison and copious amounts of alcohol felt like risky behavior.

She nodded like she didn't buy my excuse either. "Okay, I gave it a shot. I have everything packed that I can. Why don't you go help with the cupcake party?" Brooks thankfully changed the subject.

I checked the door but hesitated.

"What's wrong? Is Harrison not the Mr. Mom we all want him to be?" she asked.

"What is this reference? Because this is the second time I heard it."

"There's no help for you."

"It feels vaguely sexist." I frowned.

"It was the eighties." Brooks pushed her blond waves over her shoulder. "Why are you changing the subject? Are you avoiding the house again?"

"I'm not." I glanced at the couple debating a charcuterie board. I lowered my voice. "I just don't want to leave you hanging."

"Or is it because you're so thirsty and don't trust yourself around him?"

"You have to stop saying that."

"I'm not the one eye-banging the manny," she said.

I glanced to where an older couple looked away to chuckle with each other.

"Brooks." I groaned and felt my ears burn.

"What? John and Phil are cool," she said with a wave in their direction.

"Still. Speaking of vaguely sexist and outdated terminology ... it's not that." *At least not all that.* "It's hard being there. Harrison is great with Collette. Honestly, better than I ever thought, but he doesn't ..."

"Do things the way that you would do them?"

"Yes!" I said excitedly and then contained myself when I saw her skeptical eyebrow judging me. "Is that not what I'm supposed to say?"

"You have to accept the help you're given," she said sagely.

"I don't love that." I twirled the postcard rack. "He never loads the dishwasher the right way."

"There is no right way," she said with a laugh.

"Agree to disagree. But he also forgets to start it when he does actually load it. As I say this out loud, I see that it makes me sound anal-retentive. He's just so messy and distracted. Even Collette has already figured this out, by the way. She fast-talks him into all her whims."

"God, I love that kid."

"I know. She's going to rule the world. But for now, this tenacity is draining. I would love it more if I wasn't the person who had to clean up behind them," I said.

"Can I play devil's advocate for a sec?" she said, hip cocked.

"I've always hated that expression. Does the devil need an advocate?"

Brooks blinked with unimpressed impatience.

"Fine. What?"

"He's an actor who's literally come out here just to help. He knows nothing."

"Yeah, but neither did I, and I've had to figure it out," I said, hating how shitty that sounded out loud.

"And wouldn't it have been nice if there was someone there to have compassion and patience to help you? Sort of like George did?"

"Oof," I said, feeling crappier by the second.

"Maybe this is less about Harrison and more about your own fears in being tied to this place," she said blankly.

I thought of the intimacy I woke to. How he brought my tea somehow knowing exactly when I'd needed it. It was too much. It was too much to already feel myself relying on him. Wouldn't it feel all that much harder when it came to its inevitable end?

"Damn. Okay. Maybe. But I have to protect Collette and

myself. Harrison isn't a bad guy, that much is clear, but this isn't his life either."

"Just like it's not yours?"

She held my gaze, and I stuttered, stomach clenching. "Y-yeah. Exactly." It felt sour on my tongue.

She mumbled something about lies we tell ourselves when my phone rang loudly through the store. The other three gave me a look.

"Why are you looking at me like that?" I asked at her flared nostrils.

"We don't even have our ringers on," Phil or John said, with more attitude than I appreciated.

Brooks cackled. "See!"

"How else will I hear if there's an emergency?" I showed my phone to Brooks. "See, it's him."

"He is actually calling. Gawd, there are two of you." She shook her head.

"Hello?" I said. "Is everything okay?"

"Is he calling to ask how to use the white pages?" Brooks whispered, and I pushed her face away.

"Everything's fine," Harrison said with pep. "Question. Do we have those doohickeys for cupcakes? I'm not sure what they're called," Harrison asked.

"A mixer?" I asked.

"Those papers with crinkled edges," Collette called out in the background.

"She knows what I meant," Harrison said.

I had no idea that was what he meant. Little giggles followed after whatever he did on the other end.

"Maybe he forgot where the checkbook is," Brooks said to the guys.

They all laughed their heads off.

I stepped away, covering my other ear. "I don't think we

do. Need me to get some?" I asked. A wave of unease passed over me. Had he ever baked cupcakes before? I thought of the burned microwave popcorn I found in the trash.

"Nah. We can figure it out. Can't we, ladies?" A chorus of cheers went up.

"Oh. Um, I really think you need them to make cupcakes," I said, already imagining smoke billowing out of the oven.

"How do we feel about a cake instead?" he asked. A chorus of boos broke out.

"Just hang out. I will hit the store and head home now." I was already grabbing my bag.

"No. No. I didn't mean to interrupt," Harrison's voice sounded muffled as though he held the phone with his shoulder. "Everything is under control here."

"Is that Frankie?" George's voice joined the background chaos. "Can you ask her to get those cookies I like. But tell her they're for you. She won't let me have them if she knows. Too much sugar."

"Me neither," Collette said.

"That's rude," another little girl voice said.

"I can hear you, George," I said loudly.

"Really, Frankie. Everything is fine." Harrison laughed.

Clearly.

"I don't mind," I said. "Brooks doesn't need me anymore anyway. I'll be home in a jiffy. Please don't try to make cupcakes without them."

"Okay." There was a muffled shuffling and laughter, and the call went silent.

"Harrison? Did you hear me?" He was gone. I sent him a text to wait until I got home.

"I have to go help," I said to Brooks as I made my way to the exit.

"You're going to have to let them learn on their own!" she called after me.

"Great thought, in theory!" I yelled back, making my way out to my car.

I went as fast as I could, but somehow, the quick trip to the store was anything but, and with the drive up, everything ended up taking almost an hour.

When I pulled up, I heard the screams of laughter coming from the large wrap-around yard. Three little girls with sparkling dress-up gowns chased Harrison with fake swords as he held on to his pirate's hat, yelling, "Avast ye, maties! Avast!"

Shrill cries filled the air as the little women tackled him.

"Aye! Me booty!" Harrison shouted as they dogpiled on him, causing a chorus of laughter.

I shook my head and laughed. Everything was fine. I rushed and stressed for no reason. Brooks was right. I should give him more credit than that.

With arms loaded, I made my way to the side door and into the kitchen. The smell of burning was the only warning I had.

All at once, the deafening tones of the smoke detector pierced the air. I dropped the groceries on the table to cover my ears and quickly found the source.

Smoke billowed from the oven. The attempt at cupcakes was all over the pan and spilled over the edges of the rack, sending streams of smoke into my face. I coughed and waved, eyes burning. Everything was burned to a crisp, and a small pile was actually on fire.

I scrambled to cover my hand with a dish towel and pulled the pan out of the oven, but I missed my pinky and realized too late as the searing pain shot through my finger. I yelped and dropped the pan, at the same time slamming back into the table where I just set down the groceries, causing the bags to spill over and onto the floor.

"What's all the ruckus?" George shuffled into the kitchen.

"Everything's fine." I grabbed the pointless towel and waved the smoke toward the open side door. I leaned over the sink and shoved the window open, freeing more of the smoke.

"Are the cupcakes ruined?" He frowned at the still-smoking tray on the ground.

"It's not looking good," I grumbled.

He nudged the bags on the ground with his cane. "Did you get the cookies?"

I groaned as I sucked on my now throbbing pinky with one hand and continued to fan with the towel with the other.

"Why is the alarm—" Harrison stopped short just inside the kitchen, still panting from playing outside. His tricorn hat sat askew on his messy hair, and an eye patch covered one eye. His loose smile instantly fell off his face as he registered the scene.

"The cupcakes—" I shouted just as the smoke alarm finally stopped, my shout hanging in the now silent air. "Seem a little well done," I finished. Shoulders slumped. Defeated. Growing anger bubbled under my skin.

"Bloody hell." He pushed the eye patch up and scrubbed his face. "I forgot. I'm *so* sorry. I forgot."

His gaze roamed the scene; groceries spilled on the floor alongside a tray of burned cupcakes. Flour and mixing bowls all over the counters and not a single clean surface. His face crumpled as he saw what I had already registered. It was like a tornado had ripped through the kitchen.

"Yeah. I gathered." Absurdly, my frustration manifested as tears I fought back. I glowered at my burned pinky instead.

"Did you hurt yourself?" he asked. His pitiful face moved to me, where I cradled my hand to my chest.

"I was trying to get the cupcakes out." It came out as a growl.

"Well, that was silly," George added. "Where are we at on dinner?"

I took a steadying breath in and out.

"It'll be just a minute, George." Harrison turned to me. "Christ. I'm so sorry." He moved to the freezer and got an ice cube, then wrapped it in a paper towel.

Collette and her two friends came running in from outside, their hair was plastered to their sweaty heads under bandannas. The smell of little kid sweat and fresh air was just noticeable over the burning that filled the room.

"Oh, no," they all chorused. "The cupcakes!"

"We will just have cookies," Harrison offered helpfully.

"I didn't get any," I said emotionless.

"Noooo!" they yelled, and I had to close my eyes as the chaos inside me threatened to make me snap. I had been rushing, and I completely forgot about the cookies. And I thought we would be making cupcakes. I wanted to explain. But found my jaw welded shut.

"We want cookies! We want cookies!" the girls chanted, and George joined the uprising.

"That's lame, Frowny Frankie," Collette said.

Heat burned my cheeks. She couldn't know how those words hurt me. She was just a child—

"No," Harrison said sharply in a tone he'd never used. I flinched to look at him, but he was kneeling in front of Collette. "We don't call her that. That is not kind, and we do not talk to each other like that."

"But Mommy calls her that." Collette tugged on her ear, glancing at me for backup.

I opened my mouth to interject, but Harrison held up a hand. "It doesn't matter. We can't control how other people speak, but we can control how we talk to each other. Okay?"

"Okay. Sorry, Frankie," Collette said quietly. I nodded at her, too surprised to say anything.

I'd never been defended like that, and the gentleness of it in the heat of the moment only added to my overlapping emotions. My tears were closer to the surface than ever, and I was too shaken up. I needed to move. Get away.

Harrison stepped toward me tentatively, handing me the ice cube wrapped in a paper towel. "I'm going to clean all this up." Frowning at George, he added, "Really, George, encouraging mutiny?"

The older man shrugged with a mischievous grin before straightening his shoulders. He slammed the cane down once. "All right, mateys, fall in line. I run a tight ship." The three girls lined themselves up, lifting their chins, trying to be serious as they giggled. "Now." He sniffed. "Who wants to see my secret treats stash?" They hooted their delight as George managed to get them out of the kitchen.

My mouth fell open, but the girls were following him, marching and chanting, "Chocolate!"

One crisis at a time.

I was too flustered to speak. I couldn't even move. The place was a disaster, and I was the bad guy. I came home on a literal black cloud and ruined all the fun. Or at least that was how it looked to all of them. My throat bobbed on a swallow. A pattern was forming, and I was already so exhausted.

Harrison tugged on my arm to get my hurt hand, where I kept it tight to my body, like prying open a clam. "Let me help you," he whispered, and I unfurled.

"It's your help that got us here in the first place," I said numbly.

Hurt flashed over his features. I sucked in my lips.

"I'm sorry. I was just trying to make them happy, and then we had the treasure, and they were trying to steal it, and we forgot about the cupcakes."

"The cupcakes that I asked you not to make," I said through clenched teeth.

He winced. "I know. You try saying no to three sets of puppy dog eyes. I looked online, and it said that as long as we greased the pan, it would be fine."

"That worked out."

"I got distracted. I'm sorry." He shrugged and looked so miserable it only made me feel worse.

"I hate being the bad guy here. I really do. You obviously didn't mean to do it, but that doesn't change the fact that it happened. You could have caught the house on fire. George was in there sleeping. Little children who we are responsible for are over." I pointed outside, my voice breaking. I took a breath to collect myself. I hated being this person. "I shouldn't have left. Even for the day." I glared at the ground and shook my head. "You're supposed to be helping me. Not adding to my load. I can't do this."

"Frankie, I—"

I couldn't look at him. I couldn't look at this place that, at this moment, felt like a prison I would never escape.

"I just need a minute." I walked out of the house before I could see his hurt and feel any worse.

15

———

Harrison

"Be right back, George," I called into the living room.

"I'll man the ship!" He was being swarmed, lifting the box of chocolates above their grasping hands.

That should give me a few minutes before they tie him to the chair and riot.

Ice in hand, I chased Frankie down the garden path, through the back gate to where she briskly walked away, hands clenched at her sides.

"Frankie!" I yelled.

She didn't stop. I understood she wanted to be alone, but I needed to fix this. I couldn't stand the thought of her being mad at me or thinking I couldn't handle things.

"You know, walking this fast, I get the impression you don't want to talk!"

She stomped with more vigor. The setting sun cast the surrounding hills in shadow. The sky was a glorious shade of pink.

"I'm removing myself from the situation," she called over her shoulder. "I need to think."

"This is a great place for it. Gorgeous out," I panted, catching up. "The sky is amazing. You know, I'm pretty tired from entertaining the kids. Christ, you're so fast."

She stopped suddenly and turned. "I would like to be alone."

"Okay." I followed to jog after her when she started again. "I'll join you."

She flicked a glare at me. "I don't think you understand what *alone* means."

"You won't even notice me." I smiled.

"Oh my God." She laughed but without humor.

"I mean, I wouldn't complain if you walked slower. I just quit smoking, and this is high altitude."

Her jaw dropped. "Are you for real right now?"

"About the altitude? No. It's much higher than sea level. If you can't slow down, I guess I can jog."

"Harrison," she growled.

"You seem frustrated."

"I can't imagine why," she said, walking again but noticeably slower.

"So. What's new with you?" I asked, panting.

"Harrison. I don't want to talk. I'm so mad right now," she said with admirable calmness. Emma was constantly telling me I tended to push people's buttons without meaning to.

"Rightly so. Should we wrestle about it?" I asked.

She coughed a laugh and quickly tried to cover it. She stopped and threw out her arms. "This is serious!"

I stopped, too, and nodded. "I can tell you're upset."

"Then why are you laughing?" She gestured to my face.

I tried to relax my features, but I think I might have just smiled bigger. "I'm nervous." I shrugged. "I don't know why I'm like this. When I get nervous, I make jokes. Let me shake it out."

I bent over like a rag doll to shake myself, arms out, and shuddered my whole body. I did that until I was stood upright, but when my head popped back up, my grin pulled wider. "I literally cannot stop smiling. You know how dogs sneeze when they want to show submission in play? This is a submission smile." I flashed a very disarming and cheeky smile.

"Harrison." She groaned my name, but when she ran her hands down her face, she was definitely trying to rub away amusement. She finally came to a complete stop on a rocky ridge where the setting sun cast shadows on her cheeks from her long lashes. The anger and exhilaration flushed her cheeks. The golden hour lighting illuminated her like an angel, making her even more mesmerizing.

"I feel like this isn't about the cupcakes," I said after a long and loaded silence.

Her jaw ground before she said, "No. It's definitely about the cupcakes."

"Okay. But maybe not entirely?" I ventured. "I was going to clean up, you know. I just ... I got distracted."

"I don't think you did it on purpose." And the sincerity in her voice only made me feel worse.

"I try so hard to do the right thing yet constantly muck things up. I wanted you to be able to get out of the house for a while. I wanted to prove I could handle it all."

"I shouldn't have left. I have so much to do anyway," she said, not meeting my gaze.

"George is fine. The girls are fine. It could have been worse. Just a little mess. I'm going to clean up."

She winced.

"You don't like my cleaning?"

She just shook her head. "I don't know how to talk about this without hurting your feelings."

I frowned. I didn't want to talk about it either, then. "Are you worried about Joey?" I asked instead.

She blinked at the sudden change in subject. "I mean ..." She shook her head, eyes looking up and to the side. "I'm always worried about Joey. And Collette. And George." She frowned and looked down, wrapping her arms tight around her middle. "And that's why I needed help."

"I promise I'll pay more attention. Those girls are like wild animals." I thumbed back to the house. "They have these big pleading eyes, and when they beg, it's impossible not to give in to them."

I did my best impersonation of them.

"I'm familiar with the tactic," she said flatly as her gaze moved over my face.

"I'm so sorry. Please forgive me." I tilted down my chin and begged.

She blinked at me. "You're a ridiculous person ..."

"I've been told." I made my bottom lip jut out. I grabbed her hands, remembering her injury. "And let me put ice on this," I said, pushing the almost melted ice at her.

She sighed and gave me her hand. I felt hopeful as I placed the damp kitchen paper on her red finger.

"I think the ice melted."

"It's the gesture that counts," I said.

"Not always." She studied our joined hands. A sense of dread accompanied the tension growing in her features. "Listen, Harrison. I just ... this isn't what I wanted for Collette. She shouldn't have this pseudo-family filling in for the real thing."

"We're doing our best." Fear tugged at the muscles in my neck.

She chewed her lip. "It just feels like there's no structure. It's all chaos. It shouldn't be like this. She should have her mother here."

"She should," I agreed tentatively, afraid to speak my mind about the woman who was wholly absent.

"It's complicated with Joey. She's been such a mess in the past. This is the longest she's held a job and not indulged in harmful behavior. I worry about putting too much pressure on her to return. But she should have told me," she said.

"She should have told you." I blew on her finger without thinking. She swallowed and looked away. "I have a friend who has struggled with addiction. One of the things I had to learn was my actions, one way or another, couldn't stop his addiction. It had to be his choice to get help."

"I just feel like if I can make things easier, she will stay on track. She hasn't had it easy."

"I understand." I began rubbing her palm, not ready to let go or end this moment when she was opening up to me. "Where's Collette's father?"

She shrugged. "He was never around. He was a random guy in a random city. He made it abundantly clear that Collette wasn't any of his concern. Joey was in a better place when she found out she was pregnant. She thought Collette would make him change his mind or maybe change her life. I don't know. She has been better. Mostly."

I made a sound of sympathy. She pulled her hand back.

"I owe it to Collette to have some stability." She took a deep breath in and out. "I don't think this is working out, Harrison. It's almost been two weeks. And I love how fun you are with Collette. You are *so* fun, but I need something serious."

"Something serious," I repeated. My smile trembled.

I never thought those words could hurt any more than they had in the past. I thought I had come to terms with the expectations people had for me, but hearing Frankie say this hurt in a way I never imagined.

"I'm sorry I got so mad about the cupcakes. I know you didn't do it on purpose." She reached out her non-hurt hand as though she was going to pat my shoulder but dropped it to her side. "This is me letting you off the hook. You don't need to stay here. I think we were caught up in the moment when we came up with this plan, but this is too much to ask from anybody. Let alone ..." She flicked a look at me and then away.

A muppet like me.

"I'm letting you loose," she finished.

This was why I tried never to take anything serious. All I did was end up hurting people. Nobody could count on me. You couldn't let anybody down when they didn't hold you to any expectations.

I swallowed and nodded.

"I really appreciate all that you have done. And I know Collette and I would love for you to come visit as much as possible, but I need someone I can count on. Someone who is going to help and not add to my responsibilities. Do you understand?"

"Of course." I smiled easily. "What does a guy who's been acting his whole like know about raising a kid in a stable environment anyway?"

"I'm sorry," she said, looking down.

"Nah, love. Nothing to be sorry about. We'll get in contact with George's team and see what we need to do to get someone down here to help."

She let out a breath. "Okay. Sounds good. Well, I better get back before things get too out of control."

I gestured back to the house, my other hand behind my back like an usher. "After you."

I felt numb. Not even two weeks, and I had already ruined everything. If I had just paid better attention. If I only didn't get so distracted. If only I wasn't such an absolute idiot.

I thought of not seeing Collette in the mornings when she stumbled out of her bedroom bleary-eyed and mussed hair, mumbling whatever nonsense was on her mind first thing in the morning. This morning, she asked if her stuffies could wake her up. I had an entire cast of characters helping her get ready for the day. I pictured her sweet features as she scolded a particularly ornery stuffy.

I thought of how Frankie chewed her lip in thought as she typed notes. Or, when she was working on the book, she mimicked the silly faces that her characters were making. How she hummed as she cooked but pretended not to have any clue what you were talking about when you asked her what she was singing.

Or how George whistled "Fly Me to the Moon" when he was in a happy mood. Which had been often lately.

My throat was suddenly so tight it was like I couldn't breathe. I wasn't ready to leave this place. It was more of a home than I had ever known. It was like the last day of shooting *Terraformative*, knowing the magic was coming to an end. The pain was a physical ache in my bones.

We were silent as we walked back to the house. I held open the door as we were greeted with the sound of the girls' laughter.

We followed the cacophony to the sitting room, where George was tied to a chair with scarves and feathered boas. The girls danced around him with chocolate-covered mouths, loudly belting out a song about candy.

"Hello," he said happily.

Frankie covered her mouth, hiding a smile.

"Okay, girls, let's untie George," Frankie said. "And maybe clean your faces. Your parents will be here any minute."

They shouted their disapproval of this new plan as I sensed a new person enter the room behind me.

"Well, so glad to see you have everything under control here," a woman's voice said.

Frankie turned to the entryway to the kitchen, where the woman entered the room. Her eyes widened just as Collette looked to see who spoke.

"Mommy!" Collette screamed and ran toward the woman.

16

Frankie

"Joey?" I said numbly. "What are you doing here?"

The last person I would have expected to walk in the room was my sister, and there was a chance this was some sort of stress-induced hallucination. I was meant to feel happier, but all I kept thinking was, how was Collette handling this? What did this mean? Was she back for good?

All these questions would only be a fraction of what Collette must be worrying about.

But then I looked at the little girl. There was nothing but pure joy written all over her features, excitement bubbling over as she squeezed her mom so tight that Joey had to hunch not to tip over.

It was that simple for a daughter. Her mother was there, and she was happy.

I pushed a pain deep down inside me and focused on the present.

"Aren't you always asking when I'd come?" She patted

Collette's head to where her chin was jabbed into her thigh, staring up at her mother. "I didn't think I needed a reason."

"No. Of course not. I'm so glad to see you." I stepped forward and hugged her, all too aware of the audience.

She bent to look at Collette. "Who is this gorgeous model?"

"Mama." Collette laughed. "It's me. Look, I have another loose tooth. And Harrison tried to make cupcakes and almost burned the kitchen down. And Frankie was gone. She was supposed to get cookies but didn't. And Claire and Annabelle are here, and we are pirates—"

"Looks like I got here in the nick of time," she said, interrupting Collette. "This place is a madhouse."

Harrison ground his jaw but didn't speak. He looked at me, but I brought my attention back to my sister.

"You can stay in your old room. I'll get your sheets washed. Is the tour over?" I asked.

"No, but I had a quick break and had to see my baby girl," she said. "I can only stay through Sunday."

"Tomorrow is a weekend. We can play dolls and get ice cream. Let me show you my room—" Collette tugged on her mom's arms, causing the weekend bag to slip off her shoulder.

"Okay, baby girl. One thing at a time. I haven't even gotten settled yet." She tossed the bag to the ground at my feet. "I would love to spend the day with you tomorrow." She spoke to Collette but shot a look at Harrison as she finished.

He didn't seem to notice as he untied George from the chair.

The timing of Joey's surprise visit was suspect. My gut told me that her reasons for coming here weren't entirely centered around Collette. My stomach hollowed in anxiety.

"They really get away from you, don't they," she was saying to Harrison.

Harrison chuckled. "That they do. I shudder to think what we'd find if we got here any later."

George stood a little shakily and made his way over to Joey. "Good to see you, Josephine. Beautiful as ever."

All the while, I swirled with a sense of unbalance. I was glad my sister was here, glad for Collette, and proud of Joey for making the effort. But selfishly, I could only think about how this would disrupt our wobbly routine.

She air-kissed his cheek. "You too, George." She straightened and extended her elegant hand toward Harrison. "Nice to finally meet you in person. George always talked so much about his superstar," she said it friendly, but I could hear the hint of ice behind the words, having known her my whole life.

Joey hadn't stayed as long with George and William. She aged out of the system a few years before me. And even before that, she ran off, determined to find our mom. But she always made bitter comments about the prodigal son who was "too busy in Hollywood to even visit." George, being the lovable peacekeeper, never seemed to notice. It was William who expected more of us and had stricter rules set up for the foster kids.

"Nice to meet you," Harrison said perfunctorily and then twisted away quickly to scoop up Collette. If he had noticed Joey's extended hand, he was convincing at playing like he hadn't. "Come on, girls, let's clean up before your parents discover you like this."

The girls giggled just as the doorbell rang. They screamed and ran to hide.

"Too late," I said with a sigh.

"You can run, but you can't hide!" He chased the kids as I went to the door to greet their parents.

I eventually wrangled the girls back to their parents after apologizing about the chocolate and making small talk. Harrison made himself scarce at pickup as he had at drop-off. We hadn't discussed it, but I assumed he didn't want a mom or dad recognizing him and spilling the details to any news source that would listen.

It was moments like that which acted like reminders of who he really was and how this was all just a hiatus in his reality.

When I returned to the sitting room, Joey was leaning into Harrison, talking in a low voice, close enough that Collette wouldn't even fit between them. She snapped back when she saw me.

"Harrison and I were just talking shop," Joey said. "I'm sure you'd disapprove."

"Not at all," I lied.

"Frankie abhors the industry," Joey said. I don't know that I'd ever heard her use the word "abhor" before today. Especially not with such emphasis.

Harrison, for his part, was still uncharacteristically quiet. I worried about him. He hadn't seemed upset when I told him things weren't going to work out, but he hadn't been his normal silly self either. If anybody knew what it was to keep things locked down, it was me. I never thought about his effervescent mood, taking it for granted, but it was notably absent now.

Letting him free had been the right thing to do. He had to see that things weren't working, and this was all too much for him. I thought he'd have been more relieved, but with the sudden arrival of Joey, I was glad we hadn't determined when he would leave. I found a shocking amount of solace in his closeness.

I felt myself longing to stand next to him, like two soldiers in battle, a united front.

"So," Joey said, turning around the room, "it looks exactly the same." She nudged a stack of old papers, dusty on top of a bookshelf. "I thought you were *hired* to clean up this place." I tensed on the strange emphasis she put on "hired." As though I was somehow taking advantage of George.

"I'm archiving. I'm working mostly in the extra office and attic for now. It's been slow going." I bit my tongue from over-explaining. Joey always made me feel defensive in one way or another.

She wasn't even listening anymore.

"What should we do tomorrow?" she asked Collette. Looking again at Harrison, she said, "Are you visiting long or ..."

She was seconds from rubbing herself against him like a cat. She'd always been an unapologetic flirt. With my boyfriends. With the fathers of our friends. She'd flirted with every guy who she could somehow wield power over. Her internalized misogyny kept her victim to the patriarchal lie that women only had power if they were sexually desirable. It didn't anger me as much as I got older. I pitied her more often than not.

I rationally knew all this, yet never had her flirtation caused this reaction in me. There was a strong urge to tackle her to get her away from Harrison. She was probably the exact type Harrison went for in his industry. Leggy. Blonde. He had a history, if Brooks was to be believed.

Harrison looked at me, a furrow between his brows. "I'm actually about to—"

"He's here for the weekend," I said quickly.

Joey was the last person I wanted to know about any of this setup. And anyway, it hadn't worked out, so she didn't need to know the details. But it also didn't mean I wanted him to go.

Not just yet.

"I'm so glad I got to catch you on a break. I know how the demands of our work can really tie us down. Good timing. You'll have to join Collette and me on our outing tomorrow."

"He can't." I said it so fast that Harrison didn't even have a chance to open his mouth. "We have to go into town to ..." My mind raced, trying to come up with an excuse to keep him out of her clutches. I wasn't exactly eager to spend the day with

Harrison after I basically asked him to leave, but the thought of him spending the day with Collette and Joey without me caused an uncomfortable feeling all over my body, like rubbing Styrofoam together.

As Joey crossed her arms, waiting for my excuse, a smile started to spread on Harrison's features. It'd been the first smile since I came home and ruined all their piratic adventures.

I didn't trust it.

Too late to backtrack, I saw the moment the idea formed in his mind.

"Oh, that's right." He snapped his fingers as he spoke. "Frankie promised to go to the Watermelon Wine Fest with me."

My smile twitched. My relief at him helping find an excuse dissolved into panic. It was spending time mingling with towns-people in the hot sun, drinking wine with this beautiful man, or freeing him up to spend the day with Joey. My options were that. And he knew it. His smile grew.

"Yes. That is the thing I agreed to do," I said.

"Since when does Frowny Frankie like wine," Joey said with a skeptical look.

"I ... I like some wine. It's grown on me since I've been staying here. But Brooks is going to have a stand there, and I told her we would help."

Harrison frowned in appreciation of my quick lie.

"Who's Brooks?" she asked.

"I told you about her. Sometimes I help—"

She waved her hand in the air. "Never mind. I don't care. And you both have to go?" Joey pouted in her cutest fashion toward Harrison.

"I'm committed, I'm afraid," Harrison said.

"Oh boo."

"And actually the timing is fortuitous indeed. George can't be home too long alone. So you and Collette can stay here and have a lot of quality time," he added.

"Mommy-daughter day!" Collette called.

"Why can't George be alone?" Joey asked.

Harrison realized his mistake too late. We weren't sharing the details of George's health. The man in question was now snoring in the chair he had just been freed from.

"He had a fall recently, and we don't like to leave him too long in case there is another accident," I said, not exactly lying.

Harrison nodded.

"Doesn't he have one of those life alert necklaces or something? Cell phones are also a thing."

"Joey, he misses you," I said with a hard edge to my voice. It was one thing to aim her anger at me. But not George. Not after all that he and William did for her. "Spend time with him."

She glanced away. "Yeah, okay. Jeez." Her cheeks flushed, and she turned away from Harrison.

"It's important you and Collette have uninterrupted time together anyway, don't you think?" I said. "The three of you can catch up."

Collette grinned up at her mom. "I'll share all my toys, Mama. Don't worry."

"It'll be great," she said. "I'm going to go change, and then I'm starved. What's for dinner, Frankie?" She stepped over her bag to leave.

"Shrimp scampi," I said.

"You know I'm allergic, Frankie." She scoffed.

"Oh. That's right," I mumbled.

As she passed Harrison, she said, "You better be free in the evening. I would love to pick your brain more about your last movie."

Harrison ignored Joey's comment and aimed a soft smile in

my direction. It felt like a small victory for me, but then, when had it happened that Joey and I weren't on the same side anymore?

17

Harrison

No matter how I tried to get away from her, Joey was at my side most of the following morning after her arrival as Collette stood in her shadow, begging for attention. I was more than ready to get away from Frankie's sister, but I never wanted to be directly rude to her and risk upsetting Frankie even more.

Since the fight yesterday, we'd hardly spoken. Fight didn't feel like the right word for what happened. She very gently fired me from my volunteer position for being an extra burden. I almost wished it was more confrontational. I wish *I* had put up a fight. I wasn't ready to say goodbye. Especially not now. Frankie hadn't specifically asked me to stay while her sister was visiting.

But she hadn't asked me to leave either.

She carried a tension I'd not seen in her with the arrival of her sister. Shoulders hunched, jumping at the slightest sound, she acted like an animal in fight-or-flight. It made me feel sick. It made me want to do what I could, even if that only was distract with a good time.

Collette gave up on trying to get her mother's attention

where she was taking a selfie and came to sit on my lap. Joey was trying to "accidentally" catch me in the background, but I made it very clear that my team would sue if a picture of me "accidentally" leaked to the press. She stopped trying after that.

"When are you leaving?" Collette asked, accidentally elbowing me in the stomach as she got situated.

"Oomph." I repositioned her away from fragile areas. "As soon as Frankie is ready."

Collette sighed loudly.

"What's wrong, Princess Leia?"

"I'm Uma now. She's a pirate. Argh," she said but half-heartedly.

"Hey. What's with the lip?" I flicked my finger up and down on her pouting mouth, producing a funny sound that got her to smile.

"I just wish I could go with you guys to the carnival," she said it quietly, but I glanced up to see if Joey heard. She was too absorbed in the angle of her face to notice her daughter's wishes.

"It's a wine festival. Not a carnival. No rides or anything fun like that. And it's very dull. A bunch of grownups discussing wine."

Collette scrunched up her face. "Old people make no sense." She shook her head in pity.

"Profoundly astute," I said. "Plus, you and your mom are going to have a great time together today."

Collette shot a skeptical look in her mother's direction.

"All right. Let's get this over with," Frankie said, stepping into the room.

My head snapped to the left at the sound of her arrival. My mouth went dry as I took her in. She was beautiful in a brown gingham sun dress with hair down and wavy under a straw hat. Her smooth skin was more exposed than I'd seen her to date.

The clinging fabric tugged in tight at her waist, emphasizing the swell of her hips. As well as her breasts. Very full. Very lovely breasts. She even looked to be wearing makeup. Not that she wasn't always lovely, but she tended to the side of joggers and worn tees since she worked from home.

It reminded me more than ever how important it felt to get her out of the house. That had been my original intent when I asked her about the Watermelon Wine Fest yesterday, before the almost-not-quite-a-fight. I wanted her to relax, but instead, she opted to go work in a different location. Frankie deserved some time off. And maybe to get smashed, if I could assist.

"What?" she asked with a single-shouldered shrug. "It's just an old dress. Figured it's supposed to be nice today."

I closed my mouth and stopped staring at her ... oh, Christ, where had I been staring?

Collette gasped and hopped off my lap. "Frankie, you look beautiful!"

"Aw, thanks, Uma."

She scratched her elbow. "You guys act like you've never seen me in a dress before." She scoffed. She turned to fill her tote with a few things.

Collette and I looked at each other. She matched my features, raising her eyebrows and frowning with a slow headshake.

Frankie chuckled, catching the shared look. "Whatever. I'll have you know I used to get dressed up all the time. It just seems ... pointless now."

Another reason to get her out and about.

"You look great," I said, finally managing to speak. I had been about to ask what she meant about it being pointless when Joey finally looked up from her phone.

"You're wearing that?" she asked, her tone neutral, but the words undercutting the sentiment.

"Why?" Frankie glanced down to tug the ruche at her chest. I swallowed.

"No. No. If you think it suits your coloring. I mean, I just wouldn't want you to look washed out," Joey said.

"You look incredible. That color suits you wonderfully," I said, holding her gaze.

Frankie started to smile, but her gaze flicked to her sister. The smile faded as Joey cleared her throat.

I stood and collected my keys. "Ready?" I interjected before Joey got any more jabs in. And before I lost my cool.

"Yeah." She grabbed a water bottle and added it to the bag. She turned to Joey. "Okay. Just make sure you don't leave George. Or take him with if you leave. But make sure he isn't in the sun too long. And bring snacks. And make sure Collette washes her hands if she—"

I tugged her elbow to bring her out to her car.

"She can figure it out," I mumbled in her ear.

She blinked up at me.

"I am her mother you know," Joey said.

Frankie flinched. "I know. Sorry. Of course. You got this." She took a deep breath in and out. "Okay. Just call if you need anything."

I felt her restraining herself from going to hug Collette goodbye as she would have every other time. Collette took the liberty and launched herself at Frankie's legs.

"Love you," Collette said.

"Love you too," she said quietly.

"Bring me back something."

Frankie smiled down at Collette. "If they have anything for kids, I'll try."

Joey stood to collect her daughter by the shoulders. "You two go have a nice time." She squeezed Collette's shoulders. "We're gonna have the best mother-daughter day ever, aren't we, sweetie?"

Collette looked up at her and nodded eagerly. "We can get ice cream, right?"

"Not too much sugar—" Frankie started, but I pulled her out the front door before she could give any more instructions.

"They're gonna be fine," I said.

"No. I know. Of course. She's her mother," Frankie said as she tucked herself in the passenger seat of my car.

"Really. They'll be okay. George and Collette will be there to make sure."

She relaxed her shoulders and let a long breath out. "Okay. You're right. I'm worrying for nothing."

I went around to my side, noting her furrowed, worried expression hadn't quite melted.

The closest spot I could find to the event was a few blocks away from the park where the event was being held, and so we walked in with a large group queuing up for tickets.

"What's the big plan here?" she asked.

"How do you mean?" I used the excuse of the crowd to press myself closer to her side. She smelled like vanilla and warm weather and a little bit of sun lotion.

"I didn't think events with a bunch of people would be your thing. You know, with the fame and all that."

"Actually, it's pretty easy to be in larger groups without being noticed. Most people don't expect anybody of notoriety to be strolling about."

"Plus, you have your super-secret disguise." She pointed at the hat and sunglasses I sported.

"I have many tricks up my sleeve. I've been doing this for a while. And it worked on you, if you recall."

"True." She pursed her lips. "But I wouldn't have known who you were at all, were it not for George."

"Ouch."

She laughed and nudged me to move forward. "No offense. You know, I'm not really a movie or TV person. And horror of all horrors, I never watched the show."

"Are you ready to tell me about that?" I asked her, hopeful that she'd share something about her life. "It does seem odd since your association with the creator."

Her arms were behind her back as we slowly moved forward. She tilted her face to the sun before lowering again to be protected by the hat. "I read the books when I was a little older. They were ... very important to me."

"Me too," I said. "To many people."

"True." She took a deep breath in and out, and I knew she was formulating her words just right. "I was not in a good place when the show came out. Like physically. I was still with my mom, and it was a whole thing. Finding a place to stay was sometimes an issue." She looked away at a passing family of three, a little girl in the middle holding both parents' hands. "I definitely never had consistent access to cable TV." She cleared her throat. "This was all before George. This was—" She cut herself off. "It was a long time ago, but the show wasn't on my radar. I actually didn't read the books until I moved in with George and William. I was fifteen, and the show was over by then."

The pieces clicked into place. I had wondered about their closeness. And I knew he had many foster children over the years.

"Where'd you go?" she asked, nudging me.

"I was thinking about how strange it was that we never met before recently," I said.

She nodded. "I think your career had really taken off. You were like twenty and the last thing you'd care about was a teenage nobody passing through."

Agree to disagree. I found myself wishing I'd met her ages ago. She went on.

"I felt embarrassed to be that age and reading them even though now I know millions of adults read them too. God, I hated being a teenager."

"It's a rough time," I said. Though my teenage years were likely completely different from most peoples', I was enthralled to be listening to her. She'd not ever opened up like this, but maybe being away from the house and all the pressure it represented freed her to relax. I loved her thoughtful, cautious way of speaking. It was the easiest thing in the world to stay focused on her as she spoke. The way her mouth moved as she formed words. The way her heavy lids conveyed subtle emotion, unlike so many people. I was beginning to learn the meanings of her smallest movements. But I'd only just begun to understand her ways. I had so much that I still needed to learn.

"At that point, I was stubborn about watching the show. It was this stupid point of pride for me," she said.

We scooted forward in the line.

"Stubborn?"

"Inwardly, I was just embarrassed not to have the means to watch it, so if I made it my choice ..." She shrugged. The thin strap of her dress fell, and I pushed it up her arm without thinking. The pads of my fingertips blazed a trail up the smooth, sun-kissed skin of her shoulder. Her head turned, those hypnotic eyes following the action, her lips a breath away from my lingering fingertip. Just as quickly, she turned back, pretending to study the crowd, her teeth digging into her luscious bottom lip. "Thanks." Tiny bumps formed on her arm where the fine hair stood on edge. "But also, it was such a phenomenon by that time. I labeled myself alternative and purposely hated popular things because I thought they made me special somehow. I was very concerned about trying too hard."

"Well, that sounds like most of us at that age. At least you grew out of it."

"Not enough to watch the show." She tilted her head and smiled. "Now it feels too late. The power of it for so many I think was the timing. The magic of youth."

I made a sound of thoughtfulness. "I wonder about that a lot. Why it became so massive. I think you may be right about the timing. People found something within themselves to connect with one character or another. It was just a giant sandbox for the imagination. That's why there's so much fan fiction around it too. Have you ever read any of that?" I was secretly curious if she'd read any Adam Abotts stories.

She laughed. "No."

"I don't read it either. It makes me feel a bit skeevy. Don't tell Charlie I said that."

"I'll take it out of my meeting notes for our next call," she said dryly.

"It is now my life's mission to get you to watch the show. I will convince you yet."

"You can try." She smiled sweetly. "When has any movie or show been better than the book? Zero times," she added before I could answer, looking smug as she pushed up on her toes. "Ask any reader."

"Right. Sure, because that's not a bias sample group."

She shrugged, pert nose still in the air. "I'm a purist."

"You're a snob." I poked her rib cage, and she stumbled on the uneven earth.

I pivoted to catch her in my arms, my hands on her waist, heat burning through the thin dress material. "Am not," she said quietly as her gaze moved over my face.

"You're not," I agreed but wasn't even sure of what I'd said.

We stayed like that for a moment, where I let myself pretend this was an ordinary first date between a beautiful woman and a regular smitten man. My thumbs rubbed in a circle, and I couldn't move. I was so entranced.

A throat cleared behind us, and we realized the line had moved, but we had not. We broke apart to move up.

We finally made it to the front of the line. We walked to the table under a setup tent, and I said, "Two tickets, please."

Frankie's head shot to me. The volunteer said the amount due, and I thanked her as I handed her the cash. I asked her about her day, and she said it was hot but fun working the event. We were each handed our drink tickets and our collector wineglasses. "Thank you, darling. Have a good day."

The woman flushed and waved the next person up.

We were roughly two steps away when Frankie whisper-shouted, "What was that?"

"What?" I asked innocently.

"The new accent?" Her usual sleepy-looking eyes were wide with humor, her full mouth open wide in shock. She tugged me to the side on the edge of the field for privacy.

I couldn't believe how it made my heart kick up.

"Oh. That's Hank," I said easily. "And it is an American Southern Coastal accent to be precise," I said teasingly.

She blinked, waiting for more information as she shook her head. I enjoyed this way too much.

"It's another way I go incognito." I continued to use my low, almost drawl, but not quite, as I explained. "Sometimes I use it so that I don't have to make conversation about my accent," I continued.

"I can't believe she didn't notice who you were. You had a whole conversation." She leaned closer to whisper, "You sound like a totally different person."

"Therein lies the rub, darlin'," I said, making my voice rumble.

She shivered and stumbled back and into a pole. "Unbelievable. I thought you were super famous? Can't go anywhere level famous," she asked, laughing.

I gently tugged her forward by her waist but didn't release her.

"I think it's all relative. But to your point, I probably shouldn't play with fire, you know what I mean?" I leaned over her, resting my other forearm above her head, my glass dangling.

She started laughing so hard I had to take her wineglass before she broke it. "Stop. Stop. It's freaking me out." She shoved me away playfully, and I turned to the rest of the festival.

"Oh my darlin', oh my darlin', oh my darlin', Clementine," I began to sing loudly, exaggerating the twang. A few people glanced in our direction, but the festival had been going on a few hours already, and drunken yodeling was likely the least interesting thing to be found.

"Stop. Stop." She grabbed my shoulder, turned me back toward her, and covered my mouth. "The whole point is not to draw attention to you."

She was up on tiptoes, the front of her body pressed against me. She was so warm and soft. Would she let me bend her back and kiss her silly? I swallowed against her hand, wondering if she noticed the way my breaths came faster under her touch.

I held her eyes, and the smile relaxed from her features. She lowered her hand, her gaze moving over my face to where she had just been covering. I swallowed and licked my lips without thinking. I swore her dark pupils dilated.

"I'll only use Hank when I'm talking to strangers," I said, returning to my normal voice.

She lowered off her toes as she stepped back. "That's better."

"Some skills are too powerful. I have to be careful."

She rolled her eyes. "Come on. I have tickets to burn."

18

Frankie

THE SUN BURNED HOT ON THIS LATE SPRING DAY, AND IT FELT LIKE all of the town was out. It didn't matter that I'd been in Sandia almost two years. It still surprised me to be recognized by locals as "George's granddaughter" or "the woman from Brooks' Baubles and Books." I hadn't expected several people to come chat with me, especially with a mega-star standing, head tucked at my side. But the fresh air and sunshine—and probably the wine—made me chatty and friendly. It was nice to see this social part of myself again. More surprisingly, not a single person recognized Harrison. One guy stopped him but only to ask where he got his kettle corn from, and as he walked away, "Hank" made a show of winking at me.

We went from vendor to vendor, trying various nearby wineries until the sun started to make me feel woozy—and probably the wine. Harrison had stopped drinking his samples a few vendors back. He'd either spit out the taste or give them to me instead. I honestly couldn't tell any of them apart at this point.

"Wine is so good," I said, hanging onto his arm as we walked. "I don't know why I thought I didn't like it."

"We might have to reevaluate that sentiment tomorrow," he said with a smile.

I loved this smile that he used with me. Like I was doing something especially charming when I was only being myself.

"They really shouldn't have a wine festival on such uneven ground. Seems like a liability." My short wedge sandals were unstable in the grass field. I leaned further against him. It felt so nice. A little voice told me that I might regret all the touching tomorrow, but I told her that Frowny Frankie was off duty today.

"I'll write a strongly worded letter to the event organizers," he said.

"Tell them there needs to be more free water stations too. Oh! There's Brooks. You remember her?" I tugged him toward her table, where there was a decent crowd.

He stumbled as I dragged him to follow.

"See. Uneven," I said.

"Right." He chuckled, but I wasn't sure what about that was funny.

"Brooks!" I whisper-yelled. "Brooooooks!"

Several people in her line turned and looked at me. Harrison ducked his head, shoulders shaking.

Brooks's eyes went wide. "You came!"

"My friend, *Hank*, made me. We'll talk later," I called back. She looked back and forth between us, and I winked. She shook her head, and next to me, Harrison gestured something to her that I was too slow to catch.

She laughed but finally caught on to my subtle message. "Nice to meet you, Hank. Talk later, Frankie!"

We took a break to wander under a tent with misters to cool off. Despite the sun hat, my exposed shoulders were growing pink and freckly.

Joey got the genes that made her glow after time in the sun. I got the genes that made people concerned I needed a doctor, I turned so red in the heat. Harrison pressed a finger into my shoulder, leaving a white impression on the warm skin. As if we just touched each other freely all the time. I guess I *had* been a little touchier than normal today. "You need sun lotion," he said with that same soft smile on his features.

I wanted him to check my body all over for sunburn.

Frick, frack, fruck. This was why wine was dangerous. I was a thirsty bird.

"This is with sunscreen." I tugged off my hat to fan myself, giving no figs about how flat my sweaty hair may look. I leaned back, head against the cool metal pole holding up the tent. I felt a tiny trickle of sweat fall from the strands of my hair and into my cleavage. When I opened my eyes, Harrison was watching that droplet like he hadn't seen fresh water in months.

He glanced away and back again.

Men.

I pretended not to notice but arched my back, pushing out my breasts, fully under his gaze.

Women.

"I need it not to be so warm," I added. "And maybe four to seven less samples of wine. I forget how quickly it adds up."

I was not thinking clearly. I was thinking with wine-saturated lady bits. Lady bits who had been wandering the desert for years ...

"I'll get you some water." He glanced at my cleavage again, then furrowed his brow and spun away quickly.

"Good idea."

After he left, I collected myself. Just because Harrison was looking like a snack in his simple white tee and shorts that showed off incredible calves and thighs, and I was hard up, and we had both drank maybe a little too much and were finally alone with no distractions, and there was no hurry to go back to all our responsibilities, and we totally had plenty of room in the back of the car if we folded the seats down ... *wait, was I selling this or stopping this?*

I genuinely could not remember what the right thing to do was. I felt loose and free and just wanted to give in to what I wanted at the moment instead of thinking at all. Thinking was overrated, and this had been so lovely.

I blew out a puff of air as a man swaggered up, an arrogant smile on his forgettable face. My internal feminine alarms rang even through the wine haze.

"Hey," he said. "You doing okay? You look hot."

"I'm just fine." I blinked too slowly. I knew how I came across. Vulnerable. And I hated it. It was a flashing beacon to a certain type of man.

"You really are," he said with a grin and stepped closer.

Real smooth, mister. He wore woven brown leather Huarache sandals that looked like they made his feet smell like Collette's school shoes after a day of playing outside. He was the kind of guy who felt entitled to any woman at any time. I should knee him in the balls. Instead, I used my tote to push him back out of my bubble.

I was just about to tell him to go away when Harrison was back with two bottles of water. Once again, I felt a whoosh of relief to have him at my side rather than to handle things alone. Even though I totally could handle this guy.

"Darling," he said in his Hank voice and slipped an arm around my waist. I gasped when he pressed the ice-cold water against the back of my neck with no warning. Goose bumps prickled down my whole body all at once. What was he playing at? "Did you make a new friend?" he asked.

I wasn't a fan of his Hank voice. It reminded me that his

normal voice felt like home, but I had to say there was something about it now, like naughty role-playing.

The new guy looked at him, sizing him up as all tough guys do. Harrison was Hollywood fit, I'd seen that firsthand, but there was an air of affability about him that made him incredibly approachable and not the least bit intimidating.

"Hello," I said to Harrison, looking up at him with lusty eyes. That wasn't acting, but it worked for the situation. His gaze moved over my face, and he swallowed. I relaxed into his touch the longer he looked at me. Too intimate for a third party to witness.

He rubbed his thumb along my hip, lifting my dress slightly. The newcomer's face moved to follow the action. "Did you find a friend for us to play with?" Harrison asked.

I stilled. That was *not* what I was expecting.

The man stepped back. "Uh? I wasn't—"

"What're your thoughts on nipple clamps?" he asked, tilting his head to look the man up and down. He licked his lips as he did.

"We didn't get that far," I added, quickly understanding the game. "But he seems very open." Harrison squeezed my side as though to signal that he was impressed.

"Uh. I have to meet my friends." Stinky Shoes was gone in no time.

I turned in Harrison's grip, happy that he hadn't released me yet.

"You know most men would just try to punch him," I said once it was just us.

"Trust me, I wanted to." He rocked his head side to side, neck popping as tension melted out of him. He opened the water and handed it to me. "But nothing makes insecure blokes like that run faster than toying with their masculinity. Plus, as much as I love to tease you, I actually wouldn't want to make you uncomfortable. He'd been doing that plenty." His jaw clenched as he glared in the direction of where Stinky Shoes went.

"Hank really does have his uses." I gulped the water down. Mine was spent long ago. After I finished, I gasped a breath. "Fame is so weird. That guy would have never bailed like that if he knew who you were. He would have tried to tell you about his daddy's company and spew corporate lingo to impress you."

He shrugged. "Yeah. At the end of the day, looking at things from a forty-thousand-foot view, the metrics will all tell the same story." This time, when he spoke, it was with a different type of greasy American accent.

"You're freakishly good at that," I said in awe.

"I know. It's all make-believe. This fame thing."

He finally let me loose after one last squeeze. "How do you stay so grounded?"

"Am I? Most people would say I'm ridiculous." *I* had said that to him. I felt a wave of shame even through my fuzzy goodness. He smiled, but it was the distracting one that said he was trying to be charming. I didn't have a chance to answer. "Notoriety has been a part of my life for so long, I actually don't know anything else. Also, I have two best friends who help keep me humble."

"Aw."

"No, don't *aw*. They're terrible." He smirked.

"The ones I met around Christmas?" I asked, pulling my hair up off my neck. That night felt so weird. We hadn't really talked about it.

"Yep." His gaze moved along my exposed neck and arms. "Charlie and his Kate. That's a wild story for another day. And Emma and Wesley. You know, that's actually also a bit of a tale too. These people and their drama," he said it lightly enough, but that tension remained around his eyes. I wondered if it was hard to have two best friends find their soulmates. At least I was used to solitude.

"It's good when your people find their people," I said.

"I'm chuffed for them." A darkness shifted over his features as he turned away. "Onward?"

We started walking again, this time just milling through the throngs of people, but close enough that our arms were constantly brushing. "That's the weirdest thing about fame. To answer your question."

"What is? The thing with the guy?" I gestured back to the tent.

"Sort of. No. Well. The thing is. It's as though everybody thinks they know me, but ... I don't think I'm explaining this well. I'm somebody to so many people, but not the *one* to anybody. So it sometimes feels like I'm a nobody. I'm just a nobody that everybody recognizes."

I stopped, and he looked at me. There was a look on his face like he hadn't meant to say that. It wasn't the first time he'd hinted at the loneliness that accompanied being so famous.

"Oh God, not that pitying face," he teased.

I fixed my features to arch an eyebrow. "I'm hardly pitying the super mega-celebrity," I lied.

The truth was I felt an ache of loneliness for him. I remembered how he'd shared his minimal family life. About the interview I'd archived where he talked about wanting a big family. How quickly he seemed to fall into this paternal role. At first, I had assumed he couldn't wait to get out of here and back to his real life. But being here was special to him, and he liked being here, away from the life he'd always known. I wasn't sure if that made me feel better or worse. Like we were some sort of family experiment. A trial run before the real thing. It caused an uncomfortable pressure in my chest.

"Sorry—that was—that was too much wine." He laughed and looked like he was seconds from running.

"No. It's refreshing. I never thought about it like that." I reached out and brushed his shoulder. "I don't feel like anybody gets me either. But it's easier to think that's because I don't have that many people in my life. You're constantly surrounded by people who think they know and that might actually be worse."

"Right." He scratched under his hat. "I love what I do. I'm not complaining. It's odd, is all."

"I could see that. Thanks for that perspective," I said honestly. "I assumed all actors were self-absorbed egomaniacs."

"No, that part is true."

I laughed as we made a final turn that would bring us to the exit.

"We should probably head back," I said, not thrilled to leave. "Yeah."

"They've all been suspiciously quiet," I said, reaching for my phone for the first time in hours.

A sudden rush of nerves sobered me. I'd been so distracted, having fun with Harrison, that I wouldn't have even heard if they called. I had no notifications. Some of the anxiety melted away, but my heart raced under my palm.

"No news is good news," he said, reading over my shoulder.

"Or sometimes it's a fire in the kitchen." He winced. "Sorry. Too soon."

"No. It's good that you're to the teasing stage." He looked down as we walked out the gates and back to his car. "Sharp tongues run in your family."

"You should have met my mother." I realized as soon as I said it that I didn't want to continue down that road. "Wait. What do you mean?"

"Your sister isn't very nice to you," he hedged, shooting me a look.

It was a strange thing to notice. Nobody else ever seemed to think she treated me in any sort of negative way.

"That's just how she is. It's fine. She was there for me so much when I was younger." I shook my head. Joey was just mean to the people she loved. It wasn't hurtful. It was just the way she was. "Sometimes Joey talks, but I'm not even certain she pays attention to what she's saying. It helps me not take things so personally."

"Right," he said, but I got the impression he wanted to say more but stopped himself.

Instead, it was me who had all the words today.

"She has a soft spot for George. I know she doesn't act like it. He helped her in the past. But she was closer to William. William didn't let her get away with as much. She needed that sort of structure. And to be fair, George has always been a little distracted with the show and writing. Joey thrives on attention."

"You don't say."

I nudged him with my elbow. "She always wanted to be an actress. Ever since we were little. Collette reminds me so much of her sometimes." A pang made my heart thump hard in my chest.

"Is that why you don't want Collette to be an actor? Because of Joey?"

"Did she tell you she wanted to be an actor, and I said no?"

He nodded.

"I'm not totally against it. I guess I worry that she doesn't understand the breadth of what that would mean or the work involved. I worry about her being disappointed."

"That's understandable. It is a very hard industry to get a foot in. But ... I may know people."

I stopped and shook my head frantically. "I ... I can't think about that right now. No offense. There's so much upheaval in her life. Collette deserves stability. And consistency," I said firmly. I swallowed down the emotion bubbling to the surface. Damn this wine. "She deserves to be a child as long as possible before the outside world takes away her spirit. Being in front of a camera from a young age has to mess you up."

Harrison nodded, looking at the ground.

"Crap. I'm sorry. That's not—"

"No. You're right. My life was far from normal. And I agree that this wouldn't be a good time for Collette."

Harrison took off his sunglasses as we came to a stop in front of the car. "Plus," he said with a smile back in place, "you know what's best for her."

"No. I'm just me. I mean, I'm not her mother. If Joey was here more ... I don't mean to decide for her." I felt panic grow. I was doing my best, but it wasn't the best for her.

"She's lucky to have you," he said again. As he had before. This time, I wasn't sure who he was referring to. He opened the door for me. "Is there anywhere else you want to go before we head back?"

I couldn't think of any other place I'd rather be. Even just a day away, and I missed Collette. Joey could decide to take her back at any point, which was what should happen. That's the way it should be, but it made me not want to waste another minute away from her.

"No. Let's get h—back to George's."

"I'm ready to see that kid." He held my hand as I lowered into the passenger seat.

And for a minute, I had the fantasy that this was my life. A day out with a handsome man before going home to our little family.

I closed my eyes and leaned back. The wine was starting to make me feel queasy.

This wasn't my life. This was a moment in my life. Joey and Collette would eventually be gone. I would move on from this town to find where I'm meant to be and get back to the person I used to be.

Harrison would be gone.

"I'm sure they're all fine, having the time of their lives," Harrison said, and for the first time, it felt as though he was trying to tell himself that and not to comfort me.

Was it possible that Harrison was already as wildly protective over Collette? She was just so rare and wonderful and special, and every person who met her felt the same way. Or maybe he worried about leaving George all day?

We pulled up to the house as the sun was setting. I hopped out of the car, not waiting for Harrison, nerves rushing me forward.

"We're back," I called loudly once inside over the blaring, rarely used TV.

The living room was strewn with clothes, dolls, and various toys. Nobody responded for a minute. I shut off the TV and called out, "Hello?" just as Harrison came in behind me.

Collette came running out, still in her pajamas, now covered in miscellaneous colorful substances, a dripping spoon clutched in one hand and what I thought was Joey's phone in the other. "We had the best day ever! I had all the ice cream! And we went to the park. Mama's letting me watch videos on her phone."

She was fine. She was fine. A little dirty and high on sugar, possibly being exposed to content for people much older, but fine. I knelt, and she flew into my arms. I peppered her tangled hair with kisses.

"Ah, you're squeezing me too hard."

"Sorry," I said, releasing her.

Harrison kissed her head and ruffled her hair before stepping around us to go back into the house.

Joey sat up from the couch, surprising me. "I'm exhausted."

"I bet," I said, feeling only a little bit validated. "How's George?"

"He's napping in his study. He's been in a crap mood all day."

Maybe us both being gone was too much for him. "Glad you two ladies had fun."

"Honestly, she is nonstop. Just like a little too much." Joey spoke as though Collette wasn't right there. Thankfully, Collette was using sticky fingers to press play on a video. The child shouldn't feel like a burden by just being herself.

"She's an imaginative kid, for sure," I said, jaw grinding. One day, and Joey was already throwing in the towel. My good mood evaporated with every second.

"No wonder you're always begging me to come get her."

I opened my mouth to snap that I wanted her *mother* in her life, but Harrison was back in the room, his hat and sunglasses replaced with a fierce look of worry.

"Where's George?" Harrison asked.

Joey rolled her eyes and gestured to his study. "He's in his office napping. He's a grown man. Geesh."

She flopped back onto the couch.

"Collette, can you go wait for me upstairs for a bath?" I said, and Collette left. Tension was rolling off Harrison. My own control was slipping the second I walked back into the house, and I didn't want her to feel any of it.

She glanced back to her mom, and just as she was about to leave, Joey's hand shot up. "Phone."

Collette started to whine.

"Time for bath, sweetie. You know you can't have electronics up there," I said.

"Okay," she moped but handed the phone to her mom before sprinting upstairs.

"Gross. Why is it sticky?" Joey mumbled.

Harrison, who looked like he was seconds away from

screaming at the interruption, ground his jaw and spoke in Joey's direction.

"He's not. I just checked there. And his room," Harrison said in a flat voice, but his posture was stiff.

"Well, he *was* there." She tossed an arm in the air.

My heart dropped into my stomach, and a tingling sensation spread over my extremities. "When was the last time you saw him?" I asked, hardly able to talk, let alone move.

"I don't know. Around lunch I asked if he wanted food. He started, like, freaking out on me. Acting like I was an idiot or something. I told you he was in a shit mood all day. So I left him to his pity party."

"Joey," I gasped.

"I was not about to be disrespected like that. God, you never take my side on anything." She shot up from the couch.

"That is not true." My voice shook.

"I don't have time for this. I need a break. I'm going up to my room and don't want to be disturbed." She made her way to the stairs, not concerned with Collette or George.

A sudden wave of fury overtook me. I couldn't stand any of this. How could she say I never took her side when that's all I ever did? This was too much.

"I'm going out to go look for him," Harrison said, grabbing his coat and collecting the keys he just set down.

"I'll just clean up all the messes," I snapped. "That's what I do, right?"

Harrison turned sharply to me. "Are you mad at *me* for this?"

Was I? I didn't know. I felt furious and out of control and shook with anger, and the remaining wine in my system blurred my rational thoughts. And all of the boiling inside me just shot out to the nearest victim. "You told me that it would be fine. You made me feel ridiculous for being worried."

"How could I have possibly predicted that your selfish sister would lose track of an entire person?" He threw out an arm with anger I'd never seen from him.

"She didn't know—"

"Don't defend her. Not now." He snapped his mouth shut, nostrils flaring, almost surprised at his own words. "There isn't much light left. I have to go."

I balled my fists, rage burning my eyes. Just before he walked out, he turned to say, "Eventually, you're going to have to stop making excuses for her. Before somebody gets really hurt."

I clenched my fists even tighter and closed my eyes. I wanted to throw something at the just-closed door. But he wasn't saying anything I didn't already know.

19

Harrison

I STOMPED TO THE CAR AND THREW OPEN THE DOOR, TRYING TO
decide where to even start my search. My brain moved so fast I
couldn't pin down a single thought. Fear over George. Frustration with Frankie. Fury with her sister. Collette, not even being a
second thought to her own mother. It all piled and twisted on
top of each other, tangling like Jack's beanstalk in my mind as I
tried to make a plan.

"Where are you, George?" My voice shook as I spoke out
loud.

It had been hours since Joey had last seen him. He could
have wandered into the surrounding forest and fallen down a
slope. He could have stepped into the nearby interstate. A
hundred worst-case scenarios piled up, each more awful than
the last. How could anybody be so irresponsible? How could
Frankie accuse me of anything when it was her spoiled, selfish
sister who caused this?

A sudden icy truth washed over me.

Because it was my fault.

I pushed her into going to the festival today. I distracted her when she might have normally called to check in. Or *I* should have checked on them. This wasn't on Frankie. It was on me and Joey. But even I should have known Joey couldn't handle both of them. She was a woman who cared only about herself. I shouldn't have pushed Frankie to leave. I shouldn't have tried to convince her it would be okay. I just wanted her to smile. I wanted her to live for herself, even for a few hours, without feeling responsible for every person.

Once again, I'd mucked everything up just by trying.

I distracted her because that's what I was—a useless distraction. It was all I was good at and all I would ever be.

A soft light from around the side of the house drew my attention. Was the outside light for the pool house always on? It hadn't even occurred to me to check the pool house.

I rounded the house on a tear, and relief flooded me so fast my knees almost gave out as the casita came into view. The lights were on inside, and soft music drifted from the windows. I jogged the rest of the way down, shocked at my reaction and how utter my terror had felt. Through the curtains, George sat on a chair, staring into space.

I sent a text to Frankie rather than call like I preferred. I found I wasn't ready to talk to her on the phone.

"Found him. Everything's okay."

I knocked on the door as I walked in. His head shot up, and he blinked at me with cloudy eyes.

"Oh, Adam. I lost track of time. Are they waiting for me?" he asked after a few moments too long.

"Harrison. I'm Harrison," I corrected, but the residual tension of the last half hour made my words sharp.

"That's what I said," he snapped back just as sharply as fear and confusion made his defenses rise.

I took a deep breath and steadied myself. He reflected my

mood. He wasn't sure what to feel when in this state, so he absorbed the emotions of the people with him. I had to shake this anger. I wasn't mad at him, after all. It wasn't his fault his brain tricked him. It was my fault for not correctly handling the situation.

The tiny house consisted of a bed, a simple desk, and a kitchenette in the corner. Just off this area was a half bathroom and shower we would always use as kids. It had been renovated since then, but I still distinctly remembered shivering and being soaked, running in here to use the loo as fast as possible before going back out and cannonballing back in the pool. So many happy memories from this place. All thanks to this man.

I smiled and released the tension in my muscles. "This is a snazzy tune. What's this song?" I gestured to the record player on the desk. Soft, crooning music filled the air. A slow version of a popular classic.

George sat back and closed his eyes. A shaky smile turned up his lips as he rocked gently back and forth. "'Fly Me to the Moon.' By ... Well, it doesn't matter." He waved his hand in the air. "William and I used to dance to this all the time."

"He was a great dancer," I said.

"That he was," he said, still smiling. "He'd play this song whenever we had a spat. It was his white flag. We fought so much back in the beginning." He sighed loudly. "God, what I wouldn't give to fight with him again."

"I'm so sorry," I said roughly.

"I miss him every day." George's voice was as watery as his eyes. "Sometimes I feel the loss of him, like a task left unchecked, so I stop and look around like I was meant to be doing something? Then I realize it's the aching loss of him that I'm feeling. Like my body remembered before my mind caught up."

I couldn't speak, my throat was so tight.

"I don't want to forget him. I'm afraid of so many things, but that scares me most. I can't forget him," George said, surprisingly calm for my turbulent sadness.

I took a shaking breath in and forced myself to get it together. "You won't. You never will." I swore it, though I could never promise something like that. "I will never let you forget. I will play this song, and you will remember the dancing."

George nodded over and over, tears gleaming in his red eyes. "Good. Good. Such a good boy."

"And the fighting," I teased.

He chuckled. "Well, the fighting led to the making up and the reminder of what we really fought for. Most times when we got to the root of the argument, we just realized we missed each other."

We sat in silence as the record played on and on, and I thought about the countless injustices of the world and how it was always the gentlest, more innocent people who took the brunt of them. I wanted to assure him that he would never be alone. That I would always be there. That I was so bloody sorry for not being here every day, but I couldn't find anything remotely encompassing for all the regret I felt.

George needed something more than I could provide. After all, it would be an empty promise. Frankie wanted me gone. Today hammered that fact in. George had to find people who would help him. I would never be enough.

"I'm so sorry, George," I said, defeated and lost. It just slipped out.

He looked up and smiled. "Don't be sorry. I'm not. I have no complaints. William and I got more time than most."

I sucked in my lips and nodded. He'd still been thinking about his partner.

"There weren't many men like us who had the luxury of living together back then. We lied about him being my business partner to protect us. Fought often about it. But we also fought to make us work. Even when we were so mad, we could spit, we were always a team. We had nothing but challenges ahead of us but nothing felt more important than being together."

He shrugged, still rocking slightly to the music. "We got more than most," he repeated. "And we got to help raise all you kids."

"Those memories of coming here in the summer, between filming. They're the best memories I have. Charlie and Emma too," I said, still raw with all this emotion.

He looked at me for a long moment. "That's lovely," he said, "but I hope that's not true."

I frowned.

"Don't get me wrong, I'm so thankful too. And it means so much to me. But you need to start making your own family and new memories. You can't have your best memories be from all those years ago."

A new pain gripped my chest. Another year passing where I still hadn't found my person or started the family I thought I'd have.

"I don't know that that's in the cards for me, George." I felt that realization deep in my bones. I peaked early in life, and though my career still thrived, I hadn't felt alive like I had those summers in decades.

"You are so young, my boy. I don't think I'd even met William at your age. Don't act like your life is over. Young people make no sense," George said.

It mirrored Collette's words from just this morning, and I chuckled to myself as I somehow was lumped into both observations of other generations. "Profoundly astute," I repeated.

"You act as though your life is over," he said. "You have so much life left. So much time. Yet it gets faster every year. The absolute worst thing you could do is waste any of it."

I sucked in a slow breath.

"I know life is tragic." He reached out a shaking hand to grab mine. I held him as tightly as I could without hurting his dry, crepe-paper skin. "I know what's happening to me is ..."

"Utter bullocks," I said with a sniff.

"Indeed." He chuckled. "But you have to understand, I don't regret a thing in my old age. Not a damn thing. I was luckier than most," he said. "But I think that's because I always acted as though it could all change in an instant. And instead of being fearful of that fact, I embraced it and lived, my boy. I *lived*." He nudged his cane at me. "It's time you decided to do the same."

I held his gaze a long moment, swallowing with difficulty.

"Okay," I said, wondering how somebody just decided that. I didn't want to leave here. Not yet. I wasn't ready to throw in the towel. "I'll try, George."

"You owe me that much," he said with a wink.

We sat a little while longer, not wanting to leave the comfort of this moment. Eventually, the cool spring evening started to bring a chill.

"Let's head in and get to bed," I said.

George nodded and let me help him back up to the house.

Inside, the house was straightened up, and the mood was silent with nighttime.

Frankie stood just inside the threshold of the kitchen with her hands clutched in front of her as though she'd been waiting there. The kitchen smelled like cleaner and *home*.

"George," she said on an exhale and went right to him. She hesitated as she reached him and then, deciding something, tentatively hugged him.

"What's all this fuss about?" he said lightly, but a little worry laced his words.

"Nothing," she said brightly and pulled back. She discreetly wiped at her eye and smiled wide. "Nothing," she repeated. "Just happy to see you is all."

"Well, in that case, I'll never say no to the rare and elusive Frankie hug." He extended an arm, and she stepped close, closing her eyes as they hugged again.

I hovered on the edge of the exchange, waiting for my moment. George's wisdom had a way of being aptly timed, and there was so much to say.

"Off I pop to bed," he said and made his way to the back of the house to his room.

"Night, George," I called softly.

Frankie waited until the sound of his cane was no longer audible before she stepped forward. I met her in the middle of the kitchen. A small lamp in the corner filled the room with a buttery glow.

Frankie worried her thumb. "I'm so sorry about tonight. I have been going over and over everything in my head. I never should have—"

I cut her off by scooping her into my arms. I pulled her so tight to my body, my arms shook.

"Oh." She gasped in surprise.

I nuzzled lower into her hair, smelling like the sun and Collette's bubble bath and everything good in this confusing world.

"Okay," she said as I didn't loosen my hold. Eventually, some tension melted from her, and she returned the hug, wrapping her arms around my middle.

"Okay," she repeated this time in what sounded like a sigh.

I didn't want to fight or argue or hear her apologize for something that wasn't her fault. I just wanted to hold her a little while longer. I wanted to show her without talking what she meant to me. I was overwhelmed with sadness. I didn't want to leave this place or George. Everything felt so real tonight. The complete terror of losing him and the palpable relief to find him.

Then came the understanding that I already lost parts of him. He wouldn't ever be the same man I knew as a child. Bits of his brilliant brain drifted away every day, and there was nothing I could do. Anything any of us could do.

I held her for as long as she could stand it. Far longer than I'd ever held her. But she showed no signs of letting me go. A part of me shouted that *this* was what George had been talking about. The feel of her chest rising and falling against mine. The way she held me without hesitation. When nothing else made sense, this did.

I shuddered a breath in.

"Harrison? What's wrong? Is he okay?" she asked, finally pulling away to talk to me.

I leaned back, and she gasped when she saw my tear-streaked face I hadn't even tried to hide.

I shook my head, face crumpling. Because he wasn't okay, and there was no way to deny it anymore. That conversation in the pool house felt like a final word of advice. Like on some level, he knew that this was the last time he could impart this wisdom.

"Harrison." Her eyebrows fell back in matching sadness as she understood my meaning. She always understood the subtext and worked so hard to keep the balance. She understood that the reality of George finally got through to me.

"It's not fair," I gasped out. The tears flowed faster. My throat was so tight, my heart so constricted.

"I know." She cupped my cheek and held my face. Her eyes filled as she nodded with me, chin trembling. I closed my eyes to nuzzle against her softness, unable to bear her sadness. "It's not fair."

"I-I can't fix it—"

"Nobody can."

"I wasted so much time."

"It's okay. It's okay. You're here now. He's not alone. He's got us."

I let myself fall into her again until it felt like I could breathe. I wanted it to be true. I wanted to ask if that meant I could stay. I wanted to place soft kisses on her neck. I couldn't end this moment. I didn't want to risk losing her arms around me.

So we stayed in each other's arms, holding each other up, as the sadness passed through us.

20

—————

Frankie

THE FAINT TRACE OF HIS AFTERSHAVE WAS STILL IN MY HAIR. EVERY few inhales, the hint of him tickled up my nose, sending a fresh rush of memory. I turned in bed, burrowing my face into my pillow, unable to stop thinking about that hug. It started so innocent, so cleansing, yet carried so much more unspoken.

He'd been shaken and angry when he left to find George. When they came back, he'd been desolate. He reached for me without hesitation. He needed *my* comfort. More surprisingly, I needed his in return.

The way he held me, the words not spoken but so tangible in the air. A man mourning.

Until he became a man ... wanting? Hungry?

His arms were strong, and I'd never felt as tethered to the earth. His body was hard and flat. All my softness felt like it was designed to melt against him.

The longer our bodies sought comfort in each other, the more the sadness melted into heat. By the time we broke the hug, my body was on edge. My breaths came fast, and his eyes were dilated as he looked back into my eyes. It would have been so easy to open up to him, to find physical comfort in the distraction of our bodily needs.

Distractions had caused enough trouble.

That heat in his eyes was what haunted me as I tried to sleep. I tossed and turned for what felt like hours.

"Ugh." I glanced at the clock. It was after midnight. After the day we'd all had, I should have passed out the moment my head hit the pillow.

You know what would help you sleep ...

Nope. Nuh-uh. I ignored that horny little voice. If I took care of my physical needs, I would not be able to look at Harrison in the morning without blushing. He'd know exactly what I did. I could already see his knowing little smirk ... the way he'd bite his bottom lip, look up at me with his head tilted down. Those emotionally fraught eyes stared at me like he wanted to devour me. The way he looked when we broke the hug.

GAH. No!

I throbbed with need to just get myself off. A simple human function, nothing to it. I wouldn't even think about him or the way his breath tickled the small hairs of my neck or the brush of something against my center that inflamed me ...

Maybe I should see if he was awake. Maybe I should go see if he felt better ...

Well. That answered that. I couldn't be trusted.

I sighed again and stilled when the downstairs door clicked shut.

Adrenaline shot me up in an instant. My heart hammered blood through my ears as they tried to hear anything in the silent night. Had I imagined the sound? But sure enough, a moment later followed the sounds of steps on gravel.

I sprinted out of bed and to the window.

Outside, Joey tossed her bag into the trunk and quietly shut the lid.

I couldn't move fast enough. Coat, bra, shoes, all be damned. I sprinted out of my room and down the hall to Collette's, fear like I've never felt propelling me.

No. No, please. I can't say goodbye yet. I'm not ready. Please let me make it.

I pushed open Collette's bedroom door and a silent sob broke out of me like a gasp.

Collette was there. Sound asleep, mouth partially open, little hands curled by her face in the purple light of her moon lamp.

I closed my eyes and pressed a hand to my hammering heart.

Take a breath. It's okay.

She wasn't gone. She didn't take her.

But then—

I was sprinting again.

Joey was just about to drive away when I came to a stop in front of her car. She looked up and rolled her eyes. I couldn't hear her but saw her mouth, "Shit."

I held up my arms wide as my stance, like I was stopping a charging bull, the headlights blinding me.

She shut off the car, and I blinked in the now darkness.

She got out of the car and leaned against the driver's door, for once not speaking.

"Joey. What are you doing?" My voice shook with fear and rage and desperation.

"I'm leaving," she said the words I dreaded.

"When are you coming back? Did you tell Collette?"

She looked over her shoulder and sighed. Her silence told me everything. "You can't do this," I said.

"I can't do this," she agreed. "You're right."

"You have to stay," I demanded.

She shook her head. "Today proved it. I'm just not built for this. It's too much. It's too loud and hard and messy, and I can barely keep myself alive, Frankie."

My head shook back and forth, refusing to accept this. Tears I didn't think I had left filled my eyes. "You cannot leave her again. She won't understand."

My eyes adjusted to the night, and she was visible from the light of the back door flood lamp. She looked to the side. "She's young. She won't even remember me."

"That is not true. You *know* that's not true. She remembers everything now. She remembered the one time I burned a piece of toast, and literally every time I make her toast, she tells me not to burn it. She's so smart. And talented and sweet and funny and precocious and she needs her mother."

"I'm nobody's mother, Frankie. You know that," she spat the words in defense. As an excuse to give up.

"That's not true. Please, don't do this. Please." My knees shook as I begged her.

"I'm not built for this. I couldn't even handle a day. I lost George. I couldn't take Collette after just a few hours. I felt like pulling my hair out. She was driving me crazy, and I know that's shitty. I know I'm fucked up, but I can't do this." Her voice broke. She wasn't stupid. I never thought she was. That made this all so much worse.

"If you go, she will always blame herself," I said. We held each other's gaze, knowing that truth more than anybody else.

"She'll understand when she's older. Things aren't so simple," she said.

"You know what this will do to her. You *know*. We both know all too well."

"And you know that some people just shouldn't be mothers."

The words hung in the air. Pain lashed through my whole body.

"You don't have that choice," I yelled before quieting myself.

"Frankie," she said my name gently. "You have to see that just because I'm her biological mother doesn't mean I'm the best fit for her."

"You just have to be here," I whispered. Then louder, I added, "That's all that matters. Just stay. Just try. It will take time, but I know you have it in you. You just have to give it more time. You will miss so much. You will regret it. I promise if you just try —that's all that matters." I babbled as fear made me incoherent.

We held each other's gaze for so long. Shivers wracked my body, but I prayed I got through to her.

"Just stay a little longer, please," I begged. "Don't give up yet. Don't run away. Be better than her."

I regretted the last words the moment I said them. Her features hardened in defense.

"She did her best. She was fucked up, but she did her best," she shouted.

She left, I thought, but if I said anything else, any hope of keeping her would be gone. "I know she did," I said.

"We aren't the staying sort. We both know that. It's not in our blood. The only reason you want me to stay is so that you can get her off your plate and you can leave too. Don't act like you haven't been running your whole life. You are just too damn proud to admit it." She tossed her hair over her shoulder, glancing up to Collette's room.

"That's not true. Collette is wonderful."

"Then you keep her."

"I'm not you. I will never be you," I said and understood just how true it was.

"I can't." She cast out her hands. "I'm sorry. Okay? I really am. I wish—" She shook her head, and for once, I felt her sincerity. "I wish I wasn't such a shit person. I know that I am, okay? I know it. I hate it, but I can't change it. She's better off with you. It's fucking obvious, but nobody will just say it." Her familiar heat returned after the sudden show of vulnerability.

The reality of what this really meant closed in on me. "Are you ever coming back?"

Her lack of answer told me everything. "Look. I'll sign whatever I need to. But she's more yours than she'll ever be mine."

"I'm not a mother."

"And neither am I. Maybe it's just not in our blood." She huffed. "But there's a better mom out there for her. It's just not me. I hope you'll find her a good home."

Like she was a lost puppy. Any moment, my knees would give out. This was too much.

"Just promise me that you will be careful with Harrison."

"What?" I guffawed.

"He's not family material, okay? It takes one to know one. He's the good-time guy. Don't let Collette get too attached."

As if she could dictate anything about her daughter when she was the one leaving. I had so much rage stuffing my mouth like cotton I couldn't express a single thought except one. One thought rang clear above them all. It was as true for her as it had been for my own mother.

"If you leave, I will never forgive you. There is no coming back from this, this time."

I knew my sister, and I knew when she was determined. She shrugged sadly.

"Goodbye, Frankie. I'm sorry I couldn't be better. At least now you can ride that high horse for the rest of your life." She got in the car and drove away.

I stood for a long time staring, trying to process what this all meant.

———

Harrison

I WAS DREAMING.

This was a favorite recurring fantasy of mine. Frankie turned up in my room in the middle of the night. The moon shone bright enough that the look of desire was clear in her eyes. She wanted me. She wanted me as desperately as I wanted her.

Next, she would crawl toward me. She would pull the blankets back and take off her shirt. I would lavish her with kisses. I would bring her pleasure like she'd never known.

Only this wasn't a dream. Frankie really was here at the foot of my bed, whispering my name.

And the look in her eyes wasn't desire …

"Frankie? What's wrong?" I sat up and fumbled to flick on the table lamp.

She stood, arms wrapped tight around herself, head shaking subtly. I kneel-walked to meet her at the edge of the bed.

"Is it Collette?" Fear rushed adrenaline through me. I gripped her shoulders until she looked up at me with red eyes.

She shook her head. "Joey left. She left."

"What?" I rubbed her arms up and down. My sleep-addled mind struggled to keep up. "Is she coming back?"

"No." It was like the final tether that had been holding her together snapped, and she gasped a loud sob, hands shooting to her mouth as though she could put it back in.

I grabbed her and held her to me. I rubbed her back in circles as she trembled in my arms. Joey left. "It's going to be okay."

"It's not. It's not." She gasped between sobs. "I didn't think I could cry anymore about this. But I can't stop."

Nothing I could say would possibly make right the devastation Joey's actions caused. I could hold Frankie. I could be here. I let her sob for a while, as she had done for me only a few short hours ago. Eventually, her breaths steadied.

She leaned back, wiping at her face. I handed her a tissue. "Thank you."

"What happened?" I asked.

"I caught her trying to sneak away. In the middle of the night."

I sucked in a breath and let it out steady. She blew her nose.

She tossed her hand up. "You can say it. She's awful and a coward. I'm done defending her. I'm done hoping she'll change. I'll never forgive her for this." The vehemence in her voice was something I'd never seen from her. I was glad to see her angry. Anger felt easier somehow than the crushing pain of abandonment.

"I pity her," I said eventually.

Frankie looked up at me, confused.

"Imagine being so self-centered that you can't even see the gift right in front of you," I explained, voice rough.

Her chin trembled, and she nodded. "She's missing it all. Collette changes every single day. And it's all so amazing and scary and impressive. You know?" She dabbed at her eyes with the fresh tissue I handed her.

I nodded, throat tight. Even in the few weeks I'd been here, Collette's mini phases and preferences changed daily. "Remember how she said scrumptious about every single thing she ate for five straight days?" I asked.

She laughed and wiped her eyes. "Sometimes I look at Collette, and I'm just in awe. She's this whole person. She was a baby, and now she has thoughts, feelings, and opinions."

"So many opinions," I said, and she laughed.

"I don't understand her. I really don't," she said, and we both understood she was referring to Joey.

"I don't either," I said.

Frankie finally sat on the edge of the bed, and I moved to sit next to her. She hadn't made a comment about me being only in my pants, so I wasn't about to draw attention to it, as distracted as she was. As much as I enjoyed my fantasy, having her come to me in search of solace felt all the more rewarding.

"She's missing all the magic of these early years. It's going so fast." She balled the tissues into her hand on her lap. "And I get that it's hard. I know I couldn't handle it either, but she isn't even trying. She doesn't even try. Just stay. *Stay.* It's the easiest thing you could do."

She broke again and collapsed into herself, head down, looking like a lost child.

I scooped her up in my arms as she shivered with silent sobs. I grabbed the duvet and cocooned us both into it.

"It's the easiest thing a mother can do for her daughter. Just be there," she said out loud, but I knew she wasn't really asking me. There was no answer. No explanation. "Don't they understand how easy it is to stay?"

"I'm sorry," I mumbled into her hair. "I'm so sorry."

"How could anybody leave their own child?" She moaned.

My heart was absolutely shattered for this woman. For the child that she once was. For all the unshared burdens she carried.

"I don't know," I said.

"Collette loves her so much. You saw her when Joey showed up. How simple it is to make her happy." She sat up and looked at me questioningly. "How can I possibly explain this to her? She will be devastated."

I wiped a tear from her cheek. "Collette is an incredibly loved child. She's resilient."

"She shouldn't have to be. Nothing in the world should ever cause her pain. Is that too much to ask?"

I huffed. "Life is going to throw many awful things at her. But she isn't alone. She has you." I wanted to say more than that. I wanted to make declarations I couldn't possibly support.

"I don't have any idea what I'm doing. I can't do this."

"You are doing it."

"I'm not her mother."

"More than most."

"She needs her real mom."

"She needs you."

She took a shaking breath in and out. "I don't know what to do."

"Nothing has to be decided right this moment," I said, and she chewed her lip, nodding. I brushed another tear away.

"I'm so sorry to unload all of this on you." She rolled her eyes to the ceiling. "I never planned for any of this. None of this."

"I know. It's okay." Despite the sadness and anger I felt, having her come to me for comfort made me feel worthy on a level I never expected. It felt like a gift to be the person who took care of her. "What do *you* want to do?"

She licked her lips. Her eyes flicked around my face. Something about that darkness in her features sent heat down my spine. I cleared my throat. This would be a terrible time to misread a situation.

"I just need to forget for a little bit. I just need to leave my mind behind," she said, shifting closer. She lowered her forehead to my chest.

I stilled, blinking at her in surprise. My entire body was fully online and awake now, instantly taut with tension. "Frankie ..."

"Please, Harrison. I'm so tired. I need a distraction." She scraped her fingers through my hair as she brushed her lips along the line of my jaw. I felt my throat move under her warm, soft lips. "Please, let me forget it all for one night. Tomorrow, I will figure things out."

For one night ... a distraction.

In any other scenario, this would have been my literal dream come true, but I hesitated with an unexpected pang of hurt. My body warred with my mind more than it ever had. I wanted her, *Christ*, I'd wanted her for so long. But her pain was visceral. How could she possibly be thinking clearly? The day had been long and emotionally exhausting. If I gave in to her now, I would only ever be seen as a distraction. I didn't want to be a distraction from the real world, I wanted to be her whole world. I had hoped she had come to me tonight as a sort of partner—a person to count on and trust in.

I wasn't her partner. I was a way to turn off her mind and turn on her body.

But the truth was that this was Frankie. She was here and so bloody gorgeous, and I would be whatever she needed me to be. Even if it hurt me later.

She leaned back to watch me expectantly, fragile, hopeful, vulnerable.

My hand lifted to her shoulder as the duvet fell away. I slowly let my thumb drag down the column of her neck, to her shoulder, and down her arm. She was incredible. She tilted her head to give me more neck to touch.

I spread my fingers as I palmed as much of her exposed skin as possible. She was breathtaking.

"Frankie. Are you sure this is really what you want?" I asked. The tether of restraint was seconds from snapping. She sighed as I moved my thumb to tilt her chin up, gaining her attention.

She blinked slowly at me with her heavy-lidded eyes. "Please turn off my brain. Make me feel good, Harrison. I know you can."

Maybe I wouldn't ever be more than a distraction. Maybe I would always be the person to make her forget the world.

But I could be damn good at it.

I leaned forward slowly, giving her plenty of time to change her mind. Her eyes watched me as I moved in, finally fluttering shut when my mouth hovered just a centimeter from hers. I felt her soft exhalations as I took in the features in the low light.

"How could anybody be so beautiful?" I asked myself, but the words came out as a whisper.

She swallowed under where my palm still cupped her neck. My lips barely brushed hers as the bedroom door whipped open.

Frankie shot away so fast it didn't seem humanly possible. I hadn't even heard the sounds of Collette leaving her room. Her tiny frame filled the doorway. Light pouring in from the hallway cast her in shadow.

"Collette? What's wrong, sweetie?" Frankie asked.

I shifted to cover myself and blinked as I processed the sudden interruption. I felt ... relieved? I would have given Frankie whatever she thought she wanted, knowing I would never be able to come back from it. She wouldn't be happy in the light of day. She wouldn't even look at me if we crossed that line.

"I threw up," Collette said and started to cry.

21

Frankie

THE SOUR SMELL HIT A SECOND AFTER COLLETTE'S TEARS CAME. I moved into action immediately.

"Oh, baby. It's okay. It's okay." I scooped her up into my arms and brought her straight to the bathroom off her bedroom.

"I'm going to clean her up," I said to Harrison, who was surprisingly right behind us. "Did you throw up in your bed?" I asked her.

She cried harder and nodded.

"I'll get the sheets," he said without hesitation.

"I'm sorry," she said, still sobbing.

"It's okay, sweetie. It happens when you get sick. You can't always make it to the potty."

She nodded, her lip trembling. In the light of the bathroom, her lids were heavy, and her pallor green under damp skin.

"I went to your room, and you weren't there," she said pathetically.

"I'm so sorry. You poor thing. I'm here now. It's okay."

She nodded and curled deeper into me. I noticed she hadn't

asked after Joey, and I wasn't about to bring her up. I couldn't think about anything but making her feel better and getting her out of these soaked pajamas. I had been singularly focused since the moment she appeared in the bedroom.

"Why were you in Harrison's room?" She rubbed her eyes against the bright light, her crying temporarily halted by her curiosity.

"We were talking," I said smoothly, wondering if Harrison could hear from next door.

"I don't feel good." She started crying again. I gently set her on the edge of the tub.

"I know, sweetie. Let's get these off." I tugged the shirt over her head, careful not to get any sick on her. She shivered with tiny goose bumps all over her body. I tossed the shirt into a ball and tossed it in the corner. I breathed through clenched teeth, desperate not to smell anymore. I was not a throw up person. I was the gagging when people even pretended to gag, person.

"I shouldn't have had all that junk food. You were right." She sniffled.

"Oh baby, I think you're just sick. This isn't your fault."

"I need to throw up." She moaned and sat forward as I opened the toilet seat lid.

"Okay, see if you can go in here."

She gagged. And a roiling nausea made my neck go icy. I had hoped that if she ever got sick like this, instead of the normal colds and fevers, I would be able to power through, focusing on her. It was a fear that sometimes kept me up at night. But with every passing second, the saliva gathered in my mouth, and my stomach tightened. I wasn't going to get through this without losing it.

Right then, Harrison peeked in the doorway. "How goes it in here?"

Collette vomited—into the toilet— but the sounds. The smell.

The sick rose in me so fast that my stomach cramped. I covered my mouth with the inside of my elbow.

"Oh boy," Harrison said, noting whatever he saw on my face. "Are you sick too?"

I shook my head. "Sympathetic pu—" I couldn't even finish the words. Bile rose higher.

"Okay. You out." He pointed at me. "I'll take care of this."

"I can't let you," I said, but he was moving me to leave, and I was all too eager to get away from the smell.

"You won't be helping if you get sick too. Go finish the sheets," he said brusquely and shut the door in my face.

I gulped the fresh air and burped—terribly unladylike—but instantly feeling better. The sheets were already off Collette's bed.

"Just start the washer. I already ... uh, sprayed off the worst of it," he called through the door.

A sound came out of me that I wasn't proud of.

I heard him chuckle before a splash and sympathetic sounds.

"La la la," I sang loudly as I made my way to the laundry room, not willing to risk even hearing her gags.

I started the wash and gave Collette and Harrison a few more minutes as I opened her bedroom window and cleared some of the air. I was mostly composed when I cautiously went to the bathroom door.

"How you feelin' now?" Harrison asked gently.

"Better," she said.

"Good. I think you got all the evil out of ya."

"Will you stay with me?" Collette asked around a yawn.

"Of course. I will stay as long as you want me."

I closed my eyes and leaned against the door. It was such a

contrast to Joey. He chose to be here for the worst. He stepped up to help her without even blinking an eye. How could I have ever thought that wasn't enough?

He carried her out a moment later; she was already sound asleep in his arms.

"Poor thing," I whispered. I kissed her damp forehead.

"I think the worst is over," he said.

"I'm sorry you had to take care of that. I thought I could handle it ..."

"It's fine. Trust me, I've seen much worse. My best mate used to drink so much that—" Whatever he saw in my features cut his story short. "Anyway. I washed her best I could but didn't want to get her hair wet."

"Good idea." I pushed back her sweat-damp curls, and she sighed in her sleep.

"Thank you," I said, meeting his gaze. He broke away first.

"I'm going to lay with her for a little while. Just in case," he said softly.

"Okay. I put a bowl next to the bed."

"You should get some sleep," he said, looking at Collette and not at me. The unspoken truth there. It was the first chance I'd had to gauge his reaction to things since our kiss happened. Or rather didn't happen.

I hadn't been thinking clearly. I was so distraught, and he was so warm and comforting and *here*. But it was a good thing we'd been interrupted. There was no going back if we crossed that line. Collette was the reminder I needed. I couldn't even think about how I threw myself at him without humiliation flaming up my neck. Best to pretend it never happened.

"Good night," I said.

"Good night, Frankie. Everything will seem brighter in the morning."

I hesitated only a minute before I stood on tiptoes and kissed his cheek. "Thank you."

He smiled sleepily at me.

I went to bed for the second time that night, thinking of Harrison. He was so much more than I'd given him credit for. So much kinder and more of a good person than so many I knew.

It had been incredibly selfish and cruel of me to push him away or think he was anything less than sincere in his endeavor to help George and Collette. The man cared. So much. And I had scorned him like a child.

I had to hope it wasn't too late for me to apologize.

Harrison

IT WAS JUST AFTER SUNRISE WHEN I FINALLY STUMBLED BLEARILY out of Collette's room and into the kitchen. I should have crawled my way back to bed, but the smell of strong coffee wafted down the hallway like a siren song.

"I fell asleep," I said on a yawn to Frankie, who stood staring out the kitchen window. I often caught her staring out windows, lost in thought. At first, I assumed she was thinking about her ever-growing to-do list, but now, I wondered if she wasn't imagining another life where she wasn't responsible for so much thrust upon her.

She startled and glanced up at me with a shy smile. "I'm glad you got some sleep. Coffee?"

"Intravenously, if possible," I answered.

She chuckled, reaching for a mug.

So glad it won't be weird at all now. No reason to even mention the fact that we almost kissed last night. No reason to ruminate over the fact that we almost did so much more than that. No reason to think about how the briefest brush of her lips against mine lit me more than anything I'd felt in years. Maybe ever.

This was all going to be totally normal.

"As it turns out, that bed is not meant for a grown man." I rolled my head side to side, cracking my neck.

I stopped when I felt Frankie looking up at me. Her gaze moved over my exposed chest and shoulders. I wasn't one to preen—well, yes, I was—but now, I actively tried not to flex. Her gaze sent shivers down my spine. I cleared my throat, and Frankie blinked, glancing away.

Nope not weird one bit.

"I think the princess canopy would have been a dead give-away." She handed me the hot coffee prepared just how I liked it.

"Bless you," I said. After a sip, I sighed dramatically. "I think I would have been okay if her stuffies didn't take up half of it. That Ellie the Elephant is a real bed hog."

She sipped her own coffee and nodded. She seemed particularly lost in thought this morning.

"Did you get any sleep," I asked after a few minutes, remembering my manners as my brain fully woke up. Still not bringing up the other Ellie the Elephant in the room.

"Yeah, a little." She set her mug down and stepped toward me. "I was up thinking for a lot of it."

I stilled as she came closer. My throat went dry. "Yeah? It was a strange twenty-four hours."

She let out a breath through puffed cheeks. "No kidding. I feel a little punch drunk this morning. Loopy."

This was it. The final straw had been her making a pass at me last night and me more than willing to meet her halfway. It was some sort of test, and I'd failed. She would be giving me the official boot. After all, it had been two *very* long days since our conversation about my leaving. The two-week deadline was here and gone.

"You were incredible last night," she said.

The swallow I'd just taken snagged in my throat and I coughed. When I collected myself enough to talk, I said, "I, uh, didn't even get—"

"With Collette," she added quickly with a flush.

"Right. That makes more sense." *Oh Christ*. That was close to humiliating. "No. That was nothing."

"And before that with George."

"Well, he trusts me." I scratched the back of my neck. This was far from the boot to the bottom I'd been expecting.

"That's exactly what I mean. I've been thinking. I would have been absolutely lost without you yesterday," she said, holding my gaze.

I shook my head. "George wouldn't have even gotten lost without me."

"That's not true. And Joey would have still showed up, so don't beat yourself up." I frowned. "Though if I'm being totally honest with myself, deep down I don't think she would have even showed up if not for learning that you were here."

And when she realized she couldn't get anything from me, she abandoned her advances. We'd been thinking the same thing.

"But none of that was relevant to the point I was trying to make," she said.

"The point being?" I asked, hesitantly.

"I was wrong," she said simply. "I do need you here. We need you here," she added when my eyebrows shot up. "I know this is a big ask, especially since ... now with Joey leaving." She lowered her voice even though Collette wouldn't hear a train running through the house when she was asleep. "I don't know what I'll do about Collette yet ... but even before *that*. I was lying there thinking about how crucial you've become in running this household. You don't add too much to my plate. You make George happy and feel safe. You add stability to Collette's life."

I set down my mug with a frown. "I make things more difficult for you."

"No," she said sharply. "I wouldn't have survived the last two weeks without you. The trial period is over, and I hope that you will stay." She propped her fists on her hips, chin lifted, determined. "If you want. I think I just worried that if I counted on you and then you couldn't handle it, it would be much harder to deal with everything. But you've stayed. Time and time again, when you could have left at any point, you have proven that you take this all seriously. There are so few people that I feel like I can rely on. But you are one of them."

A warmth spread through me to know she felt that way. I had finally proven myself reliable to her. It was all I wanted, but I continued to frown at a spot on the floor. Now, I began to doubt my own abilities.

"I understand if I'm too late," she said. "With everything I said before. But I was so wrong. You don't make things harder. You're not a child playing make believe. And I like the way your brain works. I like how you act with Collette. So you're a little messy? We can see about getting the housekeeper to come more often if I'm really that uptight about it. But I'm understanding more than ever that a clean house doesn't mean a happy life. Being here, laughter and presence and showing up. That matters so much more than a tidy kitchen. The being here is what is important."

"I feel like I make things worse. That I'm stupid or a burden somehow." I spoke honestly, humiliated. "It's like every time I try, I make things worse."

"None of that is true. And I am so sorry if I ever made you feel that way. I don't know who said that to you but it simply isn't true. Everything about who you are makes you a perfect fit to stay in this temporary pseudo family. Until the book is done. Until ... I have a plan for Collette's safety." My heart clenched painfully at hearing those words. "I want you here. I know the others do too. If you'll have us."

I looked at her for a long moment. This may not be forever, but George often spoke of not wasting the time we had. I would help as long as I was needed in any capacity I was useful. Then, I would let them be free of me.

"I'm not going anywhere," I said.

She let out a long breath, shoulders rising and lowering with a long sigh. "Good."

We stood close, smiling and hopeful. "Except," she added, and I tensed. Her eyes flicked over my chest and shoulders again. They moved slowly and without bashfulness. "Maybe put on some clothes before Collette wakes up."

22

Harrison Evans: Hey, Frankie. Remember Wesley Cole? (He's Emma's *lovah* you met at Christmas.)

Wesley Cole: It's weird when you use that tone of voice.

Harrison Evans: How can you tell in a text message?

Wesley Cole: I can tell.

Frankie Ricci: We can all tell. Hi, Wesley. Nice to chat with you again.

Wesley Cole: Same to you.

Harrison Evans: Wesley has lawyers who specialize in family law.

Wesley Cole: I'm not sure they are experts in custody, but if they don't have answers, they can find someone to help.

Frankie Ricci: Thank you so much. I just want to keep her safe.

Wesley Cole: Of course. Emma told me to tell you ... actually hang on

Emma Flynn has been added to the chat.

Emma Flynn: Sorry to butt in, but Wesley was getting tired of me talking over his shoulder, and I thought this would be easier.

Wesley Cole: I was not. I like having you over my shoulder. You smell nice.

Emma Flynn: Awww.

Harrison Evans: Gross. Stop. She's right there. You could have just told her that.

Wesley Cole: I could have, but then I would not have been able to annoy you.

Frankie Ricci: Oh, I like this.

Harrison Evans: Listen. Frankie really wanted this all to be a need-to-know basis.

Frankie Ricci: It's okay, I trust your friends.

Harrison Evans: You shouldn't.

Emma Flynn: Harrison is just grumpy because he doesn't like to share.

Frankie Ricci: He does look really grumpy. He's got his arms crossed and that pouty lip going.

Wesley Cole: Take a picture.

Harrison Evans: I regret this so much.

Attachment "harrisonpout.jpg" has been sent.

Harrison Evans: At least it's a good picture. Weren't you going to say something important, Emma?

Wesley Cole: Give her a minute. She's laughing too hard to type.

TheRealRealCharlie has been added to the chat.
Kate Dubois has been added to the chat.

TheRealRealCharlie: Hey, everybody!

Kate Dubois: Who took the awesome pic of Harrison?

Harrison Evans: What is even happening right now?

Emma Flynn: It's easier this way. If we weren't all here, I'd just have to relay it to Charlie.

TheRealRealCharlie: And then I'd tell Kate. Work smart, not hard.

Harrison Evans: There is the option where we do this without taking the piss out of me?

"Help Collette" group chat has changed its name to "Too Many Cooks"

TheRealRealCharlie: Hey, remember that time I brought Kate around, and you told her about my embarrassing childhood memories?

Frankie Ricci: You can't hear him, but he just groaned.

TheRealRealCharlie: That's the sweet, sweet sound of karma.

Harrison Evans: This is hardly the same. I'm trying to help Frankie, not *woo* her...

Frankie Ricci: You were trying to say something, Emma?

Emma Flynn: The most important thing is to keep a paper trail of everything. If your sister so much as tries to contact you or Collette, keep a record in any way you can.

Frankie Ricci: She hasn't yet, but I will. Thanks.

Harrison Evans: The issue now is that she's gone MIA. We even reached out to her theater company, but apparently, she was fired last week for missing so many shows.

Wesley Cole: Just keep an eye out. We will see what we can do on our end. Family has a way of causing issues when you least expect it.

Frankie Ricci: Thanks, everybody.

Emma Flynn: How is Collette doing?

Frankie Ricci: She's okay. Asking about her less and less. Unfortunately, this is normal for her.

Wesley Cole: Kids adapt quickly.

TheRealRealCharlie: And grow even faster.

Frankie Ricci: You have kids? I don't think I knew that.

TheRealRealCharlie: Thirty-four and counting.

Kate Dubois: Chickens.

Harrison Evans: Chickens are hardly the same, Charlie.

TheRealRealCharlie: I didn't say they were.

Kate Dubois: Aw, now he's pouting.

Emma Flynn: Just know, whatever you guys need, we are here. Please don't forget that. George is family, so that means you, by extension, are too.

TheRealRealCharlie: We will do whatever you need.

"Too Many Cooks" group chat has changed its name to "Lucky in Love"

Harrison Evans: Thank you.

Frankie Ricci: Thank you all <3

Agata Wisniewski has been added to the chat.

Agata Wisniewski: What'd I miss?

23

Frankie

Time moved quickly from spring to summer. Collette asked after her mother less and less, especially when the calls stopped with her sudden departure.

Every time she wondered after Joey, the ice forming over my heart grew thicker toward my sister. While transparency was important regarding Collette—I always promised to be as age-appropriately honest with her—there was just no easy way to explain that her mother wasn't coming back. I told her that Joey couldn't come back right now and that she loved her very much. It was a cop-out of an answer, but I didn't know what else I could say.

For now, until I had any clue what to do, I would stick to the plan. The plan was to keep Collette safe right now, with Harrison and me at George's place. Harrison had a friend looking into family lawyers to figure out where to go next. Joey had, surprising absolutely nobody, completely dropped off the map. Her phone number was no longer in service, and she had sent no further information on her plans for Collette. I researched child abandonment laws just in case but found that at least six months would need to pass without a single word from Joey. That would be right around Halloween. Hopefully, we'd hear from her soon. If nothing else, to officially relinquish her rights. Then we could make a new plan.

For now, all I could focus on were the tasks at hand. Finish George's Magnum Opus. Finish archiving his life's work.

Ultimately, I was being selfish. I wasn't ready to look for the stable family Collette needed. I wasn't ready to say goodbye to her. I understood that I could never be the best option for Collette. Somewhere out there was a complete, stable family with loving parents who knew how to give her the best home possible. That was a reality I couldn't seem to process. Not yet. We still had months together where I would be her main person, not an aunt she saw from time to time if her new family allowed it. Even thinking about it caused a pain so sharp I physically pushed the thoughts away.

The four of us settled into a routine. George was at his most calm. When George was officially diagnosed with Lewy body dementia by his team of doctors, we slowly introduced a part-time occupational therapist, Otis the OT, who worked with him on moving his body and keeping his mind sharp.

Collette continued to thrive in the Sandia community, making friends and learning so much. Her school year ended, and Collette was enrolled at a summer camp a few days a week. There weren't a lot of kids in the more mountainous area where we lived, especially this time of year, and we didn't want her to get bored. She was getting fresh air and exercise and not being cooped up in the house, constantly pushing Harrison's boundaries. Poor guy.

Harrison and I were ... two separate planets rotating around the twin suns of George and Collette, careful to never collide, never talk about the night I threw myself at him all those weeks ago.

I worked on archiving and writing; he helped in his domestic capacity, and things were moving right along.

Most things.

There was still the issue of finishing this book.

George snoozed on the covered porch while Collette was at day camp.

I eventually found Harrison in the pool house, which was weird. He had earbuds in and a laundry basket of freshly cleaned smelling towels that he was folding. Or maybe attempting to fold by evidence of the single towel in his hand and the unfolded stack next to him.

A guitar was propped in the corner that I had yet to ever see him play. Occasionally, while I typed in the office, notes of the acoustic guitar would drift through the window but not loud enough to recognize. For all my teasing about the actor's natural tendency to show off, Harrison was stubborn about not playing for anyone, claiming he wasn't good enough.

"Hey," I said. He continued to stare off into space. "Harrison."

His head was turned, looking at a spot on the wall so he couldn't see my approach. I got the impression he wasn't actually looking at the wall, just lost in his own brain. This was a different form of handsome on him, still and quiet like this. Such a rarely-seen side of him. His eyes were unfocused, features soft. Strongly angled jaw, protruding Adam's apple, thick lashes, kissable lips.

I was so glad I had put all thoughts of kissing him behind me. Never even crossed my mind. Except when I looked at him. Or thought about him. Or smelled him. Or when he would gently touch me as he brushed passed me in the hallway.

Honestly, once the dam of horny thoughts broke, I couldn't put them back in. I just let myself indulge in them now. I didn't even kid myself that I wasn't attracted to him. It was okay to have a little brain fun from time to time. I wasn't about to act on it.

We were playing with fire, dancing around each other like this. I wouldn't be the person to get burned.

"Harrison," I repeated. He jumped when I put my hand on his shoulder.

He took his headphones out. "You scared me."

"We've been living together for over three months. At what point will you stop jumping when I walk into the room?" I asked, cocking a hip to lean against the chair across from him.

"When you stop being so scary."

"Aren't you funny? Why are you folding towels here?"

He shrugged. "I like it down here. It feels like a little getaway," he said.

"A getaway from your getaway?" I asked.

His face darkened, and I regretted saying that. He'd been working so hard lately with George, with Collette. Helping me around the house. "What are you listening to?" I grabbed the earbud and brought it close enough to hear. "Is that a robot?"

He reached to grab the earbud back, but I leaned out of his way. "It's my girlfriend, I call her AIV—artificial intelligence voice."

"Wait. This sounds familiar," I said.

"It should. You wrote it."

I handed it back. "Blech," I said and stuck out my tongue. "How did you do that?"

"I have a software that reads for me. Honestly, I'm still trying to explain the shared doc to you. At this point, it won't be worth the time."

"Listen. I'm not technologically ignorant." I cocked a hand on my hip. "Need I remind you that I am the one digitizing everything? I'm firmly in the twentieth century."

"Twenty-first," he corrected.

Dammit! I always got that wrong. "Oh, you're snarky today."

"Never," he said.

But he was.

"Go on." I grabbed a towel and snapped it at him. "Tell me about your fake girlfriend."

The tips of his ears went red as he finished folding, avoiding my gaze. "The short of it is that I can't always process words on a page. She reads it to me so I can focus."

"You didn't seem to be focused when I walked in."

"Actually, just the opposite. I was so into it, I lost track of what I was doing." He gestured to the unfolded laundry. When he finally looked at me, I noticed his eyes were red-rimmed. "This is the chapter about Adam's decision to leave. It's really good."

I swallowed down the compliment, unable to fully digest it, so it stuck like heartburn in my esophagus.

I shook my head. "It's mostly George," I mumbled.

"It doesn't seem like it's him."

"Don't say that," I said, instantly worried. "Wait, does it really not sound like him?"

"I meant ... never mind. Trust me, readers won't notice. Now that I know what to look for, the hints of you are all over this. It's good, though. Don't worry. Fix your face." He leaned up to press a finger into my cheek. I pretended to bite it.

He put the earbuds away and started to fold another towel. Was the story really that good that he got lost in it? Or was he just that bad at staying focused?

I was debating what I would prefer when he cleared his throat.

"What's up, Francesca?" He rolled my name off his tongue. I couldn't be sure, but ever since our almost kiss, I swore he'd turned up the volume of his flirting. It was at a solid eleven. (That was a movie reference I understood now because of the mandatory movie night that was imposed after the whole *Star Wars* "I am your father" debacle.)

"Well. It's about that, actually." I gestured to his headphones. "The manuscript. I'm stuck, and George is having a tired day. I really don't have time to get behind." I sighed and looked anywhere but at him. "And as much as I hate to admit it, your notes always help."

Harrison gasped, forcing my attention back to him. He grinned like he just won an Oscar. "I make you a better writer. I am a critical component in your creative process. You need me. You can admit it."

"I do," I said easily. "Your ideas are just so terrible that it helps me decide what direction to go in."

His smile turned into a pout. "Now, who's snarky?"

"Sorry. Sorry. I do need your help." I proffered the laptop tucked under my arm. "I was going to ask you to read this scene really quick. Please? It's just like five pages."

He cleared his throat, and a flush spread up his neck. "I-I can't always read fast. It's not that I can't read. I have a hard time reading *and* processing at the same time. I'm not an idiot."

I flinched back. "I would never think that." I didn't even want to say the word. I wouldn't even let Collette say it. Was that what he thought?

He scratched at the back of his neck. "Some people think that."

"Those people are wrong. And what did you tell Collette? 'Other people's opinions are none of our business.' But I'm sorry, I didn't know. You got through the other chapters so fast, I assumed you were reading them."

He pointed at the headphones again. "I can adjust the speed."

"Frick. Well, okay, never mind. Sorry. I didn't realize ... I wouldn't have ..." I trailed off awkwardly. I was stuck on this scene, and Harrison had a knack for getting me rolling, all joking aside, and now I felt like an insensitive jerk.

"I have an idea," he said.

"I don't love that look in your eyes." I started to back away to the door.

He cleared the spot on the couch next to him and patted the cushion. "You could read it out loud to me."

I blinked at the spot. Then at him. "It's like you went into my brain and plucked out my literal idea of what hell would be."

He laughed freely, and my guilt abated. I had to admit that few things made me feel as clever as when I was able to charm the charmer. "You know I'm reading it anyway. What's the difference?"

"The difference is crucial. Trust me."

"Come on. It won't be so bad."

"I think I would rather get Collette to try foie gras."

"So dramatic." He cocked his head and used his most Harrison Evans face on me. "I'm offering to help. I won't even look at you. I'll be over here folding the wash. Hardly even noticeable."

"Hmm," I grumbled. I really did need help. I chewed my lip, staring back in the direction of the office. "Fine. But no jokes. Of any kind. I won't be able to handle it in my fragile state," I warned.

"Your ego will be handled with kid gloves."

I sighed but opened my laptop.

After spending way too much time trying to find a position to sit where I could read without being able to see him in my periphery, I cleared my throat. "I'm thirsty. I should get water."

He handed me his. "Stop stalling."

I grumbled a few obscenities under my breath but eventually started reading, voice shaking. My voice was so high and tight in my chest I forced myself to pause and take a slow, deep breath in and out. He waited patiently, not making any comments. When I started again, I slowed down and focused on getting through this. After a few lines, I glanced up at him, but his features were neutral, fully focused on the towels, for all intents and purposes.

After several paragraphs, I began to relax and read. A few pages in, I stopped to take a sip of water and risked a glance at Harrison.

He was on his phone. My jaw dropped. So much for riveting storytelling.

"Why'd you stop?" he asked without looking up.

"You aren't paying attention," I said, sounding indignant even to my own ears.

"Trust me, I am."

I leaned over to look at him. "You're playing jewel heist on your phone!"

"This is how I focus."

"You aren't even looking at me."

"I could look at you." He finally set the phone aside to meet my gaze. "But then I wouldn't be paying attention anymore."

The words were like a bird that seemed to swoop into my stomach and flutter around my chest.

"Oh. Ah." A blush burned up my cheeks as I stumbled.

"Carry on." He picked up his phone again, and I read until I got to the end of the first scene, awaiting feedback.

Harrison blinked back to himself and spoke. "Your voice is incredible. You know that? It's so feminine but rich that even when you drop into the male voices I'm so lost in the story I forget you're even reading it."

I let out a sigh, trying very hard not to feel flattered. "But the story?"

"It's great."

"I need real notes."

"It is. You're killing it, Francesca. You really are."

"Why do you keep using my full name?" I flustered.

"Because I like how it flusters you."

I balled my fists and let my hair fall to block my smile trying to escape. "You are incorrigible," I mumbled.

"Where were you thinking this scene was stuck?" he asked, getting us back on track.

"The whole fight? It didn't feel, I don't know, forced?"

"Nah. It only feels that way to you because you know what it's leading to."

I let out a long breath. "Okay then. Well, thank you. For, uh, listening."

"You have an extra arm, though," he dropped in casually.

"What?"

"Yeah. During the struggle with the trooper. You added an arm."

"I did not." I frowned at my laptop, quickly scanning the page. "Did I?"

"Read through when he's grabbing Adam."

"No. I don't see."

"I can't really explain." He shook his head. "Let me just show you." He stood up and stretched. He popped his back and then gestured to his side. "Come here."

"What?"

"You heard me." He gently put my laptop to the side. I glared at him. "Come on. You'll be Adam in this scene, and I'll be the mercenary." He pulled me to stand.

"I don't think—"

Just then, he lunged at me. I froze. Too late, my body caught up. My arm shot out.

"Ouch. Not very Adam Abbotts to sucker punch." He rubbed his pec.

"Sorry. Habit."

He raised an eyebrow at me. "One day, I will unlock all your secrets."

I waved him off. "That day is not today," I teased. "Also, you attacked me." I shifted on my feet, feeling slightly defensive but mostly playful.

"We're acting out the scene." He dropped his arms to the side, sort of hopping in place like a boxer preparing in the ring.

"I'm not an actor, Harrison."

"You don't have to be. Just think of it like writing. Close your eyes and play the scene in your mind."

"God, please let's go back to the reading out loud. Why do you keep making me do stuff?" I whined, still a little jittery with a post-adrenaline rush.

"You'll see that I'm right."

"Writing is way more physical than I ever signed up for."

"Okay. So I attack." He came at me, slower this time.

I closed my eyes to play along. Even though this was stupid.

"It's not stupid. Stop mumbling," he said. He grabbed my right wrist. "This is where he gets the weapon, right?"

I nodded, eyes closed tight with focus, but really to avoid awkward eye contact for this silly activity.

"Then Adam pivots." I nod. He sighed. "Pivot, Adam."

"Oh. Sorry." I took his hand and turned slowly, matching the action in the book so that my back was now pressed against his front. "Adam elbows bad guy," I say and pretend to elbow Harrison in the gut.

"Oof." He bends forward dramatically, still in this weird underwater slow-mo, taking me with him so that I'm forced to brace my hands on the nearby wall.

"Wow. Great acting," I said dryly.

"Tell the golden statues at my house, love."

"Mr. Cocky. Okay. Wait. This wasn't how it went. I'm falling."

I tried to stand back up, but the angle was weird, so I flailed as Harrison was forced to brace his hands on my hips ... as I bent over in front of him. My ass bumped into his groin. Desire crashed over me. This was the fire I referred to. The fire I tried to avoid.

Humiliating. Exciting. Illuminating. There was no denying how attracted I was to this man.

"Sorry," he said gruffly and tugged me upright.

"Weird how doing this in slow motion gives this story a totally different vibe," I said, trying to lighten the mood.

"This is fan fiction territory."

I snorted. "Maybe I should try reading it, after all," I said without thinking.

He stiffened behind me. "Where were we?"

"You got the weapon from me, er, Adam," I said.

"Right." The heat that radiated off him as he stood barely an inch behind me was fuel to the fire. He held each of my wrists in both of his hands. He kicked my legs apart, spreading me, and instantly, a switch was flicked to life. Heat pooled low in me. My knees felt like they might give out. His panting breath behind me burned down my neck, tightening my whole body. I wanted to fall back against him. Let him catch me. Watch his hands roam my whole body ...

"Now, this part." His voice was low and rumbled along my shoulder blades. My whole body throbbed. "He reached around Adam." He matched the action, his own hand coming across my chest. "Grabs hold of him." I'm yanked up tight against Harrison.

A gasp escapes me and it takes all my power not to throw my head back on his shoulder and grind myself back against him. My thoughts came blurry and slow, muddled with desire.

"Now he's got Adam in his grasp, right?" His voice came out breathy.

I throbbed, standing like this. I felt myself growing wetter with every exhalation. Harrison's scent was all around me, making my mind cloudy.

"Right?" he asked, and I could honestly not recall what he'd even asked.

I made some sort of sound of assent, avoiding the question.

When Harrison spoke again, his mouth was so close to my ear that if I turned my head a fraction, I could cause our faces to touch. "But then he reaches for his own weapon. But with what hand? Unless he's got an extra set of prehensile arms," he joked, slightly strained. "I mean, in this universe, that could be possible."

"I-I see what you mean," I said. But really, I was so checked out I had no clue what he was talking about. What the crap did prehensile arms mean? Who cared about arms at a time like this? Except his. I wanted his arms to come back across my chest and graze my nipples again. I wanted to turn and rub myself against him until I got off.

"You could always, um, have him, grasp both wrists in one hand. Like this," he said, his chest rose and fell rapidly.

"Yeah?" I asked, breathy.

"He could brace him against the wall. Like this." He stepped us both up to the wall. His entire front now pushed me into it. Only I didn't feel scared or claustrophobic. I felt seconds away from humiliating myself. "And his other hand would be free to search for Adam's backup Taser." Harrison's other hand landed so gently on my abdomen that I almost didn't notice.

I stayed completely still. So silent. I thought he would pull back, but he didn't.

"What do you think?" he asked, his hand still pretending to search me. It grazed up and down my thighs so slow I thought I could cry.

"I like it." In case he was actually still trying to work and I was the one perving up the scene, I added, "Makes sense."

"Yeah." He was still pressed against me. "Good."

As his hand softly caressed my abdomen, his pinky caught on the top of my leggings, stopping its movement. I heard him swallow hard behind me. I wanted to arch my back and press my core against him to see if he was hard. But I was also so afraid to move and risk this moment coming to an end.

We both stayed perfectly still. Maybe waiting for the other to stop things first. Well, it wouldn't be me. I'd lost rational decision-making the moment he kicked my legs wide. Or maybe the day we met. Hard to say.

Either way, the air felt thick and on the precipice of something. I wasn't alone on this. His breath was quick next to my ear. He vibrated with similar tension thrumming through me.

I wasn't sure at what specific moment this pretense all ended. There was no doubt we were crossing lines now. His hand caressed the skin of my lower belly, tickling and tightening me. I clenched at nothing, desperate for him to go lower. He hesitated. Waiting for a sign? Permission?

I turned my head slightly to look at him. His gorgeous eyes burned with an intensity like I'd never seen.

"Okay?" he whispered.

I nodded and licked my lips. His gaze moved to watch the action. His head lowered as his hand continued to softly pet my sensitive skin. Our lips met. I was half pinned in the strange position, head turned awkwardly as was his to meet my mouth, but it didn't matter.

How was it possible that this was our first kiss? His lips were familiar. They were right and true. As though all these months of studying the way they moved forming words, or wrapped around a spoon, or crooked with a smile somehow foreshadowed just how they would feel pressed against mine.

I feel like I've known you ...

His mouth slanted, opened. Mine matched. Our breaths shared. Tongues as teasing as our banter has been.

He gripped me hard with both hands, desperate in their gentle strength. But that mouth. It moved me. I wished I was free to run my hands through his thick hair. To pull him close and not let him go. I wanted to touch him as he touched me, but the thrill of not getting what I wanted, of letting him control, was too great. And he seemed to sense that.

I flipped without warning, tugging him immediately back on me, my body now against the wall. One hand still braced my wrists. But now I writhed into the hand that was at my waist. He groaned, never breaking my kiss, but his hand started to explore more boldly. He spread his palm across my stomach. He took his time moving up under my shirt to cup my breast through my bra. He spread his fingers across my chest and collarbones. He took his time. And it drove me wild.

He grabbed my ass and squeezed. His hand went back to the front of my pants, and I gasped.

He grunted. A finger teased up and down the seam of my leggings. He palmed me, feeling the needy heat, but it wasn't enough. I met his hand with roughness and rubbed myself, wishing his palm would press harder.

"Harrison," I gasped.

"Tell me."

"More. Please."

He complied. His palm passed more firmly against my clit, and I threw my head back to moan. It was obscene and ridiculous and exactly what months of pent-up desire would do.

I could actually come like this. Him rubbing me through my clothes and kissing me like this. I really could, and I wouldn't even be ashamed. He had to feel how wet I was. How desperate I was for him.

"Okay?" he asked, panting. I brought my head down to study

his blown-out pupils. Intense focus flared his nostrils as color rose high in his cheeks.

The way he looked at me.

"I'm so close."

"Good. Let me feel you."

I broke the kiss to bury my face in his neck as I came.

"Oh my God," I moaned as the pulses subsided. "I cannot believe that just happened."

"It's okay." He kissed the top of my head, finally releasing my arms as blood flowed back to the tips.

The reality of what we just did crept in like morning fog. Stupid horny brain should never be allowed to make decisions. Where was the crypt keeper now? There should be some sort of fail-safe that engages when you get so turned on that you can't function. At least now I understand how humanity made it this long. We were all just a bunch of dumb, horny animals.

"I don't even know what to say." I struggled to meet his eyes. I needed to be an adult about this.

His phone alarm started buzzing.

"Because of course," I said.

"I need to go get Collette."

"Oh God," I groaned, burrowing my face deeper into the neck of his shirt.

He chuckled. "Will you look at me?"

"Probably never again, to be completely honest."

"Francesca." He rolled my name off his tongue, and to my utter horror, I was still so horny for this man. "Look at me," he demanded.

He tilted up my chin until I was forced to meet his gaze. "I don't think that will work for this scene."

"No jokes," I said but was relieved to feel a little bubble of laughter escape me.

"Okay. I will try to refrain," he said with a cheeky smile.

I closed my eyes, knowing my face was fully flushed from orgasm already. "But this is so fun for me."

He chuckled. He didn't move away. His gaze moved over my face. "Beautiful," he said, still panting.

I made a sound. And leaned forward to kiss him. I wrapped my arms around his shoulders this time, and the kiss was quick.

"I better go," he said.

"I'm going to pack so I can join a nunnery in the Alps," I said.

He groaned this time and dropped his forehead to mine, laughing slightly.

"We should talk about this when I get back," he said maturely.

Suddenly, he was the grown-up, and I was the pants-creaming immature one. "A fun dinner conversation starter."

He laughed with a little growl that made me bite my lip. "It's fine. Don't worry."

"If you say this happens all the time, I will punch you."

He was backing out of the room. "We *will* talk about this. When I get back."

"Sure. Can't wait." I slumped into the chair.

Right as he was about to leave the room, he stopped and turned. "I told you. Extra arm."

There wasn't a moment's hesitation. I wouldn't let this stray too far into the mortifying territory.

"Is *that* what I felt? So modest," I said with a lot more cheek than I felt.

Relief washed over me as he chuckled his way out of the house, strategically arranging the laundry basket over him.

"Ohhh, that's what prehensile means," I called out.

He laughed even harder.

24

———

George's Terraformative notes: The planet is a perfect utopia. The trio is celebrating the success of the crops and cataloging native the flora and fauna. The Intrepid Trio can't see danger lurking just around the corner.

NOTES:

FRicci: Unlike this book. His publisher asked for more pages. It has been two months of me helping George and not making any momentum. Maybe the publisher won't notice if the entire middle section is missing. George told me how this all will end but getting there is the problem. I don't have any clue what I'm doing. Why are the middle parts so hard?

HEvans: I disagree. Adam is moving forward, hopeful and naive, but the undercurrent that something is wrong is humming just in the background. You're doing it. Stop being so mean to yourself. I won't stand for it.

FRicci: You again.

HEvans: Don't pretend you don't love my help.

FRicci: *grumble, grumble*

HEvans: Honestly, Frankie. It's sounding good. It feels like a

G.S. Sedar *Terraformative* novel, but I can absolutely see your influence now in those last few books. Which might I remind you were some of the best-selling in decades.

FRicci: Those books were a fluke.

HEvans: The Impostor Syndrome is strong with this one.

FRicci: Is this another movie reference I don't get?

HEvans: It frightens me that I can't tell if you are kidding. Collette and I are watching *Star Wars* for this precise reason. Can you believe she doesn't know the big reveal about Darth Vader? I don't know that I've literally ever been so excited about anything. Her little mind is going to explode.

FRicci: Should a six-year-old be watching these?

HEvans: Good point. Let me ask her ...

HEvans: She said she's almost seven and it's fine. Also, she wants a snack.

FRicci: What else is new?

HEvans: Come join us. Bring popcorn. Her demand, not mine. But I wouldn't say no.

FRicci: I really need to hit the word count goal.

FRicci: Stop distracting me.

FRicci: I can't find the words today. It's so rainy and cozy. I should be curled around a book reading.

FRicci: George is not having a good working day anyway ...

FRicci: Where did you go?

HEvans: You told me to stop distracting you.

FRicci: And you listened?

HEvans: I have my moments. George has joined us. Look at this super comfy spot on the couch ...

FRicci: Maybe you shouldn't be letting her watch so much TV.

HEvans: I've stopped listening again. Also, I refuse to let this child go through life without understanding pop culture references. It's sad enough living with you. Imagine I'm Darth Vader, and finish this sentence: No, I am your __.

FRicci: Biggest nightmare?

FRicci: Did you just scream?

FRicci: Fine, you can watch. But take breaks and get fresh air.

HEvans: *This is the way.*

FRicci: The way of what?

HEvans: Helpless ... I tell you.

FRicci: Does the world know you're such a *Star Wars* nerd?

HEvans: Pretty sure it's part of my charm. Come join us. Please. You need to rest that big old brain of yours.

HEvans: Imagine I'm doing my puppy dog eyes.

FRicci: Ugh, you wield that power irresponsibly. You're lucky I already wanted an excuse to quit early.

HEvans: Movie day! Movie day! Movie day!

FRicci: I can hear you all chanting.

FRicci: You're ridiculous.

FRicci: I'm on my way.

25

———

Harrison

WE DIDN'T TALK ABOUT WHAT HAPPENED.

Not for lack of trying on my end, but Frankie was determined to avoid me the rest of the night, an ever-present flush on her cheeks. She refused to make direct eye contact, even as we went around the dinner table and each of us said our favorite thing from the day.

"Harrison did his funny monkey face at pickup," Collette said, and I made said face, causing her to giggle.

"I dreamed about William," George said, cloudy-eyed.

"Aw, that's lovely, George. My good thing was ..." She cleared her throat.

"Can I guess?" I asked.

"I had a successful writing day," Frankie answered quickly, still avoiding my gaze as her entire face went crimson. "Also, the sunrise was exceptionally pretty."

"Why is your face pink?" Collette asked.

"Sometimes it's hard for Frankie to get her words out."

Collette frowned. "You should practice more. Practice makes progress," she said with her all-knowing six-year-old confidence.

"Yes," I said, being a cheeky little monkey. "I was there to help her get those words out. I definitely think more practice would help. Though really it was hardly any effort on my end—"

"I forgot the salt." Frankie stood up suddenly. "I'll go get that." She woodenly stepped away from the table but not before shooting me a very clear warning look.

It wasn't my finest moment, but I couldn't help myself. To me, the moment in the pool house had been wonderful. It had been a release of building pressure, and I couldn't wait to do it again. Her jokes made me think she was at the same place, but once we returned to the house, she slipped back into her responsibilities and away from me.

I regretted my teasing when she refused to be alone with me to talk. I didn't stop thinking about getting her off, but I couldn't find the right way to bring it up. I wanted more. I wanted to be the person who got her off like that every day. Instead, after the chaos of dinner, cleanup, and bath time, Frankie went to her room and shut the door.

Message received.

I lay in bed, staring at the ceiling and thinking about her. Replaying the sounds she made. The incredible feel of her, how wet and how turned on she was, so that the little effort on my end had her falling to pieces. The heat that poured out of her as she arched into my hand. How desperately she needed the relief that I provided her.

I groaned, palming my erection through my shorts, still remembering how good she smelled.

She shouldn't be embarrassed. She should be proud. I certainly was.

I hadn't known Frankie for very long, but she wasn't the type to let go like that. I couldn't even believe what was happening until it was too late for me to stop. Touching her had meant more to me than any accolade or acting award. Touching Frankie meant that she gave me part of her nobody else had.

She wouldn't open up about it, but I wouldn't be able to sleep. Possibly ever again. Especially if this erection never went away.

The phone on my bedside table lit up. It must have been my personal phone because I couldn't remember the last time I'd seen my work phone. I'd been letting Collette use it more and more. She liked to make videos of herself performing the same song over and over and then have me watch them and give critiques. So long as the critiques were me complimenting her.

The phone lit up again.

I slid it open to read the awaiting messages.

"Meet me in the pool house in ten."

"Unless you are sleeping."

"Are you seriously sleeping?"

I chuckled and responded. "Not anymore."

She responded with an eye-roll emoji.

"Be there in eight," I sent.

Instantly, my palms were sweating, and I tried to calm my body. Just because she wanted to meet in the pool house didn't mean she wanted to continue what we started earlier. She would want to sweep it under the rug and pretend it never happened. She'd been so embarrassed after, which was absurd because I'd never seen anything so beautiful in my life. If I told her that, would she even believe me?

Down at the pool house, I found her waiting just inside the door, standing awkwardly, hands shifting from resting in front of her to her pockets and back.

"Hey." I smiled at her.

She sighed and looked at me with her familiar yet unreadable expression. "Hi."

"Why here?" I asked.

"You were right. It feels like being here isn't *here*." She gestured up to the main house. "There's nothing but reminders of everything that I need to decide and do and finish."

"Are you okay?" I asked.

"Yeah, of course." She gestured to her laptop on the side table. "I finished another scene. I still need your help to move forward."

"Move forward?" I held her gaze.

"Yes, this is my very subtle way of pretending like earlier never happened."

"Ah." I had thought this was the route she would take. "Because it was bad?"

"No, not because it was bad." She lifted her chin. "Obviously, I enjoyed it immensely."

"Didn't think so. I just wanted to hear you say that."

"Oh my God."

"Let's do it again." I flopped onto the bed, kicking out my feet before patting next to me.

She laughed a growl. "It wasn't appropriate. Don't you think it will make things more complicated?"

"Is complicated bad? My favorite movies are the most complicated ones. *Life* is complicated." I wanted more. I wanted her to know I wanted more. There was no need for awkwardness. "Maybe we should make out about it?"

She rubbed her forehead, her smile large and tugging at my heart. "It was really out of character for me," she said.

"I'd argue you were very much in character."

"Harrison."

"Adam would totally let that happen."

"I think you lied when you said you didn't read fan fiction," she teased.

I chuckled. But she was warring with herself. It was my job

to keep her smiling even when she couldn't. I rolled up off the bed, showing that I was listening. "I won't push things." I tucked my hands in my pocket. *Look at me, cool as a cucumber.* "Just know, I'm always going to want to touch you. I've wanted to touch you since the moment I mistook you for a fan and you accused me of stealing. Making you come will fuel my fantasies for the rest of my life. I won't ever stop wanting you."

Her mouth fell open before she closed it to swallow.

"But I'm in no rush." I shrugged.

She wanted someone to play it easy, be at her beck and call. I could do that. No pressure from me. I stepped closer, and she didn't move. I lowered my head to her ear and said, "When you need me, for anything at all. I'll be here."

She shivered. "Okay." She let out a breath and put her hands on my shoulders. "Okay." This time, she took control, backing me up until I hit the bed. I fell back, my mouth going dry. My pulse went mad as I sat back on my hands, looking up at her. "Anything?" she asked.

I could only nod. Dear Lord, please let her need to be ravaged, preferably by my mouth.

"Because I really need to finish this scene. So get your listening ears on," she said.

I fell back onto the bed with a groan. "Cruel woman."

She laughed but moved to the head of the bed and patted the pillow beside her. "Get comfy. It's a long scene."

"I know you think you're toying with me, but this is my second-favorite thing we did in this room today anyway. So win-win."

She bit back a smile and started reading.

I got myself comfortable as I lay on a pillow next to her. Her soothing voice read on in the calm night. The heat of her warmed my side. I fell into her story, in awe of this incredible woman next to me. Thrown into everything, prepared for nothing, and managing it all.

She read. I laughed at a joke. I mentioned a line that felt off.

"I don't think he'd say it like that," I mumbled so deep into the story I couldn't open my eyes.

"I thought you fell asleep."

"How could I sleep at a time like this?"

"How would he say it?"

"'My whole life has led to this moment. Nothing could stop me.' He thinks they will understand later. The mission is all he's ever known."

"Good. I like that." She lightly tapped a note on her keyboard; the sound was as meditative to me as an ocean sound machine.

Her rich voice continued, her yawns coming more often. I wasn't kidding when I said she had an incredible reading voice. She could easily do this for a career if she chose.

"That's the end of the chapter," she said eventually. I heard the soft click of her computer shutting.

"Hmm," I mumbled.

"We should go back up to the house," she said as she settled onto the pillow next to me.

"Maybe we should cuddle about it." I peeked open an eye to see her reaction.

She yawned. "I'm too tired to fight your charm."

She clicked off the light, and I shifted to pull the blanket out from under me. She tucked herself in, and I instantly scooped her into the little spoon position.

I was just on the verge of sleeping but could feel her mind awake.

"It's all going to work out. The book is really good. Trust me, I played a writer once," I said.

She laughed against my chest. She grabbed my arm and held

it to her chest. I was almost never gifted Frankie PDA. Not that this was exactly public. But her touches were so rare. Maybe there was some magic to this pool house. To the darkness. I would take whatever she would give me.

"I hope so," she said softly. "Thank you for this. For helping. For everything."

"It's nothing," I whispered, and she sighed into sleep.

"It's not nothing, Harrison. Not even a little."

I squeezed her a little tighter. But it was nothing to me because meeting her needs was a natural impulse, like catching a ball flying at your face. I would do anything for this woman. I'd never felt like my life had a purpose until I met her. If there was any doubt before, holding Frankie in my arms and listening to her sleep was the final clue.

I was so in love with this woman. In hindsight, I sensed it the moment I saw her that first day.

And with that came the horrifying knowledge that I would never be enough for her. I couldn't be. I was filed in her mind as a distraction.

I may not be forever material, but I could be what she needed right now. I inhaled her scent and let myself drift off to sleep.

I would love this woman the only way I could, and then when she left me, I would try to find a way to survive.

The day would come when she would realize my best was not enough for her, but until then, my best was everything.

26

Frankie

I WOKE UP GROGGY AND CONFUSED BUT INCREDIBLY RESTED. Possibly the best sleep I'd gotten in years.

Hot breath exhaled against my ear, and an arm pulled me closer. I blinked open my eyes, and pre-dawn light was just coming over the surrounding hills of the pool house. Sleeping in Harrison's arms was like being wrapped in the world's most comfortable blanket, fresh from the dryer on a day off.

I closed my eyes again and let myself imagine a life like this. One where we weren't playing house and fake family, where I woke up like this until I forced him out of bed to go make coffee for us. Or better yet, he'd wake me up with a tease of his fingers or tongue. Maybe he'd roll me onto my stomach, grind his hardness into me, and find me wet and ready.

It caused such an acute longing in my chest, I forced the thoughts aside and sat up.

Harrison mumbled sweetly, grasping for me in his sleep, as though he couldn't help himself from reaching for me. It was enough to make me fall back and lay down facing him as I studied his quieted features.

One more minute wouldn't hurt. I kept my fist tucked under me to keep from running a finger down the slope of his nose or over his softly pursed lips.

Maybe my thoughts were too loud because he blinked open his eyes.

I smiled bashfully, having been caught staring.

"Hi," I said.

"Morning," he mumbled.

"We better get back to our rooms before the others wake up," I said because it felt safer than *We better make out about it.*

He grumbled and rubbed his eyes. There was a moment before he was fully awake when he was looking at me in a way I couldn't define. His usual silliness was gone, and there was a rawness in his expression that had me almost launching myself at him. That same patch of hair stuck straight up.

I grinned and ran my fingers through it before I realized what I was doing.

He smiled sleepily at me. "I'm still dreaming."

My heart clenched.

"We're both awake. Let's go get coffee."

"Shh. Don't wake me. I like this part."

He leaned forward to kiss me. It was an innocent press of lips, but it made my pulse ricochet. I wanted to deepen it, wanted to fall into this warmth, but we really did need to get going before having to explain to the others. Also, I really needed to brush my teeth.

"Harrison," I said ,trying to be firm but, as always, weakening under his charm. "The sun is almost up."

He blinked again, really rubbing his eyes. "Sorry. I—"

"It's okay. I just have a lot to do today, okay? I'll meet you back up there."

He nodded and glanced at his lap. "I'll be up in a minute."

The rest of the day only got worse from there. George and Collette both woke up on the wrong side of the bed. The changes I made to the story in the pool house glitched while saving to the cloud—yes, I did understand how the cloud worked, in theory—and I had to redo a bunch of work. Collette cried about every little inconvenience, and honestly, I got it. Some days were just big feelings days. I was having one of those.

I wished I could go back in time and redo the morning. Instead of rushing out of bed, I would let myself have just a few more minutes in my Harrison fantasy. Warm and comfy and responsibility free.

Brooks texted that afternoon. "Karaoke night at the bar. COME OUT WITH ME!"

I sighed loudly.

"What's wrong?" Harrison asked.

"Nothing. Brooks."

He looked over from where he peeled potatoes, a hand towel slung over his shoulder. I turned the screen so he could read it.

"You should go out," he said. "I'll get Collette down."

"What part about me screams, 'OMG karaoke!'?" I asked.

He snapped the towel at me. "You could use a night out. It was a rough day."

"It was rough for you too," I said, lowering my voice.

George threw a fit with Otis the OT and Harrison had to spend almost an hour talking him down. Harrison shrugged. "I've had plenty of nights out. Plus, it's really unfair of me to do karaoke. I hate to make everybody else look bad."

"Are all actors so humble?"

"Yes," he said simply.

I chewed my lip, debating. "I'll think on it."

As it turned out, I didn't have much of a choice. Harrison

ended up conspiring with Brooks—I'm sure his call was the only call she wouldn't balk at—and made plans for me to get out.

So here I sat, in my fanciest jeans and dress top, alone at the local bar, as I waited for Brooks. I nursed a spiked seltzer and hotly debated with myself if I should share with Brooks all the details of my recent adventures with Harrison. She would find my over-the-pants O an absolute delight. I could already hear her claiming to have *felt it*. As though she could lay some sort of claim to the death of the crypt keeper.

But it was the other things I wasn't so sure I wanted to share. It was one thing to laugh off an easy orgasm, but I couldn't so easily explain the rest. How I seemed to notice everything about him, thought about him constantly. The way his arm muscles flexed as he spun Collette around the room as I pretended to hate it and told them to be careful not to break anything. Or his morning bedhead and sleepy smile when he tried to beat me to make coffee. He never did.

Every time I handed him his cup, he'd ask, "Was I close?"

"This close," I'd pinch my fingers together when, really, I'd been up for an hour or more writing in the early silence of the house.

"Tomorrow, I *will* make it first."

"Sure." I'd boop his nose and go back to work.

Or the way he almost always fell asleep reading to Collette at night, and I'd find them asleep in the same position, one arm flung over their faces. Or the way he talked to George about William, about the past, constantly reminding the older man of all the beautiful things in his life. Or the pride in his voice when discussing Charlie's sobriety and Emma's charitable endeavors. So very many things I noticed about Harrison. I wanted this man. More so than ever. I wanted him like I never wanted another person. And he told me that I could use him for whatever I needed. He made himself available to me.

I imagined him finding me in the hallway, pressing me against the wall, gasping my name into my neck as his hand reached into my pants. I imagined him visiting my room in the middle of the night to slip under my covers and bring me to orgasm with his mouth. I imagined him taking me from behind, one hand curled into my hair, one grasping my hip as he rocked into me, making me come. He'd have to cover my mouth to keep me quiet as he thrust into me slow and steady, bringing me to the brink as he rubbed my c—

Wait. That was three arms. Okay, I really did have a problem with adding extra arms.

"This seat taken?" a rich, familiar voice asked.

My heart jumped, feeling like I'd just manifested Harrison.

"Hank," I said before I turned to see him standing in his cap and sunglasses. "Nice shades. Inside this bar. At night. Very incognito."

"They'll never know." He took off his glasses and folded them before he slid into the stool next to me and his knees bumped mine. "Maybe too much with the shades."

"Is everything okay with George and Collette?" I was already reaching for my bag to leave.

He gently settled me with a hand to my shoulder. "Everyone is fine. Brooks pulled a switcharoo. She insisted."

I took a long pull of my drink, taking a moment to steady myself against the growing excitement of his unexpected company.

"That doesn't surprise me." In the months since the Watermelon Wine Festival, Brooks took back her warnings toward Harrison, pointing out that he was still here and that meant something. And after Joey, I didn't disagree.

He looked sheepish. "I can be fun too." He waved to the bartender to get their attention.

"Only if you just be you. No Hank," I said, wanting the man

I'd become close friends with, even though it felt silly to think of them as separate people.

He smiled. "Deal." He looked me up and down, taking his time. "You look gorgeous, Francesca," he said in his normal voice, and heat spread up my cheeks. He ordered a beer, then nudged me with his elbow. "Is this okay? Instead of Brooks?"

"It is," I said. He smiled so big I had to look away. "I just can't drink too much."

"Why?" he asked hesitantly.

"Remember me at the wine fest? Brooks told me I was hammered. I think I may have embarrassed myself." I scrunched up my face in a wince.

"You were adorable."

I swallowed down the compliment and stored it with all the others he gave me, hiding them like little treasures on a secret shelf. "I used to be fun."

"I think you're fun now," he said easily as his drink arrived. "Thanks." He held it up to mine. "Cheers."

"Cheers. Oh yeah, I'm fun? Was it the mean game of Go Fish or the way I organize my work in excel?"

"Spreadsheets are sexy."

"You're a ridiculous human." I smiled as I turned so my legs were more firmly pressed between his.

"That's what they tell me."

We sat in silence as they set up the karaoke.

"You keep alluding to this wild side. Does that mean you're going to sing?" he asked.

"Not even a little."

"Lame."

"I am now."

"But not before?"

I sighed. "I guess it's all relative. If my younger self saw me now, I don't think she'd recognize me. I was a wild child for a while. Or maybe I was just young." Maybe this crisis of identity swept every woman rounding thirty, and this wasn't even about the sudden changes in my life over the past few years. I couldn't be sure, but I felt removed from myself, like I was acting out "adult character number one."

He turned so our knees bumped again. I finished my drink. He ordered me another.

"I've always been a free spirit. A rolling stone. I thought that settling down was a form of giving up," I shared.

"Is that what you think now?"

I sighed. "I still feel like that person but also completely removed from her. It's like I'm in this holding pattern, waiting to get back to the person I used to be, but I get further from her every day."

He nodded. He didn't seem sad, but a pensiveness behind those emoting eyes made me think I wasn't explaining myself well.

"All of this happened so fast," I went on. "I hit a rough patch. I came to George, and he offered me a job on the spot."

"That's George."

"It is." I softened, thinking of how George hadn't even hesitated. "I had no résumé to speak of, but he found a place for me."

Harrison moved closer as a group waiting for drinks crowded us. "He can sense good people."

"I don't know about all that. I think he just has a huge and generous heart. He always assumes the best of people." I took a sip of my new drink. "Maybe even when he shouldn't. But I'm determined to prove myself. I never thought it would all lead here. And then." I took a large pull of my next drink, letting the heat loosen my tongue. "One day, not long after, Joey showed up with the most incredible little kid I ever met. Then she left." The terror I felt that first night washed over me. A crippling fear that made it impossible to sleep. I checked on her a hundred times that first night, convinced that something terrible would happen the moment I took my eyes off her.

"Joey said she'd be back in a couple of days," I explained. "Collette was four. I had never even babysat. I was not what you'd call a kid person. Then all of a sudden, I had this whole tiny human to take care of. I had no idea what to do." My throat tightened, and I took a break to have a sip and find a breath. Harrison waited patiently, thoughtfully. "But, as you can imagine, Collette has always been very sure of what needs to be done and helped guide me. It always made me feel like I was fumbling and she was the adult." I couldn't even think about those days without feeling anxiety, a sort of traumatic callback to those first nights. When I looked at pictures of myself, I couldn't even remember what it felt like to be that person. "I would lay in bed just terrified I would accidentally hurt her."

"But you both made it and are doing great." He scooted closer as the bar grew louder, the music starting. "And Joey?"

"Days turned into weeks. She would at least check in back then. George wasn't struggling as much with things at that time and was incredibly helpful. Just like with me, he stepped up and helped with everything without even a word of complaint or hesitation. It seemed whatever phase she was in, he quickly adapted. A natural father."

Harrison swallowed, eyes squinting. "He really is."

"Some people just have that instinct for it, you know?"

"Yes and no. I think taking care of each other is human nature. Even if you don't know what shows to let her watch, you would know how to keep her safe. You let her be herself and love her without trying to fit her into a box. The fact that you even worry is a pretty good sign."

"Okay, well—" I flushed. "What about you?" It was harder to store his compliments about how I raised Collette. Those felt too heavy to sit on the shelves with the other light and shiny ones he gifted me.

"I don't know that anybody would find me particularly suited to be a father." A shadow moved over his features so fast, but he didn't give me a chance to interrupt. "But I have always wanted kids."

Whatever that look had been about, it was obvious he didn't want to delve into it. We both avoided talk of our parenting skills. Probably because we both knew we were treading too close to a topic that would have to eventually be discussed. What would happen with Collette? How would we ever find the right home for her?

Instead, I smiled. "You've always wanted kids?"

"Loads of them. Just as many as safely possible."

"Good luck to your poor wife."

He smiled against the lip of his beer, taking another drink and staring at me after he swallowed. "You never saw yourself as a mother?"

"No. God no. I didn't exactly have the best role model."

When I didn't elaborate, he said, "That doesn't necessarily mean anything."

I raised a skeptical eyebrow at him. "But then you met Joey, and you realized 'oh, yes some things are genetic.'"

His jaw ground. "You're not like her."

"More than you know." I shrugged my shoulder. "I'm just not a settling down person."

He seemed surprised but didn't comment. No time like the present to set the record straight.

"This was all meant to be temporary before I got back on the road. But I never meant for this layover to last so long. I just—I don't want you to think that I'm using George."

He leaned back, another look of surprise crossing his features. "I don't think that."

"But you did. At first."

"Yeah, but that was a million years ago. Why would you think that?"

"Just with Joey and everything. It's sort of in my blood. My mom left us. Joey left Collette. We aren't the staying people." I shouldn't have said that. His features darkened.

"You keep saying that but I haven't seen any evidence. You are still here."

I bit my tongue. I was more like her than he could know. We were cut from the same moth-eaten, poorly woven cloth. He can't understand how un-maternal this family was. The line of family trauma stopped here. I would get Collette a good home. I would make sure she had safety and stability. I wouldn't let her pay for the sins of my sister or mother. Or me. Even if the thought of not seeing her every day caused a painful ache deep in my marrow.

I cleared my throat and risked another look. "I just want you to know that the plan was never for me to stay. This was all temporary. I would never leave like they did. I would never do that to Collette." I swore it, and it was a truth I felt in my bones. "But I'm not staying at George's when the work is done. I will find Collette a home with a real family." Saying it out loud made my tongue feel sticky and heavy. It was what I'd been telling myself for months. It was the *truth*. So why had it felt like a lie?

It was important that he understood the plan. It was the attraction I felt to him. I could actually feel it growing roots in me, those roots growing out of my feet and into the earth. If I didn't set those boundaries, then I'd risk being planted here only to be ripped painfully apart when we left again.

"I guess we never really talked about the after." He swallowed, and it was audible even in the loud bar.

"Yeah. I'm sure we will still see each other, but you have to get back to LA and your career, and I need to figure out what the hell I'm doing." I laughed nervously, hearing the strain in my own ears.

I glanced around the bar, feeling awkward, grasping for a subject change. He had that subdued energy that he had the night I told him the arrangement wasn't working. Not sad, exactly, just more like his brightness levels were brought way down.

I couldn't stand doing that to him.

On stage, a group of women my age were having a great time blasting "Wannabe" by Spice Girls.

He opened his mouth to speak just as I asked brightly, "What are you going to sing?"

He blinked at my sudden topic change. "Oh. Um. I don't know. You want me to sing?"

"I love your singing," I said honestly, even if I never admitted it before.

He smiled like I'd never seen, full face, brightness turned all the way back. *If you give an actor a compliment …*

He sat up and snapped his fingers. "Good sir! Your finest karaoke menu," he called loudly to nobody in particular.

I laughed as he made his way to the DJ. He flipped through the book, and as the ladies finished up, he grabbed the mic and went to the stage. He got the attention of one of the ladies and whispered something in her ear. She cackled loud enough to be heard across the bar and gestured for her friends to come back on stage.

I wasn't jealous at all.

As soon as the song started, I understood why he kept them on. It was "Love Shack" by the B-52s. Harrison sang the guy part with a goofy eighties affectation, bobbing his head not unlike a rooster strutting.

"Cocky," I mumbled.

The women all sang the backup vocals, including the little

yells. It was pretty cute. Soon, the whole bar was laughing and clapping and singing along. This was the draw of karaoke. Okay, I got it. If people recognized him as Harrison Evans, they weren't making a big deal out of it.

"He loves this," I said out loud, but it was lost in the cheers.

Was he being cheeky referencing our own "love shack"? Not that it had been completely christened as such.

Not yet.

I flushed at my own thoughts.

The performance was great, but I was slightly disappointed he wasn't using the opportunity to show off his incredible talent. Of all the times to show restraint ...

When the song ended, he made the ladies all take a bow. They gestured to him in return, and he bowed deeply. He was about to hop off the stage when I yelled without thinking, "Encore!"

It was as though everybody went silent, so my shout rang loudly through the air. Half the bar snapped their heads to me, and I wished I could melt into the earth. But then Harrison looked at me, he held my gaze, and for a moment, there was only us. The rest of the crowd began to chant in support of another song. He nodded slightly and went back to the DJ.

He chatted with the man in headphones, who looked at the stage and nodded. He gestured to an acoustic guitar sitting next to a stool. Harrison took off his hat and scrubbed his hands through his hair as though shaking out nerves. This surprised me because I would have never in a million years guessed he had any sort of hesitation. He had been weirdly shy about his practicing, though.

"This is a song I've been learning." He cleared his throat as he strummed and tuned the instrument. "I'm not brilliant at the guitar, so bear with me."

The women from the previous performance wooed calls of

support. He nodded at them with a nervous chuckle. "Cheers." He blew out a breath and rolled his shoulders. "Here goes nothing."

He started strumming notes of a familiar tune, but I couldn't quite place it. His eyes were squinted in focus, almost closed. As soon as his voice rang through the air, the hairs all over my body stood on end. He sang low and quiet at first. A somber lyric about being in the way if he stayed. I frowned, and after another line, there were a few chuckles as people started to realize the song. They whispered to each other with nods of understanding and would smile and clap.

His voice was incredible. The song was so melancholic, and his rich voice was tentative and beautiful.

Then he got to the chorus, and the bar went silent. Any trepidation vanished as the song went on. The air was sucked from my lungs. "I Will Always Love You," closer to the Whitney version than Dolly's original, even though it was acoustic with a rock edge. All his own. His voice rang out so clear and gentle, yet powerful through the air. When he hit a particularly long note, his voice cracked. He shook his head, but the crowd cheered so loud he grinned and went on.

He sang on about loving this person forever, and I couldn't remember the last breath I took. It was wholly his own version of the incredibly popular song. His voice was unlike anything I'd experienced. When he hit the highest, longest notes, the strain of his neck muscles did something to me. I loved how his mouth pulled to the side when he sang the high note on the word "please." The way he strummed the instrument, as he poured his soul into the song, was enthralling. Not only to me.

Harrison should be charging for this. Every person was awestruck. Soon, couples paired up to rock to the song. Some sat in their chairs, rocking and watching, eyes gleaming.

It was absurd to think he chose this song for any other

reason than he wanted to show his vocal chops—and, my God, the man had chops—but a part of me, a very big part of me, wished this was for me. I wanted it more than anything to be for me. The climax of the song had the whole bar swaying, and I couldn't look anywhere else. The way his hand held the microphone. The way his eyebrows contorted as he sang. His hips that rocked gently to the soft melody. Even when he fumbled over the mini guitar solo he was going for in the middle, not a single person stopped watching.

This man had offered himself to me. Had told me I could take from him anything I needed at any time.

What sort of idiot would I be not to take the offer?

A big one.

I was entranced. We all were. The song was an absolute classic for a reason, but I was convinced no other person could sing it like Harrison did.

Then he opened his eyes fully and met mine. Across the whole bar, he found me in an instant. He spoke of leaving and not being what was needed. Then there was that chorus. He absolutely belted it out, never breaking my gaze as his whole body poured itself into those notes.

My heart beat itself against my chest, as if it was trying to crawl to him.

If people were looking to see who he sang to, I didn't notice. I only saw him. I only heard him. His eyes never left mine for the rest of the song. Each lyric felt more powerfully poignant and heartbreaking in connection to the conversation we had just had.

At the climax, he nailed the highest note, and the whole bar lost their minds. I felt tears burning my eyes.

"Phew, thank you," he said at the end, panting slightly, his voice now hoarse from those high notes.

They tried to get him to do another, but he just shook his head shyly, tugged his hat back on, and made his way to me.

His voice had cracked open a truth in me that couldn't be put back together. I wasn't drunk. I wasn't lying to myself.

I was just a woman who wanted this gorgeous man. My whole body was electric from the energy of his voice, his looks, and months and months of casual touches. If I thought one stray secret orgasm would ever be enough, I was the idiot. I needed to be run through, torn apart, and used until I couldn't move. I needed him in me. Over me. Biting, tugging, pulling.

He came back to the bar. I had been lost in thought. I couldn't sit still.

"We need to go back to George's," I said.

"What's wrong? Did something happen?" He glanced around where a few people were staring in our direction, but I saw none of them. Nothing else mattered.

When he looked back to me, something was written all over my features that made my intentions clear.

"Anytime?" I asked. I didn't need to clarify.

His gaze darkened.

"Let's go." He rubbed a hand over his face before throwing down cash for the tab.

27

Harrison

SHE WAS SILENT DURING THE DRIVE BACK UP TO THE HOUSE. I wondered if I had misread the lust in her eyes when, really, I had gone too far. Had somebody in the bar recognized me and said something to her that made her shut down? I had noticed a few not-so-subtle flashes and phones pointed in my direction.

Was my song a little on the nose? Maybe. Would I always love her? The lyrics were so perfect. I knew she would leave me; I knew I wasn't the best for her. Maybe that was why I'd been practicing that song in secret for the last few months. I sensed from the beginning that I would never be able to hold on to Frankie the way you can't hold on to the most perfect moment of a sunset.

The way Frankie was so tied into my every fiber of being made it impossible to imagine a time in my life when she wouldn't always be my first thought. It was always Frankie. Before my eyes even opened in the morning, my mind focused on her, how she would be feeling, and what I could do to make her life easier. It never even felt like a chore. It felt like a gift I was given.

"Thank God, you decided to be an actor and not a rock star." Frankie's declaration was out of nowhere, but her tone was light.

I laughed as I turned into the gravel drive up to George's. "How's that?"

"You'd be too powerful."

I laughed, feeling the tension ease from my body.

"I'm serious. You were seconds from getting panties thrown at you."

"Well, you know how it is."

"No, I don't." I felt her look at me.

"Did you like it?" I hadn't actually gotten a reaction from her. Or if I had, my brain was afraid to misinterpret it.

"I loved it. I told you, I love your voice," she said. "You're incredible."

"Thanks," I said. For somebody so fleeting and rare with physical affection, she doled out compliments like it was nothing. Maybe it was nothing for her. I wanted to ask her to elaborate, to tell me in particular what she liked because I had put a lot of my soul into that song. I had hoped it would come across tongue in cheek, but as I performed for her, I felt the truth of the words.

But had she felt that?

"No. Don't go to the main house. Go to the pool house," she instructed.

I swallowed with difficulty. "Right," I said, feeling a tightness of anticipation.

"I don't want them to know we're back yet. I don't want this night to end," she finished.

Don't overthink it, Evans. Play it cool.

I put the car in park and turned to her, finding her watching me.

"Harrison. When we go in there, I'm going to ask things of you. I'm going to take you up on your offer. I'm going to show a side of myself that you've not seen. I want you. I want to touch you and be touched."

I stared at her mouth. Then her neck. I started a list of all the places I would start with. There wasn't enough time in all the infinite universe for the things I wanted to do to and with her.

"Is that okay?"

"Was I not talking? I thought I was talking," I said.

She licked her lips with a smile. "I'm just warning you now. What happens in the pool house, stays in the pool house. That's going to be a different Frankie than you're used to."

"Your tone says warning, yet all I hear is beautiful music."

"Is your offer still open? If not, we can go back to the house—"

"No. Nope. Offer is wide open." I let out a breath through pursed lips.

"What's wrong?"

"I just lost a lot of blood to my brain very quickly." I flexed my fingers on my knees. She reached for my fingers and laced them with hers. When I looked at her again, I said, "I want to be sure this is happening."

She squeezed my hand. "It's happening. It can stop whenever either of us wants it to, but it's happening."

Yes. God, yes. Please let me lick every inch of your body.

"You've stopped talking again."

"Did I? Actually maybe better that time." I took a steadying breath. "And you're sure you won't have any regrets?"

"My only regret is wasting the time I already have. I need this. I need you. Harrison, I can't wait any longer."

I was out of the car and around to open her door before she had even taken off her seat belt. I scooped her up into my arms, hefting her like a bride, as she squealed a laugh and then buried her face into my shoulder.

"Slow down," she whispered.

"Nope."

Her laugh vibrated against my chest.

Once inside, I gently placed her down, but her arms remained linked behind my neck. She placed a soft kiss on my cheek before she broke away to close the blinds on the two windows. She clicked the one lamp light on, filling the space with quiet light.

She turned back to me. I scanned her as she slipped out of her heels, losing an inch of height. There was a determined set to her shoulders. The jeans hugged her ass so perfectly that I wanted to slide my hand into her back pocket all night long and squeeze. The satin top she wore highlighted her cleavage.

I dropped the keys on a side table and slid out of my trainers.

"Penny for your thoughts?" she asked, taking out her earrings and setting them next to the keys.

I tucked my hands into my jeans and looked up at her. "If I'm doing this for you, then I get to control the speed. You follow my instructions. You are off tonight. No choices. No responsibilities. Your only job is to say when something doesn't feel good."

She stepped closer and tentatively played with the button on my shirt. "I'm so not worried about that." She looked up at me, and her normally half-covered eyes were even more lustful, almost closed. "Can we get naked?"

"And I thought you were great at following instructions," I said roughly.

"I don't ever remember saying that."

"I've waited way too long to rush this. We're gonna be here for a while."

She moaned a petulant little sound.

I gently collected her face in my palms and lowered my face

to kiss her. I went slow. Just to feel her lips against mine. Our last kiss had been too brief, too long ago. I needed these lips that consumed most of my waking thoughts. We tilted our heads in tandem to deepen, mouths opening to let our tongues caress. Her arms wrapped around my waist. We stood for minutes just kissing. When she stumbled and broke away, I looked at her with dark eyes.

I slid the strap of her shirt off her shoulder, bending down to inhale her neck.

"Am I allowed to touch?" Her hands flexed at her side as she sighed into my lips.

"I'll think about it," I said.

She blinked slowly. I straightened as her hands explored my chest, running up to my shoulders and down my arms. It felt incredible to be touched like this. I closed my eyes and focused only on her exploration. I was desperate to take it slow. I didn't know if this would be a regular thing or a singular event. I would treat it as my last night on earth.

"Okay." I grabbed her wrists, holding them with one hand down in front of her. It had the bonus of pushing her breasts up and together. She bit her lip, and I was right to think she wanted me to take control.

I used a single finger to push the other strap of her top off her other shoulder. It slid to reveal the straps of her bra, revealing the tops of her breasts. I dropped my head to inhale the space between her cleavage. I pressed a kiss to her sternum, feeling the soft but quick beat of her heart under my lips. I released her hands, and they stayed loose at her side as I took her neck in both hands. My thumbs pushed her chin up, the tips of my fingers massaging the back of her neck. She sighed and relaxed the weight of her head back.

I moved behind her until I could rub the base of her skull at the top of her spine. I couldn't remember the role, but at some point, I'd researched pressure points and was easily able to find this one. My thumb stilled and pressed gently into it as she shivered a moan of pleasure.

Her pants came faster, and we had only just begun. My other hand brushed from one shoulder across her breastbone to the other side.

"Relax back," I said. She leaned her head back onto my shoulder. "So much tension."

I searched her shoulders for knots and found several, rubbing out the tension. I dug into one spot. "That's the book." I found another. "That's the archiving work." I moved around. "Here's Collette and George."

She gasped as I found a particularly large knot and rubbed it out. "Ah, there's Harrison," I teased.

"No. I find the tension I carry for you is a lot lower," she whispered.

Her eyes were closed, and I placed a soft kiss on her temple. "That's a shame. All I ever want to do is make you feel good."

"This is an excellent start."

I kissed down the side of her neck exposed to me to her shoulder. My right hand went back to her collar and reached into her bra. I pulled out her breast and rolled her nipple gently in my fingers. She felt better than all my wildest fantasies. I fought to go slow and luxuriate in her body when my own was desperate to take her apart piece by piece until she couldn't speak.

"I'm never going to make it through this night," she said, pained.

"I want you so out of your mind, you can't think. Only feel."

"How can you be so patient? Haven't you felt ... haven't you wanted this for months?"

"So long. That's why I can't rush it."

I pushed her shirt and bra down so her arms were trapped,

but her breasts were free. I moved to sit on the bed, bringing her forward to stand in front of me. I rubbed my lips over her nipples, one at a time, then pushed them together so I could lavish both at the same time. There was no way this felt better for her than it did for me. She put her hands on my head and pulled me closer.

Maybe I was wrong. I sucked one breast until she groaned louder. I freed her arms by sliding her top down over her jeans and unhooking her bra. I ran my hands over every inch of exposed skin, my head at just the right height. Her skin was warm and soft and smelled lightly of vanilla and laundry detergent. I nuzzled just above her belly button, breathing out as I reached for the button of her jeans.

My tongue trailed along her stomach, hips, and ribs, teeth occasionally scraping to cause a gasp above my head.

"I don't think I can stay standing much longer." She sighed.

"Perfect." I grabbed her hips and flipped her onto her back on the bed. I pulled her jeans off, leaving her only in black lace underwear. I lowered my mouth to her sweet cunt and put my whole mouth over her, breathing my hot breath onto her.

She groaned and arched up into me. Goose bumps broke out over my body. I gripped her hips and rested my forehead against her abdomen.

"Harrison. Please get naked."

"Love, I'm hanging on by a thread. These clothes are the only thing keeping me sane."

"Let's get crazy." She arched up again, and the sweet smell of her desire engulfed me.

I groaned and pressed my nose and mouth over her core again. "Behave," I commanded, letting my low voice vibrate through her. "You've been doing so good. Don't want to start misbehaving now."

"I don't think there's a right answer to that."

She writhed under me. I slowly, torturously peeled back the last piece of fabric that kept her from me. I drew it down her legs, kissing every inch of her along the way.

"Harrison," she moaned.

I smiled as I nipped my way back up her body.

I stood up to see her in all her absolute gorgeousness. She was naked and perfect, sprawled on the bed. I was dizzy and overwhelmed and on fire. I palmed myself, pushing roughly to get my erection under control.

"Please," she begged.

"We've only just begun, Francesca." She watched my hand as I worked myself over my clothes. Her nipples were hard, feet kicking her up higher into the middle of the bed. I took a breath to steady myself before I kneeled on the bed. I inched closer, grabbing her ankles to rest them on my shoulders. I brushed up and down her long legs, trying to memorize every moment of this.

Rush nothing. Remember everything.

I would be the best distraction ever. She would be so out of her mind she couldn't possibly worry about a single thing. This was what I was made to do. When the pressure got too high, I was the release valve. This was my purpose.

I lowered to her core and licked. I listened to every hitch of breath. I paid attention to every sighed demand.

"There.

"Oh God.

"Softer.

"Faster."

This was the only time I would heed her demands. She was soaking on my fingers as my tongue lapped her up. I was greedy for every part of her she gave me. Her arousal coated me, and I swallowed it all.

She dug her heels into my body, and the pain helped keep

me focused. Not that I was even remotely distracted. Say what you would about my brain, but when I had a singular focus, nothing could take my attention away.

"You're so hot. You look so hot," she said.

When I looked up at her, tongue still teasing her, she looked down at me. She cupped her own breasts, her mouth parted as she rocked her core against my mouth. I smiled up at her, and she threw her head back. "Harrison. I'm so close."

I refocused on what I knew she needed. I felt the clenching seconds before she screamed out. I let her ride it out on my fingers, softened my mouth to feel her final pulses.

Sweat dampened my whole body. I licked my lips and sat back, watching her as she threw her arms out wide. Her knees were still spread, revealing her swollen wetness. I wanted to take my cock out and slam into her right then, but this was about her pleasure. I ran a hand over her thigh as I pressed against my cock, trying to calm it down. I'd never been so hard in my entire life. It was almost painful, but every single thing I just experienced was worth it. I rubbed her stomach and breasts as I made my way back to lay by her side.

She lay panting for a while as I stared at her. The rise and fall of her breasts. Her perfect nose and the way it led down to her top lip and the sweet point of her chin.

"I can feel you staring at me," she said.

"Just admiring my work."

"In that case, carry on."

She shivered, and I pulled the blanket over her.

"Harrison," she said, turning to stare at me. There was a look in her eyes that made my heart thump loudly in my chest.

Don't trust any post-orgasm looks. I swallowed. "Yes, love?"

"Please. For the love of God, will you get naked now?"

I pretended to think about it.

She smacked my shoulder. She pulled me in to kiss me

deeply. When she ended the kiss, she looked between my eyes. "This isn't only for tonight. You don't have to gatekeep."

I didn't realize how much I needed to hear the words. I nodded once, somberly. A final thread of tension was snapped free. She began to unbutton my shirt, sitting up to kneel at my side. I shifted higher in the bed, gaze moving from her focused eyes to where she bit her bottom lip to her breasts.

I shifted to help her tug off my shirt. She straddled my hips. Painstakingly slow, she divested me of my layers.

"For being so verbal about all my clothes, you're taking your time," I said, body rigid but not actually in a rush. She placed kisses everywhere she tugged off clothes to reveal skin. She exhaled hot breaths against my neck, my pecs, my abs.

"Your body ..." Her hands never stopped running over me. "All these muscles."

"I'm embarrassingly close," I choked out.

"Like over the panties, close?" she asked.

I bit my cheek. Thoughts of her first orgasm here were not helping.

"Welcome to my world," she finished.

"I had that coming."

She grabbed my cock and stroked down and cupped my balls. "No, you have this coming."

"Word. Play," I gasped between strokes. "Love it."

"Your turn, Harrison. You get to feel good too."

We were kneeling on the bed. Her hot, bare skin against mine. My cock was so hard it rested against her belly button. I gripped the back of her head, my fingers spreading through her damp hair as I pulled her forward for another bruising kiss. I couldn't get enough of that mouth. I was wild now. Tense and shaking. We broke the kiss to watch as she grabbed me, stroking me with a firm grip. Her heated gaze met mine briefly before she returned to watching her work. I gripped her hand and helped her move it, never taking focus from her face. It was too much; she was too beautiful. My focus locked on her features, biting her lip as I finally came hard, spilling over the soft skin of her stomach.

As my breath collected, I cursed myself for losing control. I needed more. I pulled her in for another kiss, meeting her mouth as her gasp melted into a moan.

This couldn't be over yet.

28

Frankie

I CAME BACK FROM THE RESTROOM AND INTO THE WELCOMING, warm bed. The familiar guilt was trying to nag me into leaving, but I wouldn't listen. The night wasn't over yet.

I quickly checked my phone, just to make sure there weren't any problems back at the house.

I had one text from Brooks.

"Everyone is asleep. I take it that because you haven't called me ten times that you're having fun. Please, Frankie, just enjoy yourself."

What was it about seeing your name in a text that made it feel all the more serious?

"Fine. If I must," I text back and set the phone down.

I rolled over to find Harrison propped on one elbow, watching me. His hair was messy, but not the same way it was in the mornings. His cheeks were still flushed, and the muscles of his upper body were on full display.

"Everything okay?" he asked. There was a worry in his tone that I suspected wasn't about the others.

He was waiting for my retreat, waiting for me to hurt him, and that broke my heart. I nodded and scooted forward to him.

"I'm not ready to leave here yet," I said.

His Adam's apple bobbed on a swallow. "Okay."

I loved his big, serious eyes and how they displayed so much emotion.

I leaned forward and kissed him deeply. He matched my kiss until we were both panting.

When I broke it to lean back and look at him, he repeated, "Okay."

I pushed him back and straddled his thighs. My hair fell around us as our kiss went on. My nipples brushed his chest, and as my own heaviness returned, his length hardened against my thigh. It wasn't only my desire for him that made my heart feel this way. The look in his eyes as he gazed up at me, brushing the hair out of my face, was one I had caught on him many times over these months. A look that I couldn't ignore. A look that matched the same longing deep in my bones.

I reached down between us to stroke him. The muscles in his neck that had strained when he sang were flexed now as he sucked in a breath, head thrown back. This power was a heady thing.

On the table next to the bed was a condom that I noticed on my return from the restroom.

He followed my gaze. "Not to be presumptuous. We don't have to—"

"Oh. But we do." I licked my lips, and he watched the action closely.

"Good point." He reached for the condom as I scooted to make room. I leaned back to watch him roll it on. His brows furrowed with focus, and every muscle in his body was on edge. I watched him take his time with heavy-bodied admiration. Task completed, I bent forward again. His eyes shone as he swallowed hard. He was reverently quiet as I used him to tease and coat my entrance. It took no time until he was lined up, and without anything but wordless assent, I slowly lowered onto him. He threaded my fingers in his as I settled.

We stilled, hands clasped at his temples, as I adjusted. His muscles were coiled, but he never made any move to rush. I luxuriated in the full feeling, relaxing to take him more fully. Eventually, I clenched, and he took the indication for what it was, and in tandem, we began to rock.

We kissed until it became too difficult to get the motion and maintain the rhythm. We laughed as we were forced to break apart before we accidentally gave the other a bloody nose. He rolled me onto my back and rocked slowly, hitting something incredible. He pushed deep into me and didn't pull off back, pressing hard against that spot that sent me wild.

He was incredibly tender and vocal. He praised me and told me when he felt good too. Normally, eye contact was too intimate, but I couldn't look away when I tilted up to meet him and pull him deeper into me.

I loved the heat of him. I loved his praise and words of direction. I loved every movement.

He was above me, hands on my spread knees as he looked down at where he slid in and out of me. "You're so perfect. You feel so incredible."

The muscles of his abdomen flexed and contracted with every wave-like thrust, and I allowed myself to be taken away. To let him lead the show. It was so nice to be folded and bent, told what to do and how to take pleasure.

"Just like that. Spread wider. Good. God, yes. Like that. So good. Better than I dreamed. Gorgeous. So perfect." A hundred words of praise.

When I came again, he followed right after with a groan of pleasure, and my name gasped from his lips.

———

"Remember that first day we met?" I asked, a question popping into my head that I only felt comfortable asking after he'd been inside me. I was a deeply strange person.

"No. Refresh my memory? Ouch. Nipple."

"What did you mean by I feel like I've known you?" I asked.

We were back in bed, showered but not dressed.

He rolled to prop his head on his elbow and study me. "It was a weird way to say that," he admitted.

"Was it because of George? Maybe because he had mentioned me?"

"I don't think so." He grabbed a strand of my hair and rubbed it between his fingers. "I can't explain it, really. I felt like something in me recognized something in you."

I lay on my back and looked at the ceiling and felt him shift back too. "Brooks believes in something like reincarnation. She thinks that sometimes you meet people you were close to in past lives and your souls recognize each other."

He was quiet for a while before he found my hand in the blanket and held on to me. "I like that."

My throat felt inexplicably tight. "Yeah," I whispered.

I kept waiting for Harrison to say more. I felt tense with something I wasn't sure about. I was too lost in my thoughts to know how I felt about all this. I am sure it would make things more complicated and harder down the road, but I couldn't regret it. Not even for a second.

I had thought about telling him that when he started to speak.

"Hey, before I forget. Not to talk shop at a time like this." He grabbed my boob, and I rolled my eyes. "Don't forget that trip I have to take is in two weeks. I have to go back to LA. I've been avoiding my team for long enough, and they can't push it back anymore."

"Okay, I remember." I sat up. "Wait. Two weeks? That's Collette's birthday. You didn't forget about that, right?"

He rubbed my back. "I'll be back before that. It'll just be four days during the week. She'll be in camp every day, and with everything starting to settle down, I figured I couldn't keep pushing it off."

Four days. I felt so heavy. The lightness that made me feel like I was floating off to space crashed me back to earth, and even the safe cocoon of the pool house couldn't stop the realities of the outside world from crashing in.

I didn't want to think about how this would end. I didn't want to have to be strong and make hard choices. I wanted to be cared for and taken care of like I had been. I wanted someone to love me above all else and choose me every time. Make choices for my needs to keep me protected and happy. I wanted to be loved and love.

No. A visceral fear settled into my bones. A gripping of my heart so sudden it felt like I'd fallen off a cliff.

No.

I wanted independence. I wanted no weight, no responsibility, a life on the road with nobody to abandon me. I wanted to find myself again.

"Right. No. Of course. We know the realities of your work," I said and managed to keep my voice light despite the growing ache and turmoil inside me.

Harrison pulled me into his arms, lifted my chin, and lay a soft kiss on my mouth. "I'm just going for a bit. Not leaving. I feel like it's important to make that distinction."

"You don't have to explain. You don't owe me, us, anything."

He chewed the inside of his lip. "Right."

I wouldn't weigh down this glorious evening with my

Frowny Frankie energy. It had been so good. More than good. Incredible. *Let yourself have this.*

If I were a woman of freedom, living a life of adventure, never tied down, I would need to be able to make physical connections and let them loose. I wouldn't be able to have an emotional crisis every time. That wasn't who I wanted to be.

I straddled Harrison's lap with no warning. His eyebrows shot up.

"I guess we just have to take advantage of our time."

I crawled farther down his body, planting kisses as I went.

"Oh. Well, who can argue with that," he said.

29

Harrison

Frankie used to say that my stay at George's was a getaway, a temporary escape, but I hadn't ever been as restless and home-sick as I was in LA these last few days. It was never more clear to me that we'd had begun to build a life at George's, whether she was able to admit it or not.

Leaving Collette, George, and Frankie—even for this short trip—was harder than I thought it would be.

Especially Frankie.

She hadn't been kidding when she said the first night in the pool house was not going to be a one-off. She found an excuse to meet up almost every day in the past two weeks. A quickie while Collette was at camp and the OT was with George. We had making each other come down to an exact science. Frankie had freed a side of herself, and there would be no going back.

But I missed her. Every moment of every day, during meetings and costume fittings and rehearsals.

I'd been so busy I'd not even been able to see Emma and Wesley. However, they would be at George's this weekend for

Collette's birthday. Charlie and Kate were in the States for a while too and had planned to visit.

LA was loud and crowded, shiny and fake. I talked to more people in three days than I had in months, and for once, it drained me instead of filling me up. No conversation felt real, nobody genuinely seemed to care about me. It made me feel entitled and isolated. How could someone with my life feel so empty? It was shallow and ungrateful, but it felt that way to me. I felt half alive in LA. Fake and sterile.

I missed my home.

Not my mansion in LA. Never had it felt so cold and empty. I felt so sick at the thought of it that I almost asked Emma and Wesley to stay with them at the place they were renting until their new home was built, but I worried how needy it would make me sound.

The evenings were the worst. The days were so long it was too late to video call Collette since she'd already be asleep and texting with Frankie was ... well, there was no texting with Frankie. Unless she was typing on her laptop, electronic conversations were impossible. She would respond with a thumbs-up, which everybody knew was a slap in the face, a conversation death.

My last meeting on my last day was with my manager. I was exhausted and twitchy with the desire to get back to George's. My thoughts were too loud, and my skin itched with overstimulation. I'd gone most of my adult life living the LA lifestyle, yet now it felt like my brain couldn't handle it. It was as though I'd pulled off a mask, and now it no longer fit my face without extreme discomfort.

I sat in Chad's gleaming office, overlooking the hazy LA skyline. Matching his trendy office, Chad had a trendy haircut and an expensive suit. He was a brand and that brand was money. Chad had been managing me the last few years after my first manager had retired. At the time, the bidding war that ensued over representing me had been flattering, but much like the mansion, it all felt flat now.

"Wanna talk about this?" He turned his phone to show the viral video of me singing to Frankie.

I winced, unable to watch more than a few seconds. I was a fool in love. It was as clear as anything. Written all over my face, my undying love for a woman who had no idea. Or if she had the slightest clue wasn't ready to accept it. What did she think about being linked with me? Would this make her a target of obsessive fans? Another layer of stress hung on my shoulders like a sopping blanket.

"So much for laying low," I said.

"This was your family emergency?"

"It's complicated. It's been a rough few months. We needed to get out." I ran a hand over my face.

"Well, you're back on the map. You can't hide out anymore. The good news is, people are eating this up. ChicChat did an entire episode on this little love song and the mystery brunette with sleepy eyes who you serenaded. They love that you are gaga over a nobody. It's a good look after being MIA—a normy for a girlfriend."

"She's not my girlfriend. She'd be the first to tell you."

"Well, whatever she is, I hope she's prepared for all this. You are a mega star. You need to get back to reality."

I thought of Frankie in LA, and it was like imagining Wes Anderson wanting to make a movie with Michael Bay. She would hate it here, every aspect of it.

"It's been almost a year, Harrison."

"Eight months." Eight months in which time had stopped moving at normal rates. Some moments were so fast, too fast, and others dragged on painfully. Some days were hard and full of tears, and others were packed with giggles and laughter. It was all worth it. Every second.

"Regardless. It's an awfully long hiatus. I've hardly heard from you."

"That's the point of a hiatus." My work phone had been decidedly silent, and it was nice not to even think about it.

"Time to get back to it. You've made a splash. You can't miss this opportunity to ride this wave."

"Damn the capitalist consumer culture," I grumbled.

"It's a well-oiled machine. A machine that benefits you greatly, I might add."

"I know." I leaned forward, elbows on my knees, to drop my head in my hands. Acting was my life and had been since I could walk. I wanted life in Sandia to be real, but was I too stupid to see the truth? I was being ungrateful for the life I had. Wishing for a life that I couldn't have when I had the literal American dream. Somebody's dream, anyway.

"You committed to this role two years ago. You were stoked about it before. What happened?" he asked softer.

I shrugged. "I have just been dealing with a lot of stuff."

"Look. I'm not going to ask about what's going on. Quite frankly, we aren't those kind of friends. But I need to know how this will impact your career. Are you going off grid like your buddy Charles?"

"No," I said. "I've just been helping out."

"Seems like you and that chick are awfully cozy."

"It's just a distraction." I felt sick with the regurgitated lie.

"Look, plenty of celebrities have lives. I'm not asking you to choose. But you have to make an effort here. You committed. I was warned you can be a little flighty, but you aren't a flake. Bring the bird to set if you want."

"Yeah." I thought of asking Frankie to hang around a film set where I'd work twelve-hour days, and she'd have to make small talk with actors. I could already imagine her slow blink of disbelief. She wouldn't even consider it. But then I thought of all our shared moments. How good they felt. How she looked at me when she was about to come. Maybe it wasn't absurd to ask her? I could just ask.

I imagined her head thrown back, laughing in my face. Calling me pathetic for making these hookups more than they were. I felt instantly sick.

"I know you were trying to lay low for a bit longer. But the cat's out of the bag. You're back on the map and trending. All good things."

He stood.

"I'll see you next month when filming starts. These short visits aren't going to cut it anymore."

"Yeah, I know."

"You get distracted. I get it. It's fun. But your commitment is here."

There was nothing else to say because he was right.

I made my way back up to George's feeling reality like chains. I tried to shake it. Smiled for the paparazzi. Shook hands with fans. Did the things.

It wasn't until I was driving up to the house that I felt anything close to joy again.

Frankie waited for me at the front door. She was beautiful in a sundress, and I was conceited enough to think she wore it for me. The second I parked, she ran to the car door and pulled me out to kiss me with ferocity.

"Hello," I said against her kisses.

My entire body lit up. Not only because, yes, I wanted this so bad, had missed her so bad, but because *she* missed me. She wanted me. It was euphoric. I pressed her against the car, grinding my already hard cock into her.

"Hi." She smiled shyly at me, lips swollen, eyes bright.

I glanced back at the house.

"George?" I asked.

"OT. Collette is at camp."

"Pool house?" I asked.

"God, yes."

We barely made it through the door when I was on her. I couldn't even wait to get her clothes off. I pushed her up against the wall. I kissed and teased her breasts until all her sounds told me she was wet. Sure enough, when I shoved up her dress to slide my finger into her knickers, she was soaked and ready for me. I pulled myself out of my jeans and tugged her knickers out of the way. We'd stopped using condoms after the first few times when we both had good bills of health, and Frankie said she had an IUD. And I was never more grateful. I shoved into her with a hard thrust.

She gasped out my name. I stilled only for a minute, letting her relax around me, feeling the flutters of her adjusting.

"Are you okay?" she asked as she cradled my head to where I lavished her breasts.

Was I? I didn't think I was. I didn't think I would be ever again. I hurt for her; my body screamed for her even while I thrust into her. I loved her and wanted her in my life forever.

These desperate flings in the pool house wouldn't be enough forever, and I understood that more clearly now.

"I've missed you," I said instead.

"It's only been four days." She smiled against my mouth.

"Too long." I slid out slowly to slam back into her.

"Fuck," she screamed out.

I covered her mouth with my hand, hot breath and groans vibrating against my palm.

And I did. I fucked her hard and fast. I couldn't get deep enough or close enough. My entire body burned from the inside out. I was out of control. Feral.

The sounds of me smacking into her were as loud as her gasps and groans filling the air.

"So beautiful." I dropped my hand to roughly grab her face and kiss her.

Her eyes were dark and unfocused as I took what I needed, as I gave her what she needed. Her roughly squeezing hands gripped me anywhere they could find purchase. I gave hard, but she gave right back. I left red patches on her damp skin. Using my momentum to keep her upright. She was flushed, the straps of her dress down, both breasts spilling out, bouncing as I thrust harder, faster.

She held on as best she could. It was rough and dirty, and we both came sharply and loudly. I settled her to the ground, tucked myself away, and kissed her again, slower. Her eyes studied me closely when we finally stopped to breathe deep. There was a furrow between her brows as her hand cupped my face.

"I missed you too," she said.

I let out a shuddering breath and dropped my forehead to hers.

30

Frankie

I STOOD ON THE FRINGE OF COLLETTE'S BIRTHDAY PARTY. THE POOL overflowed with raucous girls and splashing. The backyard was decorated with streamers and fairy lights as Harrison grilled food for the small gathering. Harrison's best friends and their partners were also in attendance. I would have thought there would be a separation between the big celebrities and the locals, but everybody was vibing, and the atmosphere was light and happy.

Especially Harrison. He wasn't exactly a grumpy guy, to begin with, and now he vibrated with joy and happiness. He was fully in his element, cracking jokes and making everybody around him laugh. He flitted from person to person, checking on food and drinks, kids constantly shouting after him to come play with them between hosting duties.

I wished I could be in the moment with him. I wished I could turn off the building worry and stress that occupied my mind. I wished I could stand here and imagine this life for myself. But this wasn't my life, and it wasn't his. And things were beginning to feel so perfect in this role-playing that I wasn't sure either of us could stop now. We were on a train barreling down an unfinished track.

The few days Harrison had left to go to LA, I had missed him so much it hurt. It changed me. It couldn't be normal to miss him as hard as I had. I was a wild animal meant to roam. It was in my blood, and all this domesticity felt surreal. I didn't know this person. Who was I?

But at the same time, it was because of him that I re-discovered part of myself.

It wasn't just sex. It was great sex too. Lord, it was so good. We could not get enough of each other. There were muscles in my body that had long been forgotten. Like how my calves cramped for days after he took me roughly from behind one late night in the pool house. I'd taken to wearing dresses more and more just for convenience, and he'd taken full advantage. Hands on my hips, he tugged me up and high on tiptoes as he roughly slammed into me. Or when he'd laid me out on my side, one leg propped on his shoulder, and my abs were tight the next day. Or when I rode him up and down, hips grinding and sore for a week. He showed me parts of myself—sometimes literally, like that time with the mirror—that I hadn't even seen myself.

It was freeing.

Okay, yes. So, this was a resurgence of my sexual side, but it wasn't only that. I hadn't felt connected to *myself* in so long. I had been shoved into all these different roles I didn't fit into. Harrison made me forget all that. He was freshly fallen snow to my mind, blanketing the ruts and worn paths to let me sit in silence with parts of me I missed.

I connected with my physical being for the first time in years.

I was beautiful, desired, lustful, adventurous, spontaneous, wild, and wicked. I could make the world's most wanted man get on his knees with the point of my finger. This was the Frankie I remembered. These were the aspects of myself that had defined me for so long.

I missed myself, and I hadn't even known it. And it was all thanks to him.

Later, as the sun started to set, Harrison and Collette performed another song together. The Beatles "Birthday" of course. All the little girls danced around, getting crazy, shaking their heads all over like mini-moshers and squealing with delight. All the adults laughed from the sidelines. When they finished the song, she bowed, and he did too.

"Happy birthday to our queen, Collette."

"Thank you, Papa Harrison."

The world seemed to tilt, and I reverted to that same frozen reaction I hadn't needed in some time. Harrison hugged her tight, and there was such an emotion written all over his face. He didn't correct her and say that he would be leaving again for LA. That he wasn't her father. I glanced at his friends. Emma and Charlie exchanged a look that matched my own reaction. Had she really said that? Was Harrison in too deep? Was Collette going to get hurt after all I had done to protect her?

My heart stuttered and skipped. That tightness in my chest all week at his absence rooted deeper into my bones, mixing with the marrow. The roots squeezed my lungs, taking my breath away. I had to leave before the roots strangled me alive. A plant ripped from its roots would never survive. Collette was still young enough that she might be okay if she found the right family. She had known love and, so maybe, it would be okay. I was forever changed after my mother left me. I couldn't let sweet, fragile Collette have her whole life ripped apart.

All at once, it was like I watched this party from the outside, like I was watching a film of a life that wasn't my own. The characters and setting looked familiar, but I was outside my body as it played out around me.

How did I get here? Whose life was this?

Harrison came up to me and hugged me after. I looked up to see his friends and the guests watching us. I stepped away. What was he doing? Why had he been so touchy-feely today? This wasn't what we discussed. What happened in the pool house stayed in the pool house. He played this role of a family man all too well. It wasn't real. This wasn't real.

I wiped my sweating palms on my dress and ignored the hurt that flashed over his features.

"I better go get the cake," I mumbled and stepped away.

In the kitchen, I prepared the utensils and plates. The sounds of the party drifted in through the open window, along with the smell of summer, causing a preemptive sense of sentimentality. I knew if I ever had this combination of senses, I'd be sucked back to this exact moment, and it already hurt.

Brooks came in, arms spread. "I'm here to help."

"Here, warm this up for the ice cream cake." I handed her the cake knife.

"That kid. Already seven. Hard to believe."

"I know."

"She's incredible. I just love her. I wish I had half the confidence she has."

"Don't you?" I asked with a smile.

"Fake it until you make it, baby. You should feel proud."

I mumbled something unintelligible as I opened the freezer to take out the dessert. It occurred to me that I had been one of the most consistent things in Collette's short existence so far. I spent almost half of her life with her, but it was impossible to take any sort of credit for it.

"Still no word from Joey?" Brooks asked softly, glancing toward the door.

"No." I sighed, and the tightness grew. "She hasn't sent any papers. She won't respond to the lawyer." A very expensive lawyer. "After six months of no contact, I can file abandonment charges," I said flatly.

Wesley's lawyers had prepared everything. The moment it hit six months of no contact, Joey would no longer have claim over her daughter. It was for the best, but the facts still gnawed at me. Still made me question everything.

"That has to be soon," Brooks said, brow furrowed.

I nodded, arms wrapped tight around my middle. "Next month."

"Wow." Brooks stepped closer to me. "And then? Are you filing for custody?"

There was a twinkle in her eyes that looked like hope.

"I-I don't know. I want her to have a family. A real family." My thoughts were all mushed up, and I couldn't even say what I dreamed about in the deepest, darkest secret chambers of my heart that I thought had long been sealed over with scarred tissue.

Brooks glanced out the window and back to me. "I think she has a real family."

My head shook back and forth.

"Have you thought about maybe staying here in Sandia?" she asked softly, eyes gleaming with hope. "You all make a pretty good trio, if you ask me. And maybe I'm being selfish, but I would love for you to stay." She carried on speaking, but I could hardly hear her for the ringing in my ears. "... You've had one foot out the door since you got here. You won't even call me your best friend. Even though I totally am because there is literally not another single person on this planet I would answer a call for. Even my own mother. You're always looking out windows, dreaming of far-off destinations. I get it. Some people are just rolling stones." She frowned with a final shrug. "I don't want you to go."

I gripped the edge of the counter hard to keep myself from

tipping over. The air around me wasn't working right. I couldn't seem to pull it into my lungs, and it was making my fingertips go numb. People didn't stay. Harrison couldn't stay. If his week away had shown me anything, it was that this needed to end sooner than later. I had become so reliant on him that I couldn't function without him when he was gone.

But I knew I was already lying to myself. Things were already too deep. That inability to breathe were those same roots that had spread through my body, pinning me to this place.

"Hey, hey." Brooks placed her hands on my shoulders, and I flinched hard. "Frankie. Look at me. It's going to be okay. You don't have to figure it out at this exact moment. Just enjoy this party. One step at a time. One day at a time, okay?"

I was biting my bottom lip so hard that I tasted blood, but I nodded.

"Take a breath for me, okay? Big one in and out," she demanded. "There you go. One more."

Tears balanced on my eyes. Humiliation spread through me. All I could see was the image of my mother driving away one last time, blurring over this moment, making them indistinguishable from the other.

"It's okay. You know you aren't alone, right?" she said. "You aren't alone," she repeated.

I nodded, breathing until the tingling sensation left my fingertips and gravity righted itself. "I'm sorry."

"Don't be. It's okay. You have time. Let's change the subject." She hugged me and then moved to grab the plates and napkins. "How's the book going?" she asked, and I stumbled.

It was like she could see all the many worries currently swirling through my brain and plucked them from thin air. One after the other. The publisher had called again and all but demanded that we send what we had so far. They needed to start promo. They needed as much as we could provide to start on auditioning audiobook narrators and a hundred other things I didn't understand about the publishing process. And didn't want to.

"What d-do you mean?" I fussed with the cake on the table.

"George's book?" She leaned against the sink to look at me. "It's all the whole world is talking about. I haven't heard this much buzz about a book. Probably ever. I've already gotten dozens of preorders. I think they're hoping he'll sign some. Him being a local and all."

I swallowed the panic that had gripped me and released slightly. The secret was still safe. "I think he's almost done. He sent some of the pages off to the publisher."

"Great news! And you've made a ton of progress around here. See, everything is going to be okay," she said.

"Yeah," I said tightly.

"Speaking of things abuzz on the interwebs, I saw that video of karaoke night." She wiggled her eyebrows.

"Oh yeah, I heard about that." Someone said something to Collette, which was exactly what we were trying to avoid. I'd been avoiding watching it. Some part of me still rejected the reality of his other life. I was putting on blinders, and that wasn't the best way to handle the situation.

"Have you watched?" she asked.

"I don't need to."

Plus, I didn't want to confirm every scary and wonderful feeling I'd had that night was all over my face and his. I would rather keep things as they currently were, neatly organized on a shelf labeled *denial.*

"I can show you."

"It's okay."

"So you and Harrison ..."

"Brooks. Not the place to talk about it." I glanced around to make sure nobody else was around as I arranged candles onto the cake.

"The man is gaga over you. I totally called that. You two have old souls."

I laughed to myself. I couldn't deny that Harrison wore his heart on his sleeve, but he also lost his shirt a lot. I hadn't told her about our sex-a-thon. I could still smell him on me from the quickie earlier as we put extra towels in the pool house. "Put extra towels in the pool house" will forever be a euphemism to me.

"I think it's nice. You're happy. I don't understand why you're fighting all this so hard," she said sadly.

"I'm not this person," I said too fast, like something in me snapped. Why was it on me to make sure that nobody got hurt? Why was I the one who had to make the hard choices and do the hard things? It was like all the boiling up tension and sadness in me spewed up and out. I glanced to the door, making sure nobody was around. "I just spent this past week moping around. I felt like one of those women standing on the cliff looking out at sea waiting for her soldier to come home."

"Why is it bad that you missed him?" she asked patiently, not rising to meet the bait of my outburst.

Because I have grown to rely on him too much. Because the house felt cold and empty and quiet. Because I missed his stupid comfort as much as I missed our physical bond. I missed having a partner.

"This isn't a real life, Brooks."

"Not if you never give it a chance."

I shook my head. "I don't want to talk about this right now. They're waiting for the cake."

She couldn't understand. She didn't have the facts. From her point of view, I was just a woman with a perfect life to slip into, and all problems would magically be solved.

"Harrison and I aren't anything. He starts filming next month. He'll probably stop coming up here since I won't need him to help with Collette. My work here will be done, and I won't have an excuse to live here."

"It's not like George will kick you out. Grandpop George loves and welcomes all."

"I don't want to take advantage of him."

"I'm just saying there is no rush." Brooks looked at me flatly.

"This has a deadline. This has an end. I wish he wouldn't act like we were some sort of family. It's just messing with Collette."

"That's not his intention, and you know it." She crossed her arms and glared at me, her cool demeanor finally slipping.

"I know." I pressed a thumb to the growing headache in my temple. I couldn't help the panic, and it made my brain freak out. But she was right. Harrison wasn't trying to hurt anybody. I smoothed my palms on my dress. "No. I know. Harrison wouldn't ever intentionally hurt anyone. But I also don't think he gets it. He doesn't always think things through. He's all passion and impulse. This was a fun way to fill in the time before filming. He is going back to his life. We both talked about that. That's always been the plan."

"Plans change."

"Not this one."

31

Harrison

I stumbled away from the kitchen window. The pain that gripped me was breathtaking.

The day had felt so perfect. I hadn't felt this happy in so long. Maybe since the days of *Terraformative*. I let myself imagine this as my life. I hadn't overheard anything in Brooks and Frankie's conversation that I hadn't already known. This was temporary to her. I didn't think things through. I had been trying so hard today to make her see how good things could be. Let her imagine a life when I really let myself hope, but she thought I was still pretending.

None of this was pretend for me. I had missed her so much all week. I was in love with her but had no idea what I was to her. I was a plaything. Cut to me in a month's time, back to LA alone and worse than before because at least I hadn't known love like I felt now. I wouldn't survive this. I really didn't think I could leave her and survive this.

My insides felt brittle. I was seconds from shattering.

"Okay, come here." Emma was at my side, tugging me to a cove of trees away from the house and the party.

I hadn't even seen her come up to me.

"What's going on?" Charlie asked from next to her. I hadn't noticed him either.

"I don't know. He looks like he's going to be sick."

"Heya, mate, all good?" Charlie lowered his head to look at me.

I shook my head. I collapsed onto the base of a tree and dropped my head to my knees. My two best friends crouched beside me.

"What happened?" Emma asked.

"I heard her talking to her friend." I shook my head, throat tight. All these weeks, I had been her lapdog. She'd call, and I'd come like a good little boy. I knew how to make her feel good, and she couldn't get enough. "I thought ... I thought I would be okay—"

I cut myself off, not even sure what I was trying to say.

"With what?" Emma rubbed circles on my back.

"Her—we—I thought just having her would be enough. I want more. I want everything and I'm a glorified sex toy to her," I spat out. My anger grew.

"When did that start?" Charlie asked, then shook his head. "Doesn't matter. What do you mean?"

I knew every gasp she made. I knew what every moan meant. I could do things to her. I would let her come back time and time again. I never fought it. I told myself she would eventually feel it too. How could she not? But she didn't feel anything for me. She was always looking for the way out.

The worst part was I would still let her come to me. Even now, even admitting it out loud and knowing I would only ever be a joke to her, I still wouldn't be able to fight her. I loved her too much. I would take any scraps I was given.

"She thinks I'm an idiot. Good for one thing," I said, unable to look at them.

I felt the heavy silence of Charlie and Emma exchanging a look.

"I'm sure that's not true. You've been here for months. She's really come to rely on you, I can tell." Emma spoke softly and gently.

"I thought that I would be okay with just giving her what she needed. But it's not enough anymore."

"You caught feelings," Charlie said.

"No." I slumped my head back against the tree. "They were always there. I just realized that she hasn't caught them. It's like this virus that's eating me from the inside out, and I thought it would be contagious, but she's totally unaffected."

"So romantic," Charlie said with a grimace.

"Okay, well, first," Emma said. "Rule number one is never trust anything you overhear. Who knows how close she is to Brooks. Frankie's a closed-off person, right? She doesn't share much at all. She's not about to gush about feelings with her bleeding heart on her sleeve. It took me years to get the truth out of Wesley. Not everybody was taught how to be free with their emotions. Trust what you feel when you are together."

"She is just having a good time. Because that's all I am and all I'll ever be," I growled, unable to absorb her advice.

"Harrison, that is not true. Nobody thinks that," Emma said firmly.

Everybody thought that outside of these two. And maybe even them. Emma never trusted me to tell me about her lifelong love for Wesley or her struggles with her life. Charlie hid his addiction for so long and then his relationship with Kate. My own relatives, by blood, only saw me as a paycheck. I was just the pretty accessory for people in my life.

"I wanted to make a difference here. I wanted to help, but I think me leaving this week made everything worse. I feel torn in two," I said.

"Your career is important. Nobody faults you for that," she said. "Acting has been your whole life. Nobody thinks you should give it all up. You came to help, and you *have*."

Was there anybody who thought I was capable of anything besides acting? A life in LA.

"If she asked me to quit and stay here with her, I would," I said.

Charlie and Emma blinked back at me.

"Are you sure? We didn't think things were so serious," Charlie said.

"I didn't tell you guys. I didn't want to see that look on your faces." I dropped my head to avoid the worried pity in their eyes. "I love being here with her and George and Collette. The time I have with them all feels so precious and fleeting, and I hate that there's this ticking clock in the back of my brain at all times, telling me this too will end."

"We don't know what's gone on between you two. Only you two do, but you need to ask her. Don't make choices for her. That's not fair," Emma said firmly.

"Give her a chance to explain her feelings," Charlie said.

Her fear kept her so locked down. I wished she would open up and let me in, but I wasn't that person to her. Someday, somebody would be able to pry her open and insert themselves. I felt sick for that future life. I would be off God knew where, and she would find the person who got let in.

"Time for cake!" Frankie yelled out as everyone started to gather at the outside table.

"Talk to her. Tonight," Emma insisted.

I nodded. Not like I'd be able to sleep anyway.

They stood up, and both extended a hand to help me up.

Charlie placed his hand on my shoulder before pulling me in for a hug. Emma joined us.

"You aren't alone, Harrison," Emma said. "You never were."

I closed my eyes at her words, holding them a second more before we had to go.

Wishing I could feel them.

The rest of the party went smoothly. I avoided Frankie. I had come on too strong and gave her space and gave myself time to make a plan to talk to her. After a day of activity and company, she would need some time alone to decompress.

That night, I couldn't sleep. The house was silent. The advice of my friends swirled in my head.

I made my way down to her room, ready to bare my soul and be rejected. I couldn't live in this in-between anymore. I needed to know what happened with us, with Collette.

There was so much hurt and anger warring in me, but I wasn't mad at her. I was just sad. I wanted her to pick me. I wanted her to admit that these last few months had meant as much to her as they did to me.

I was a changed man. I didn't want to go back to the life that I had. It wasn't a fulfilled life.

I knocked lightly on her door, and it swung open to darkness. She wasn't in her room. I frowned and spun in a circle. I searched the downstairs, and from the kitchen window, no lights were on in the pool house. Back up to the second story, I heard the creaking of shifting floorboards coming from the attic. I wouldn't have expected her to be working tonight after such a long day, but maybe she couldn't sleep either.

Light poured from the open door, and soft sniffling drifted down. I climbed up the drop-down ladder, poked my head over the edge, and found her. Frankie sat on the floor, head in her hands.

She was crying.

My heart dropped, and fear made my feet close the remaining distance.

She gasped when I broke into the room, face shooting up to reveal tear-stained cheeks.

Whatever fear-based anger motivated me was gone in an instant. I dropped to my knees to pull her into my arms without the slightest hesitation. "What's wrong? Frankie, what is it?"

She sobbed harder and let herself crumple into me. Her sobs wracked through her body as she gripped me tight.

I noticed her laptop open, credits rolling on the screen, and music I recognized.

Terraformative.

Frankie was caught red-handed watching the show she swore she would never watch.

I wasn't sure what it meant, but it meant *something*. It was like a dam broke, releasing all the pent-up fear and emotions from the day. I threw my head back and started to laugh. I felt unhinged, but this was too much. It was too perfect.

Frankie leaned back in my hold and shoved at my chest. "It's not funny." She looked so pitiful with her chin trembling, trying to be stern with red-rimmed eyes.

"It's a little funny."

"No, it's not." Her chin wobbled as she protested and it just made me laugh harder. "Harrison!" She sniffled and wiped her cheeks. "It's so sad."

"Was that the series finale?"

Her face crumpled again as she nodded. "I can't ... believe it's over," she spoke between shuddering breaths.

"It was a happy episode, I thought? The Intrepid Trio off and on to their next grand adventure."

Her shoulders shook again as she hid her face. "I can't believe how much you're enjoying this," she said muffled.

"I'm sorry. I'm just so happy. Have you watched the entire thing?" I was losing a battle to stop smiling.

"Yes. I can't believe you caught me. This is humiliating."

I lifted her chin. "Why? This is amazing."

"You're so smug."

I laughed again but handed her a tissue from my pocket. I'd learned to keep them on hand to avoid Collette wiping *things* in various places.

"I knew you'd be like this if you found out," she said, wiping her nose.

"When did you even find the time?" I rubbed her shoulders as I looked down at her. I couldn't ever feel mad when she was in my arms. Whatever hurt had been causing my anger dissolved when she looked up at me with gleaming eyes and held on to me like I kept her safe.

"I've been sneaking up here at night," she explained.

"Since when? There are eight seasons!"

"I started shortly after the Watermelon Wine Fest. I only meant to watch one"—she tossed her arms out—"and then I couldn't stop." She rolled her eyes. "It's stupid good. I really wanted the whole world to be wrong."

"I did try to tell you." Silly, beautiful, stubborn woman.

"I can't believe you *lived* this. I can't believe I missed this. It's so good too, you know?" Her eyes welled again, voice warbling. "Different from the books enough that it worked for TV but also loyal to the tone of the books. I just want to curl up and live in this world."

"I understand." I rubbed my thumb over her cheek, drying the tear streak.

"I hate this feeling. Now stupid reality feels insufferable."

"Not totally." I pressed a soft kiss to her temple, and she sighed. "But I will say, all these years and not one project I've worked on has come close."

"How did you guys handle it ending?"

"I don't think we did. We were all changed."

"You were so good, Harrison." She shook me roughly but playfully. "So good. You were so young. I can't even fathom what your life was like."

I chuckled but pulled her back to hold her.

This meant something. I had to ask her. I had to have hope.

To endure was human, and my heart wouldn't give up on us yet.

———

Frankie

I LET OUT ANOTHER LONG BREATH, TRYING TO SCRAPE UP ANY remaining fragments of dignity. He caught me, and based on the grin that hadn't left his face since he found me, I would never hear the end of this. I couldn't even be mad, though. I had to eat crow. I deprived myself of pop culture significance to prove some point to myself and was wrong.

Harrison leaned back on his hands, legs sprawled in front of him. No hurry to leave the attic despite a long day and the even later hour. "What made you want to watch the show finally, after all these years?" he asked.

"I don't know," I said honestly. "I actually told myself this would be the worst time to start watching. Because of trying to finish this book. I didn't want to be influenced by it. But it was like I couldn't stop. I felt like an addict. Between this show and uh, putting extra towels in the pool house, I have seriously lacked some sleep. I made good progress while you were in LA." I scratched my elbow.

I wanted to feel close to you. I wanted to understand you. I missed you.

"And did it live up to the hype?" he asked.

"I loved it." I tossed out my hands, head shaking. "I get why the fan fiction for this world is so abundant. I never want to leave it. I loved that it was a little corny at first, and by the end ..." My throat got tight again, but I physically could not cry anymore. I took a breath. I shifted focus. "Was it hard to be on the other side? Did you feel like you saw the sausage being made, and it took the magic out?" I asked.

He looked at the roof, eyes closed. "Not at all. It was harder, maybe. Because our lives were so intertwined with this world. The cast and crew were my home and family for all of adolescence. When it ended, it was like this defining moment, like I could pinpoint the exact moment my childhood ended." He rubbed at his sternum with a frown. "I think that's why I'm always happy to do any press, or reunions, or interviews for it. Maybe it's a little silly to hold on to Adam so tightly. Hard to know where he ended and I began."

"Not silly." I squeezed his hand. "But you and Adam are so different, it's interesting that you feel so intertwined. Not that I really know the others well, but of the trio, you're the least like your character."

"Because he's so serious? So clever?" His face fell. The humor that had been there since he found me dissipated.

"Serious, maybe? That's part of it." I watched him closely, wondering if my attempt at a compliment was accidentally hurting him.

"Yep. I'm the good-time guy, the joke. He's the leader. The one who gets shit done." He leaned forward to start to stand, dusting off his hands.

I put a hand on his arm. He frowned at it. His sudden mood shift knocked me off balance. "What did I say?"

"Nothing I didn't already know. That you think I'm a joke."

I flinched. I shuffled for him, the wood panels hurting my

knees through my pajamas. "I do *not* think you are a joke." I poured all my sincerity into the words. I wasn't explaining myself well, and the angrier he got, the more I felt my tongue stick to the roof of my mouth. I placed my hands on his shoulders. He looked at them before bringing his soulful gaze back up to me. "Let me explain what I meant."

"Okay." He shifted again and pressed me back onto the comfortable pillow I'd been sitting on.

I took a moment to collect my thoughts as he studied me, face flat. "I meant that Adam was always so cold. Kept people at a distance, focused on the task." If anything, I related to Adam the most of the characters, but I wasn't about to admit that. I understood Adam's fears. "You're so warm and caring. You command a room like Adam, though, and everybody instantly listens to you and trusts your opinions on things. You are insanely attractive like Adam. Obviously." I felt heat rising up my neck as I spoke, but I couldn't stop until I saw the worry release from his crinkled forehead. "But you are *not* an idiot. I don't want to hear you talk like that again. What did you tell Collette when she called me Frowny Frankie? We don't talk to each other like that in this house. Only kind words.

"I've watched you jump into the deep end here and handle it with aplomb. You are tender-hearted and charming. You are creative and passionate. You love and are loved easily in return. Do you know how rare that is?" I whispered. His nostrils flared, and his focus was searing me. His chest rose and fell faster with each declaration. "Adam was wonderful as a leader of the trio, but not like that." I glanced away. "You are impossible not to love." My throat closed. It was as close to a confession as I could bear.

"Frankie," he said. He held my gaze and licked his lips. "I—" It moved around my face, and he was on the verge of something big. My heart kicked around my chest.

"I was almost a father," he blurted.

I flinched back. Of all the things, I hadn't expected that. "Wh-what?"

He brought up a knee and wrapped his arms around it. "It was leaked to the media at one point but my team swept it up quickly."

"Brooks had mentioned something about that early on." I took a steadying breath.

"Don't look at me like that. It's not true. Not exactly," he said. "Contrary to the short-lived and false accusations, I never lived a crazy bachelor lifestyle, floating from one woman to the next, leaving babies in my trail. There was one woman who I was close to. She was ..." He stopped himself from whatever he'd been about to say. Maybe to stop from giving too much personal information away. "Not an actress. But we did see each other a lot during shooting one of my films. We got really close."

I nodded, and a burning sensation tingled up my neck. Nonsensical jealousy turned my stomach.

"A few months after we wrapped, we were, uh, still seeing each other. Never seriously. She never wanted any sort of commitment. She had been separated from her husband and didn't want the press. I understood. Never put any pressure on it." He rubbed the back of his neck and looked around the cleaned-up attic. "Anyway. She came to me and told me she was pregnant. I was thrilled. I naively thought she'd come to tell me in hopes of taking things to the next level. Like I said, I had always wanted to start a family. Even if she only wanted to co-parent and not be together, I was up for whatever. I feel like I have all this love to give, and nobody wants to receive it."

Did he really not see how beloved he was? Did he not see how we all rotated around him like planets around the sun? Same with Emma and Charlie. Same with the ravenous fans.

I sat perfectly still, waiting for him to continue. He cleared his throat. "This is ... well, nobody knows this besides Emma and Charlie. But it's—"

I put my hand on his. "Only tell me if you want."

His jaw flexed, and he squinted. "I want to tell you." He pulled me into his arms, positioning me between his legs, my back to his chest. "I started making plans. The excitement poured out of me. And she was just looking at me. She blinked and then started to laugh. She actually laughed," he said, his voice tight. "She told me it wasn't mine, but even if I was the father, she'd still go back to her husband. She said some people were meant to be fathers, and others were there for a good time. She told me I was pretty but dumb, and I could not raise a child."

"What a terrible thing to say," I whispered, my heart absolutely shattered for him. I could picture the way his eyes would have been lit with joy, unable to hide any emotion passing through him.

"She was right. I never did well in school. I always got in trouble with my teachers and later the set tutors for being flighty and not paying attention. I couldn't finish any book. I told you how I have a hard time focusing. But I always knew that I wanted to be an actor, and the stuff they were teaching me never interested me. Until it did. I got roles, and I'd dive deep into researching them. I can't stay focused. Only if I'm curious, then I'm so focused the rest of the world goes away. She knew I was too irresponsible to raise a child."

"Oh, Harrison." I held his arms close to mine and squeezed him tight. "That doesn't make you stupid. Not even a little. She was wrong to say that."

"She just came to tell me she was going back to her husband, and I completely projected an entire life on her. I thought I was finally going to be a father. But what sort of father would I be when I can't even remember what I'm doing half the time?"

"She was wrong." I twisted around, a leg on either side of his hips to grab his face. "Look at how wonderful you've been with Collette. So many times I've watched you play with Collette and been so envious of how easily you connect with her while still being able to guide her. It's instinctual."

He leaned into my palm and kissed it. "You know, it's funny, when I first met Collette, one of the first thoughts I had was, 'this was how old my daughter would be.' I think Collette is always how I imagined this pretend daughter I never had. They are the same age." His voice broke off.

I made a sound of pain. Inhaling felt like shards of glass. Poor, sweet Harrison. His bond with Collette made even more sense. I couldn't even imagine how awful that pain would be. "I've felt my whole life that I'm stupid because of the things I struggle with, the fact that I have just the most basic education. I've spent my whole life acting, and that's all I'm good for."

"You are not stupid. You are wonderful, and I love the way your brain works." I leaned forward to kiss his cheek. "You're an incredible man, Harrison. Anybody who can't see that is the real idiot."

He grabbed both my hands and swallowed, studying my sternum. "It's just that, I've projected a life onto a family that wasn't mine before. It was one of the most painful things I've lived through. I don't want to misunderstand a situation again."

He lifted his eyes to hold my gaze. All at once, I understood why he'd shared this wound with me, what he was getting at. I wished never more than at that moment that I could take all his pain away, that I could make promises to heal him.

This was the terror I felt when Collette was hurt because of her mother, and there was nothing I could do. I wanted to take everything awful away and wrap her in happiness. Was this love? Was this being in love? Because if it was, then this was shitty. I hated it. How could I be able to love somebody so viscerally, with my whole being, and not be able to make everything right? That was supremely unfair.

But I couldn't fix this for him. I couldn't take this life and make it his. Collette wasn't ours. This life wasn't ours. We were house-sitting and role-playing.

And never has this reality been so unbearable. A taste of a perfect life that he couldn't have and I could never provide.

I closed my eyes and dropped my forehead to his. "Harrison. I wish I could—"

His shoulders slumped forward. "I understand."

"It's not that I—" Not that I what? What did I want? What was it that Harrison meant to me? Could I pivot? Could I let go of all that scared me and planned for? It felt so easy, so simple right now with him in my arms. This was it. This made sense more than anything. "I can't offer a life that isn't mine," I said.

He nodded against my forehead, eyes closed in pain. "I understand," he repeated.

"I really wish—"

"It's okay."

"I hate seeing you hurting." I kissed his lips. "I want to make you feel better." I kissed his neck, inhaled his smell, and made myself memorize it.

I grabbed his hands and tugged him to stand. The house was dark and silent as I took him downstairs. He followed me hesitantly, never speaking, just a warm, constant presence all the way to my bedroom.

I shut the door behind me and leaned against it.

His throat worked a swallow as he watched me wearily. "This isn't the pool house."

I shook my head but moved to step in front of him. I reached for the hem of his T-shirt and lifted it over and off.

"Are you sure?" he asked.

I pressed a finger to his lips.

There was no doubt in my mind. Harrison in my bed. Inside me. Holding me. This was what made sense. This was the next right step. Harrison deserved to feel loved and be cherished. He was so free with his love. He too, deserved this solace. Maybe I couldn't promise him the family he always dreamed of, but I could show him what he meant to me. Show him that despite everything, he'd found a way into my battered and abused heart.

32

Harrison

FRANKIE BROUGHT HER LIPS TO ME SLOWLY. WE KISSED LONG AND deeply. There was nothing here like our previous frenzied coming togethers. She held my head and poured a gentleness into her kiss. And I accepted it.

She had tried to be gentle with me in all things. She folded me into her life and took me as I was. She wouldn't tell me lies or what I needed to hear. But she cared for me. That much was obvious. I was wrong to think that she was using me. She loved me as perfectly as she could, and I was being greedy. Maybe I was set to always suffer in my extremes. I was all or nothing. Extremely single-minded, focused, or completely disinterested. I felt with my entire being or ... Well, I would always love Frankie. That much I already knew to be true. She was as woven into me as my years on the show. She'd come into my life to show me my full capacity to love. That was her gift to me.

There was love here. In her own way. A tenderness that Frankie rarely gave except for the lucky few. The four of us in this house were lucky in that way.

Our mouths only separated when we needed to pull pieces of clothing off the other. We stood naked, memorizing each other with our hands and mouths like we were archiving this moment.

When we fit our bodies together in her bed, it was slow and tender. My gaze never left hers.

It was intense and deep, and it felt like love. It was our version of love, of course.

She cried my name softly as she came apart on me, a tear in the corner of her eye. I kissed it away and came a moment after.

Later, in her bed, I held tight and practically heard her thoughts in the air around us.

"What's on your mind?" I asked. My heart was hammering with hope.

Tell me we can stay like this forever. Tell me you love me. Tell me how we can make it work.

If I told her how much I loved her now would she believe it? Would she accept it, or would it feel like pressure to make a promise to me?

"I was just thinking about the cruelty of life," she said.

I blinked. "Wow. Was I that bad?"

She laughed and pulled me closer to rest her head on my chest. "I think we both know it wasn't. Don't fish. It's gauche."

"Gauche is my middle name."

"It is so unfair. How a family could want a baby so bad and never have one. How someone could feel that pull so sure and never experience it. And then there are people who have children without thinking about it. Like it's ... I don't know, a side effect of living. Something to be dealt with. Something to cure yourself of," she whispered as she got to the end.

"Or how a mind that created an entire world that made a million or more people happy could start to kill itself."

She squeezed me tighter when my voice broke. "Exactly. It's cruel. There are a million examples of how unjust life is."

"George would tell us that the beauty is there to balance it out. That we have to take time to notice it and enjoy the good while it's here." I inhaled along her neck.

"He's so good at that. I feel so scared all the time," she admitted softly.

"Really?" I lifted my head to look at her. She nodded, hand running over my abdomen. "You always seem to know exactly who you are and what you want."

"I guess I'm just good at faking it."

"Christ, I hope not. My ego would never take it."

She kissed my pec, and I felt her smile. "You have nothing to worry about, Captain Modest."

"What are you afraid of?" I asked, running my fingers through her hair.

"Everything." She huffed. "Collette being alone. George being scared or sad. You being gone," she said.

I swallowed the tightness and fought the urge to understand what that could mean.

"Me being ..." She faded off.

"Being too beautiful?" I asked.

"Yes. Yes. That's what keeps me up at night," she said dryly.

"Seriously," I nudged her.

She grabbed my hand and looked at our intertwined fingers. She lifted one and put it down, then the next, one at a time, only to start over again. Taking her time to say what she needed.

"My mom left me when I was fifteen," she started. "It was never exactly stable before that. But when she drove away that last time, there was such determination in her eyes. I knew I would never see her again. Joey still tried. Even though she was older, maybe because she had more time with her, she always had hope. Tried to find her for years but my mother was done with us. She told us she didn't want to be a mom. That what happened to her wasn't her fault but it would be better if she left us."

I let out a long breath. Her breakdown after Joey left became even more clear. There was no doubt that she had feared Collette was living a shadow of her same life. This made it all lock into place.

"I'm so sorry," I said.

"For the longest time, I kept waiting for something. I don't know. Not her. I knew she was gone. I was waiting for a grown-up to come and tell me everything would be okay. I had hoped forever that someone would come and scoop me up and tell me that they would take care of everything. I gave up by the time George and William took me in. I understood the truth."

"The truth?"

"We are alone. We are totally alone."

"That's what you think?" I asked, in surprise. How could she think that when she had George. She had *me*.

"It's how I feel. Felt," she added, and I held my breath. "I don't know. I'm so afraid to hope. I just want to make sure Collette has everything I never did. I want her to have the perfect family that will be there every day and buy her new backpacks and school supplies, ground her for talking back, and take her on family trips and just all that stuff. She deserves normalcy and love and consistency."

"I know, it's not the same." I sat up and she did too. We faced each other, naked but not distracted. "It doesn't take the pain away. But you are that grown-up for Collette. You and George. You are here out of selfless love and not obligation. You see that, right?"

Her mouth parted and her eyes glistened. "I never thought about it that way. I feel like I've just been this holding pattern."

"She could have been another child lost but you were that

adult that came and told her she was loved and special and taken care of," I said.

She pressed a hand to her chest. She opened her mouth to speak but ended up sucking in her lips and looking to the side, nodding, tears welling in her eyes.

"There are good people in the world. There is good to balance out the horrors," I said. "We exist to take care of each other. We aren't designed to be alone. Some people are just hurt and scared. Like you were, but you chose to reach out with love and make a different future for Collette." I swallowed as my words sunk into her. It was as though a weight was lifting from her, and I could almost see something changing in her body.

"You too," she said.

"Me too, what?"

"You choose hope and love every time."

"I've had a charmed life. It's easier for me," I said.

"I don't think it's ever easy to choose to have hope in this world," she said.

We fell asleep holding each other. Nothing had changed, we still had no answers, but Frankie had shared a deep part of herself. I knew her better than ever. I drifted asleep feeling hopeful.

"Why are you naked?" I blinked my eyes open to see Collette standing above me, rubbing her eyes. "Why are you in Frankie's room?"

Next to me, Frankie woke up and looked at me and then Collette. She didn't speak. Her eyes went wide.

George shuffled in a moment later. "Come on, Collette. I'll teach you how to make pancakes. And about young people wasting time."

I glanced over to Frankie, she grabbed a pillow and covered her face, falling back. This would undo all the distance we covered last night. Surely, this would cause her to—

"Wait, are you laughing?" I tugged the pillow off her face.

She nodded between laughs. "I have no idea what I'm going to tell her."

My chest swelled with pure joy. She was beaming. She was lit from within.

"I don't suppose we can use the restocking towels excuse?"

Her laughter melted away but her smile remained. She was watching me with sleepy eyes and bed head.

"You're beautiful," I said.

She flushed and looked down. "I'm happy," she said. "I feel lighter this morning. I don't know." She glanced to the window.

"Good." I pulled her close to kiss her, but she held up a hand between our faces.

"Gah, sorry about my breath."

"Since when does that matter?" I cocked an eyebrow at her blushing.

"Since I didn't wake up an hour before you and have time to brush my teeth. I'll be right back."

I stretched in bed as Collette walked in. "I'm trying to watch my show but this keeps ringing."

"Oh, boo." I reached for my work phone Collette handed me.

"Keep it short," the little girl demanded.

"Yes, your highness."

Frankie was dressed and back in the room as I ended the call. Collette snatched my business phone back and dashed out of the room.

I looked up at Frankie, and she watched me tentatively. "Who was that?"

"Agent." I winced. "I have to be back in LA today. I'm sorry. The other lead dropped and they want me to do some last-minute screen tests with the new actress, test our chemistry. I'm so sorry."

She took a deep breath and came to sit on the bed. "Okay." She held my gaze.

"Okay?"

"Yes. You have to go. We'll be fine. School starts Monday. The book is almost done." She lifted her chin, nodding. "Actually, no offense but it would probably be best for my productivity if you weren't here."

I leaned forward and kissed her forehead. "You have got this. And hopefully, it will go fast."

She kissed me back.

"I will miss you," she said.

I grabbed her tight. "God, I'll miss you too. And I will be back just as soon as possible. Everything will be okay."

She nodded against me, tension back in her shoulders.

33

———

Archive File: **6724**

George's Terraformative notes: The planet is a tropical utopia. The trio is celebrating, they don't see the truth.

Notes:

FRicci: There is something that must be done that will bring all the glory and fame. Adam wants to go. They need to send out a message or get the plants or something like that. He tells the others that they need to go. This was supposed to be the last mission. He is tired. They are tired. They are fighting all the time.

HEvans: You're pulling the punch.

HEvans: Also. I hate LA.

FRicci: No, I am not.

FRicci: Also. I thought you loved LA?

FRicci: What punch?

HEvans: You don't want the Intrepid Trio to fight. But they have to fight, or Adam won't get his head out of his ass.

FRicci: Whoa whoa whoa. Watch how you talk about Adam. They don't need to fight. They have been best friends their whole lives. Why would they fight?

HEvans: Erm, Emma just snorted out loud reading that over my shoulder. She said even more reason that they need to fight.

FRicci: I disagree. They can talk amicably. Like adults. (Tell Emma hello!)

HEvans: Snooze. Adam needs a push to change. You know this. You just don't want to make them fight. (She said hello back.)

FRicci: You're right. I don't want to. I want them to hold hands and stay together forever and go back to the academy, where everything was simple and easy.

HEvans: You sound like me. Things change. Change is inevitable, and we all know this.

FRicci: I am pulling the punch.

HEvans: Bingo.

FRicci: I miss you.

HEvans: I miss you more. I'll be back soon.

FRicci: Breath is bated.

34

───────

Frankie

Two weeks. Two weeks and Harrison still hadn't been able to leave LA. I was unmoored and restless. When Collette was at school and George was napping or with Otis the OT, I paced the house, looking for tasks but unable to focus on anything.

I thought I was okay. I had made peace with these feelings. This *love*. But love shouldn't feel like this. It shouldn't grip me like panic and terror. This wasn't right. Maybe I'd been confused. This shadow loomed just behind me, and no matter how many lights I turned on, I couldn't burn it out.

I'd grown too comfortable. Let myself adjust to the roots but felt more adrift than ever. We were just about to hit six months of no word from Joey. The lawyer had the documentation ready for the courts. Without the child abandonment filing, I couldn't get custody granted. There was no official paperwork tying Collette to this house or George. As far as the courts were concerned, he was just a man in mental decline. It shouldn't be as hard since I was related by blood if I wanted to keep Collette.

I couldn't decide what was right for Collette. Was I being selfish, or were Harrison and I really the best family for her?

How could I be the best choice for her?

How could I be the best choice for anybody when feelings of love and devotion caused me to panic? I was this hump-backed little Gollum gripping to love, waiting for it to be ripped from my fingers.

And now this. This stark reminder of what real life would be like with a movie star as a parent. It would be all on me, and wasn't that defeating the point? George and Collette would be dependent on me twenty-four seven. Yes, the book would be done any day now, in theory, but could I do this all alone? Be in this house alone in my mind that would never stop wondering about the countless other paths I should have taken.

I paced back to the office and tried to work on the book, but I was too anxious to focus.

My phone rang, and I answered it immediately.

"Hey, Frankie." I could tell by Harrison's tone that it wasn't good news.

I closed my eyes, and the looming shadow blurred the edges of my vision.

"Hey, are you headed back?" I asked, already knowing he'd let me down.

"I'm sorry. I'm so sorry," he said. "This movie has just been one disaster after another. I *will* be back by this weekend at the latest. I just have to do some damage control."

With every promise, a layer of ice grew over me. I'd heard these excuses before, time and time again. Another actor, another broken promise.

Protect yourself.

"Don't bother," I said. My voice sounded distant, unlike my own.

"Don't bother? Are you serious?" His voice cracked, and I

could hear his own exhaustion. I knew he was working hard. I knew he wanted to be here. Yet I couldn't stop the sharp words that flew out of my tongue. It felt like it cost something to just admit that I was flailing without him, that I had grown to rely on and need him this much. It made me feel weak and pathetic.

"There's no point," I said.

His background grew quiet as I heard shuffling and a door close. "Frankie, please don't shut down. Let me turn the video on. Let me see you."

"This was always supposed to end," I said.

Visceral panic took over, gripped my throat, and it genuinely didn't feel like me talking anymore. I watched another person operate my body. I watched my mother drive away for that last time. I'm alone. I'm alone. Nobody to care for me. Nobody to keep me safe. I was both numb and tingly. Like I was dying but aware of every cell in my whole body. I couldn't move.

This wasn't a normal reaction to bad news. This wasn't normal or good.

"I don't want anything to end," he said. There was a beeping as he tried to video call me. I ignored it. "Please let me see you, Frankie. I-I know this is bullocks but please don't push me away. Is that really what you want?" The panic in his voice had me squeezing my eyes shut tight.

"It doesn't matter what we want. We aren't happily ever after people. At least not together," I said.

"Says who?" I flinched at his anger. "You need to make a choice," he said with vehemence. "Stop letting your past define you. Stop letting your sister rule you. It's your choice. This is *our* family." His voice broke, and I bit my lip to keep a sob from escaping.

Why was I fighting him so hard? Why was I chasing the pain?

"That's not fair," I whispered.

"No. You aren't being fair. We've come too far for you to act like this. Like we aren't a family. You told me that I was easy to love. Let me love you. Let me love you, Frankie. Be the courageous woman I know you are. You can choose this for us. Please. Have faith in me," he begged.

Giving in to him, no matter how much I wished I could, felt like cheating somehow, like the wrong choice. It couldn't be good and easy. It had to be hard and bad.

"I don't get to make this choice. I can't just pick a family who doesn't belong to me. This isn't an open casting call for a family, Harrison. These are real lives and real people, and Collette isn't mine." I sobbed out, surprising me so much that I covered my mouth with a hand.

"You are wrong about that," he said. "I know it's scary to love her that much. It scares me too. But Collette is *yours*. Even if I'm too much, even if you don't want me"—my head shook as he spoke. He had no idea how wrong he was—"don't let her be wrapped in those fears. Remember that you are the person she needs. Be the person you searched for as a little girl. And I hope you can figure it out before it's too late. That child loves you. I love you. I don't know how many different ways I can say it until you believe it. But I love you."

"Stop. Please stop." I shook my head, and my whole body shook. This was too much. Too awful. Love shouldn't feel like this. "I can't keep doing this. Every time you leave, I feel less like myself."

"Then I will quit. Is that what it will take for you to have faith in me? I would have quit when I met you. Say the word and I will."

"That's not funny."

"I'm not kidding," he spat. "I want you, Frankie. I want you and Collette and George and that bloody messy house and folding towels and corny jokes and burned cupcakes and chaotic mornings. I want getting her ready for school and steamy summer days by the pool and back pain from falling asleep in that kid's awful bed and everything else that comes with it. I'm not a joke. I want you to believe that."

I laughed and cried. "I'm not asking you to quit your job, Harrison. I just—I want to do the right thing. What are we even thinking? This was always meant to be temporary."

"Does that help? If you keep saying it over and over. If that's the lie you need to tell yourself?" Harrison was rarely this sharp, only when he was absolutely rigid about something.

"Harrison. I'm trying to do the right thing here." I closed my eyes tighter, and tears streaked out. "But you're breaking my heart."

"Yeah, well, you already fucking broke mine," he shouted.

The line rang in the silence. I turned my head away so he couldn't hear the gasp of pain. Still hiding my feelings, still afraid to hurt and be hurt.

"Just-just wait, okay?" he asked. "Fuck. I have to go but please just trust me that we can talk through this. I'm not going to leave like your mother. Okay? I'm not Joey. You *know* me. Stop trying to push me away so you can be right. Would you rather be happy or right?"

"I told you that in trust."

"I told you things too. Because we are in a relationship, Frankie. That's what people do. They share and argue and they communicate. Just because you're scared and we're fighting doesn't mean I'm leaving and not coming back. That's not how people operate. Will you please just tell me that you understand that?"

All this was to avoid pain and here we were both miserable. What am I supposed to do? I wished somebody would come in and tell me what to do and fix all this. "Can we really have this life?" I whispered. "It feels too good to be true." And as I said it, I realized how real that fear was.

It wasn't that I believed it was meant to be temporary. It was that I didn't believe anybody could be this happy. Certainly not me. Who was I?

"God, I bloody hope so." He sounded so much lighter, and I was able to take a deep, shuddering breath in. "We're in this together, okay?"

I gasped out but nodded.

"Are you nodding?" he asked softly.

I sniffled a laugh. "Yes."

"Okay." He let out a sharp breath. "Okay. Fuck. I have to go. I'll be back this weekend. Please. Just please, let's talk then, okay?"

"Okay."

"I love you, Francesca. It's all going to be okay. You aren't alone," he said.

I shuddered in a breath. "I'm sorry." I shook my head. "I'm so sorry. I'm just all alone here and all in my own head. And the deadline for Collette and the book is coming, and I don't want to screw everything up, and I'm sorry."

Once I said it out loud, I understood that was what was happening. That was the pressure that caused me to lash out. Trying to control one aspect of my life when I felt no control over the rest.

"It's okay, love. It's okay. I will be there soon. I love you," he said.

I steadied myself, deciding for once to be brave like he was. Strength in a way I never imagined for myself. A different sort of courage found only through vulnerability. "Harrison, wait." My whole body shook as if I'd been out in the Arctic. "I-I love you too."

There was a beat of silence in which I thought my stomach

might liquefy. Then he huffed a deep gasp of relief. "Bloody brilliant." The smile became full brightness through the line.

I'd said it, and it was okay. I was okay.

The doorbell rang.

"Who is that?" he asked.

"I'm not sure. Call me after you wrap for the day?"

"I will."

Harrison was right. It would be okay. Whatever happened, I would be okay.

I wiped my face and collected myself before I went to the front door.

I checked the peephole first and found Joey standing there, massive black sunglasses on as she looked around, arms crossed as she waited impatiently.

My entire world tilted on its side.

———

Harrison

I SAT WITH MY HEAD IN MY HANDS, SHAKING BREATHS IN AND OUT. That was too close. Too close. She was so scared. I understood fear, but when would she let herself fully trust me? How many weekends away until she couldn't be talked back down? And how could this setup ever be enough?

I scrubbed my eyes, exhaustion weighing down my shoulders and making my eyes blur. I wished I had time to call Emma or Charlie and talk this through, but we were on hour ten of this day and somehow still two hours behind schedule.

A hand on my shoulder made me jump.

It was my agent, Chad. "Harrison? What's up, man? You gotta be on set."

I stood up and felt the blood rush on delay, causing me to

tilt. I needed to sleep and eat and had time for neither. I'd been burning the candle at both ends in an effort to get back home sooner. Not my empty mansion in LA, but *home*. Whether or not Frankie called it that, nowhere else was.

"Yep, sorry," I said. "Personal call."

Chad had an intense fake smile beaming from his sweat-covered face.

"What the fuck, Evans? They were about to roll."

"I needed to check in at home."

"That was twenty minutes ago," he said.

"I just—"

"Let me guess, lost track of time?" He used his left hand to reach over and scratch at his right eyebrow, put out and annoyed. "Listen, man. I get it. Family is obviously most important, but every minute here costs the studio thousands of dollars, and they won't hesitate to take it from your check."

Embarrassment burned the back of my neck. "I'm sorry. It's been a rough few weeks."

"And you're distracted."

I ground my jaw.

"Where's your work phone?" he asked, at the end of his tether with me.

I winced. I couldn't remember the last time I even saw it.

"That explains why I can never get ahold of you." He scoffed with a shake of his head, making me feel smaller with every word. "Listen, I get it. You're a pretty important person but other people's time is valuable too. You need to hear the truth. I was warned about your flakiness."

"It's not—"

Chad held up a hand. "Did something happen? Like, do you need to go? Is it pressing at this moment?"

"No, I—"

"That's what I thought. So, then, let's let that sit and focus on your job, on the people who are counting on you here and now."

I swallowed, feeling like a scolded child. After all, I had been acting like one. I'd been making a pig's ear of everything, trying to be everything at once. I was under contract. I owed it to this movie. Frankie would be okay. I would be home this weekend and would remind her of all that we had.

"I'll look after your phone." Chad held out a hand.

"I need to have it if something happens."

"Let me hang on to it. I'll keep an eye on it. If something comes up, I'll let you know right away."

"Okay." I hesitantly handed it over.

"You can come get it any time," he said, gripping my shoulder.

I nodded.

"Let's get you back to set."

35

Frankie

"You can't come in here," I said, blocking the door.

My sister rolled her eyes. "Come on, Frowny Frankie. I'm your sister."

Those large sunglasses covered half her face, and she couldn't stand still. She glanced over her shoulder and back at me, lower lip pouting.

That old familiar tug wanted to just give in, knowing that it would be easier.

But no. This wasn't about her or me. This was about her messing with Collette's head, and we were done with that.

I used my body to block her path as she tried to push past me. She was frail and easily bounced off. "If you want to be like that, I'll just call the cops, and they will give me my daughter."

Two weeks. Less than. Only a few more days she had to be a deadbeat, and she wouldn't have an ounce of power.

My fingers balled into fists. "I told you last time that there was no coming back."

"Well, you aren't the fucking boss of me, are you?"

I stepped out, shutting the door behind me. "Just tell me what it is you want."

She scoffed and paced the porch.

I sat in a rocking chair, leaning forward with my palms flat together, squeezing them between my knees as she ranted so quickly I could hardly follow. She was even thinner now, and I knew she likely wouldn't take off her glasses because they hid bloodshot eyes.

Had I caused this? Had I pushed her back into her addiction? She told me often enough I didn't support her—

No. I told that voice. I thought instead of Harrison's words about addicts. Words I knew all too well to be true. I wasn't responsible for her actions. I wouldn't take this on.

"I hated the company I was touring with anyway. They honestly were so jealous of me they kept doing things to fuck me over. It's fine. I've been living with some cool people down in LA. I thought about saying hi to Harrison while I was in town but hadn't gotten around to it."

She'd been ranting for twenty minutes, explaining her absence and delays in getting the paperwork to me.

I didn't care for her story. I cut her off. "I will not let you take Collette," I said firmly, not when she was clearly back in an unstable place.

She scoffed. "She's my daughter, and you really don't have a choice."

I stood up and balled my fists at my hips. "You lost your rights to her last time. I've been trying to find you for child abandonment and get custody like you promised I could have when you left."

"Now, you don't have to worry." She gnawed at a nail already chewed to the quick. "And anyway, I'm not taking Collette. I know I'm shit at being a mom, okay? Calm down."

Tension melted out of me. She wasn't taking her. Maybe she

just wanted money. I would scrounge whatever I'd earned. I would give her whatever it took to keep her away.

"I found her a family," she said.

I stumbled back. This was so much worse. "What?"

Just shy of six months, and she was back. Just shy of deciding what I wanted, the choice was ripped from my grasp so that all my stupid mistakes became clearer.

"No." I shook my head. "No. I-I want to keep her. Let me have her, please. I'm family."

Joey sneered at my breaking heart with disgust. "You're as much of a mother as I am."

I placed a hand on my heart. "No." I focused on Harrison and our life that we built. Thought of how he comforted me and told me I was enough. I loved her, and that was enough. "I am *here*. I love her," I said.

Joey shook her head and shrugged. "Yeah. And? You don't think I do? I literally made her. I birthed her. And it sucked." She turned her head away and swallowed, a flush spreading up her neck. "I love her enough to know that she deserves better, okay?"

It was everything I had been telling myself. Everything I feared to be true. What if Harrison couldn't understand? He was good and loved and saw the world through his star-studded glasses of privilege. Our romantic relationship made him incapable of seeing the ugly side of me. This inherent dirty truth of who I was and where I came from. I would eventually make him leave too.

"It's not your fault, Frankie. We are cut from the same cloth. But this is a legit family, okay?" Joey came closer and pulled out her phone. She smelled like yesterday's booze and sweat and something bitter. "Look." She pulled up YouTube and played a video from her recently watched. It was a video of a family doing some sort of obstacle course in their massive backyard.

"I don't—Why are you showing me this?" I asked.

"This is the family who wants Collette. They are legit. They have like three *million* subscribers."

"What do they do?" I shook my head, not understanding.

"That's it. They just record their life. Dumb, boring shit. But like, for some reason, kids watch the hell out of it. These parents have seven adopted kids and a shit ton of money. And they want Collette."

"But why?" My head was throbbing. The family on the screen were laughing and running around, challenging each other. They seemed happy.

"They're a theater family. I showed them some of the videos Collette made. The ones of her singing and dancing around."

"You shouldn't—"

"You and I both know she's insanely talented. Just because you don't have any dreams doesn't mean you should squash everybody else's. Stop sucking the joy out of everyone else. That's what you do."

"That is not true." My voice shook. "I just want to protect her. I am here. I am the one trying to help her."

"Then help her." Joey tossed out her arms. "This is a real family. And they are stupid loaded. They want Collette. There isn't anything more to understand. How are you not excited?" She shook my shoulders, and I had to turn my head away to avoid her sour breath.

"You don't think it's weird that they record their kids all the time? They're children, not content."

She shrugged a bony shoulder. She had a break out of painful-looking bumps. When she caught me noticing, she tugged up her sweater. "It's just how things are now. Everybody is online."

"I don't know. I need to think. I—when do they want her?" I asked incoherently.

A tension headache throbbed at my temple. I needed to talk to the lawyers. Was this even legal? Had they even met Collette? Nothing about this seemed normal. What were my rights? All my thoughts were swirled up.

"As soon as possible. And it's not your choice. I'm trying to be a good sister and tell you."

I pressed a hand to the acid burning up my throat. "You want to take her now?"

"The quicker I do, the quicker I get paid, and I can get some stuff. I'm low on cashflow at the moment. I need new headshots and clothes." She scratched her neck and looked away.

"Joey, *please*," I begged.

Please what? If she had just stayed away a few more weeks, I could have taken control, but now I felt so powerless. What could I say against her own birth mother? I needed to think. I needed Harrison. I needed Collette and George.

I needed my *family*.

This wasn't my choice, but it didn't feel like Joey's either.

"Just stay. Just a few days. Eat and rest. And, and we can talk to Collette and see what she thinks?" I sat up straighter, nodding. "Don't you think Collette should have a say?"

Joey raised her eyebrows at me in a way that told me she thought I was an idiot. "Sure. Let the six-year-old decide if she wants to move to the house full of toys or stay here with an old man."

"Seven," I said sadly.

"Whatever." Joey rubbed her head. "We can talk to her tonight. But that's it. I'm leaving in the morning. You can ask her, but it's on you when it doesn't go your way."

I nodded, immobile with dread.

"I'm going to go lie down for a little while," she said.

As soon as I was alone, I called Harrison. I knew he was filming, so I wasn't surprised it went straight to voicemail. I begged him to come home and explained everything as fast as I could. I had no idea who else I could contact to reach him. I didn't even know his work phone number. That aspect of his life was so hidden away. Because of me. He pretended it didn't exist because I was too fragile to handle the thought of him ever leaving. He kept his career like a dirty little secret because I had made him feel that it was. I had taken cracks at his acting and hurt him. He'd done so much, and I continued to let my own issues dominate me. He was right. He wasn't going to leave like my mother. I would have to trust that.

As Joey napped, I waited in the pickup line for Collette. I pulled up YouTube and watched more videos of that family. I had already decided that I would fight for Collette, but watching these videos confirmed it. There was nothing outwardly rotten. By all accounts, they were a large, happy family. Their house was massive, with mountains in the background, somewhere in California? No, the houses seemed too McMansion for that. Utah or Arizona maybe. Somewhere in the Southwest. The more videos that played, the stronger of an off-putting undercurrent I couldn't put my finger on. The strained smiles. The forced challenges. The older children growing more sour as the years passed, smiling less often. I watched a video of one of the children undergoing minor surgery, waking up groggy and crying, reaching for his mother, only to have a camera shoved in his face and obnoxious animations inserted about his incoherent ramblings. Making a joke of it. It made my stomach churn with frustration and pity.

Was it ethically responsible to publish every private and sometimes incredibly awkward moment of adolescence online for millions of strangers to watch? Was I projecting my own issues on this new form of entertainment?

Or was I correct in my assertion that these children felt like they were being sourced like commodities for social currency? It didn't feel *right*. And where were the laws protecting these children? I couldn't imagine the same strict child labor laws that Hollywood, at least, *finally,* had being applied to these "fun home videos." But looking through these time stamps, they were being produced rapidly, sometimes more than one a day. How much choice would they have? Would Collette be forced to perform for a camera, even if she didn't want to? Would a camera be there as she developed her first crush or got her period instead of a loving parent? I made the mistake of scrolling deep into the comments. I saw several questions asking after a private Patreon account for the littlest girls.

"No!" I threw my phone to the passenger seat, feeling sick to my stomach.

There was no doubt. I would not allow this life for Collette. I would do whatever it took to keep her safe and loved. That had always been the most important thing that wouldn't change now.

I scrubbed at my face until a honk behind me told me to pull forward.

I tried not to let my nerves show as Collette chatted happily. When I parked at George's, I gestured for her to climb in the front seat as I sometimes let her do.

"I just want to let you know that Joey—your mom is here."

"Okay." She shrugged a shoulder but tugged on her earlobe in the way she does when she is nervous.

"We're going to have a grown-up conversation, and you're going to make a big decision. But you aren't alone. And no matter what you decide, I love you. Okay?"

She nodded. "Can I have cheesy crackers?"

I huffed a laugh. "Yeah."

"Really?" Her eyes lit up.

Junk food was the least of my worries. "But not too many. You don't want to spoil dinner." Apparently, I couldn't turn it off completely.

Inside, George and Joey were arguing.

"I don't know what is up with you lately, but you can't talk to me like this." Joey had her arms crossed, leaning in as she snarled at the older man. When she saw us, she tossed out her arms. "Finally. He's being weird again."

"Heya, George," I said. "Everything okay?"

George turned on his walker, leaning heavily on it. "There are my girls."

I let out a quiet sigh of relief. At least he was doing okay.

Collette dropped her backpack and started to run at them. Joey braced herself, arms out, but Collette ran to George.

"It's okay, Papa George. We're home now. You can have cheesy crackers, but only a few. You can't spoil your dinner." He let her tug them to the kitchen.

Joey blinked after Collette, jaw open in surprise before she snapped it shut.

After dinner, I still hadn't heard from Harrison. This was typical on a shooting day, but I had wished he was here for this conversation. Joey refused to spend any more time waiting.

We sat George and Collette down, and Joey cleared her throat. I thought she was about to explain the situation, but she pulled out her phone instead. "Hey, Collette, wanna see something cool?"

I opened my mouth to speak but decided to wait. George frowned, hands clasped at his chin and studying the interaction.

Joey showed Collette a video of the family. Collette watched with intent and laughed. With every second, her attention stayed rapt, and my heart fell. Had I overestimated her desire to stay here? This whole time, I'd been worrying about being enough for Collette, and it was only just occurring to me now, that given the choice, Collette may not actually pick this weird, little family.

"This family wants you to come live with them, Collette. Would you like that?" Joey asked, using that artificially sweet voice adults sometimes used with kids.

Collette looked from the video to me.

"Or you can stay with me," I offered simply.

I wanted to stay here at the house and with Harrison, but I couldn't promise any of those things. I could only promise that I would love and take care of her, and there was absolutely no doubt for me. George's brows furrowed, creating a deep wrinkle. I could tell he didn't understand the situation and was staying quiet.

"You want me, Frankie? You'll keep me forever?" Collette asked.

My throat was so tight I thought I might get sick. The hope and love in Collette's eyes almost broke me.

"Of course. I love you, Collette."

Collette looked back at her mother. "I want to stay here with Frankie." A shadow moved over Joey's face. "I don't want that other family."

"Collette. You're being stupid. This family has a mansion and toys. You'd get to sing and dance all the time and be on TV."

Collette hesitated only a minute. A little crease formed before her light brows. "We don't talk to each other like that in this house. We talk to each other with kindness."

Joey growled and tossed out her hands. "You're making a mistake."

She shrugged. "All my stuff is here."

"You'll get new stuff. Better stuff."

"And Frankie and George and Harrison?" she asked hopefully.

"Well. No." Joey rolled her eyes.

"Nah. It's okay. I want Harrison and Frankie. And George. This is my home. I like my school and my friends, and I don't want to go."

Joey opened her mouth, and I snapped, "Enough. That's enough, Joey."

I turned to Collette and smiled, opening my arms. "I want you too, kiddo."

Collette ran to me. A surge of love poured through me. Even if I had to fight, I wouldn't ever let her go.

"This is bullshit." Joey stood up as Collette flinched.

I closed my eyes and held Collette as long as she would let me. Joey shook her head and stomped upstairs. I would deal with her in a minute. For now, I let my love flow into Collette, and I wouldn't release her until she let go first.

"Well, now that that's settled, we should probably get some cookies," George said.

"Great idea," I said and smiled at him over Collette's head. He smiled back, but the crease was still furrowing his brow.

———

JOEY HID IN HER GUEST ROOM FOR THE REST OF THE NIGHT. I KEPT waiting for her to stomp through the house and dramatically announce that she was leaving. I kept my ears pricked, and my body was tense with high alert. I wouldn't let her leave without some paperwork saying she had to leave us alone now. I would tackle her to the ground and tie her up if I needed to. Collette made her choice.

There was no doubt in my mind that Collette was my daughter. I was an idiot to let it take me this long, but I was her person.

After bedtime, I paced the living room, watching the front door.

I'd spent so much time these past two years waiting for

things to end, waiting for this holding pattern to be over so that I could get back to my real self.

I had been desperate to find myself, to recognize something in the person I was now. But there was no going back to who I used to be, and for the first time, I was completely okay with that.

I liked who I was now. I loved the life I had fallen into, and more than that, I was proud of the person it helped me become. I was proud of my capability to love and be loved even though I had never been shown how growing up. Harrison and Collette and George all loved so freely that it helped me be courageous. I would always be afraid, but I would lead with my heart. Maybe the girl I used to be was gone, and maybe this version of myself would be someday too, and that was okay. For once, I was excited about the present, not just wishing for something else.

I stopped my pacing and blinked. "Oh."

It occurred to me this was the same issue that Adam Abbotts struggled with in our currently unfinished manuscript. He was so desperate to hold on to the past and what the plan had been that he was missing the life and family he had created. There was no need to find a new earth when his life with the people he loved was enough.

To be human is to endure. But it wasn't. It was to live and love. It was to dance around the kitchen pretending to be pirates and laugh until you thought you might be crying. It was singing so loud your head hurt, holding tiny hands, kissing the person you loved, and watching the sunrise as you sipped coffee. And breathing. Just breathing.

I snatched my laptop and began to type and type, glancing up occasionally, listening to the quietly sleeping house.

I got lost in the story. The final chapters of the final book flowed out of me as though George stood there dictating them. Tears blurred my eyes as I wrote the final words.

Then, I immediately went back to the beginning to read through everything I had written. Over a hundred thousand words, all sucking me deeper into the world of *Terraformative.*

I woke with a start, my neck stiff from falling asleep on the old couch. Though the house was as quiet as ever, an instinct told me something was very wrong. Head still spinning from being sound asleep, I fumbled forward off the couch and to the door.

Outside, Joey's car was missing. I hadn't caught her in time.

I swore under my breath, but that little voice ringing loudly in my head didn't stop, it grew until it was screaming, blurring my vision.

"No. No." I sprinted up the stairs.

I threw open the door to Collette's room.

The air was knocked out of me as I fell to my knees. Her bed was empty. Her dresser open and messed with hastily searched drawers.

Collette was gone.

A loud, agonized sob filled my ears. It was my own body making that sound.

Loving this much, this big, so hard. It's too much. The pain was unbearable. How could people have children? Weren't they terrified all the time? How had we survived as a species?

I wanted Collette. I wanted this family. This messy, silly, difficult life. I wanted it all.

I didn't think I could feel a pain worse than being abandoned by my own mother, watching her drive away, but I was wrong. The pain at this moment was so intense I felt like I was dying.

I grabbed Ellie the Elephant and pulled her to my chest. It smelled like her. I curled my body around it, and the sobs started.

I let myself cry for several more minutes and let myself feel the pain tear through me.

But that was it. I wasn't giving up. I wouldn't.

I dialed Brooks despite the incredibly early hour.

"What's wrong?" she asked, sleepily.

"I need my best friend," I gasped.

"Oh." She sucked in a soft breath. "I'm on my way."

36

———

Harrison Evans Voicemail Inbox

Francesca Ricci (mobile)

2:40 p.m.

Transcription

"Harrison. I'm really sorry about calling at work again so soon, but it was Joey that showed up at the house. Please. Call me back as soon as you can."

———

Francesca Ricci (mobile)

3:33 p.m.

Transcription

"She wants Collette. She said she has found a family for her. I'm stalling her as best as I can. I am so sorry to ask this, but is there any way you can get back as soon as possible? I told her that we needed to talk to Collette about what she wanted, but I can tell Joey ___ isn't herself. She's not good when she gets like this."

———

FRANCESCA RICCI (MOBILE)

7:50 p.m.

Transcription

"*Collette is brave and so strong. I love her so much. ___ She picked us. She picked us even___ and Joey is not happy. I'll have to keep an eye on her. I hope you are doing okay. I am sorry for my panicked calls earlier. ____ What? __ Yeah. I'll get Ellie. Did you brush your teeth? Okay, sorry. Talk to you soon, Harrison. So proud of our girl. I love you. I love our life. I'm so proud of our girl.*"

———

FRANCESCA RICCI (MOBILE)

12:50 a.m.

Transcription

"*Starting to worry that I haven't heard from you. Usually you call by now but it's okay. I know how things are when you are focused. Also maybe you mentioned a night shoot? It's okay. I just had to tell you that I figured out the ending to the book. It's good. It's really good. I cried. Like so much, I could hardly see the keyboard as I wrote. I think the readers are going to like it. I hope. I have had so much coffee. I'm afraid to fall asleep when Joey gets like this. I probably won't sleep until she leaves in the morning. So much coffee. Can you tell? Oh man, I can't believe I finished the book. I feel weird and light and sad. No. Not sad. Hollow but relieved? Like the words were wrung out of me and all that's left is my husk. I don't know if that even made sense. It's weird. I'm going to read through it one more time before I send it to Kate, she said she'd read it right away before I send it to the editor. Ahh!*"

———

FRANCESCA RICCI (MOBILE)

3:35 a.m.

Transcription

"_ son. She's gone. _ Oh God. Oh God. I fell asleep. ___ Harrison. I fell asleep and she's gone. I messed up. I messed up so bad___. I can't_ and __ . Where are you? I need you. Where are you?"

———

Francesca Ricci (mobile)

4:13 a.m.

Transcription

"I found the address of the family. I'm going to get her. Brooks is here with George. He was sleeping last I checked on him. I won't let her be taken from me. I'm going to get my daughter and bring her home."

37

____

Harrison

"Harrison?" Emma found me in a near catatonic state.

I wasn't sure how long I'd been staring into space, mind racing, a thousand choices to make, yet the order to make them was a baffling puzzle that I was incapable of solving.

I needed to get to Frankie. Frankie was driving to Collette. Find Collette. Contact lawyers. No. First, call Frankie back.

"Harrison?"

"Emma?" Emma was here. Why was Emma here?

I stood up and threw myself into her arms. "I'm here. It's going to be okay." Her voice shook as she held me tightly.

I released her and tried to form coherent words. "I don't know what to do. I-I don't." I scrubbed my hands over my face, wishing like hell I hadn't quit smoking.

"Have you slept? Or eaten?"

I shook my head. "What time is it?"

"A little after nine."

Hours. Frankie had been trying to get through to me for

hours. With each of her voicemails I'd listened to, the more I spiraled out of control.

I tried to figure out how far that meant Frankie would be? Still in California? I had no idea. I just knew that the complete devastation I felt made my useless brain even more inept.

"How could I ever think I could take care of them? That's my job, and I failed. Because I lost track of time. I lost my phone." I scrubbed my hands through my hair, tugging until the pain distracted me from my breaking heart.

"That's not true. Chad took it," I said, remembering.

Why was Emma even here? She wasn't meant to be here. I blinked at her, finally meeting her eyes.

"And I should have gotten it back. I just forgot. I was so into that bloody scene that I just forgot to get it back from Chad. And then I fell asleep. When I got it back, it was too late. I was too late."

"It's not too late. Listen—"

Chad walked into my trailer.

"You're needed on set," he said.

The pressure in my brain felt like it was about to crack in my skull.

"Chad, this isn't a good time. There's been a family emergency," Emma said softly as she came to stand in front of me.

"Yeah. Right. Sure." He sucked in his lips and looked around. "As there has been for almost a year. You took your time off, Harrison." He looked around Emma, not even acknowledging her. "You've cost this movie enough. You have to get your shit together, man."

I was still locked in place, debilitated by infinite options. "I just need—"

Chad lowered his voice and stepped closer. "Let someone else handle this. You don't need to worry about it. This is why you have a team. Whatever it is, your people can handle it. Nobody else can replace you on that set, though."

"I just—what if they need me?"

"You're an actor, Harrison. What could they need from you?" I rubbed at my chest, knowing he wasn't wrong. "Acting is what you're *meant* to do," Chad said. "Are you really the best person for this crisis anyway? Are you sure this is something you can handle?"

"Okay, that's enough." Emma's cheeks burned bright red, spreading into her matching hair. "Harrison. Don't listen to him. This place is work. It will be here, or it won't. But you know Collette and Frankie need you. Don't let him make you feel bad. You're what they need."

"I'm not enough," I said, shaking my head. Frankie left without me.

"That's not true. You are exactly what they need."

"I don't know what to do." I shook my head.

Emma stood in front of me and grabbed my hands. "Yes. You do."

"Tell me?" I asked. If I just knew what to do. But I'm not smart enough ...

"You know, Harrison."

Chad started to speak, but her head whipped to him. Whatever he saw on her face stopped him from talking. She'd dealt with men far worse.

"You need to trust that Charlie and I need you and care about you. But more importantly, you need to have faith in yourself."

My jaw clenched, and I couldn't find the words.

"Ignore what you think I want, or Chad, or the whole production team. We'll figure it out. Remember what Wesley told you?" She held my gaze.

I swallowed and shook my head. I couldn't even remember my own name right now.

"He told you to be the person you want to be, and not who the world has painted you as," she said.

"That's right," I said, remembering how they drove me to action before.

She smiled. "You have this story in your head that you can't possibly be enough for the people who love you and that's simply not true. You listen to yourself. Trust yourself to know what you want to do."

I thought of what Frankie told me about how easy I was to love. I held on to that.

"I'm going to get my family," I said.

Emma nodded. "Excellent. Wesley's got the jet ready."

"Oh, come on." Chad threw up his arms.

"Chad, you're fired. No offense. It's business," I said.

He shook his head. "Good. Because you've fucked yourself on this set, and I don't want to be associated."

"Let's go," I said, ignoring my former agent.

Once on the jet, I was pleased to see Charlie and Kate. They stood to engulf me in a hug once I was on board.

"What are you doing here? How did you guys know?" I said, tears burned the back of my eyes.

"Frankie emailed me last night and then sent a message to the group chat," Kate said.

"I got the jet ready and picked them up." Wesley checked his phone. "If she left around four a.m., we just might make it around the same time as her."

"Thank you. This is ..." I wanted to say it was too much, but I knew that I would do it for them. Was it so hard to believe that they would do it for me in return?

"I talked to the director," Emma said. "They weren't happy but they understood and didn't want to lose you. They were able to shoot some other stuff and use a stand-in for some of the scenes. Until you have a new agent, I'll help with all this."

"I can handle it," I said weakly, but wouldn't even know where to begin.

"You probably could. But you don't have to. I got you. I'm living that semi-retired life and don't mind." Emma squeezed my hand.

We were in the air and headed to Nevada in no time.

"My lawyers have the address, but listen, we may not have the rights," Wesley said. "The law isn't on our side with Joey still in the picture. I just want you to be prepared for that. Unless there is evidence of ..."

He didn't finish that sentence, and I couldn't handle the thoughts of any harm befalling Collette.

"Has anybody been able to get ahold of Frankie?" I asked.

"No. Straight to voicemail," Kate said.

I sat in silence, leg bouncing. I looked around to see my best friends and their partners.

"Tell me it's not going to be too late," I begged them. Looking at each of them one at a time.

I didn't care for the worry and concern on their features.

"We aren't leaving without a fight," Charlie said.

"Whatever happens, we're together, and we'll figure it out," Emma said.

"So, no sugar coating then?" I joked, but it sounded forced to all of us.

My phone rang loudly.

"Thank God for in-flight Wi-Fi," Emma said and squeezed Wesley's hand.

"Is it her?" Charlie asked.

I was patting my pockets and checking for something I knew I wouldn't find. "No. It's my work number."

The others looked around, as confused as I was.

"The last time I saw it was ..." I answered the call as it dawned. My work phone had been more Collette's than mine these last months. "Collette."

"Harrison?" Her small voice said. It absolutely wrecked me. Fear and relief to hear her sweet little voice and pure rage at her mother all battled in me at once.

"Collette, I can't see you. Where are you?"

"I'm in the closet." She sniffled. "Where grown-ups cry."

"Are you crying, sweetie?" My heart began to race, formulating plans of how to get to her.

"Where are you?" she asked.

"I'm on my way to come get you."

"Okay." She sniffled again.

"Love, are you okay?"

"I'm hungry."

"Where's your mom? Can you turn on a light so I can see you?"

"She's sleeping. She sleeps a lot and doesn't like when I make noise."

"It's okay. You can be quiet," I said, voice tight in my throat.

"I want to go home. Is Frankie with you?"

I sucked in a breath. "She's on her way too. We're coming to get you. Right now. Just. Hang tight, and we'll be there as fast as we can."

"Okay. Frankie said she wanted me to live with Papa George, but Mama says Frankie doesn't want me. This family wants me." I swallowed.

"That's not true. Frankie loves you and wants you."

"They have a dog," she added.

"We'll get you a dog. If you want a dog, we can get a dog."

"Frankie said we couldn't get one because they're a lot of res-respons—work."

"I bet we can change her mind," I said. "Are you at the new family's house?" It was quiet as I looked up to my friends hopefully. "Did you nod?" I asked, smiling to myself. Much like her mother. Her real mom, not Joey.

"Yeah. Sorry." The phone speaker crackled loudly like a sleeve rubbed against it. "I have to go. They're calling me."

"Okay. I love you. I'll see you soon," I said.

"'Kay. Bye."

When the call ended, I looked at the others. "Did anybody else record that? About being hungry and not wanting to be there?"

All of them nodded and held up their phones.

"Okay. Good." I slumped back against the seat.

I didn't like the worry in her voice. I didn't like her being hungry and too afraid to make a sound. But it wouldn't be much longer now. I was going to get my girls.

38

Frankie

THE SUN STARTED PEEKING OVER THE HILLS, NOT QUITE UP, BUT MY
eyes adjusted to the gray morning pre-dawn light. My phone
battery was in the red hours ago, so I shut it off to save what was
left instead of searching for coverage in these stretches of desert
highway. Of course, in my rushed state, I'd not grabbed a
charger.

I hadn't heard back from Harrison. In my desperation, I'd
reached out to his friends. Maybe that had been a mistake. The
more I drove, too stressed out to even listen to music, the more I
thought about how alone I was. I had spent so much of my
energy making sure that nobody got close, so this was what I got
alone on a desert road at the crack of dawn.

I rubbed at dry eyes that felt like they vibrated out of my
head. I ran on pure adrenaline, and the pressure behind my
temples grew with every jaw-cracking yawn. Aside from the
three-hour nap on the couch, I hadn't slept in over a day.

"Are we there yet?" George popped up from the back seat.

I screamed and had just enough time to pull over into a gas

station before accidentally swerving into incoming traffic. "George! What are you doing?" And how the hell had I not seen him?

"I'm here to get my girl," he said and yawned. Calm and collected, he looked out the window curiously, like he hadn't hidden in the car.

I placed a hand on my runaway heart.

"Oh, George." The disappointment was evident in my voice. "How did you—When did you? I thought you were sound asleep."

I thought of the panic that would be all over Brooks's face, finding George missing.

"I have to call Brooks." Dread filled me as I checked the clock and did some math. It would add at least four more hours to take him back and then all the way down to Nevada.

"I want to help, Francesca." He held my gaze in the rearview mirror.

"George, I have no idea what I can even do, let alone…"

"An old man? I'm not useless yet. Stop treating me like I'm already gone. I'm not." His voice shook with anger.

There was unbridled strength behind those gray eyes, so much love and compassion; they held power still. Yet, seeing him in the car, outside the house, there was no denying how frailer he seemed.

I shook my head, pulling out my almost-dead phone. "I need to get you home. I have no idea how long this will take. We don't have any of the stuff you need. This isn't safe."

I called Brooks. She answered right away. "Frankie, I was trying to call you." Her voice was panicked and filled with tears. "I just went to check on George because you said he'd usually be up by now—"

"He's with me. He snuck into the car," I said on an exhale,

fingertips pressed to my forehead. "My phone is about to die. I had it off to conserve battery."

"Oh, thank God." She sucked in a shaking breath. "Thank all the things." After a frantic laugh, she added, "Cheeky old fella."

"Yeah." I scrubbed my tired eyes.

"Wanted a grand adventure, I take it? What are you going to do?" she asked.

I thought of the additional hours. "What can I do? I'm going to turn around and take him back." I looked in the rearview mirror. George's brow furrowed, his fierce gaze locked onto mine.

Adam Abbots, of all people, popped into my head at that moment. He had the determination to save the people he loved. A final adventure. My throat tightened.

I sighed loudly. "After we go get our girl," I said, holding his gaze.

He grinned and gave a thumbs-up.

We got some crappy coffee and used the loo. Thankfully, the gas station had an old-fashioned paper map because my phone died just after I wrote down the address.

"I know you don't want to hear it, but don't do that again," I said to him.

"This was too important for you to go alone. You aren't alone." He shifted on his feet with his chin lifted in defiance.

"I'm so glad you're here," I said and threw my arms around him.

He held me tight, trembling slightly.

He kissed the top of my head. "Such a good one," he said softly.

George was tired around the eyes when I helped him into the passenger seat. The rest of the drive, he slept on and off. At one point, he woke up to ask where we were going, and I squeezed his hand. "Going to get our girl," I said.

"Yes, yes, I know. Of course. Josephine will give me gray hairs," he said, tipping his head back. I didn't think he was here with me when he said that, and I wondered how many times George and William had to take middle-of-the-night adventures to help my sister.

Collette's well-being plagued me. Joey shouldn't even be driving, let alone trying to take care of a child. I should have never fallen asleep. I gripped the steering wheel and focused on getting there.

We made it to Lincoln County, Nevada. My eyes burned as I tried to navigate the map and drive. I wasn't even sure I held it right side up.

"Come on, let me help." George took the paper stubbornly. "Don't forget, when it comes to this old-school stuff, I'm the expert."

I huffed a hollow laugh, too tired to fight him. Honestly, I wasn't sure I could figure it out without help.

I had no idea what time it was when we pulled up to a large but boring house in a suburb with perfectly xeriscaped yards.

I took a steadying breath and stared at the front door.

"You can do this," George said.

"I just really thought I'd have a plan by now."

"You did have the whole drive."

"I panicked. Now I'm not sure what I'm going to be able to do."

"You are that girl's mother. I love Joey. I know she has her struggles, but you love Collette like nobody else."

"I do love her." I let that feeling strengthen my determination and yell louder than the fear.

"Have as much faith in yourself as we all have in you."

"Okay. I can do this." I nodded, shoring myself up. "I'm going to get her."

"Yes, you are." George squeezed my shoulder. "I'll be here if you need me."

As I made my way to the door, I was disheveled and out of place in this cookie-cutter neighborhood. But I kept my chin high. Fake it until you make it, like Brooks said. I rang the doorbell, aware of how ragged and worn out I looked. A woman around my age, but far more put together in her pencil skirt, blouse, and gleaming gold jewelry, answered the door.

"Can I help you?" she asked cautiously.

"I'm here for Collette," I said.

I didn't have a plan but it didn't matter. I wasn't leaving without my little girl.

"Um. I don't understand." Her large smile stayed in place as she spoke.

"She doesn't belong here. She belongs with me," I said.

The woman glanced into the house. "I think there's been a misunderstanding. I'll be right back."

Before she could close the door, I screamed, "Collette! It's Frankie!"

The door shut in my face.

I banged with both fists. I looked like a crazy person. I didn't care. Let the neighbors see. Call the police. I wasn't leaving.

A second later, the door ripped open. "What are you doing?" Joey hissed and pushed me back away from the front porch stairs, slamming the door.

"You can't have Collette. You can't take her in the middle of the night. She picked me. You had no right," I said. Maybe yelled.

Joey was pale with dark circles under her eyes. Her hair was limp and greasy. She looked as though she hadn't slept either.

"Did you think you'd just show up here and take her? Was that your big plan, Frowny Frankie? You're not her mother. You have no rights."

"Joey. I *am* her family. These people are not. Let me have her. And I will go. We can go our own ways."

"Fuck no. Are you crazy? I'm not losing this money," she growled.

"You told me you love her. Let her be with me and George."

"You think that's best? You're just like me. You're an unloveable mess who doesn't know how to mother. And you think I don't see what is happening to George? You think anybody would give him custody?"

I took a breath in and out to settle myself, shaking my head as the realization hit. "You hate me so much, don't you?" I balled my fists. "You blame me for everything that happened with our mom. I don't know why I took so long to see it." I lifted my gaze and held hers. She glared back at me, shoulders heaving, a tiny muscle above her mouth twitching. "I always thought we were this unit. That we shared an unbreakable bond. But you genuinely hate me." My voice broke as I realized just how true it was.

"You ruined everything." Her hands slashed out. "We were perfect until you came around. You made it too much for me. You demanded all her attention, and you drove her away."

"She was sick," I said sadly.

"She would have pulled herself together."

I looked at my sister in a different light then. Somehow, I'd held a different image of her for so long that I was unable to see the truth. She was a stranger who hated me and didn't care who she hurt. Even if it was her own daughter.

"Maybe she would have, I said. But we will never know because she never came back," I said. "To either of us."

Her shoulders flinched.

Soft steps approached me from behind, but I didn't take my focus off my sister. "I'm sorry for everything that happened, but it's not my fault, Joey. Blame me or don't. I really don't care anymore." I stood up straighter and poured every ounce of vehemence into my words. "I love Collette. She is my daughter. And I'm not letting you sell her just to prove some twisted point. I'm going to protect her and love her like every little girl deserves. Like we deserved."

Her eyes filled with tears, and I was shocked at the emotion. "You-you have no right." Her teeth bared as she spoke.

"I'll find a way," I said simply. And I knew that I would. If it took throwing every cent and legal battles for the rest of her childhood, I would deal with them so Collette never felt anything but safety and love.

"She'll never love you like she loves me. I'm her mother, and that's one thing you'll never get."

Maybe before those words would have struck out and hit their intended mark. Now I knew better. Family is created through love and commitment and not always by circumstance of birth. "I hope one day, you'll realize how wrong you are," I said calmly.

"That's enough," a voice came from behind me as fingers laced through mine.

"Harrison?" I sucked in a breath and turned to find him coming to my side.

Not just Harrison.

Behind us, just a few feet away, were Emma and Charlie holding George, along with Kate and Wesley. All of them here.

"Wh-what are you doing here?" I asked.

"We're here for you," he said.

My chin trembled as I smiled at him. Immense relief at having him here filled me. I would do this alone if I had to. But I didn't have to.

The front door opened to reveal three kids, curious about the scene unfolding on their doorstep. The parents tried to corral them back and into the house, but they were greatly outnumbered. The children poured onto the porch, staring with eyes wide and mouths parted as they looked at all of us. The older kids looked shocked at Emma, Wesley, and Harrison. Understandably.

"Oh my—" the mother started.

"Joey, Collette is coming with us. You lost your privileges to be her mother," I said. "This child is not available for sale or whatever it is that you want with her," I said, not hiding my disgust as I spoke to the mother.

Harrison squeezed my hand harder. He gave me a nod, but his features were more serious than I'd ever seen as they glared down at Joey.

"You can't buy a child. We won't let you." Of all the people, I was shocked to see it was Wesley who spoke to the parents of the other children. His words had a vehemence that I hadn't expected from the usually subdued man.

"We—I think there was some sort of misunderstanding. We were under the assumption—" the mother started.

"We don't want any problems. Nothing has been signed," the man I recognized as the father said, appearing at her side.

How quickly they gave up fighting for a child they supposedly wanted was so bad.

"Just, listen. Please. Can you take this somewhere else?" The mother glanced across the sprawled-out suburban neighborhood. Several neighbors were pretending to wash their cars or walk their dogs to glimpse the action.

Collette came barreling out and into my legs a moment later. "Frankie!"

I almost fell over. She was still wearing the same clothes. It hadn't even been twenty-four hours, but I had been so afraid she would have been hurt. I shuddered in a breath as I squeezed her, my heart hammering, close to tears but keeping my strength just a little bit longer.

As soon as she was in my arms, the family quickly gathered and went inside. The door slammed, and the lock clicked loudly into place.

"We're leaving." I stood, unsteady with Collette in my arms. It wasn't easy. She was over half as tall as me now.

Wesley glared at the front door, and something told me he had done his own research into this "family," and this wasn't the last they'd hear from him. But at that moment, all I cared about was the little girl in my arms who smelled like someone else's home and needed me, who chose me.

"No. No!" Joey screamed and took turns between yelling at us and banging on the front door. Nobody in the house responded, and I suspected we were moments away from having the police show up.

"Joey, we are leaving. You can come with us, and we can figure out a plan, or you can go your own way," I said, one arm balancing Collette and the other wrapped around Harrison.

"What about my money?" she screamed. "You think that I'm going to give up that easily?"

Harrison finally spoke. "If money is all you care about, then we'll get you some. You've already lost the biggest treasure you had." He gently took Collette from my shaking arms and held her fiercely. I stepped closer to both of them, and he pulled me in, still balancing Collette. I wrapped myself around her, another protective layer. Poor Collette tucked her head on his shoulder and looked at me with wide, confused eyes.

"It's okay, baby," I smiled at her, talking softly and just to her. "You're safe. And we're going home, okay?"

She nodded sadly before burrowing her face back into Harrison's neck. Kate handed me a blanket, and I tossed it over her to protect her from the cold and stress of the situation.

"Fuck off," Joey spat at him. Then turned to me. "You think I don't know about George and the book? You think you can just cut me a little check and send me away because I'm just some idiot? If I go to the press and tell them who is really writing that story, I'd make ten times as much as they were offering."

Harrison and I stilled. We were so close to leaving. Dread locked my feet in place. The book seemed so far away. I never thought she'd pull out this last-minute bargaining chip in a million years. George was another victim of her manipulation, and I wasn't sure how to make this better.

I looked at the others, all sharing equally somber combinations of worry and not quite hidden anger as we looked at one another. George leaned over and whispered to Emma.

If I could have protected Harrison and his friends from this, I would have, but they chose to be here. Standing there with the man I loved and the people who loved him because they were his family and, by extension, mine. I felt like I belonged to a group that loved unconditionally, a family formed through pure love in a way that wasn't beholden like blood family was.

I belonged.

"Fuck all of you. I'm taking my daughter, and I'm telling everyone that Frankie is the one writing this book." Joey stomped and moved to walk down the sidewalk past us.

I glanced at the others. We knew we had very few legal rights. I couldn't hurt George's book, but I wouldn't lose Collette.

Harrison squeezed my hand. I had been fighting for so long. My brain raced to think of a new plan or some distraction to keep her away. I didn't know what to do.

39

Harrison

FRANKIE'S ARMS DROPPED FROM WHERE THEY'D BEEN HOLDING Collette and me. The moment Joey made her declaration, Frankie's face drained of color. Joey was making her choose between the two people she loved more in the world than anybody. The two people she had done all of this for from the very beginning.

Without discussion, the others came forward to step around the three of us, forming a protective circle.

"Enough!" George shouted, breaking the silence. "That is enough, Josephine!" His deep, booming voice carried, and we all turned to him as he broke from Emma and Charlie to step determinedly forward.

"George?" For all her bluster, Joey barely held it together. She looked strung out and exhausted. When she looked at George with confusion, I could almost see the little girl she must have once been.

Frankie was right, Joey wasn't in a good place, and that made her unpredictable. I slowly pulled Collette and Frankie farther away.

"Josephine. What are you doing?" George shook with emotion when he finally came to a stop in front of Joey at the bottom of the stairs. "I know you can't want this. I know you want what is best for that little girl. Why are you doing this?" He jabbed a shaking finger at her. He was several inches shorter than her but seemed to loom over her.

"I-I—" Her eyes filled with tears, and her lip trembled.

"I need a moment with Josephine," George said. "Please collect everyone and wait for me in the car."

We were all too stunned to do anything but obey.

We walked down the long driveway to the street, where we all waited silently near the two waiting cars.

George spoke to Joey, her arms crossed, lips protruding in a pout. Her chest rose and fell quickly. Her nostrils were flared, but she'd stopped yelling and listened to him. As he spoke, I recognized the body language of one of his speeches, imparting wisdom. I'd been lucky enough to receive many in my life. Joey crossed her arms and tried to act like he wasn't getting through, but her chin trembled, and soon her face cracked.

George put a hand on her shoulder; he held her gaze, gently lifting her chin until she met his eyes. Whatever he said flipped a switch. All at once, her shoulders hunched like she'd been punched, and she collapsed forward into his arms. I wasn't sure who was holding up who.

Frankie sniffled quietly at my side. I turned to check on her and found her eyes red-rimmed and welling with tears. "I know. I'm hopeless," she said, rolling her eyes at herself.

I pulled her tighter against my body, soothing a hand over her back. "I think you're the opposite of hopeless. I think you're hopeful. You want her to be the sister you always thought she could be."

She swallowed but didn't say anything more.

Joey helped George back down the driveway.

"We'll meet you guys at the hotel," Emma said. "We'll take Collette so she can get some food and rest."

After many, many hugs, Charlie, Kate, Emma, and Wesley got in the other car. When everybody was gone except Frankie and me, Joey dropped her head and spoke to us.

"I'm going to rehab," she said and wiped at her eyes.

"Okay, good," Frankie said. She balled her hands into fists.

"Maybe this time, it'll stick." Joey rolled her eyes, but tears were still falling. "I do want to be better than this."

"I know."

"I think there's just something broken in me."

"Broken things can be fixed," Frankie said and squeezed her hand.

Joey didn't look like she believed her sister. "Anyway. I'll sign the papers or whatever. You will have full custody of Collette."

Frankie sighed a sharp breath. "Thank you. Thank you so much."

"She's coming with us back to California," George spoke confidently. "There we can meet with the lawyers and then get her set up at rehab."

Joey lifted her chin and looked to the side. "I want that rehab with the spas and stuff. The nice one in the Hills that all the celebs go to."

I exchanged a look with Frankie that spoke volumes. You couldn't expect her to change too much in one day.

I personally wanted to handcuff her to us, but whatever George said to her seemed to have stuck because she helped the older man into the back of the car and waited for us, leg bouncing as she looked out the window.

When it was just Frankie and I, we held hands, aware that we still stood in front of a stranger's home. There was so much to say, but we were both so tired and worn out from the last twenty-four hours.

"I need to get back to set," I said weakly. "Emma gave Chad hell and negotiated some leeway, but I really can't stay."

I swallowed and wished I could go home with her. Wished I was invited.

"Right." Frankie nodded at the ground, tucking back her hair. "I appreciate all of this. All of you so much."

"Of course." I shook my head. "I'm sorry I was so late. I'm sorry I missed your—"

"You were right on time." She stood on her toes to wrap her arms around me.

I held on to her and sighed into her hair. I loved this woman so much. I wasn't ready to be parted from her.

We held on to each other for a long time.

"I was so scared," she said.

"Me too," I said.

"I never thought I could love somebody so much. I didn't think I was physically capable." I rubbed circles on her back as she spoke. "And now I love so many people with my whole heart. It feels so good. Terrifying, but good."

"I know." I laughed and squeezed her closer. "I think I loved you the moment I met you. And just fell deeper every time I got to be near you."

"Harrison?" she asked. "When are you coming home?"

I leaned back to look her in the eyes. "Home?" My eyebrows lifted in hope.

"I love you, and I need you back at our home with your family."

I took a shuddering breath in, letting her words wash over me.

Our home.

Cut to me opening the front door to George's, dropping my

bags as Collette comes barreling toward me, Frankie right behind her with a gentle smile on her lips.

"I can't tell you how much I love hearing you say that."

"I'm sorry if I ever made you doubt it. I need you. Collette and George need you. We are a family, and we need to be together," she said, our foreheads pressed together. "I love you."

"I love you too." My whole body shook with emotion as I kissed her deeply.

When George wooted from the car, we broke our kiss, and Frankie turned away bashfully. Joey rolled her eyes and sunk lower in the seat.

"I have to take care of some things. This movie but then I'll come home. To our home," I said.

"Okay," she said with tired understanding.

I wasn't ready to leave her yet. Not after everything that happened. I simply needed to be near Frankie and Collette and George and know that everybody was okay.

I made a decision. "But that can wait one more day." I cupped her face. She blinked tiredly. "Let's get you some sleep."

"That sounds nice."

I would go back to work tomorrow.

Back at a nearby hotel, Frankie slept soundly curled on her side next to me. I watched her slow breaths move her chest up and down. Her mouth was slightly parted, her eyebrows pinched like always, yet she looked more peaceful than I'd seen her in some time. Maybe ever.

Wesley and Emma flew with George and Joey back to LA to get started on that process. Charlie and Kate took Collette for the day, practicing their new roles of aunt and uncle. Based on their updates, Collette loved the attention as they took her shopping and to lunch.

Frankie stirred and shifted, removing one of her hands

where it had been tucked between her knees to search the duvet between us.

"Where are you?" she half-mumbled, eyes closed.

I slid down to lay facing her, threading our fingers. "I'm right here."

She let out a deep breath and hummed contentedly. "Gets-somesleep," she slurred.

"If you insist." I tucked myself in and she turned so I could spoon her. I inhaled her scent as I closed my eyes and let myself drift off.

40

———————

Frankie

THINGS SETTLED DOWN AFTER WE ALL GOT BACK FROM NEVADA. BY the time Harrison finished shooting his current—and last project for a while—it was almost Christmas again. I was never more grateful to have a boring, old, consistent schedule. I stopped looking over my shoulder for the shadow, waiting to take everything away, and instead turned my face up toward the shining sun.

Collette and Harrison were playing outside, building a snowman. I watched from the kitchen window with a smile on my face. I'd only heard from Joey once since she was checked in at rehab. She didn't sound happy, but she sounded stable. She also made sure to mention how nice the spa was. I would take that for now. She asked that I didn't talk about Collette or tell her where she was. Collette hadn't asked.

"Francesca?" George snuck up behind me.

"Hey. You okay? Want some tea?" I turned to him.

"Yes. The good stuff. And some biscuits. Meet me in my study." He shuffled away.

Tray loaded a few minutes later, and I met George in front of the fireplace in his office. I loved the smell of this room. I loved sitting in here with him. Maybe he'd want to write another book, something new. Instead of the idea filling me with high expectations or dread, I felt a strange sense of giddiness at the idea. Kate had also mentioned possibly working on something together.

But there was another little nugget of an idea swirling in the back of my brain. So precious and tiny that I didn't even tell anyone but Harrison about it. I had an idea for a children's book about a lost pirate, orphaned at a young age, who travels the seas, and along the way, meets the family she never had.

Harrison thought it was *bloody brilliant*, but for now, I just let it percolate in the back of my mind.

"Penny for your thoughts?" George asked, bushy eyebrows raised.

"Just wool-gathering."

"Let's chat," he sat across from me. Interestingly enough, our last grand adventure perked him up a bit, so we decided to take him on more day trips when Harrison was back for a weekend or a few days at a time. It seemed to be helping his energy more than we expected.

I focused on that instead of the last time I was in his office to have a serious conversation, and we talked about ghosts and deadlines.

"I wanted to show you this." He reached around to hand me a heavy hardcover. "Now, it's just an early proof. That's not the most recent manuscript, so nobody else can read it, but I wanted you to see."

I gasped as he handed me the last book in the *Terraformative* series. My heart lodged in my throat as I ran my hand over the matte cover.

"It's beautiful," I said. My heart skipped as my fingertips ran over the title. "Wait. No. George."

"Yes. It's only right," he said, already cutting off my protests.

Under G.S. Sedar was the printed name "F. Ricci."

"But ... Won't this hurt sales?" I asked, shocked at how lovely it was to see my name there. Evidence of the hours and heart I'd put into this story.

"I've had more preorders than I've had in my entire career. The warehouse has already said they won't have enough for additional orders. But even if that weren't the case, I would still want your name on that cover," he said.

"This is too much."

"No. It's what's deserved. I would have had you bigger and centered on top with mine, but intellectual property and all that. The publisher wasn't having it. You wrote this book, my dear. It is your book as much as mine."

My mouth opened and closed before I shut it entirely to keep from crying.

"And just so you know. From here out, the covers of the last two books are getting updated as well. You co-wrote those. The publishers were less thrilled, but I threatened to take my name off altogether, and they were flexible."

"Oh, George. You wonderful, silly man." I shook my head.

"There is one thing though." I looked up when I heard the trepidation in his voice. "The spelling. I wasn't sure if you wanted a pen name. Or, ahem, maybe." He slid over official-looking paperwork. "I was talking with Bob and the team, and honestly, I don't care what name you go by, but I was hoping at least, legally, you'd be my daughter. You always have been, and now it's time we made it official."

I blinked down at the papers, unable to believe this was really happening. Unable to comprehend just how much it meant to me. A family already, but now a family officially. "You want to adopt me?" I was worried he was having a memory issue. "You know, I'm quite old now, George, right?"

"Oh, bosh. You're basically a baby. And it wouldn't matter if you were ninety. I still want you to be my next of kin."

My heart lodged itself firmly in my throat. I stood up to lean forward and hug him. He hugged me back and I sniffled.

"Thank you. I would love to," I said.

"Cheers," he said tightly and sighed once, lifting his chin. "I can never thank you for all that you've done these last years. And now you've brought Harrison back into my life full-time. And sweet Collette. There's no finer way for a man to spend the sunset of his life."

I reached forward and squeezed his hand. "Thank you for accepting me, for bringing me here to begin with. You gave me hope and a whole new family. I'm happier than I've ever been," I said, and then I had to stop because I couldn't speak through my emotions.

After more hugs and tears and plenty of biscuits to distract us, I finally let George rest by the comfort of the fire.

That night, after hot chocolate and story time, Collette fought sleep. So, of course, she was chattier than ever. She told me about a boy in her class with two moms.

"I'm lucky because I have two moms too. And a Papa Harrison. And a Papa George," she said.

I smiled at the ceiling, wondering if love wasn't scary at all. Love gave your heart added durability so that the more you loved, the stronger you were.

"You have so many people who love you," I said.

"I will call you Mama and Harrison, Daddy. It would be easier." She said it so matter-of-factly there was no way she could know how it made my heart soar.

"I would love that. And I really think Harrison would too."

"Why are you crying?"

I sighed and scrubbed my face with my sleeve. "It's all I do these days."

"I'm just glad it's not in the closet anymore."

I laughed and said, "Me too." I distracted her with an "attickle" and eventually got her to sleep.

I met Harrison in the hallway. "Is she out?" he asked tiredly.

"I bet you could still go in there." I yawned as he enveloped me in a hug, my head dropped to his shoulder.

"I will. She gets very stern with me in the morning if I don't sing her favorite songs."

We stood arm in arm. "I'll meet you in our bedroom. I have so much to catch you up on," I said.

"I love that," he sighed, moving the hairs on my head.

"Hmm?"

"Our room," he said.

"Our room. Our home. Our family." I leaned back to meet his eyes.

"Music to my ears." He smiled down before kissing me.

I had just finished brushing my teeth and was getting in bed when he returned.

"Still got it," he said arrogantly. "Out like a lamp."

"Speaking of, turn out the light and get to bed."

"Yes, ma'am." And I glared to make sure Hank wasn't coming out. Just before he reached for the switch, his eyebrows shot up. "Wait. I almost forgot."

He went to his dresser and dug around before coming to hand me something tucked in his hand. "Happy one-year anniversary of meeting," he said and handed me a little pile of fluff.

I grabbed the once stolen chick and ran a finger over it. "You kept it."

"I couldn't get rid of it. Not when it made me think of you."

"I'll cherish it," I said, nuzzling it with my nose, noting it smelled like his cologne. I set it on the bedside table just as the light clicked off.

Before my eyes could adjust to the dark, I heard shuffling, then yelped a moment later when he found me under the covers and pinched my backside.

"Hey," I said. Then said it again more breathily when he rubbed the area, slowly pulling me flush against him.

We wordlessly divested each other of our clothes, mouths and hands roaming. Hot breaths. Quiet moans. Safe, together, in love.

We took our time and moved in sync, eyes locked even in the low light. I came luxuriously, tenderly gripping his back, heart to heart. He followed a moment later.

After, we lay in silence as I listened to the sound of his steady breathing. It was such a cliché, but a comfort I never knew I needed.

He spoke, startling me a little.

"I love acting. It's something I've done my whole life and feel so grateful for getting to do. But even when I won awards for my acting or my best days on set, there was a little voice that would always ask 'Is this what it's all about then?' And something deep in me would answer, 'not yet.'"

I made a soft hum of acknowledgment, and he went on.

"This was never the family I imagined but it's more than I ever thought it could be. You and Collette mean everything to me. I thought it would be better for her to be raised by her family. That they would love her more. But there is no way anybody could love her more than I do. No person would lay down their life. If she asked me to give up acting, I would. My heart is so full. I am complete When we make her laugh or talk to her about her day. I feel connected. Collette and you, it's like everything slid into place. That little voice is quiet now."

I held him tight and nodded my head against his chest.

"What Joey said, about feeling like something was broken in her," I started. "I felt that way. I worry that some days, when you are gone, and Collette is older, and George is ... Well, sometimes I worry that those feelings will return. I worry that I will lose sight of everything and feel that darkness. That I'm broken in some way. That I will do something to push you away and ruin the best thing that's ever happened to me," I confessed to the night and to him.

He kissed my temple. "Lucky for you, I'm too stupid to take a hint."

"We don't talk like that in this house." I pinched his side.

"No, I know love. I'm just telling you that I won't give up. I'll follow you, no matter how dark those days get. I will be here. Just be here." He sighed, then added. "And sometimes, when I'm distracted and ruin a recipe, or worry that that will be the time, I fuck it up enough to push you away—"

"I'll be the one to tell you that it was just a recipe. And you can't get rid of me that easy. Because people stay and fight. People stay."

We sealed that promise with a kiss.

41

EARLY REVIEWS FOR G.S. SEDAR AND F. RICCI

"Along with the rest of the world, I loved the Terraformative series and have been reading my whole life. I was sure there was no way the last book could possibly live up to the expectations. I am happy to say that I was wrong. This book encompassed the love and friendship at the heart of the Intrepid Trio. F. Ricci seamlessly folded into the storytelling, adding a contemporary feel while still holding on to the classic world we all treasure. I cannot believe this series is finally over. Excuse me as I weep into my pillow for weeks."

- KS, Early Book Reviews

"NOW THAT I KNOW THERE WAS ANOTHER MEMBER OF THE SEDAR family working on these books, missing pieces fell into place for me. I loved this series my whole life and felt like the characters grew up alongside with me. This is the perfect end to a perfect series."

- CN, *Fantasy and Sci-fi Magazine*

"G*IRLS CAN'T WRITE BOOKS. T*HIS BOOK PROVES IT. T*HE SERIES IS* garbage now. If we wanted sappy romance in our books, we'd read that smut the sad housewives read."
  - Kyle, Alpha Males Book Reviews

———

"M*Y HEART IS FULL. T*HIS BOOK WAS UTTER PERFECTION. G*EORGE AND* Frankie make an incredible team. I don't know how I am supposed to function now. Well, back to the beginning to re-read the series."
  - Kate Dubois, NYT bestselling author

———

"I *DON'T KNOW WHO THIS* F. R*ICCI IS, BUT THEY HAVE BECOME MY* newest one-click author. If they're good enough to write with G.S. Sedar they are good enough for me, and this book proves it. Let's just hope this isn't the last we hear of this amazing writer."
  - Nikki, Bestie's Best Book Blog

42

———

Harrison

Many months later

"ARE YOU READY?" FRANKIE ASKED, SQUEEZING MY SHOULDER. SHE straightened my tie in the mirror before resting her head on my shoulder.

I nodded, throat already too tight. How was I going to get through this speech? "I'm afraid I'll start crying."

She shrugged. "So cry. I haven't stopped since everybody started arriving."

I wiped a tear from her cheek.

Outside, in the yard, the crowd was massive. The entire back-yard behind George's house, *our* house, was packed to the brim with friends and family, neighbors, Hollywood elite, and whoever else felt impacted by George. Hundreds of wet eyes looked up at me as I stepped up to the front, in front of a massive projector screen. A wave of unexpected nerves had me taking a large, shaking breath.

"I'm not really even sure how to start this," I said, clearing my throat. Charlie stood behind Kate, hugging her. He gave me an encouraging nod. To their side, a tearful Emma held Wesley's arm. He turned to kiss her forehead.

"It's hard to convey the absolute change that one man brought the world. We are all here because of him. Not only the books he wrote but because he was a father to so many who needed him." I glanced at Frankie at my side, Collette at her side, gripping her hand.

"I don't think I could possibly say anything that represents all the lives George has touched." My throat was too tight to continue. "So I'll just let the videos do it for me. Over the last few years, in addition to writing and wrangling us, our lovely Francesca has managed to archive hundreds of hours of film and thousands of pages of work, all in a project of love for George. Tonight, on this screen and smaller screens throughout the yard, we will be sharing some of our favorite memories."

The crowd clapped and exchanged sentimental smiles.

I gestured to the screen where George sat frozen, hands clasped, waiting to speak. He was in his late fifties, handsome, and it was the first video interview he gave about the creation of the show based on his books. We all thought it would be a great way to start the night celebrating the man.

I took a steadying breath again and spoke into the microphone.

"Happy birthday, George! Wherever you are," I said.

The crowd roared a cheers before falling silent. Frankie gave my shoulder an encouraging squeeze.

Then, in the still silent yard, a booming voice.

"I'm right here, my boy!" The crowd parted to reveal George.

He sat at the center of the party on a massive throne custom-built just for tonight's event. A shimmer of laughter went up around the party.

"Ah, right you are. Cheers! Happy birthday, then!" I held up my glass, and George did the same with his birthday chalice.

"We have to guess your age to be somewhere between fifty and one hundred and ten since you refuse to tell anybody how old you are," I shouted over the growing conversation.

"And I never will, you cheeky git!" he shouted back.

"All right then. Keep your secrets," I said.

"Oh, *Lord of the Rings*," Frankie said softly at my side. "Also a book first."

"George probably went to school with ole Tolkien," I teased.

My laughter was cut off by the crowd singing a rousing round of "for he's a jolly good fellow."

On the projection screen, the first video began to play. After George came the Intrepid Trio talking about how much they love him. First, as children, flushed cheeks on the first year on set, then cutting to us now. My throat was tight to watch twenty years pass in the blink of an eye. Charlie, Emma, and I found each other and held hands.

The videos played on as the party continued. Next to the many children who he and William helped raise, including Frankie and a healthier-looking Josephine. Collette waved at the video when it came on.

"I've digitized every piece of fan mail, also, Grandpop George," Frankie explained later when he had a break from his adoring friends and family. "You can listen to them too. There were hundreds, probably thousands. All there. All to remind you any time you want to listen."

"Mama!" Collette came running up and grabbed Frankie's hand. "I saw you on the screen. It showed a picture of you as a teenager. You had black hair." Collette looked shaken to her core.

"It was a passing phase we don't need to talk about," Frankie mumbled.

"Daddy, will you throw me in the pool later?" she asked me. I grinned down at her, surprised every time at how fast she was growing.

"Give me a few and I'll be back in."

She ran off to meet with her friends. I grabbed Frankie's hand to place on my heart. "I wish you could feel this, this overwhelming joy. I wish I could transfer it to you somehow just so you could feel it."

She nuzzled my hand. "I don't need it transferred. I feel it. Everywhere."

———

Frankie

LATER ON, THE POOL WAS COVERED TO TRANSFORM INTO A DANCE floor. The kids were all inside, sleeping or watching movies in the home theater while the adults continued to party into the night. Twinkling lights were strung up in the trees surrounding the garden, and gentle oldies crooned from hidden speakers. It was a warm summer evening, and the air smelled sweet of flowers. Brooks was whispering with a handsome stranger I didn't recognize and waved at me with a wink when I caught her eye. Emma and Wesley, Charlie and Kate, Harrison and I all found our way toward one corner, together dancing and swapping partners with each song. Even Agata managed to boogie down with Otis the OT.

Eventually, I made it back into Harrison's arms. We were both so tired at this point that I hardly shuffled side to side, resting against his chest, feeling his familiar comfort.

"I think Agata just squeezed Otis's bicep," I whispered to Harrison.

"We'll have to keep an eye on her," he said with a wink.

George sat watching with a contented smile on his face.

When the speakers began to play "Fly Me to the Moon," Otis went to George and managed to get him up for a dance. The young man held George with sturdy gentility as on-screen old footage of William and George, only a few seconds long, played on a loop. George smiled with wonder, hand going to his mouth. Harrison stopped to watch with shining eyes. The silent video showed George throwing his head back to laugh before resting it on William's shoulder. George looked my way and mouthed a thank you before resuming his dance with Otis.

"That's incredible," Harrison said in a choked voice, catching our interaction. "Where did you find it?"

I cleared my throat. Everything had come together more perfectly than I ever could have imagined. "Buried in a box. It was on old film most of it was ruined but the specialist managed to save a little."

"I feel like I'm in a time machine."

"Keep watching," I said, knowing the order of everything played tonight.

Then it was nineties camcorder footage, streaked and shaky, of children playing in the pool. A chubby Charlie danced on screen, and somewhere to our left, Charlie groaned, and Kate giggled. Emma and Wesley smiled up as the camera zoomed in on Emma in the water with Harrison. So young and happy, cheeks red from the sun, and smiles so big.

"It's so wonderful. It's all so wonderful," Harrison said. "Thank you for doing all this. I've always loved it here."

"We should stay here forever," Frankie said.

"I would like that."

We danced close, foreheads touching. Harrison traced his lips over my shoulder as I rested my head against his chest.

"We've always done things out of order, not traditionally," I said eventually, gathering my courage.

"Does that bother you? Because you know I will drop to my knee and ask you right now," he said.

I held on tight to his arms. "Don't you dare make this about us. Plus, I'm pretty sure Charlie and Kate beat you to the punch."

"What do you mean?"

"They disappeared for a while," I said, wiggling my eyebrows.

"Ew. I did not need to know that."

I smacked his arm lightly. "And when they came back, Kate had tears on her cheeks. She went to Emma and showed her a ring."

"What? She showed Emma first?" Harrison asked, outraged.

"I think she was closer," I said.

"Doesn't matter. Charlie told me first when he was ring shopping," Harrison said with a sniff.

"I feel like you're missing the point."

"The point being? Because honestly. I would have married you the moment I met you. I had been trying very hard to play it cool. And you know, trying to convince you I wasn't a shoplifter. I know you want to be free, and that's a pretty big commitment," Harrison said.

"Yeah, it is." I sighed. "Best not to rush things." I nodded seriously.

"Would you like to get married?" he asked hopefully, those expressive eyes glinting with wonder. We were hardly moving.

"I don't know," I said, and he frowned. "And I don't even know what I would wear."

He raised an eyebrow at me. "Really?"

"I can't predict how big I'll be in the next few months. A summer wedding is too soon, but I will be huge by the fall."

He stilled. "That's not—" His face drained of color. His wide eyes flicked to my stomach and then back up to my face. I couldn't stop the grin from spreading on my face at his stupefied expression. I fluttered with excitement and nerves, hardly having been able to keep things to myself this long.

"How do you feel about the name William? Or maybe Willamina, Willy for short, if it's a girl. That's sort of a thing in my family."

"Frankie. Do not tease me. My fragile heart cannot take jokes right now." He took a step back and scrubbed a hand through his hair.

"You're right, sorry. Willy is a terrible name for a little girl."

His eyes narrowed, jaw tight.

I had to stop torturing him like this. "But we will have to decide whether the baby has their own room. I could see Collette liking the idea to share in theory, but she might change her mind on nights when the baby is crying. But we can leave it up to her."

"Francesca?" His voice broke.

"I'm pregnant," I whispered.

He threw back his head and yelled in delight. A few drunk partygoers clapped and whooped even though they had no idea why. He scooped me up and peppered me with kisses.

"Bloody hell. I love you. I love you. I'm so proud of you." He dropped to kiss my stomach even though I wasn't even close to showing. "Keep up the good work in there. He stood back up. "Christ, and I just finally stopped crying." He started wiping his eyes.

"You're happy with this news, then?" I asked, knowing he was. I was excited and scared but proud to be adding to our makeshift family with Harrison.

"Unimaginably. I'll make a dozen babies with you. We will have so many kids we'll lose track of them."

"Okay. Whoa. Let's slow the roll and see how this goes, as I'm the one doing most of the legwork here."

"Fair. I'll round down to five."

"Harrison."

"Four and another dog. Two dogs."

I narrowed my eyes.

"God, I love our family. I cannot wait to tell Collette."

I beamed. "Me neither."

"She can't wait to be big sister. She's been dropping a lot of hints."

"A lot of hints. It worries me that the pool house isn't very soundproof."

Maybe it wasn't easy for everybody to stay. Maybe, like most things, love was a sort of spectrum. I was lucky enough to be in the bit that made my love the most important thing. I couldn't leave. There weren't any forces stronger than just being here for the people I loved. Even when it was hard and scary or overwhelming. Even when I wanted to run away for a few days or hide or find the bits of myself that seemed to be far away, I still wanted to stay. I needed it like breathing.

Harrison held me tight, occasionally sighing as we continued to dance.

Some people might shoot sideways glances at our strange little family, but it was ours, and it was wonderful. I looked forward to the future, I let go of the past, but mostly, I lived in the moment surrounded by love.

***

Not ready to leave the world of these three best friends? Read this bonus scene and find out what happens next to our beloved Intrepid Trio. Read HEN PARTY!

But wait there's more! Did you know I have an all new contemporary small-town series, set in the fictional town of Slippery Slopes, New Mexico? Read on if you're interested in a free sample of ALL DOWNHILL FROM HERE, a hilarious forced proximity romcom.

ALL DOWNHILL FROM HERE

Bee

"You would tell me if I were a ghost, right?" I asked Deckard before blowing out a hot breath on the café window. The tip of my finger made little snowflakes in the fog.

"Aren't you trying to clean that window?" he responded.

I spun to threaten my best friend with the bottle of glass cleaner. He flinched behind the safety of his laptop. He was a bit of a coward like that.

"You're avoiding the question," I said.

"Put the spray down." He held up his hands in surrender.

I spun back to the window I was, in fact, meant to be cleaning.

Grizabella's Café had been a pretty busy work day despite it being New Year's Eve. Lots of locals and tourists alike spent their new Christmas cash in the many eccentric shops of downtown Slippery Slopes, New Mexico. It had slowed down now and I wandered around, very ghostlike, attempting to straighten up the cat café.

Anticipatory adrenaline made me restless. Maybe because I

hadn't made plans for the night, or perhaps that magic that came with the end of one year and the hopes of a new one beginning.

Or the three mochas I'd consumed during my six-hour shift.

Upstairs, the owner, Mel, was warming up her vocals on her piano by singing a rendition of "Memory"—a little on the nose, to be honest. She did that for the tourists. Occasionally, she'd hit a high note that would cause all the cats in the café to meow in unison.

Except for Einstein, the fluffy ginger cat currently chasing a piece of paper stuck to his tail in circles—

"Oop." He fell off his wall perch. "He's okay." Sure enough, Einstein got back up with an annoyed sneeze and walked over to one of the beds lining the café floor.

All my homies at Grizabella's were fosters from the local no-kill animal shelter, Whisker Wonderland, and were available for adoption. Between Mel and I, somebody was almost always here to keep an eye on them and feed them. I usually took the opening shift and her the closing. Sometimes, Ellie from next door at Trailside Treats would come in and check on them too if need be. They stocked the pastries we offered.

Grizabella's was one of the two local cafés, in case you preferred your lattes sans cat hair. Just kidding, there was no hair in our coffee.

Usually.

"Deckard, I'm serious," I said, wiping away my breath snowflakes. Ghosts couldn't make breath drawings, right?

He turned from where he was perched on his stool, working on his laptop as always. He tilted his head with his classic half-smirk that drove the ladies wild and his brown flop of hair that fell into his eyes. He held my focus with his one green, one blue eye.

"I guess it depends on if I thought it would make you sad," he said.

I sighed and went to set the rag and cleaner on the counter. That's so typical. Trying to protect my feelings. But I was completely fine. This was why I didn't tell him about my parents leaving on their newest adventure on Christmas Day and being alone all week. He'd just give me that sad, pitying face when it wasn't even sad. My parents had me late in life, retired by my graduation, and have since lived their best life by cruising it up around the world most of the year.

Deckard looked at the half-cleaned, streaky window and back at me. "Aren't you going to finish—"

"If I'm a ghost, you should tell me. That's what friends do," I said.

"Okay, Bee, if you were a ghost and I was aware of that fact and also not a ghost, I would tell you. What's this really about? Does this have to do with your obsession with that statue?"

"I'm not obsessed." I shrugged, getting that prickly feeling when he tried to dig for information from me.

"You've asked everybody in town about it."

"You don't think it's weird that we have a giant statue in the middle of town, and nobody knows who she was or why we have it?"

"Everything about Slippery Slopes is weird."

"That's fair."

"So you're okay?"

I avoided his look.

"Of course," I said casually.

It wasn't about the statue, even though she was always on my mind lately. Not entirely. It was about the fact that all day long, I heard people discussing their exciting plans for the night, the new year bringing hope for the future and a new start. Not a single person asked me what I was doing or invited me, which

I'd grown to accept, but for whatever reason, it wore me down today.

Deckard held my stare until I felt itchy. I carefully navigated my way through cats and back behind the counter.

"What are you doing on New Year's?" I asked.

He blew out a breath through pursed lips. "I haven't decided yet." He started counting on his fingers. "My mom has her annual New Year's Masquerade Party, but I don't know if I'm up for that this year." His mom was the mayor, and he had five, yes, *five*, older sisters. He switched to another finger. "Then there's always the big party at The Tipsy." The Tipsy Trekker was the bar the locals used, affectionately referred to as just The Tipsy. "I don't know. I can't decide. Why? Do you want to hang out? It could be like the old days, where we gorge ourselves on junk food and binge-watch *Terraformative*?"

I perked up hopefully. "Yeah? I'll bring the Pop-Tarts and marshmallow fluff."

(It would be difficult to believe that both Deckard and I were almost thirty based on this conversation.)

Deckard and I met in first grade, and by the time we were in fifth, we were inseparable. Much like most of the world, we became total *Terraformative* nerds and watched obsessively in high school. Even now, we returned to the old show as much as we could despite it having just celebrated its twentieth anniversary. One of the things we had in common was our ability to enjoy things that made us happy without concerning what others thought of us—him because he's beloved by all in town and me because nobody ever noticed me.

But even those traditions were fading as we got older, and the sentimentality I felt for those old days sometimes gripped me so hard I couldn't breathe.

"I'm getting dinner with Cass first, but then we could all meet up after your shift."

I had played third wheel to many of Deckard's "not real" dates over the years, and rarely did the women he went out with find it charming that he brought around his lovable, zany, perpetually single best friend. But at least I had plans now. I came around the counter to his table, feeling more excited. We could wear our old *Intrepid Trio* shirts, and maybe I could get him to be a model for my next knitting project—

"Crap." His eyebrows crashed back down as his shoulders slumped.

The flame of hope burning inside me guttered out. I knew that look. Deckard, bless his heart, always double-booked himself. A downside to being the best friend of one of the most popular guys in town. He was always helping a sister or his mom or any of the residents around town.

In addition to the absolute lack of attraction between us, this was one of the main reasons we would never work out. He's too busy. I needed at least three to four hours a day to sit and stare out the window in silence.

Thankfully, I had that in spades.

"I just remembered one of my sisters asked me if I would babysit after dinner." He tugged on his floppy hair. "You could join me?"

"Which sister?" I asked suspiciously.

"Dottie," he said, not meeting my eyes. I bore my glare into the side of his head until he looked at me. "Yeah, okay. Now, I remember why I didn't mention it before."

Dottie hadn't liked me since we were in the eighth grade and I accidentally set fire to her bedspread. It was an honest mistake, a science experiment gone wrong.

And then again at twenty-three. In my defense, the conditions were perfect for a re-trial.

She'd never forgiven me.

"She hardly brings up the peanut butter incident anymore," he said, but still wouldn't meet my eyes.

"Oh yeah, I forgot about that too," I mumbled.

Apparently, she didn't believe I was "fit to watch her children" when I had the attention span of a—

"Look! Mr. Sparkles is snuggling with Godzilla. That's adorable. Just last week, they wouldn't even be on the same side of the café," I said and crouched down to pet the two cats with their front paws wrapped in a hug. "Look at you cute wittle babies."

"What are you going to do then?" he asked me.

"I'm just gonna let them snuggle. I should take a picture, though. Good idea." I pulled out my phone.

"For New Year's, Bee," he said with another quirk of his lips before I looked back to add to my collection of cat photos for the adoption website.

I could be honest and say I had no plans, but Deckard would feel bad. Then I would get uncomfortable and probably do something stupid like knit little paw-puppets for the cats to perform a puppet show just to make him laugh. It would become a whole thing.

And I left my knitting supplies at home.

"Hard to say. I have so many options." Lies. I had one option: be a loner. Deckard's worry crinkled his brows. "I have big plans."

I waited for an invite all day to anything, but nothing ever came, and now even Deckard was busy. I rubbed my palms on my jeans. It was fine. I had work early tomorrow anyway. It was just another day ...

"Are you sure?" He was watching me intently again with his hypnotic heterochromia stare. He knew the power of that look. The door jingled with a new arrival. Saved by the bell.

In walked Cass, Deckard's current lady friend. She was a

pretty brunette with a kind smile who worked at the hospital in the town over. She was a year older than us in school, and last year, I gave her a ride to work after her car broke down.

They greeted each other with that awkward hug thing people who weren't quite a couple did.

Then she noticed the third person standing there.

She extended her hand to me. "Hi, I don't think we've met yet."

We chatted three times last week. I shot Deckard a subtle look. Deckard refused to admit that the rest of the town could not see/remember me. He always told me that if I showed people who I was, they would love me. But I would have to be seen first.

I began to doubt his ability to even discern paranormal entities.

Deckard laughed. "Very funny. Imagine you just forgot she had lunch with us last week."

I waved at her with a flat smile. Even as she looked right at me, I could see her already Ctrl+Alt+D me from her brain to save room for more important things.

Cass laughed awkwardly. "Right. Of course. Nice seeing you again." She tucked her hair behind her ear and thumbed to the door. "Ready to eat?"

Deckard gathered his things and shrugged into his coat.

"Yeah. See ya, Bee. Happy New Year." We were too good of friends to hug, so we just waved.

"Happy New Year, Deckard."

He left without a glance backward. I stood at the door a moment too long, staring out the window past downtown. The setting sun cast a pinkish hue on the white peaks of the mountains surrounding our town. The one and only aerial tram slowly made its way up the side of The Slope, our only ski hill. I watched it creep its way up, a tiny dot, and wondered about the people in there now and their plans for the night.

"You can flip the sign to closed, Bee. I gotta start getting ready for the party," my boss said.

I startled and turned to see her all decked out in what looked to be a 1920s beaded flapper gown. Mel lived in New York most of her life, making a living as a chorus girl for a ton of Broadway shows. She retired to Slippery Slopes ten years ago to open a cat café after a "life-changing" trip to Japan. Mel always spoke like a news reporter and rocked a lot of boas. She pulled it off.

"Sure. Ready for what?" I asked and flipped the sign. "You look great."

"Thanks, Bee." She spun and then did a little Charleston kick. "The party tonight." My blank look led her to add, "'The Shake Your *Broadway* into the New Year' musical-themed costume party I'm having here tonight."

"Tonight?" I asked.

"Yes. It's why we're closed tomorrow."

"We're closed tomorrow?"

"Yes." She cocked a hip and rested her fist on it. "I swore I told you." She pursed her lips in concentration, the beads on her gown making an appealing clicking sound in the silence. "Remember that online vlogger lady from Cozy Creek, Colorado, is coming? I want the café to get a mention in whatever her next story is. It'll be a boon for the business."

My ears began to ring, and I felt like I needed to sit down. My own boss forgot to tell me about a party at my job? I'm her only full-time employee.

What was it about me that made me so forgettable to everyone in this town?

I plastered a smile on my face. "Oh. Is there any help you need or anything?" I looked around the café, still full of cats and no party decor. "I have a few minutes to spare."

"You're a doll, but no thanks. I have the gals coming over to help. You go party it up with the rest of the young ones," she said.

"Yep. Okay, cool. I have loads of things to do."

I crouched and said goodbye to all the cats, one by one, taking my time even as the others arrived to set up the party around me. I wasn't stalling in the hopes that they would invite me to stay. That would be pathetic, and I was *not* pathetic.

Eventually, though, I ran out of cats.

I collected my bag and jacket and made my way out to the town square to visit Jane Smith. The sun provided enough afternoon light, so I wasn't in the dark, but heavy black clouds rolled in fast on the horizon. The lingering snow from last week had all but melted except for the parts in the shade that never got hit with direct sun. It had been a mild winter so far, but supposedly, that would change soon. There were rumblings of a storm coming, but I'd only half listened.

Meteorologists weren't to be trusted.

I made my way to my favorite bench and sat down to share baby carrots with wild guinea pigs that roamed throughout the town. (That was a story for another time.)

There was a tight, painful squeezing in my chest. It was like this most days, but usually, it was easier to ignore. It felt worse this time of year—being a ghost in the town you grew up in.

I stared up at the statue I dubbed Jane Smith. She stood in her almost ten-foot (or thirty GPs, at least) glory just outside the roundabout in the center of town. (Important to note here that most people in Slippery Slopes measured height by guinea pigs or GPs. It was a fairly loose system and not really based on anything solid.)

Jane Smith was a bronze masterpiece of a woman who looked like she stepped out of the old-school computer game *Oregon Trail* with a baby clutched to her chest as she stared into the distance. I passed that statue on the way to work, long forgotten, covered in creeping vines and overgrown grass. Every day, I came here, ate my lunch, and looked up at her. I thought about the wind blowing her in perpetuity as the heavy strands of hair forever whipped along her face, the metal of her skirt tugged in the wind, and her ever-present maternal protection of the bundle in her arms. Was her baby okay? Who were they? Where were they going? And why did our goofy little tourist town have a statue of her? All my searching had led to dead-ends, and it was as though I was the only person who cared.

A group of passing tourists stopped to play on their phones in front of her, blocking my view. One of them almost sat on me.

"Sorry, I didn't see you," they said.

"You and the rest of the town, buddy," I said.

They shot me a confused look before the group scurried away.

I sighed.

"What am I supposed to do?" I asked Jane when I was alone again. "What would you do if you were me? If you lived in a place where nobody even knew you existed?"

I waited a beat, the cold air whipping through me, sending chills down my back.

"Probably not talk to inanimate objects," I answered myself.

Good thing I had Deckard, or it might seem sad that the second person I talked to the most was a statue.

I stared into her fierce bronze eyes. Something was shifting inside me. I was on a precipice. Maybe it was the rolling over into the new year, or the massive clouds on the horizon, or the still potent caffeine thrumming in my veins. Whatever it was, I had a choice. I could do things exactly the same and continue to feel like I was disappearing, or I could make a real change.

Jane Smith wouldn't put up with being forgotten. The weeds crept up her base, and dirt collected in her crevices. She used to be someone worth memorializing and now she was a Jane Smith. No plaque explained who she was. Another woman lost to history.

"No. I won't let that happen," I told her.

I stood and pushed off some of the dead leaves collected by her feet. "I'm not letting you be forgotten. And I won't be forgotten either," I said to her, my head tilted way back to meet her gaze focused on the horizon.

I couldn't go on like this. I couldn't roll in another year being forgotten about.

"If you wanna be noticed, then you have to do something noticeable."

Decker told me once or twice that I could be impulsive, but it was *hours* until midnight, and I was formulating a plan.

I shot another look to the tram and checked my watch. I had enough time to go home and pack a bag before the last one went up.

I would not start this new year the same. I would not go on as I had been. Bee Perkins will make an impression on this town one way or another. I could have a pity party. But I'm going to have my own party. I'm going to change everything this year.

New Year, New Bee, started tonight.

Read on, HERE.

ACKNOWLEDGMENTS

It's always hard to finish a series, and this trilogy is no different. These three best friends bombarded my brain from the moment they came to me and demanded to tell their stories. I am in love with not only Charlie, Emma and Harrison but also their partners, Kate, Wesley, and Frankie. George, Collette, and Agata and so many others I met along the way, still pop into my brain like friends I want to check in on. Especially Agata. Usually Agata.

I find solace knowing this isn't the end of *this* world, and in fact you should expect some future books from me that include side characters who are now demanding to tell a story of their own. Maybe a certain beautiful blonde who runs a shop in Sandia, or a former bodyguard from book 2, who has some explaining to do. Things are percolating, people!

I really will miss the world of *Terraformative*. So much of the notes I have for George's book and the show, and even some of the fan fiction Emma wrote, exists in various notes on my phone, or notebooks on my desk, or as background in my Scrivener files for each book. I think, if you are reading this, then it's very likely that you are a person who also gets *very* into the worlds that authors can create. The world *Terraformative* feels that way to me. I like to imagine in some parallel universe George Sedar really has written these books, and the television show was a life changer for so many people. Regardless, I'm thankful to have been included in this version of it.

As always, there are a hundred people who helped make this book possible and I always worry that I've missed someone, but be sure I am so loved and so thankful for the support around me.

Nora, my ultimate cheerleader and coconspirator in all things. You constantly inspire me.

Brooke, for listening to me ramble, feet in the air, as I hashed out this story. Also, sorry for the time I summoned a wind so powerful while telling a scary story we both almost had a heart attack when the door flew open.

Tracy, my first reader and always my most rational listener when I panic. The chickens and I thank you from the bottom of our hearts.

Karla, for the daily chats about all the things and once again for being partially responsible for sparking this series.

JR, setting the bar for all my heroes, but especially Harrison. Every day is a new adventure with you and I couldn't be more thankful to have you as a partner in our weird and wonderful little family.

Nicole, Jenny, and Marla - What is an author without her amazing editors? Nothing, I say.

All my Dramione peeps, IKYK

Speaking of Peeps, my reader group Pipe's Peeps (Piper Sheldon Reader Group) is incredible. Thank you for being the OGs. I love you all.

To all my friends and family who continue to support me on this journey. I really am incredibly lucky/thankful/supported.

ABOUT THE AUTHOR

Piper Sheldon writes Contemporary Romance and Paranormal Romance. Her books are a little funny, a lotta romantic, and with just a little twist of something more. She lives with her husband, daughter, and elderly dog at home in the desert Southwest. She finds writing about herself in the third person an extreme sport in awkwardness.

Sign up for her newsletter here!
  http://pipersheldon.com/newsletter

If you are a Piper Sheldon fan, join her Facebook reader group to get all this insider info!
  Pipe's Peeps (Piper Sheldon Reader Group)

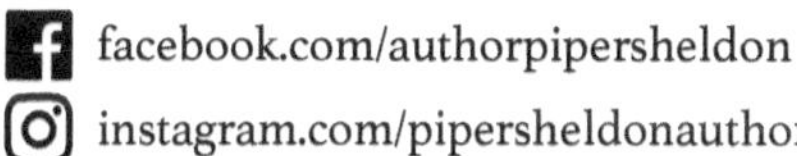

facebook.com/authorpipersheldon
instagram.com/pipersheldonauthor

ALSO BY PIPER SHELDON

Unlucky in Love Series - Contemporary Celebrity Romance

Stranger Than Fan Fiction

Better Date Than Never

Down For the Word Count

Slippery Slopes Series - Small town, Romantic Comedy

All Downhill From Here

All Joking Aside

The Unseen Series - Paranormal Romance

The Unseen

The Untouched

Cozy Creek Collection - Small Town Romance, collaborative series

Fall Shook Up

Smartypants Romance

The Scorned Women's Society - Small Town Romance

My Bare Lady

The Treble With Men

The One That I Want

Hopelessly Devoted

It Takes a Woman

The Teacher's Lounge - Small Town Romance, collaborative series

Band Together

You can find all of Piper's books at pipersheldon.com or on her author page on Amazon.